The Australian Connection

The Australian Connection

To Tim
From
Johnathon Bee.

Johnathon Bee

Pearl Press

First published in Great Britain by Pearl Press
ISBN 978-0-9568688-9-3
Printed and bound by Good News Books, Ongar, Essex, England.

Warning
This Book contains material suitable
for the Adult reader

The Killing Bone

A tribal elder carefully removed the bones
of his dead ancestor from their scared site.

Information passed down from the
Dreamtime.

Dictates that the Haunch bone represents
a copy of the original contours of
Australia.

According to custom the Bone must be
placed and face in the right direction. To
conform to the present shape of the
Continent.

Bones of the fingers are thrown towards
the all seeing Sun.

The majority that fall and point in the
same direction. Indicate the location of the
chosen one.

Once activated the power of the killing
bone can not be revoked, removed, or
recalled.

The Chosen one is a marked Man.

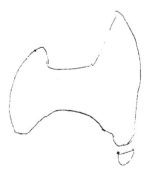

Prologue

I bought a copy of the The Australian Connection from a small bookshop in a back street of Northbridge the civilised social part of Perth, Western Australia. Written by Ray Conner, now using the name Johnathon Bee to protect his identity, he is trying to hide from me. Advertised in the Sunday Supplement of the West Australian newspaper as a 'must read'. Number one on the list of things to do.

Ray and I go back a long time, unknown to each other until recently. A grey ghost, no past, present or future, I need to stop running, retire and watch the sunset. That man has destroyed my life and my business. One more thing to do: see Ray Conner face-to-face. I received information that the local celebrity has his property on the market. I have time to kill. I can wait for years. An appointment with the local estate agent had been arranged previously but he was running late, no worries. The coffee shop next door was the perfect place to rest, relax, enjoy a Cappuccino and a shot of Bundaberg Rum, and so I began to read the following.

Chapter One

The Arrival

The heat of the sun was just too much for the long-toed lizard as it lost its grip on the underside of the corrugated, asbestos, roof. As it fell, it turned and landed on the head of Bluey, the Australian cattle dog, dozing in the shade of the veranda. The ensuing raucous, reaction, of the dog attracted the attention of Fay.

Fay was an in-between: not black or white, but of mixed race, not part of Australian society, an outcast. A full blood Australian Aboriginal has a strong family commitment. White Australians keep themselves to themselves; they don't mix, only on high days and holidays (or to use and abuse). Fay had no chance, she had a foot in both camps and was not accepted by either; she could not bridge that ever-widening gap.

Previous experience of loud, raucous noises had conditioned Fay to be prepared for any unexpected activity. The survival instinct took over, as the cacophony of sound increased, she slowly surfaced from her drunken stupor, as the alarm bells in her head prepared her for fight or flight. Her first panicky thought was has the Boss Man returned early? Hide the empty wine bottle and find the frock, forget the knickers, not enough time. The frock was frayed, tattered and torn, a calico calamity. She looked in the mirror and realised that gravity had taken over.

Fay was rotund and Rubin-esque, but no oil painting. Festooned in flabby fat, forty and finished, she was losing her looks and she knew it. Fay was a big, big lady; no place to hide and nowhere to go. This was as good as it gets: food to eat and a place to sleep, on call night and day. As she prepared herself for private inspection she had second thoughts. The alarm bells were still ringing. The dog was barking too loud, as she bent over and tried to find the besom broom which was hidden somewhere under the bed. The calico dress split again and a pendulous breast broke free of its covering.

The last time the broom had seen the light of day was etched in her memory and on her back. She thought, people pay for scars these days and they call them tattoos, I get mine for free. A bead of sweat and fear escaped and ran down the front of her dress between her ample bosoms.

Armed with the offensive weapon, (or an excuse to be working) she advanced in fear and trepidation out on to the veranda. She was expecting to be confronted by the manic macho dog barking at the open end of the drainpipe, which was in search of the long-toed lizard. After a severe beating with the besom broom, the dog departed yelping, to a safe place. Fay excused her fit of fury and a feeling of guilt, by telling herself, what comes around goes around. Violence breeds hate and hate breeds violence, the endless cycle. Having justified her reaction and calmed her conscience, she realised that she and the dog were one and the same. Both used and abused.

The hot claustrophobic quiet of the Australian outback had descended once again: the clear blue sky and the burning inferno of the noonday sun. Fay peered into the distance and watched as the bitumen road shook and shimmered in the blistering heat haze. It was just too much to take: the flies, the filth, the dust and dirt that descended on everything that moved.

'I hate it, I hate it, I hate it!' she screamed. Fay had a lot of hate. To calm down, she returned to the cool small confines of the bedroom. Then the bikers arrived.

Dez the biker was not a nice man. It could be said that he was a violent man: full of steel implants and solid muscle. A legacy of previous barroom brawls. A black patch covered the empty socket of his missing right eye, which was lost as the result of an encounter with another inmate in a prison riot at an early age, when he was on remand for dealing drugs. That prison term, the first of many, could be seen in the dim and distant past as you stared hypnotised in to his left eye. The thought of your own mortality and inevitable demise was less frightening than that black vacant staring orb. It was like a black hole in the Universe, from which no light, understanding or information escapes, it absorbs all relevant knowledge and gives nothing back. He was the leader of the pack (The Wild Dogs), your worst nightmare, been there and done that, or are about to. Dez was a schizophrenic head case, not part of a normal, sensible society. He was a health hazard; beware, lock up your daughters, every mother's nightmare or fantasy, and another social outcast. His reputation went before him: to be detained at her majesty's pleasure was an occupational hazard. Dez was an intelligent man, (on a good day) and could manipulate the system to his advantage. After attacking a rival drug dealer in the comfort of his own home, because of a financial disagreement, he broke the victim's legs with a baseball bat. He arranged for the victim to be removed and deposited over the fence into the neighbour's yard. Out of sight, out of mind. For being a perfect prisoner, he served eighteen months of his three-year sentence for grievous bodily harm. Dez had now been let loose into civilised society to continue his chosen career in the community as a carpenter: cabinet and coffin maker.

Bluey the cattle dog heard the bikers at the same time that the long-toed lizard fell on his head. Having been distracted by the interruption from above, he had to deal with the immediate problem, first thing's first. After being brutally bashed with the besom broom, Bluey retreated to the safe sanctuary and security of the dark confines under the water tank to lick his wounds. The rusting windmill creaked continuously above, revolving endlessly in a desperate attempt to supply water to the tank and the adjacent Billabong.

He was woken by the sound of the screen door banging relentlessly in the distance on its squeaky hinges. As the breeze began to increase in strength, he could taste the wind-borne sand and turned around, but there was no escape. The slight movement stirred up more dust and sand, it began to descend and sting his moist listless, eyes, forcing an annoying cloud of sand-flies to reluctantly leave his eye-lids and escape the increasing wind. The heat haze had merged with a mirage, or was it the real thing? Rod, the owner of the cattle station (he who must be obeyed) had returned. Bluey knew when to keep quiet.

Rod had seen better days. Too late to change his ways, Rod was stuck in a rut. In the beginning it was easy, but then it became so hard to keep it together on your own. He never knew his mother, she died giving birth to Rodney but his father, Patrick Conner, was a hard working Irish immigrant who made his money with a pick and shovel in the gold fields of Kalgoorlie, Western Australia. The workers in the gold fields where paid a pittance. Their paper wages were spent in the company store on necessities, boots, braces, blankets, tents and Tilley lamps. Any leftover cash was converted into the local convenient currency (nature's nuggets) or gold dust. This would be exchanged at the local watering hole. Down at the hotel they had a set of scales on the bar, to weigh your financial worth and exchange it for the foaming, fighting, future which would ensure you a good night out. But Patrick Conner knew better. He looked, learned and listened; he was a survivor. He kept himself to himself and calculated the odds.

At the local pub, on a drunken Friday night when the beer was flowing freely, the Gods were looking down on Patrick; he played a winning hand of poker and acquired more money than he had ever dreamed of. In a moment of madness he bought a god-forsaken place and named it The Happy Homestead, in the hopes of striking it rich. He found a few gold nuggets but the more he dug the less he found. When his dream turned to dust he turned to the only thing he had left, his religion. He became a man of the cloth, a fine upstanding member of society, a preacher man who believed in hellfire and damnation.

Rod had a good start: he had a devoted nanny, a god fearing full-blood Aboriginal lady named Sunrise. At an early age he was sent to Perth, the state capital of Western Australia to receive and be subjected to, a good Catholic God-fearing private and (painful), boarding school education, where he learnt right from wrong. When he returned to the 'Happy Homestead', Sunrise had disappeared and Fay had appeared. Rumour had it that Sunrise had gone on a walkabout, an Aboriginal tradition. A free spirit, he or she would walk off for no apparent reason to enjoy and embrace the space, quiet and freedom of the vast Australian interior.

In the Fifties and Sixties, the Australian government in their wisdom, operated a policy of white integration. It was designed to educate aboriginal children into the ways of the white man by snatching them at an early age from their unsuspecting parents and isolating them from their nearest and dearest for the rest of their lives, never to be seen again. The majority of these aboriginal children were placed with the great and the good of society, religious law abiding citizens, magistrates, vicars, catholic convents and the like. So Rod, being young and naïve, was not surprised to find Fay at the happy homestead on his return, it was just the way of things.

When father died, Rod inherited the lot. Thousands of hectares of scrub-and and dried up tumble weed. No good to man or beast, but only on condition that he took care of Fay and that he would provide her with a roof, a bed and one meal a day for the rest of her natural life. If he sold the property it was to be shared equally. Sell it? He could not give it away. It was, and still is a financial liability. Rod was not a happy man, full of hate, but there was a lot of it about.

Rod was a red neck, one of the good old boys; he communicated in an uncouth laconic, lethargic language, and had become a monosyllabic moron. He would be a wife beater, if he had a wife. He was drunk again, two days of buying beer, and doing business in Broom the nearest town had turned into a week of drunken debauchery, as usual.

Lightning Bob the aboriginal driver, stockman and station manager, drove the flat bed pickup truck carefully as he approached the Homestead, but it was too late. One last lurch when he changed gear to drive off the bitumen and on to the undulating dirt track, caused the contents of the Boss Man's stomach to escape. As he fell out of the open door and on to the red dirt road below, he threw up. Crawling on his hands and knees and covered in vomit he reached the steps of the veranda.

'Fay!' he shouted. 'Fix me some food, now!' Then he passed out.

Lightning Bob was one of the good guys, a good Aboriginal; they are out there if you know where to look. He came with the property, a professional tracker, employed by the Australian Army in the days of the Vietnam War as a survival instructor. Nobody knew his history or where he came from. He had always been, and always will be part of the land, it was his ancestral dream and time tradition. Settled and sensible, he had no

5

illusions, no past, present or future, but still had a need to go walkabout.

Bob enjoyed waking the Boss Man with a bucket of cold water, the contents thrown from a safe distance. Half drowned and shouting obscenities, Rod staggered to his feet waving his arms about in a feeble and futile attempt to connect with the cause of his discomfort. Bob then had the equally enjoyable task of informing the man:

'Boss Man, Fay done gone walkabout, missing, disappeared.'

Rod took one step forward missed his footing on the steps of the veranda and crashed headfirst into the screen door.

Rod woke with a hurting head.

'Bitch, Bitch, Bitch!' he shouted, which made his head worse. There was no answer, no sound, except the loud banging inside his skull. Then his memory returned. Of course the bitch had gone walkabout again, he thought. He crawled across the floor and into the bedroom. He lay there in a drunken stupor, sweating quietly all night in the stifling heat, listening to the sounds of the night, half-awake, half-asleep. Moving occasionally to the kitchen to get another tin of Tennents Extra.

The sun, that golden globe of relentless heat rose again at 5 a.m., so did Rod. Sleep, what sleep? he thought. The weather was another worry. A long hot, dry summer, and still waiting for the first rain of winter, the end of February and not a drop. Which will arrive first fire or flood?

He sat out back by the Billabong to try to clear his head. Must have a swim and try to cool down, he thought. The luxury, the relaxation the sheer joy of the all-enveloping liquid. But it didn't work; the water was too warm. Hot and dry again, he needed more beer. Just the touch of the tin, the thought of the cool contents, of that cold can, reaching the parched parts that only the Amber nectar can reach, brought blessed relief.

The clear bright blue sky, without a cloud in sight, stretched endlessly and unbroken into the far distance. No wind and not even a trace of a slight breeze disturbed the uncomfortable calm. Nothing moved except the shaky shimmering of the heat haze on the arid, deserted, dirt road. Not a sound, even the crickets had stopped chirping, it was too hot to bother. It was 80 degrees in the shade.

As Rodney went back inside to get another beer, something moved. Was it the leaves on the gum tree, or was it a mirage? Too much heat and beer will do strange things to the imagination. No! There it went again and in the corner of the paddock by the rain butt next to the water tower, a small dust storm whirling around in a random, erratic and uncontrollable manner like a mini-tornado.

A bedlam of Budgerigars had descended in great numbers to drink at the billabong. This unusual occurrence was a sign of things to come. Having been forced from their natural habitat by fire or flood, they were fleeing the advancing onslaught. Only to be disturbed by the arrival of Lightning Bob, who confirmed the opinion that mother Nnature was on the move. Aboriginal people know these things. It's a natural instinct.

So did Rod, his survival depended on it. A well-rehearsed plan of action was put in to operation. Clear the yard, front and back of all dry, loose inflammable material. The nearest gum tree will have to go. It cast a shadow and cooled the south side of the house but if it caught fire there would be no house left for it to shade. It was half-dead anyway, due to the last drought and dieback disease. The diesel engine on the earthmover reluctantly coughed and clattered into life as Lighting Bob prepared to head out into the surrounding bush to cut a firebreak, to isolate the paddock and the surrounding property.

The sun was going down, changing its golden glow, into a blood red ruby colour. The wind was getting up, a wild hot wind like a tumble dryer. It didn't last long. The wind stopped - a bad sign, mother nature's having a rest and planning her next move - the lull before the storm. Then in the still heat of the night he saw it in the distance. No sound at first, just the lighting flashing endlessly. As it approached he heard it crackling over the cane fields, coming down the canyon, north of Cooper's Crossing. Ray stayed awake all night. Which will come first, fire or flood?

Another dawn, another day, a bunch of kangaroos burst through the bush and cleared the paddock fence five feet high. Focused on one thing, filled with fear, they flew through the air into the open field beyond. They knew what he knew. There was a bush fire coming, and they were the fire alarm.

The wind returned, getting stronger. It began to howl as it bent the branches of the banyan tree and battered the bottlebrush to the ground. As it came closer, Rod could smell the oil of the eucalyptus trees, carried on the wind as it mingled with the smoke of the burning bush. Time to get ready, take down the curtains and open the windows just an inch. A fire needed oxygen, and if they were closed, it would suck them out to get the oxygen inside and equalise the air pressure. The billabong was the best place, as he sat in the cool water, to watch the fire flash over.

Rod could hear the crackling flames growing increasingly closer, fiercely consuming the canopy. He watched as the leaves wilted, writhed and withered in the intense heat as the eucalyptus exploded in a shower of sparks and burning embers, ignited by the oil in the gum trees. With the wind that strong, it would not last long. As the fire moved on up the valley, it left a trail of clean pristine virgin soil ready for new life. The wind dropped to an exhausted slow breeze, and then the rain started, slow at first then big, hot, tropical drops, bouncing on the burnt out bush and hissing into oblivion. Then, it was pouring. The big wet had finally arrived.

Lightning Bob appeared as usual from nowhere. Was he part of real time or dreamtime? Who knew? He had an ethereal quality.

'Boss Man, flood coming,' he said. It was time to get ready. Bob had been to see the tribal elders of the Balinga people up in the stone country, and was told by the wise one with the wispy beard that Fay had been taken north by the bikers. News travelled fast in these parts.

Chapter Two

Rod went looking for Fay. He crossed over into the Aboriginal Reserve with the usual attachment of flies, red dust and dirt sticking to the flat bed pickup truck. North or South of the line, it made no difference, it looked the same on both sides. Then the rain returned.

Te Tree, the next town (the only town) coming up on the way to Darwin in the Northern Territory, the highway was one long lonely road. The town was a god-forsaken, non-descriptive dust bowl in the middle of nowhere. Flies and filth corrugated iron, weatherboard shacks and mangy dogs, mostly mongrels. Then Rod saw him in the piercing beams of the headlights between the sweep of the wipers and the rivulets of rain running down the windscreen.

Sitting cross-legged in the middle of the road, just outside of town, an elderly Aboriginal, with a long grey wispy beard. Rod had seen it before: a death wish, no hope, no help, and no future. The old man was close to death, getting ready for the ancestral dreamtime. An Aboriginal elder is treated with respect and admiration as a man of wisdom, knowledge and longevity. He has earned the right to decide how and when he dies and as a mark of respect, to choose his own time and place.

Rod swore, swerved and missed the man by a metre or less and then drove on carefully and calmly to inform the police of Te Tree about the obstruction on the highway (definitely a health hazard and a traffic violation). Rod was informed later that a snatch squad had been organised and dispatched to the location, only to be confronted by members of the extended Balinga tribe, all family members of the intended victim. They were aware of the possibility of the boys in blue interfering. As the rain became heavy and harder, the man in question was still mumbling and grumbling in the middle of the highway. After the boys in blue had a brief exchange of verbal incompatibility, which led to an ignominious stalemate, members of the aboriginal family purchased from a local food store, a number of frozen kangaroo tails (a local delicacy). In the process of removing the intended victim from the middle of the highway, an undignified scuffle erupted, which rapidly got out of control. The police were set about, assaulted and brutally bashed by the Aboriginals wielding frozen kangaroo tails.

Two men were arrested and appeared in court the next day, charged with assaulting the police officers. No pleas were entered and they were remanded in custody. After an intensive investigation, a police spokesman said the kangaroo tails could not be found and used as evidence for the prosecution, as the evidence had been destroyed. Friends and family of the accused had eaten them all. Eventually the men were released due to lack of evidence.

In Aboriginal mythology, a belief survives that the dreamtime spirit will speak to you at the moment of a near death experience, to answer all your questions. The Aboriginal elders need to know these things. The one with the grey wispy beard had the answer to the questions that he had been asking. Thanks to Rod, the near miss on the highway and the dreamtime spirit, he now knew where to look for Fay.

Dez never missed an opportunity to entice a lone female by fair means or foul into his clutches. Such was his persuasive determination, that the word 'no' was not an option. Dez and his band of desperados had a commune, east of Halls Creek just across the border of the Northern Territory in no-man's land, a no-go area, on the edge of the Simpson Desert. The commune was like a parasite, it would slowly entice and surround its victim absorbing, destroying and eventually breaking down the individual's resistance. It was continuously searching for new converts, especially females. It had its own law, rules and regulations. Dez was an all-powerful warlord on his own land. He demanded respect and got it. He was living the life of his favourite fantasy film character. He really was the man in the movie Mad Max.

The Northern Territory is Australia's equivalent of America's Wild West as it used to be, one hundred years ago. The isolated wind-swept towns in the middle of nowhere; one hotel, which is open all hours, with a shotgun rack behind the bar. Farmers and the good old boys would leave their shotguns there till later in case their best behaviour and intentions became the worse for wear, due to an excess of alcohol, like leaving your car keys behind the bar in a civilised society. Never ask a local how he makes his money, it was not a good idea. Go north to the mangrove swamps, crocodiles and the sacred Aboriginal reserve of Arnhem Land at your peril, or South to the sand and the vast empty interior of the Simpson Desert.

The Aborigines define a shadow as a dark figure, cast on the ground, or a spectre or ghost, or even an inseparable companion, one who follows a person in order to keep watch on him. He records all your actions good or bad and transfers that information to the Dreamtime Spirit. The Dreamtime myths of the Australian Aborigines are an inseparable part of their life and their landscape. Their beliefs, expressed through those myths, form the very basis of their culture. Today, tribal Aborigines look upon themselves as direct descendants of those mythical beings of the past. Every Aborigine who lives in the country created by his Dreamtime ancestors is linked intimately with that environment. It is a very close personal link that dominates his entire philosophy, code of behaviour and way of life. It is the foundation of all his social, secular and ceremonial activities. As it was done in the Dreamtime, so it must be done today. These laws are clearly outlined in the Dreamtime mythology. This mythology is eternal. It identifies Aboriginal past, present and future. The great Dreamtime ancestors are an integral part of the land and life. They exist in all things and speak to those who know how to listen, leaving signposts for those who had learned how to read them, always there, like the latest DNA technology, fingerprints and carbon dating.

The Elders of the Balinga tribe knew all about the Dreamtime. Up in the stone country, the rocks weathered slowly, holding on to their history. The biggest and best of the mighty monoliths would whisper words of wisdom if the time was right. It was a sacred place, a traditional part of the Aboriginal Dreamtime legend. A member of the Balinga tribe, the Aboriginal elder with the long grey wispy beard was born in the shadow of that sacred place.

A rock or stone contains information of its history, which can be unlocked and analysed by using the latest modern technology. It is a time capsule. It can also provide information for the future, what has been, could be and maybe is a sign of things to come. To be advised on a personal family matter, a true blood Aboriginal elder would resurrect and consult the Dreamtime Spirit, which lays dormant in the bones of his dead ancestors. After consulting the bones and conferring with the Dreamtime spirit, the scared sign's could-not be ignored. The elder would use the information to locate his intended victim. The chosen one would cast a long dark shadow on the ground. The greater the sins, the longer the shadow.

Dez had a long shadow. Unleashing the power of the Spirit was not to be taken lightly. The Elder arranged a meeting with the leaders of the local tribes, to justify his impending action. Confirmation was required that the bones of his ancestor are placed in the traditional position and pointing in the right direction. After a group discussion with the tribal elders, it was agreed that the killing bones were in the required position, arranged and aligned to indicate the location of the intended victim. The last piece of the puzzle was completed the picture. Now that the killing bones were activated, there was no turning back. The elder with the long grey wispy beard knew what had to be done. The Dreamtime spirit had spoken. The word was sent out, and Lightning Bob responded to the call. He had been informed of the decision made by the elders.

Dez had detected a feeling of frustration. A hint of claustrophobic containment had infiltrated his environment. Since his return, the rains had continued relentlessly. After his arrival, the obligatory drunken debauchery had lasted for two days and nights. On the third day he was becoming bored and restless. Violence is a very volatile virus. When unleashed, it can affect and destroy the surrounding area, like a dangerous dormant volcano ready to explode. Dez was bubbling up under the surface and his temperature was rising. He had to get out.

His animal instinct was alert to something he could not understand, a feeling of unrest; something was not as it should be. He was hot, his bones were aching, and it felt like he had a fever, time to make a change and it had to be now. He had an intense desire to go and lie down in the cold comfort of the relentless rain. Shouldering his shotgun and a pocket full of shells, he advanced through the smoke-filled room towards the door. His path was obstructed; his copulating drunken desperados were oblivious to his presence. This was not the respect he required. Loading the lethal weapon on his way, he stopped and fired both barrels at two figures fornicating on the floor in front of him. A follower, a member of the fold, sighed, died and rolled over. His passion spent, his spirit heaven sent.

The high-pitched screaming of the distraught woman writhing next to the body of the deceased descended into a controlled cacophony of subdued sobbing, as she saw through the dispersing shotgun smoke. And she saw that piercing stare, the black vacant evil staring orb of the left eye, standing over her. Dez reloaded the twelve-bore shotgun, which was still pointing in her direction. You could taste the tension. Nothing moved, not a sound, not a whisper, except the low monotonous slow rumble, given off by the rotation of the smoke stained ceiling fan, as it tried to force the foetid air into the far corners of the room. At full volume, the music machine was still pumping out a continuous bass beat, causing the contents of a beer crate placed next to it, on top of the fridge freezer to rattle. It was a surreal tabloid, like cardboard cut out figures, frozen in time and fear.

He carefully stepped over the dead man and the rapidly spreading pool of blood. The tension was lifting as he continued to make his way in a sensible and civilised manner toward the door. As he reached the door, a low murmur of relief and discontent broke out and became audible from the onlookers. Then in one swift move he stopped, turned and shot the music machine. The adjacent beer bottles exploded in a foaming fountain of glass and gunshot.

Actions speak louder than words; he had made his point and retrieved his respect. Dez needed peace and quiet. Closing the door quietly behind him, he walked out into the black night and the pouring rain, he had to cool down. His bones were still aching. The more he walked the worse the pain. Mentally as well as physically, he was still hurting. He had to lie down, relax and gather some inner strength. The rain had moved on and as he looked up from his prone position he caught a glimpse between the scudding clouds of that star formation known as the Southern Cross. The clouds cleared and revealed the clear night sky. The stars appeared bright and brilliant with their luminescent lustre.

He lay there deep in thought and came to the conclusion that if you believed in a life after death and a second change, maybe there was another world up there that was better than this one, where sinners were accepted and forgiven. That must be heaven. If so, then this must be hell. Dez decided the more mistakes you make down here, the better your changes of redemption are when you get up there, (he worked in strange ways). With that comforting thought, he fell asleep, but he would never go to heaven.

The day dawned with a clear blue sky. The sun was already soaking up the steaming residue of the recent rain. Dez needed the freedom and isolation of the wide-open spaces, to escape and get back to nature, to practice his hobby of killing kangaroos. He took the four-wheel drive Toyota truck parked in the paddock at the back of the commune and drove north, up into the Stone country. Leaving behind him tire tracks in the rapidly drying red dust of the Simpson Desert. Following the tracks of the Toyota was not a problem for Lightning Bob. Whatever the weather, he could track his target in a tornado.

The saltwater crocodiles of the northern territories will travel for miles in the rainy season, they follow the flood and end up in an isolated billabong to watch and wait for their unsuspecting victims. These descendants of the dinosaur will slowly surface and silently survey their intended prey, calculating the distance and then deciding when to strike. The attack is fast and furious a lightning-fast lunge, leading to a lethal lock of tearing teeth. Which, combined with the weight of the prehistoric predator will force the unfortunate victim under the surface into the murky depth of the creature's deep domain and the all embracing death roll of the crocodile. Deprived of oxygen, the victim will rapidly relinquish their hold on life. As the foaming frenzy caused by the fight subsides, the all-embracing clear calm water will close over and once again peace and tranquillity will return, without a sign of disturbance to the deceptively quiet billabong.

Dez had found the perfect place. On the other side of the billabong, a concealed kookaburra was cackling its lunatic laughter in the shade of a coolabah tree. The kangaroos would come down to the billabong to drink at dusk. They would present a sitting target and Dez never missed, like shooting at the shapes of the cardboard cut-outs of cops back at the commune. All he had to do now was watch and wait.

Lightning Bob was doing the same thing, watching and waiting on the other side of the billabong, concealed in amongst the ghost gums with other members of the Balinga tribe.

The boomerang is a powerful weapon in the right hands, like a ballistic missile with a homing device and Bob was an expert. As the sun was setting, Dez was casting a dark shadow and dozing off by the side of the billabong. He was exhausted. He could not move. His bones, his whole body, hurt like hell and then without warning it hit him behind the left ear. When he came to, he had been stripped naked, his eye patch had been removed he was tied and trussed like a Christmas turkey. Bob had already found his final resting-place.

Lightning Bob and the elected members of the extensive family had arrived at the crack of dawn to prepare the termite mound. In the northwest part of Australia, the fully formed mature mound is an impressive air conditioning unit. From two sides, (east and west) the six feet mound is designed and built to vent hot air and volatile gases, generated from their ceaseless endeavours. Fresh air from north and south is absorbed deep into the mound and their underground labyrinth. Baked by the burning sun on the outside but on the inside soft sand are spit and regurgitated cellulose, a malleable material which can be removed or rearranged. This disturbance is guaranteed to upset the occupants. In an enclosed environment, a countless number of termites protecting their territory is an uncontrollable fighting force.

Dez was gagged and bound with his hands and feet tied together behind his back. He knew a few things about traditional Aboriginal folklore and admired the way they dispatched their victims to the Dreamtime, slowly and painfully, but this was not what he needed to know. It was part of a ritual preparation that concluded with the chosen one meeting his maker prematurely. A carrying pole had been inserted between his shoulder blades and shinbones. The Aboriginal carriers were dressed in their tribal earth colours, they were chanting an incomprehensible mantra as he was transported, safely secured like a suckling pig on its way to market, or like a ceremonial sacrifice.

After the rain, the top of a termite mound can be removed with a sharp machete, like a boiled egg in an eggcup. He was heading for one, which had been prepared earlier. Having scooped out the interior of the mound and replaced the top, Lighting Bob was waiting for the arrival of the chosen one.

Dez shook and shivered uncontrollably as he came close to his final resting-place. He had felt fear before but nothing like this, now he could smell it and taste it. Completely helpless and vulnerable, the adrenaline rush that he had always relied on was missing. For the first time in his life the situation was out of his control. He was scared.

Before the interment, Aboriginal tradition demands that the chosen one is presented to the four winds, North, South, East and West. The winds have to die down and become completely still, it is a sign of acceptance. The pole carriers with their reluctant reprobate circled the mound twice, stopping at each of the four corners for confirmation from the Dreamtime, that their intended action would be accepted. Just a slight breeze would be enough to justify the cancellation of their commitment, but there was no wind and no movement around the mound. The chanting and foot stomping had stopped, and as the red dust descended slowly with the oppressive silence, it settled on the feet of the pole carriers. Not a sound upset the surrounding silence.

Suspended in time and space, Dez had run out of luck. Lighting Bob was fully prepared to do what had to be done. In a trance-like state and still communicating with the Spirit World, he began to break the silence. Quietly, in a slow mumble, he began again, chanting to the Gods, reciting a long forgotten language. He increased his volume as he slowly approached the mound and removed the top and placed it on the ground in front of Dez. The biker was about to be buried alive and he knew it.

The end of the carrying pole with Dez still attached was placed horizontally inside and up against the back wall of the termite mound. The front wall supported the weight of his frantically thrashing body. Facing west, he noticed the last dying rays of the setting sun as it slowly descended below the horizon.

The pole carriers were lifting the front end slowly but surely into an upright position as the monotonous tribal chant continued, louder and louder. As they advanced closer, hand over hand along the pole raising it to the vertical, gravity took over. Dez began to slip in reverse, along the pole, uncontrollably towards the dark interior of the termite mound. The pole had reached the vertical position and was then removed. Dez, safely secured in the mound, could only listen to the cacophony of sound as it increased to a crescendo and the demonic dancing of the pole carriers disturbed the red dust once again with their shuffling dirt encrusted feet.

Bob slowly replaced the top and at the same time the golden glow of the sun disappeared completely. Dez watched as the light diminished and darkness descended in his burial chamber. The last thing he heard was the kookaburra cackling its lunatic laughter. The termites began to cut, bite, pick and rearrange this foreign body placed in their way. As they relentlessly advanced, the countless swarm engulfed his head in one writhing mass. Ears, eyes, nose and throat slowly became blocked. Dez lost all reason as they crawled into his empty eye socket. His mind went completely mad, even the cackling kookaburra was shocked into silence as his death scream disturbed the still dark night of the Australian outback.

Chapter Three

The Departure

As his mother had requested, Ray Conner placed the framed photograph of his coming out parade in the same prominent position as yesterday, on the table at the side of her bed, next to the old wind up gramophone and the pile of black 78rpm records. He had to admit he looked good in those days. Graduating as one of New York's finest from the Police Academy was something to be proud of: a shiny shield, starched shirt, and a straight back. The NYPD was his ultimate goal, part of the American dream to be accepted as a fresh-faced New York kid who then turned into a full-fledged fighting machine. Full on and focused, in an age of innocent inexperience, he was prepared to protect the population in accordance with the letter of the law, but that was a long time ago. How things had changed since those days. Now older, and much, much, wiser, Ray Conner was now facing retirement. Where had the time gone? Grey hair and a balding bit, which he tried to disguise, round shoulders a stoop and bad back, plus a burger-belly were the legacy of a lifetime of law enforcement. Ray had continued to receive his pension. He had a plan to take mother and move to Florida, play a round of golf, a bit of light jogging maybe to lose a few pounds. Or get fit in a Health Farm? All things were possible when you retire, but his mother had no intention of moving, the apartment contained too many memories.

'Don't forget the window and the mirror,' she shouted.

'OK,' he replied, as he left her bedroom with the breakfast tray. A regular request, it was part of the daily routine. The position of the photo frame and the mirror had to be perfect; it was an automatic reaction, the same as brushing your teeth. Ray returned as usual and released the catch.

He lowered the window the required distance: exactly six inches no more, no less, as he had countless times before. The long portable dressmaker's mirror also had to be in the right position at just the right angle. Close to the window to reflect the goings on of the street life below. The window routine kept her in touch with reality. They both liked routine; it meant continuity and security. After her stroke, his mother was housebound. The grey-haired lady had an old fashioned Victorian attitude, domineering and demanding, as she had been all her life. Right was right and black was white if she said so. A loss of feeling down the left side of her body had forced her to lie in bed, all day and every day. Only to be interrupted by the occasional short shuffle to the bathroom and back with the aid of her walking frame. For the first time in his life, Ray felt really needed, wanted, and indispensable. His mother had become even more demanding, but Ray could handle it. It had become a challenge, a part of the job.

Her bedroom was two floors above the Butcher, first door on the right. She could smell the chicken Chow Mein cooking in the Chinese restaurant opposite as it slowly permeated the apartment. She tried to ignore the gaudy neon sign as it flicked weakly and intermittently constantly day and night, advertising an oriental eating experience. It looked tasteless and tacky. She could also the cabbage cooking at lunchtime from somewhere down the hallway. It was another one of life's problems; she liked the finer things of life.

A successful seamstress and a talented fashion designer at an early age, she had moved amongst the great and the good in uptown New York City. In Manhattan, Daddy had connections; the right people at the right parties, in the right places. Bought the brownstone building at a knockdown price on the corner of 53rd and 3rd on the advice of a city planner, (in advance of a compulsory purchase order, which never happened). Rented out rooms and apartments, she was financially secure, but she was bored. Life was too easy. With time to spare, the bored little rich girl was helping out at the arrival desk on Ellis Island when she met Michael Conner (Ray's father). He changed her life completely. Just off the boat, an Irish immigrant, he was tall dark, and handsome, wearing his one and only shiny Sunday suit and carrying a bundle of basic belongings. It was love at first sight.

They moved into the apartment on their wedding day. She was eight months pregnant when Mick Conner, employed as a mechanic at the local police station, was gunned down on his way home from work. Working late on overtime, he needed the extra money. He finished his shift at nine o'clock that night, too late and too tired to change, he walked home still wearing his N.Y.P.D. sweat shirt. Mick stopped off at the local Five and Dime store and bought a brown paper carrier bag full of baby things for later, but once out on the sidewalk, he realised he had forgotten to buy the round musical rattle - the one thing his lovely wife really wanted for the baby. On his return, two raiders were robbing the register. They had taken the till and were on the run. As they passed him by, they shot him twice. He made his way home and climbed the stairs to the second floor apartment. Leaning against the door, with his lifeblood draining away, he pressed the doorbell continuously. He could see her distorted face as she looked through the spy hole. Mother opened the door and the last thing he said as he fell to his knees was, 'I have bought the musical rattle.' As the contents of the brown paper bag slipped from his grasp and spread themselves across the floor, the rattle splattered with blood, escaped and rolled around the room, playing an in appropriate musical melody. It still has pride of place even now, after all these years on top of the mantle piece above the fireplace.

But now, she was listening to the sound of the street below: the constant wailing of the blues and twos as they rushed around town, going about their lawful business enforcing law and order, protecting the good guys in another part of town reinforced her feeling of security. As they passed by, she could see in the mirror that on the sidewalk below their apartment, life was cool, calm and collected for the bad guys who were hanging around doing deals and smoking dope. At the corner of the brown stone building a religious lunatic was sitting crossed legged as usual, wearing a turban and a loincloth lamenting the loss of Jesus Christ. Already covered in cuts, he was beating his body yet again with a leather belt. His usual attire, the waterproof laminated sandwich board, which is inscribed with the information that Jesus saves, had been removed and placed like a frame next to him in an upright position, to protect his cheap plastic ghetto blaster from the pouring rain. It pumped out the information at full-distorted volume, that the God fearing Southern Baptists would

21

save you. Body soul and mind for the price of a local phone call, or a free 0800 nation-wide number backed up by a small donation, and an acceptable credit card, another normal day in the Big Apple.

Ray Conner was an independent undercover cop. Working alone, his code name was Red Rover. Having worked his way up through the ranks, he was now in a position to do his own thing where and when he wanted. He had the freedom to roam at will. He was just another faceless figure on the streets of New York City. A hobo a wino, or a city slicker, he was a frustrated actor who could play all the parts of life's rich pattern, a natural chameleon. He could change shape, creed or colour (with the help of his make-up box) depending on the job. It was a God-given natural ability to mix and mingle.

Ray could smell crime in advance; he lived and breathed it. With modern technology, the Global Positioning Satellite and a heat seeking Infrared system he was being tracked 24/7, to the nearest square metre. He also had a direct line to the Police Commissioner and the authority to call up the S.W.A.T. squad or a police chopper at any time, day or night, no questions asked. He had complete control of his day-to-day existence. No one told him what to do or where to go. There was no big boss man. Ray was on his own except for his minder. The department insisted that he always had someone follow him. As soon as he left the apartment, an undercover cop would tag along at a discrete distance. It was a game he enjoyed playing, spotting the sad soul dressed up like a male or female. A bag lady or a blind man with a stick, they had all been tried before. They were becoming too obvious and predictable. Ray would have to have words with the department. He could handle that, but he wasn't too sure about the religious lunatic on the corner of the street.

Today was not a normal day. Ray had cut his hair and removed his beard; he had to look the part. Booted and suited in a clean white shirt with a tight collar and an acceptable tie he felt uncomfortable, but wearing his concealed 38 Smith and Weston made him feel better. He was ready. He was off to work in the local bank as a passive observer in the back room. An important part of the business presentation is the black leather attaché case. It contained a pile of apparently pointless papers and marked money.

Bundles of bank notes previously prepared by the department to provide proof of identity if touched. Individually identifiable, they were all impregnated with a chemical, which absorbed fingerprints, sweat and DNA. Carefully closing the case and completing the required code numbers activated a tracking device, a transmitter concealed in the lining of the case. Undercover cops also get mugged on the streets of New York City.

Security had notified the department that a suspicious character had caused enough concern to alert the employees to the possibility of a bank raid. The man in question made a visit to the bank first thing on Monday morning to open an account with the minimum amount of money. He returned on Tuesday at closing time to talk about a financial transfer. He was back on Thursday to deposit an undisclosed package, in a security box in the bank vault. Three strikes and you're out. Ray recognised the pattern; he had seen it so many times before. Occasionally you find a completely new crime but most of them are the same old tried and tested formula of failure.

Having activated his personal tracker, Ray left the apartment and locked the door. Yesterday a tenant had been found dead in the building. He had lived in the flat below. A poor bare miserable room with a cracked window and a dripping cold water tap, dispensing a constant supply onto the dirty dishes below: congealing the grease covered patterned plates, in the over-flowing stone sink. Aggressively, the workers were removing the belongings and personal possessions of the previous occupant and unceremoniously throwing them out of the window into the street, to be ignominiously scooped up by the dump truck in preparation for the renovating of the property and the arrival of the new resident. He had died in his sleep. The tenant had nothing and left nothing, another lonely old man. No pension, no past and no future. Left alone in his tiny flat he was found dead on the bed wearing a threadbare army overcoat with a worn out frayed collar and cuffs. Covered with a cheap thin blanket, in his bony white waxen hand he was clutching a collection of military medals. This time of year the temperature can fall fast from plus to minus. Ray had heard that the last time the credit key for the electric meter had been recharged to supply the one bar electric fire, fridge and a forty-watt light bulb was a week ago. Cause of death: hypothermia and hopelessness.

Ray descended the stone steps of the apartment building. As he emerged and turned the corner, he noticed the cheap grey blanket as it was thrown through the window from the floor above. Catching a gust of wind, it opened up like a parachute and descended slowly with dignity, undulating on its final journey. Like a lost soul releasing its last breath, free of the constraints of conformity it settled silently on the rubbish skip parked under the fire escape. As Ray passed by, the blanket moved and an apparition appeared from underneath.

Peter emerged from the dust and detritus of the builder's rubbish skip and jumped down on to the sidewalk clutching a plastic bag. He began to perform his party piece, hanging over the wrought iron railings at the front of the building and throwing up. To be confronted on the sidewalk by Peter is a scary thing. The unsavoury individual had the unnatural ability to distract attention (or course it) by vomiting on demand. Always wearing the same shabby Mac and with a lazy left eye, they called him Colombo. Depending on the time of year he lived on the streets in a cardboard box, or an empty cargo container down in dock land on Fisherman's Wharf. Occasionally Peter would rent himself a room in a cheap run down boarding house. The department employed a lot of weird and wonderful people. The last time Ray and Peter worked together, they were at an illegal casino, just a front for pimps and prostitutes in uptown Manhattan. A high-tech state of the art listening device had to be attached as a permanent fixture, somewhere in the casino. The dress code was a tuxedo and a couple of giggling girlies, false names and addresses, and a big wad of money was the acceptable entrance fee.

Playing Roulette as previously arranged and on cue, Peter threw up, down the front of the black dress of the house hostess. Ray intervened immediately. Uttering obscenities he grabbed him from behind and pushed Peter to the floor. An undignified fight developed where they rolled around convincingly in the corner, next to the secluded seating unit. The hostess was still weeping and wailing and distracting attention as Ray placed the bug surreptitiously under the unit. Beaten up by the bouncers and banned from the club, they were thrown out. On the street, nursing their bruises, they decided to celebrate another successful police plant operation with a root beer and pastrami on rye at the nearest all-night diner.

With his minder in place, Ray crossed the intersection of 33rd and 3rd and stopped on the corner as usual to buy his copy of The New York Times from Pedro the paper seller. He realised that this was not good: he was repeating a pattern of complacency. Because of the disguise Pedro did not recognise him. That was a good sign but sooner or later a regular routine will attract attention.

The Chase Manhattan Bank was an impressive building. Ray could think of a lot more easily accessible targets. He climbed the front steps, pushed his way through the revolving doors and made his way into the entrance hall. In the corner of the reception area, standing next to a pretentious green plastic fir tree festooned in flashing lights, a rotund red faced undercover cop dressed as Santa Clause in tradition Christmas clothing was ringing a brass bell and saying, 'Ho, Ho, Ho, Happy Christmas.' Too obvious, it was still November; will they ever learn? thought Ray.

He presented his ID card to security and escorted to the inner sanctum: the manager's office. As he crossed the pink marbled floor of the cavernous foyer, he began to sweat; his collar and tie were too tight. Ray began to feel uncomfortable. He looked around at the wage slaves in their reinforced bulletproof glass cages. Like performing monkeys in a human zoo. Honest law-abiding folk, he realised what a soul-destroying nine-to-five existence some people lived to make ends meet. A part of the rat race trapped on the treadmill of life in the endless effort to survive.

In the back room Ray watched a continuous display, as the security cameras out front fed a continuous supply of irrelevant information to the computer screens. Provided an endless visual display, recording every detail of a mundane repetitive daily routine.

The Bank was ready and waiting. The workers had not been warned in advance, it was part of company policy. The usual rules applied: when asked to hand over the money, do not resist. The tills contained a previously prepared bundle of identifiable bank notes. To be used only on demand. The intermittent flashing lights on the Christmas tree out front looked the same as those installed around the enclosed canopy of the customer cubicles at the front desk. Each coloured canopy light contained a mini camera, when the sequence was activated by one of the feet of a

25

bank employee; each bulb took a picture in turn from right to left and back again like a brain scan. Linked to the central computer every movement was saved, examined, and analysed.

This secondary security system was activated at 10:32 a.m. A city gent with silver hair, wearing a black business suit was pointing a pistol in cubical four and sliding a briefcase across the counter, under the partition, toward the cashier. Bundles of used $20 bills were demanded and deposited into the case. He retrieved the case, concealed the pistol and turned toward the exit. Acting on information received in their earpiece, a previously prepared plan was put into operation and the security staff moved in.

Security will not challenge a suspect in the crowded concourse of the bank, but wait until after they have reached the exit. With the revolving doors in sight, he noticed two security guards approaching from opposite directions. They were too eager, they had blown it. At the same time a little old lady wearing a hearing aid emerged from the restroom and crossed in front of him. In an instinctive act of desperation he grabbed her and pulled out the pistol. It was a stand off. Frozen in time, the guards had stopped in mid-stride. The old lady reacted immediately and dropped to the floor losing her hearing aid, leaving the gunman exposed to Santa Clause who shot him at point blank range. As the sound of the gunshot disappeared in the stunned silence that followed, a small tinny voice could be heard coming from the discarded hearing aid. 'Nice one Peter, I owe you one'. Peter returned to the rest room and changed back into his shabby 'Colombo' street clothes. Placing his disguise in the plastic bag, he left the bank building and sat on the sidewalk, waiting.

Ray removed the video recording from the VHS unit and left the office. As he walked toward the front door of the bank, the body was covered and removed with the help of the NYPD. The spot were he was shot left a mark on the polished pink marble floor that complemented the colour, but as he approached and walked around it, the red oxygenated blood began to change colour and congeal. It was quickly washed away by a member of the cleaning staff. Displaying an attitude of bored indifference, moving a long handled mop about meeting the requirements of her contract. Ray paused on the front steps as he heard the brass bell ring out and Santa Clause say, 'Happy Christmas Ho, Ho, Ho!' Inside, business continued as usual. Out on the street at 11:30 a.m., he passed the video to Peter, to be viewed later at the local precinct. Sixty minutes can change your life in New York City.

Ray took time out to enjoy the autumn day. As he walked home from the bank he stopped at a downtown deli, bought a take away salami sandwich and took a yellow cab to Central Park. Just to sit, eat and watch the changing of the season. As the plants and the trees prepared for winter the leaves on the maple trees were changing colour. Those that had already lost their nutrients, the red and browns were also losing their hold on life. As the north wind blew intermittently, they were randomly discarded and descended in a disorganised manner. They reached the ground to be crunched under foot. Or if they settled in the shade of the canopy cast by the over hanging branches, they were slowly made into mulch by the multitude of microbes that thrived in the damp dark conditions.

Sitting on a park bench with the leftover scraps of the sandwich, he began feeding a flock of perfectly preened pigeons performing their feed me routine. He watched as they lost their inhibitions and came closer. Ray was in charge again; it made him feel good to be in control of the situation. It was a part of a cop's conditioning.

Set into the ground, opposite the Dakota Building, the Strawberry Fields Memorial to John Lennon contains the word 'Imagine'. Picked out in the centre of a mosaic circle it brought back many memories, from the early days of the Police Academy. Walking on the sunny side of the street, Ray had to cross over to the dark side again. Out front, and in the shadow of the Dakota building dealing dope was a young pretentious punk street kid, wearing a black fleece, the hood displaying a trendy designer fashion logo. Cavorting on a skateboard, he impressed the passing public. As they gathered and stopped to watch in admiration, he occasionally accidentally, at a given signal, bumped into a bystander, who was prepared to accept a piece of plastic wrap into a pocket as previously arranged. An onlooker, his money minder, had already received payment in advance.

Walking through the audience, Ray ignored the act and left it to the street police. He was to old to run after a street kid on a skateboard but it would be mentioned later down town at the precinct. He decided to descend into the depths of the New York subway system and take a ride on a graffiti-covered train, to Grand Central Station. Looking out on to the white tiled stopping off points on the journey, seeing the low life, the hustlers and the hobos, he reflected on the fact that anti-social behaviour, ducking and diving, wheeling and dealing took a lot of time and energy. Why waste time? You can't change the rules, so behave. You're born, you do a bit, and then you die, end of story. Is it all completely pointless?

He entered the station and appreciated the cathedral-like space: the huge vaulted ceiling and spectacular sparkling chandeliers. Ignoring the ticket-buying commuters scurrying about in a frantic effort to arrive at the right ornate, brass-windowed booths. Ray went straight to the left luggage locker that contained information and marked money. It would be used if needed, by Peter or Ray. Sign a receipt for the money, a declaration of intent and fill out a form for the department. As part of a regular routine, the paper work was cleared and replaced by a midnight mover, an unknown member of the police department. The marked money was used to incriminate criminal characters. It would be exchanged for illegal goods and end up in the hands of a suspect holding the folding, with a bit of police persuasion it was then traced back to its original source. Like fishing for fools with a baited hook, sooner or later someone would bite. They kept track of each other by leaving details of their intended destinations, writing down the day, date, arrival time and the chosen route. After leaving his allotted supply of marked money in the locker, Ray returned to the subway and took a train down town. Arriving at the local station and looking forward to an evening of domestic culinary delights, he decided to stop off on the way home and indulge in the delicacies of Leo's Delicatessen located between Lexington and 3rd Avenue.

For Ray, food and cooking was one of life's luxuries, a reason for living. Loaded up with bulging bags full of deli delights and waiting at the crossroads for, the red light to turn green, on the opposite corner from Pedro the paper seller's patch. He never gave a second glance as the ambulance with the flashing lights and two-tone horns blaring screamed by, in a frantic attempt to deliver a patient to the Accident and Emergency Department of the nearest hospital.

On the street corner and also in front of the stone steps of the brown stone apartment building the scene of crime signs where directing the passing pedestrians around the fluttering flags of the police cordon. At first glance, the Jesus-freak looked as if he was sitting silently in meditation in a comfortable position, resting his back against the A-frame sandwich board. The small round red beady spot on his forehead, just below the front of his turban and between the eyes, was not a significant sign of an eastern religion, or a weeping western spiritual or religious stigmata. Ray watched as the small bullet hole, expelled a single drop of blood. It emerged from the confines of the cranium, released like an irritating tiresome tear that had been contaminated by a speck of salt. Let loose, it slowly descended down the nose, to hang on to the tip. Rapidly followed by another, which completed the same course and combined with the other to form a big bulbous drop. By his side the ghetto blaster was still blaring out at full volume the distorted message that Jesus saves.

The street punk kid on a skateboard appeared from nowhere. He arrived at the crime scene and slowing down, he took a detour. With impeccable timing and the ability and agility of a ballerina, he ducked under the flags of the police cordon and grabbed the ghetto blaster. Without a pause or missing a beat in his perfectly performed choreography he continued on his way toward the crossroads. With his hood down and going for the green light, he never saw or heard the approaching danger from the side street.

An illegal Mexican migrant had secured his first job in the USA with false papers and a licence lent to him by a friend of the family. Driving a dump truck, and filling up the builders rubbish skip parked under the fire escape he had a problem. Engaging the reverse gear, the warning horn was not working. He never felt the bump as the rear wheel rode over the street kid and broke his skateboard.

The body and the ghetto blaster had fallen silent. Squashed and displaying their contents, they were both in a bad way. The Police and the Paramedics left the Jesus freak for later and took time out to confer and confront the latest life or death situation in an efficient manner, like a team of American football players huddled in a heap trying to make a decision. But it was too late for the ghetto blaster. The hard outer plastic shell had shattered and in a last desperate attempt to spread the word, it had disgorged its hidden secret, the reason for its distorted sound. Under the stationary dump truck, hidden from view, below the rear axle and in the shadow of the big back wheels, plastic wraps of crack cocaine were spread far and wide, lying on the street next to a ringing cell phone.

Ray intervened and took charge of the situation; it was time to take control of an incompetent collection of street cops. He issued orders and restored organised efficiency. Leaving them to deal with the recently departed Jesus-freak, he retrieved the phone and read the text message that said, 'Aussi John,' before placing it in his pocket for later. Returning in time to listen as the Chief of Police in charge of the crime scene interviewed a witness.

'I watched it all from across the street, two of them came out of the window and down the fire escape from that apartment on the second floor above the Butcher. They landed in the rubbish skip. The first one looked at the Jesus freak and shot him in the head. The man with the gun had a symbol of some sort tattooed on his right cheek a dragon maybe, the mark of a member of a Chinese Triad? Then they both ran up the side street past the dump truck.'

Ray overheard the witness statement and time stood still, his blood ran cold.

The witness was still presenting his claim to fame. Preparing and elaborating his story for the local night time TV news. Money might be mentioned. He wanted his five minutes of fame (for a price) but Ray was long gone, running up the stone steps two at a time he reached the apartment.

Without slowing down, he took the cop on guard by surprise and burst through the broken door. Before he had time to explain his presence, he was grabbed by the legs from behind and thrown to the floor. He ended up on the carpet face down, in the shattered glass of the framed photograph of his coming out parade. Hearing a continuous clicking sound, he rose up on his elbows to see the window wide open and the long brown curtains flapping in the breeze, as the old black 78 record stuck in the last groove on the wind up gramophone, repeated itself endlessly. He was trying desperately to reach the centre label.

The cop apologised and explained the situation. Opportunist intruders had reached the apartment by the fire escape. They lowered the window and climbed through, to ransack the empty room looking for cash. The old lady had disturbed them and been shot on her way back from the bathroom. Her walking frame still lay on its side between the bathroom and the bedroom. Not waiting to listen to the rest of the minor details, he realised that the ambulance he saw on his way home contained his Mother.

Ray was on the run again. He took a cab to the local hospital, looking out of the window on the way. As the rain ran down the glass on the outside, he could not decide if it was the tears escaping from his eyes being reflected in the dirty finger stained window, or if it was the continuous down pour on the other side of the glass. A hospital smell is universal: disinfectant, death and disease. Accident and Emergency had taken mother to Intensive care. Hooked up to a complicated collection of tubes and a blood transfusion unit, she was in a bad way. White as the sheet she was laying on, Ray thought of the word shroud but this was not good, he could not accept this. After an all-night bedside vigil in, which they both drifted in and out of consciousness, he woke up at the sound of his name. Mother was sitting upright in the bed and he had to listen to the painful, emotional outpouring of a person who knew she was dying, like the last confession of a convicted killer.

Holding his hand, she issued a long list of things to do, constantly interrupting his words of controlled calm, compassion and positive thought. She would not be persuaded to rest, relax and save her breath. Her time was short and she knew it. As the old lady slowly lay back and settled down again into the comfortable confines of the hospital bed, a peaceful hush descended. Ray watched as the unblinking eyes turned to look in his direction. He sat, he watched, he waited but not a sign, not a movement, nothing. Uncontrollably shaking and sobbing, he was desperately trying to get it together; he stood up and turned to leave the room. As he reached the door, he heard her voice from behind his back.

She sat up for the last time and said, 'Don't forget to send the Christmas cards and tell your Australian cousin.'

Then she fell forward and the movement removed the blood transfusion tube from her left arm. The peaks on the screen and the pings that emitted from the heart monitor resided and then the screen registered a flat line.

When he returned home, the police cleaning crew had completed their work. The apartment had been photographed, fingerprinted and secured, leaving behind the cold clinical feeling of a sterile atmosphere devoid of life. At home alone, sorting through a lifetime collection of pointless possessions which meant so much to the dearly departed, is the hardest thing you will ever have to do. Deciding to keep or discard, the treasured lifetime collection, of mass-produced hand painted porcelain figurines, carefully placed in a prominent position on the top shelf of the dresser, or the ornaments, which jostled for space beside the missing presentation pack. Sealed in a transparent protective covering, the display case contained in mint condition, a collection of Irish coins. Purchased in the year of his birth and never to be touched or disturbed, except for cleaning. Ray was told at an early age that they would be worth a fortune later. To dispose of the remaining worthless articles or donate them to the local charity shop along with the old worn out records felt like an act of betrayal. Mother kept a daily journal in the drawer at the side of her bed, and a collection of recently received correspondence, relevant to the day-to-day running of her property rental business.

Unknown to Ray, the drawer also contained an address book full of information, the names and addresses of family, friends and famous figures from the past, the great and the good of America.

Going back in time, he realised that Mother's life had been a long interesting chain of events with a very chequered past. Reading the written word opened up a history, a sealed time capsule. Her secret past was presented on a platter, a smorgasbord of titbits and delicacies on the surface, but built on a cold hard bed of despair, desperation, and dedication. Stuck to the last page a faded photograph of his granddad as a young man, cut from the New York Times on the day of his arrival in America.   He had arrived as a hero. Next to it, a faded letter explained his fall from favour. Ray read the following:

THE
S S TITANIC

White Star Line

(April 14 1912)

*B*ack in Gaol again, but I am a hero so they say. America, the land of the free, justice and opportunity. That's what I thought. Do you believe in luck? Read my story and make up your own mind

I am Mick Mulligan. I have been to Sea before, I don't think I shall go again. Let me explain. I jumped Ship in North Africa, January 1911 for personal reasons and was arrested in Cairo a year later after a bar room brawl. I escaped and stowed away to Southampton.

I changed my name and papers and signed on the Titanic as a seaman second class. On April 14 th I was on watch in the Crows Nest with Sam Smith. On watch for what, to see the Sea? They had mentioned Icebergs, any excuse to keep us there. It was getting colder by the minute. The temperature was dropping and so were my spirits. I did not need to hear the music and laughter down below in the first class Ballroom. It only made me more depressed, and then I saw it.

The Titanic was the biggest Ship afloat, but the Iceberg I was looking at dead ahead was even bigger. I was halfway down the ladder when the impact threw me to the deck below. Landing on the tarpaulin which covered the Lifeboat broke my fall and knocked me out.

The next thing I knew I was ordered to help the women and children and lower the Lifeboat, then I passed out again. When I regained consciousness I felt the cold Atlantic freezing my right hand which was hanging over the side of the Boat. Either that or the piecing scream of panic had brought me to my senses. A little lad was clinging desperately to a floating piece of flotsam which was passing by. His hysterical Mother screamed in my ear to save him.

I was not capable of rational thought due to mental confusion caused by the blow to my head. I found myself swimming towards the little lad. When I reached him he pointed back the way I had come. I turned in time to see the overloaded lifeboat slip slowly beneath the waves caused by his distraught Mother leaning too far over the side.

I can't remember much of those days that we lay on that broken hatch cover. It could have been four hours, four days or four weeks. I do remember tying us both to the cover but I don't know how or when I managed that. When I woke up I was covered in white up to my neck had it been snowing? No it was warm it was a white sheet, I was in a Hospital bed.

We docked in New York harbour and faced a frantic, force of photographers and newspaper reporters all looking for a story. My picture was on the front page standing next to the little lad. I was a Hero, for a day. The little lad's dad remembered me from the picture in the paper.

He was the Chief of Police who arrested me in Cairo and from whom I escaped after a bit of brutal bashing. America, freedom, justice? I've got six months in Gaol and lost my right hand to frostbite and Gangrene. Not much freedom and not much justice. Do you still believe in luck?

Mick Mulligan

Chapter Four

Ray sent the message far and wide as fast as possible to all the addresses in the book. He made sure that they all had enough time to respond and attend the funeral. It was short and sweet, like a wedding. You are allowed an allotted time slot, to arrive, pay your respects and go through the expected procedure, before going home for tea and biscuits. Making way for the next interment on time, according to the rulebook and running order of the day.

Conveying the dearly departed to the Promised Land without halt or hindrance. It is like a continuous conveyer belt of rejected items. For the undertaker and the gravediggers, death is a lucrative business, an uninterrupted constant supply of corpses. To be cleaned, preened and presented in the Chapel of rest before the final journey. The account will arrive later along with the junk mail and the letter from the local authority demanding extra money as the sole occupant of the apartment, (like a happy holiday punter paying a single room supplement for the privilege of being alone). We are born with a design fault, a sell by date. We begin, we do a bit and then we die. It makes no sense at all, so what is the grand plan? Ashes to ashes dust to dust, some don't try but some must.

No one from the past attempted to attend. Their cards of condolences arrived with well thought out explanations and excuses. The great and the good had failed but the real people had arrived, they stood in the pouring rain with their heads bowed as a mark of respect. Cathy the cleaner, the janitor, mother's devoted carer Mrs Mason, Mr Chang from the Chinese restaurant and Captain Luck from the Police Department were all present. Peter, at the gates, in his shabby Mac could always be relied on to be close by. That man was something else.

Paying his last respects at the side of the grave, deep in thought, Ray slowly became aware of a ringing tone from the cell phone in his pocket.

He read the text message 'Aussi John.' So much had happened in such a short time; he had forgotten to hand it over to the Department. Ray gave it to Captain Luck. After a last look at the coffin, laying in the cold embrace of the carefully cut confines of the grave, containing his history, the past and his reason for living. He slowly turned and walked away; to try and pick up the pieces of his shattered life.

Ray had to keep busy, doing the only thing he knew he could do well, the day job. When he arrived early the next day at the office of captain Luck, he realised why he had decided to go undercover. At 9 a.m., the charge room already contained a heaving hysterical collection of pimps, prostitutes, drunks and drug addicts left over from the night before. The pimps were posing and strutting their stuff. Performing like prima donnas in their gaudy glad rags, wearing their gold rings and presenting a mouthful of golden molars. Their prostitutes complained continuously. Out on the street they each had their own patch to patrol, separation gave them a feeling of control, in charge of their own small world. Confined in one small room it was an opportunity to settle unfinished business with the opposition, a meeting place for the ladies of the night. Flashy fingernails, perfectly painted and presented sharp as the claws of an alley cat, became weapons of war. Fights were breaking out indiscriminately and for no apparent reason. Hair pulling and naked flesh exposed to all the people present. Rolling around on the floor in their mini skirts, without their underwear was not a sight Ray needed to see. Bedlam broke out as the usual useless group of local drunkards became activated by the incessant noise. They decided to stand up in a wobbly fashion and made a collected effort to confront their opponents in a fight to the finish. Forming their fists and at the same time facing in all directions, they prepared themselves to fend off the non-existing threatening force. The professional drug addicts looked on in silent wonder and amazement from their elevated position, the lofty heights of their own personal planets.

In the office with Captain Luck, Peter agreed with Ray's request that he should be allowed to return to work immediately. No compassionate leave, no more weeping and wailing, that was yesterday. Ray had to carry on; he had a crime to solve. Working with the help of the service provider the cell phone memory had provided a number of interesting leads into the investigation of the death of the crack cocaine dealer, most of the numbers were already known to the Drug Squad with the exception of one. Call signals that activated the customised phone with the message 'Aussi John' were generated from a mobile transceiver. The phone contained an automatic delete, which wiped the location of the call after ten minutes. Ray realised that the man in charge had invested a lot of time and money, setting up and organising his part in the illegal business. Buying the franchise, paying for the permit and getting permission from those who must be obeyed. He would not be notified by the Traffic Police for non-payment of a parking ticket, or a final demand from the Taxation Department. This man was smart, a grey ghost, he covered all the possibilities. Leaving nothing to chance, and no trace of his existence and participation. Ray enjoyed a challenge.

Peter left the office with one intention. He was a man on a mission, to find Aussi John. Downtown had been taken over by a Colombian drug cartel, protection rackets, pornography, moneylenders, murder and mayhem. The Mafia in their day had to employ enforcers. Big heavy muscle bound men; to go out and collect payment but men cost money. Once they are hooked, crack cocaine controls the user. Like a moth to a flame they return without threat or force. On a regular basis they willingly arrive to pay the dealer the source of their supply. Like an efficient company/corporation that has streamlined and down sized its workforce, and made redundant the regular arrival of the debt collectors on the doorstep. Peter arrived as usual at the local drop in centre for people with a drug problem, to look, learn, and listen.

At the centre Peter heard the name Aussi John again. Jimmy White, a black South African junkie with a tattooed cheek, was a full-time speed-freak junkie. Peter was playing the part of a user, made a point of participating in the conversation. Rumour had it that Aussi John was providing the best buy on the street. Certain words and information provided clues and credibility, which collectively helped to complete the picture. Another part of the puzzle had fallen into place. Trying to contain the availability and supply of hard drugs on the streets down town had resulted in a turf war. Ghetto gangs with guns, fighting for their patch. Macho men strutting their stuff and making their mark to protect their image. Control freaks on an ego trip, more bullets than brain cells. The city mortuary contained an unusual amount of cocaine addicts, caused by the consumption of a contaminated supply. Cut with caustic soda and talcum powder to bulk up the buy. Those responsible were controlling the market by increasing the price for the good gear. The first rule of business: create a demand and then limit the supply, name your price and then blame the opposition for their inferior product.

Pete needed to buy a supply, so he took a trip to Coney Island. In the cold light of a wind swept winters day, it presented a deserted God forsaken façade of tasteless, tacky boarded up buildings, shedding red and gold flakes of cheap gloss peeling paint. Revealing the exposed underside to the elements. As the angry sea slowly but surely increased its wind power and pounded the properties. The continuous loud raucous rubbing sound, created by the waves that incessantly moved and eroded the pebbles on the beach, suppressed the muted sound of a flock of sad-eyed seagulls as they sat muttering and mumbling with their backs to the wind. As the gale force wind slowly changed direction and Peter approached them, they took flight, angry and annoyed at being disturbed. Crying out, they departed in unison, dispatched in desperation they flew in formation to the roof of Frankie's French Fries and Burger Bar.

Next to the weather beaten worn out wooden steps that led to the front door of the restaurant. Left over from the last summer season, discarded by some of the thousands that paid the price of the exciting entertainment on offer. An accumulated selection of litter had collected in a corner. Clown masks, paper hats and discarded polystyrene coffee cups, driven there by the relentless winds that were pushed on by the ferocious ferocity of the mountainous grey green seas that were produced by the Atlantic gales. This time of year the pickings for the feathered flock, were few and far between. As Peter approached and climbed the steps to the front door, there was no need to knock. Unexpectedly it flew open, caught in a sudden gust of wind it began to move its rusty, squeaking hinges back and forth. As the competition from the wind grew greater it lost it's audible protest as the door banged on relentlessly. As Peter forced the door into the open position, a big bold opportunistic herring gull took advantage. Swooping down, it flew by and deposited a large amount of droppings on to the shoulder of

Peter's shabby Mac. It flew on through the open door.

Peter found it sitting at Frankie's side, next to the needle stuck in his right arm. Slumped in a corner, behind the cocktail bar in the back room. Frankie had been dead for hours. The bulging vacant stare of the lifeless brown eyes protruded, as rigor mortis set in. The impressions from the wrist restraint were still visible. They had been bound, and were now black and bruised. Three empty glasses and a bottle of imported Australian Bundaberg rum remained on the counter. Peter focused his Polaroid pocket camera and took photographs. Frankie was not an addict or a user, a retired cop he passed on information about the low life and supplied the occasional bag, to be planted by the department to convict a known villain. As Peter closed the door he realised that the bad guys were getting closer. It was a warning: it was time to change direction.

The autopsy report and the men at the morgue confirmed the suspicion that death had resulted from a drug overdose-caused by an injection of contaminated cocaine. Peter had to go to ground, hide up for a while and think this thing through. No phone calls. No outside influences, and no interruptions. Ray understood the way that Peter worked. They both came from different directions, to meet in the middle and solve the problem. Opposites attract. Their lines of communication would always be open. It was uncanny the way they thought, like twins, they had an affinity. Plus they had the advantage of the latest electronic, state of the art tracking device, and immediate satellite communication.

To change the mood completely in his spare time, Peter played blues guitar (he was good) and as part of the day job he could be seen around town playing, in the subway and on the sidewalk. Collecting coins in a cap placed next to prince the police dog. He preferred animals to people. But Peter had a weakness. An insatiable craving for caffeine, his constant consumption of coffee kept him continuously alert. He was an addict, without a regular intake Peter could became very volatile, and unstable. Hyperactive, and out of control he was a force to be reckoned with. Times Square on a Sunday night was the place to be. B.B. King's Blues Club had a Gospel Choir from Harlem, and a special attraction. Peter sat in the back row to relax and enjoy the music. Looking like a lost and vulnerable out of town tourist. Sitting in the row in front, a couple of Afro-Americans began in a slow venomous whisper, to argue about a drug deal. The shot of the silenced gun could not be heard above the booming voice of B. B. King. Peter looked on, and witnessed the shooting.

Automatically, he jumped the row of seats and chased the responsible dreadlock-wearing Rasta man down the isle. They crashed through the emergency fire door exit. Out in the alley, kicking the garbage cans out of his way as he went, he sent them clattering down the dark, damp, deserted street. Running down the road at full speed Peter had a clear run. Disturbing the rising steamy fog, discarded from the subway vent, expelled by the continuous supply of below ground commuters. Bursting through the misty cloud, he saw his objective. As he went after the gunman he called out, 'Stop, Police!' and aimed his gun at the fleeing target.

Passing by the local laundrette, the man stopped and turned, a tattoo on his right cheek, a dragon, the mark of a member of a Chinese Triad, was illuminated by a sudden light. The force of the explosion blew Peter off his feet, as the first floor apartment above the laundrette erupted in a ball of flame. Blowing out the windows and covering him in shards of broken glass.

Shaking off the shock, Peter slowly regained his composure. Finding his feet again and in the light of the flickering flames, he saw a shape, a figure coming toward him. Emerging from the doorway of the burning building. A little old lady in a singed kitchen apron, still clutching a blackened, smoking wooden spoon, in her left hand, had blood running down her face. Which she was ineffectively trying to wipe away with a kitchen cloth.

Suffering from shock, she said, 'Would you like this? I have some more; I bought them on special, two for the price of one from the five and dime store on the corner. You never now when you might need them.'

Peter took the blood soaked rag and surreptitiously placed it on her head to extinguish what was left of her burnt and still smouldering, blue rinse, curly, cauliflower hair cut.

In the office, first thing Monday morning, Peter joined the usual collection of insurance assessors, forensic investigators, and fire department officials. A character from county hall, wearing a clean white shirt and a designer suit was also present; this unexpected disruption was not part of his day job. He was sent there to convince the waiting TV camera crew that it was an unfortunate accident. That it had nothing to do with the department's continuing reluctance to spend money. Modernise and replace an existing, deteriorating gas main. An ongoing local issue, which had previously resulted in the death of a passer-by, discarding a cigarette-end and unintentionally igniting the escaping volatile vapours. The media people, those that get paid by their employers to find or create a story, to fill T.V. Air time, and or column inches, were out in force. The assembled company and crew were transferred from the police department, transported uptown to view the location, to examine the evidence, and confirm their positions of importance. Peter walked uptown. The pungent smell of smoke still hung in the cold morning air, as the diminishing drizzly. Illuminated by an early morning sunbeam, pierced its way through the hole in the roof. Left over from the previous night's rain, it finally finished, and extinguished the remaining embers of the burnt out building.

A member of the Arson Department carried out a routine investigation, and confirmed that an unaccountable internal explosion had caused the fire. A gas supply was not connected to the all-electric apartment. Hearing this, the man in the spotlight, the character from county hall, breathed a deep silent sigh of relief. He rapidly made his apologies and cut short his meeting with the media. The excuse was that he had a prearranged appointment with a local charity. His expensive designer suit was now impregnated with the smell of smoke and he had an appointment with a lady, at a pre-paid hotel room for two. She was not working for charity. Desperate to depart with dignity as soon as possible, he hurried down to the ground floor.

Left behind in his wake, the media men franticly followed in his footsteps. Peter arrived in time to witness their departure. Without a second glance, they passed Peter in his grubby Mac, as he stood to one side to let them by, in what was left of the burnt out lobby, like a cloud of flies following a tasty bit of meat, prepared for the morning TV market.

When the party of parasites had departed to report their conflicting conclusions, Peter slowly, calmly, and carefully examined the remains of the previously adjacent apartments. The force of the explosion had blown a hole through the flimsy, particleboard partition wall, and carried with it the pieces of a person that was impossible to identify. Next to the hole on the other side, in the old lady's apartment, standing upright on top of the cooker. A dried up, burnt out, cooking pot, contained the charred remains of last night's evening meal. Untouched by the blast, it was still waiting to be removed from the slow heat, radiating from the electric ring. Peter pulled the plug, and returned to the remains of the room next door. Picking up and placing the remaining pieces of evidence into plastic bags the forensic team were hard at work. The remains of the fridge and freezer were scattered far and wide. A sharp pointed part of the metal casing had pierced a piece of oblong wooden furniture situated in the opposite corner of the room. Now burnt beyond recognition the blackened remains had disgorged it's hidden content. Collectable Irish coins, loose change from foreign parts and a slightly fire damaged leather wallet. The corner also contained fragments of glass. Above the burnt remains and imbedded in the wall by the force of the explosion. A part of a broken bottle still displayed the singed label of the Australian Bundaberg Rum Company. The coins were bagged and tagged by the forensic team. The remains of the broken bottle and a blob of melted metal, looking like a modern art impression of a pair of distorted dishes fused together, were also taken for further examination. After the departure of the picture-taking professionals from the media, Peter took out and focused his pocket camera and took photos for his own private investigation.

Before he left the scene, Peter poked about and picked up a piece of a dry charred, carbonised chair leg, laying next to the hole in the wall and in front of the non-existent fridge. It had escaped the deluge of water that had been laid down by the fire department. He broke it in half and released the absorbed, pungent powerful smell of gasoline. Carbon carries and contains odours and impurities. Peter did not need chemical analysis; he had an experienced nose. This was no accident. It was deliberate. Someone did not like the person that was now in pieces in the black plastic disposable bags.

Back at his room in the boarding house, Peter pasted his latest photos on to the wall with blue tack, below the ones that were still part of on-going investigations. The last in line, matched up with the one above, they had something in common Bundaberg Rum. The killing on Coney Island and the latest collection of colour prints provided another piece of the puzzle. Peter phoned Ray immediately.

When he received the call, Ray was at home doing the paper work, sorting out the final details of the last will and testament of his recently departed mother. To reply to the cards of condolences, Ray had written in the nicest possible way a standard letter on the word processor. He used mail merge to insert the addresses. To inform the great and the good that it was understandable that they could not attend the funeral due to pressing commitments and he understood. Maybe they could meet up later? The letters also contained the following information: Please accept a hand painted porcelain figure, a priceless piece of my late mother's private collection. Dispatched and on the way to you, a private security company will ensure special customer care. On arrival it must be confirmed with a signature and cash on delivery.

As the morning light broke through the bedroom window of the apartment, Ray woke and remembered that he was on his own. There was no more, 'Don't forget the window and the mirror.' No more breakfast tray and no regular routine. For the first time in his life Ray was alone. He decided not to shave and looking like a scruffy tramp, a homeless hobo he walked to work. Out on the sidewalk he passed a brown skinned bag lady pushing a supermarket trolley full of her worldly goods. He did not recognise or give her a second glance.

When they eventually arrived at the station, he and Peter would have to have words. He reckoned that Ray was losing the plot.

Ray was miles away in a world of his own. Crossing the street on a red light, not hearing the traffic frantically braking and backing up, horns honking and the drivers delivering their verbal abuse, he reached Pedro the paper seller on the opposite corner. Pedro had seen the suicidal situation about to take place.

'Man, you must be mad! You have survived all these years fighting crime. Risking life and limb and now you have a death wish? I refuse to sell you a paper until you get your act together.'

Ray had been told. Following from behind, Peter had seen the situation develop. Taking a short cut, he arrived at the police station in time to explain to Captain Luck.

Ray arrived later and walked into the office as the captain was comparing Peter's photographs. At a glance the captain knew that Peter was right. Ray needed to take time off and do something different; he was suffering from burn out. A lifetime of law enforcement had taken its toll. His retirement was long over due. That, or a desk job.

Chapter Five

The captain was amazed that there was no resistance. Ray was too old and tired to argue with the captain, he had nothing left no defence or resistance. He reluctantly accepted the desk job and become part of the Information Technology Centre. Introduced to a room full of bright young things, he felt like a fish out of water, stranded in an alien environment. It increased his feeling of isolation and insecurity as he saw the only vacant seat situated in the far corner of the back row. Out of sight and out of mind, Ray was ignored as he desperately tried to get to grips and understand the complexities of the modern computer age. A cell phone was fine, he could handle a set sequence of numbers. An international encyclopaedia of information on the Internet and working out the intricacies of Electronic Mail and understanding the workings of World Wide Web sites would take a little longer. Ray felt like a naughty boy that had done something wrong and had been sent back to school, to sit in the corner and complete his education. Peter was back on the street again. The captain had sent him out to buy a bottle of Bundaberg Rum, an expensive item that could only be purchased from a limited number of retail outlets.

To visit uptown New York, Peter had dressed to play the part of a rich eccentric connoisseur of fine wines and imported alcohol. After a hard day's work, he eventually found the outlet he was looking for: a supplier of Bundaberg Rum and European Dutch liquor chocolates, available from E.M.U. Foreign Imports Emporium, situated on Fifth Avenue.

The next day Ray began to understand and decipher the complicated world of the computer. He took to it like a duck to water he was a natural. Busy banging about at the keyboard, Peter arrived with his unopened bottle of rum. His lazy eye was twitching; he was suffering from a lack of caffeine. Ray recognised the signs and knew it was important if Peter had arrived at the office without first consuming copious amounts of coffee. He interrupted as Ray located the last known address of Lennie, the dope dealer.

The street punk kid on the skateboard had lived above the laundrette in the same apartment were the Sunday night explosion had taken place. Peter insisted that Ray use his latest technical tool immediately to search for information. He located city hall property records department and inserted the web site address. The information super-highway revealed the fact that the property belonged to an off shore investment company registered and traded as EMU Imports and Exports based in Amsterdam, Holland. Peter breathed an audible sigh of satisfaction he was on the case, he was up to something but Ray knew him well enough not to ask, until Peter had satisfied his additive craving for caffeine. Ray turned his attention again to the computer keyboard, trying to locate the owner of the property where Lennie had lived.

He pressed a few keys and was interrupted again, this time by one of the back room boys from forensic delivering a comprehensive detailed report. The team of analytical experts had completed their investigations and confirmed that the explosion had resulted from a deliberate combination of a volatile liquid and an explosive material. The report suggested that the fridge/freezer contained a gasoline accelerant. Traces of a melted silvered plastic material were also found, bonded by the force of the explosion to the widely dispersed, fragmented pieces of the cooler compartment. The forensic department had decided that the explosion had resulted from a carefully constructed pre-planed sequence of events a chain reaction. The report suggested that a three-litre cardboard wine box placed in side the cooler on the top shelf had been used. It contained a silvered plastic bladder. Filled with gasoline and open at the top to release the vapours, it had been situated next to an explosive. The detonator had been wired to the fridge light and the opening of the door activated the explosion.

The second paragraph of the report contained the information that the rare collection of Irish coins had escaped fire damage, protected from the heat by their location behind a leather wallet. The wallet contained the remains of a first class plane ticket to Amsterdam and also a couple of

Dutch guilder coins. Forensic had also decided that the bright blob of melted metal that looked like a pair of distorted dishes fused together. It was all that remained of an ornamental set of kitchen scales. It was suggested that they could have been used for weighing quantities of drugs.

Once again Ray returned to the computer. The screen displayed the answer to the previous question: the property belonged to an off-shore investment company registered as EMU Imports and Exports, Canal Street, Amsterdam, Holland. Ray was confused. He thought the computer had failed to register his latest request to find the owner of the property of Lennie's last address. He knew he was getting old but he wasn't stupid. He re-booted the PC and began again. He carefully repeated and entered the previous set of instructions the result was the same. The same company EMU Imports and Exports, Amsterdam, Holland owned both properties. They were still using the initials of the previous owners of the property. The European Monetary Union: a government department controlled by the bureaucrats in Brussels. Ray worked over time that night putting the pieces of the puzzle together.

EMU Exports was the holding company, controlled an International conglomeration of dubious business ventures, including coffee exporters from Columbia, property management in Miami, a diamond dealer in Amsterdam and shares in a South African diamond mine. Ray continued his research and discovered that a sizeable percentage of the company's collection of independent investors had received professional investment advice from the parent company and then invested money in Australia. Another south sea bubble that was about to burst, it was selling worthless paper promises in property and low laying land that was prone to flooding, or a piece of land devoid of life, swept clean every day by the insistent dry desert wind of the outback.

The captain called Ray and Peter into the office. He had a proposition. It needed a combined effort to collect the information that was required to catch the main man Mr Big. A section of the department played the same game as the CIA's undercover cops. They were employed on continuous working leave until later. Getting caught was not an option; the department would deny all knowledge of their existence.

Peter shuffled in first wearing his shabby Mac and his permanent five o'clock stubble. Ray arrived later booted and suited, clean and perfectly presentable for a day at the office. Standing together in front of the desk they were like chalk and cheese, two complete opposites. One fat and forty-plus and the other one thin and thirty-something, they looked like cartoon characters. Laurel and Hardy sprung to mind. The captain tried to keep a straight face, he was about to send them on a do or die assignment.

One last job to infiltrate, disrupt and destroy the criminal organisation. No holds barred and no interference or interruption from the department, free reign to achieve success. Money was not a problem. On completion, their early retirement and financial future would be secure for the rest of their lives.

The captain left them alone in the office to decide. Carrying large polystyrene cups of coffee, he returned from the cafeteria up the long corridor to the office. He waited outside as the augment subsided. The two inside always argued about any proposition. It was a ritual that had to be performed before they came to the same conclusion.

As soon as the captain opened the door, an aggravated Peter pounced on the coffee cups like a bird of prey. He downed three of the four cups immediately without stopping or saying a word. Leaving one for later, Peter began to perform like a barrister addressing the bench. He was in full flow, on a roll, locking his thumps under the lapels of his shabby Mac. Peter approached the captain and announced that after a sensible serious discussion they had reached a decision. Ray refused to get involved in the conversation or make eye contact with the captain. They both knew that eye-to-eye contact would result in hysterics. He gave a sly wink, a sight nod of agreement and grinned as Peter took centre stage and performed another one of his many perfect party pieces.

After the monologue, Peter confirmed the foregone conclusion that they would accept the mission. After the performance, the captain presented the plane tickets, two single KLM airline tickets to Schiphol International airport, Amsterdam Holland via Greenland. It was then that Peter realised he had made a big mistake. He had a phobia, an irrational fear of flying. It would take a lot of coffee to get him of the ground but once committed it had never been known for the man in the shabby Mac to back down, or change his mind.

They had forty-eight hours to get their act together before departure time from JFK airport. Ray had read about the explosion above the launderette. The little old lady from the next-door apartment had suffered shock and superficial burns. She was about to be released from the local hospital and put into the care of the Social Services, on her own with no friends or future and nowhere to go, without a permanent place to live. Her first name was Mary, the same as his dearly departed mother. He had no idea why he decided to visit this stranger, but he gave her the keys to his apartment.

Peter was also totally confused; he knew nothing about anything outside of New York City and the surrounding suburbs. He decided to travel light. His limited amount of necessities were an airline map, a packet of rolling tobacco, cigarette papers, matches, the ticket, passport, and a jar of instant coffee. All contained in a supermarket plastic carrier bag. Peter would have no problem with the excess weight limit of cabin luggage. He arrived early at the airport for the midnight flight. Dressed in a camouflage combat suit of jungle green it seemed appropriate for a stop off in Greenland.

On C.C.T.V. this suspicious character, after sitting so long alone, in the corner of the cafeteria had been brought to the attention of the airport security staff. The night shift arrived to take over and after a quick discussion they decided to remove the undesirable potential problem. Looking like a military man on the run or a drop out homeless hobo, Peter was approached and pounced on from both sides at the same time. Ray arrived in time to see Peter spread-eagled against the terminal wall being furiously frisked by security. He turned his head in time to see Ray walk by. A brief glance and a wink were exchanged as Ray continued his uninterrupted step to the check-in desk.

After the apologies, Peter followed the instructions on the indication boards to the departure lounge. A continual moving walkway took him past the glass fronted observation area. The KLM 707 passenger plane had parked so close he could see the pilots entering the cockpit for the return flight. One of them turned around and waved, an automatic reaction, a part of the training manual. Peter responded immediately, standing to attention and giving a soldier's salute. On the moving walkway, he suddenly realised he looked like a tin target in a shooting gallery at a local county fair. Seeing a 707 up close for the first time was an awe-inspiring sight. The size of the metal monster was something to behold; the nearest he had been to a plane before was a DIY, motorised plastic model Airfix kit, constructed with the help of his son on his sixth birthday. They tried to fly it across the lake in Central Park. Peter watched as it descended short of its destination. Close to the other side, it landed on the surface and floated within touching distance of the out stretched hand of his one and only excited son. He watched in stunned silence as his son waved, walked into the water and proudly plucked the plane from its landing place. It was triumphantly raised aloft in his left hand, like the torch in the hand of the Statue of Liberty. Peter watched in horror as his son stumbled and disappeared. In slow motion the slowly sinking arm, the small hand, clutching the mid-section of the miniature Boeing disappeared into the slowly lapping waters on the far side of the lake.

Time stood still and etched in his memory it remains the last sight of his dearly departed son.

Chapter Six

The Decision

The Dutch/South African Pilot, Jamie Johnson senior, wearing his silly grin and waving to the silent soldier on the moving walkway on the other side of the glass, had reached a decision. This job would be his last time in America.

He took his place in the cockpit for the pre-flight check. He had to go and go now. The flight scheduled for departure four days before, had been a part of his escape plan. He knew he was running out of time. The regular flying routine from North America to South Africa, the refuelling stop and the illegal pick-up for the forward flight to Amsterdam, carrying a carefully concealed consignment of uncut contraband played an essential financial part in providing his future wife with a secure future. The stop over in Cape Town also gave him a chance to bond with Jamie junior, his distant antagonistic son, and to invite him to the wedding.

Amsterdam Airport presented no problem. A taxi to the dark deserted office of EMU Imports and Exports, located above a shop in the red light district concluded his part in the first stage of the procedure. On arrival, he entered Erica's Exotic Emporium on the ground floor and in the front room, in full view of the passing public. He slowly removed his uniform, like a pornography film star. An audience began to gather which was exactly what they both wanted. The potential witnesses would confirm later that, compliant coupling was about to take place as Erica closed the curtains. Unseen by the passing potheads and perverts, the sexually satisfied pilot dressed in his new, clean, previously prepared and made-to-measure uniform. It contained a considerable amount of paper money in a secure section of the lining.

He made his way to Damme Square in the centre of town and took a taxi to Hilda's apartment. Carefully clutching in his right pocket the engagement ring safely contained in its red robust heart shaped box. On the way, he rapidly, silently and continuously repeated his previously, perfectly rehearsed speech. The original exciting adrenaline rush had changed over the years and had now become a feeling of pursued paranoia. Turn around time was forty-eight hours.

After an uneventful transatlantic flight the Boeing 707 arrived on time at JFK Airport, New York. The Hertz self-drive hire car was ready and waiting. Driving downtown, he reached his destination, to complete the final part of the plan another change of uniform. Slowly seeking out a parking place in the side street, a coloured madman, with dreadlocks ran out of the mist in front of him waving a gun. At the same time, the laundrette opposite him exploded in a ball of flame. Reversing rapidly with a squeal of smoking, protesting tires he backed out into the oncoming traffic and returned to Times Square. This was not part of the plan. Alone in New York with no where to go, he had to make a decision, hide up in a cheap motel without being recognised and stand out like a sore thumb in his uniform, or go back to JFK, where the uniform would be one of many but his face would attract the unwanted attention of his colleagues. He was not happy stuck between a rock and a hard place, in desperation as a last resort, he phoned his confidential connection Aussie John.

As instructed, the Pilot delivered the car to the nearest Hertz car hire centre. Leaving the keys on the front desk, he walked out into the night. Out in the parking lot he found the light blue Ford Falcon. The keys to the car were concealed behind the right front wheel.

A safe house owned by EMU had also been made ready for his arrival. Located in a leafy suburb south of New York City, at three in the morning the sound of silence was oppressive. A part of his paranoia began to take over as he slowly approached his resting-place. Reading the numbers on the right side of the road painted on the post box or positioned next to the front door was not a problem. Halfway down the street he found what he was looking for: a white weatherboard house, without a number or a post box. Feeling secure within the safety of the four walls, he took a can of beer from the fully stocked fridge-freezer and settled down in front of the TV.

Relaxing with his feet up, he reached for the remote control and changed channels. The local all night news stations were showing scenes from the city, of the burnt out apartment above the launderette. Concentrating on every word and deep in thought the pilot was disturbed by the ringing sound of the cell phone. The airline had a problem. The regular routine maintenance staff had downed tools and walked off the job. An industrial union dispute, the sub-contractors had a cash flow problem. It meant that the aircraft was grounded until further notice.

The pilot calmly accepted the information and then on completion of the call, in a fit of fury he threw the phone across the room. Unless informed to the contrary, he would have to take the merchandise back to Amsterdam.

When he received the call from the company, Jim Smith had just been released from the county hospital equipped with a new pacemaker; he felt fighting fit. Jim knew all about aircrafts; he was born under the flight path of JFK and worked relentlessly after leaving school to achieve an important position in the airline industry. Working 24/7 had taken its toll at an early age. A self-employed free-lance local lad, he sold his expertise to the highest bidder. He was a wizard with wire, word processors and the latest relevant technology. He could wire up your toaster and turn it into a time machine, he was that good!

The next day back on the job at the airport, he met the last minute members of the newly formed maintenance crew. Eager to prove their worth one last time, a collection of senior citizens past their prime and sell-by date were busy, adjusting their bifocals, reading the small print in the manual, and transferring modern hi-tech information into a physical application. They had all been previously employed in the airline industry.

After removing the instrument panel in the confined space of the cockpit, to install a digital altimeter, Jim began to adjust and recalibrate the replacement, a sensitive GPS receiver. Halfway through connecting the new component, he placed his hand accidentally on a live wire, received an electric shock and completed a circuit. His pacemaker missed a beat, the shock set up an irregular erratic movement. The rapid powerful pulses passed down his right arm, into his hand, and at the same time, they sent a signal to the altimeter, readjusting the original settings.

He came to strapped to a stretcher, carried by the paramedics on his way back to hospital. Passing by the tail plane he noticed a hired hand rapidly replacing rivets, completing the half-done job left by the previous employees. Unknown to the company, the contractors were using cheap, inferior materials to maintain the door of the pressurised cargo hold: an accident waiting to happen. A new member of the maintenance crew completed the installation of the altimeter. Connecting the two remaining loose wires, he positioned and secured the component in the display panel. On completion, he filled in the form that confirmed his opinion: the flight deck was fully functional and ready for the return flight.

The paranoid pilot picked up the ringing phone and listened before he spoke. His enforced confinement had increased a feeling of fear and trepidation. An audible sound, an involuntary release of satisfaction escaped his lips as he recognised the voice of Vicky, in charge of pilot personnel, responsible for informing the flight crew of their departure time from JFK.

The Pilot arrived early at the Airport. He walked out into the dark night and on to the tarmac. He noticed a forklift truck still loading the cargo hold with a consignment of corrosive material, a full strength industrial solvent.

On the flight deck, Dennis, his co-pilot continued to fill in the day's edition of the New York Times crossword puzzle. He looked up and asked a question.

'What is a four-letter word for a conveyer of contraband?'

'Idiot,' the pilot replied as he left the cockpit.

Aware of the fact that he was still dressed in his slightly soiled uniform, the pilot welcomed the passengers on board. He passed by the seated rows of the paying public, shaking their hands on his way. The last one at the back by the rear door had just taken a trip to the toilet opposite. Sitting back down in his seat, he rapidly returned to the standing position as the pilot approached. The army man hit his head on the over hanging luggage compartment. Looking dazed and confused, he gave a soldier's

54

salute. Dressed in a fighting man's uniform, covered in the camouflage colours green and brown, he unintentionally let slip a jar of instant coffee previously located in his loose fitting combat jacket. The pilot made a mental note, to inform the on-board air marshal that this one was a potential problem.

Having rearranged the flight plan of flight 101, the passengers were notified that due to limited airspace, the aircraft would be taking the northern route, for a re-fuelling stop at Godthab, the capital of Greenland. Up the in front, in Club class, Ray, reading the New York Times readjusted his seat belt, ready for the take off, as a perfectly presentable Rasta man, wearing a hand stitched, made to measure designer suit walked by. He was on his way to join the special few fortunate enough to afford and fly Business class in their secluded enclosed compartment. They were far enough away from the fellow passengers to ignore them.

After connecting his laptop computer to the movie channel, Ray relaxed and looked through the window. He watched the first white snow flakes of winter, as they slowly and silently descended to settle on the dry deserted surface of the airport runway. In contrast, the titanium blades of the powerful jet engines began to rotate. Turning rapidly, they moved the passenger plane as it began to taxi, past the terminal to take its place ready for take-off. It waited at the end of the landing strip before it received final clearance from airport control. In preparation and frustration, it increased its robust roar to a crescendo of sound. Securely held in place, it reduced power, released the brakes and proceeded sedately along the runway.

Responding to the touch of the pilot, it immediately unleashed its full potential. Rapidly gathering speed, it produced a final forceful thrust and rose reluctantly from the ground. Flying north and gaining height, it swiftly penetrated the low-lying snow cloud located above the city. Breaking through into the clear night sky, the pilot gazed in awe for the last time as he looked at the countless number of stars shining in the dark distance of empty space. He set the controls on automatic and woke up Dennis, still dozing after being informed at the last minute that he was needed for the return flight. The cabin staff had finished their routine of reassuring, replenishing and relaxing the passengers. The cabin lights were low, the majority of the passengers had settled down, contorted and trying to sleep in an uncomfortable position, under their identical blankets provided by the airline. A minority were still awake, and watching a repeat in-flight movie. All, except for that silly soldier at the back still standing upright and requesting endless cups of coffee from the exhausted cabin crew.

A solar flare had unexpectedly released hundreds, of thousands, of tonnes of repressed energy; a vast quantity of uncontrollable emissions from the surface of the sun, more than its usual display of erratic behaviour. They were rapidly approaching the upper atmosphere. Dennis, soundly sleeping and snoring continuously in his co-pilot seat, gave a grunt and snorted loudly, as he was rudely awaken by a vivid flash of lightning, striking and illuminating the cockpit, exposing the increasing amount of ice rapidly collecting on the other side of the cabin window, adding extra weight to the already over-due ageing aircraft. As it flew through a pocket of open air without the support of the head wind flowing under the wings, it dropped dramatically and fell a thousand feet. On the way down, the plane reacted violently to a down draft caused by the thunderstorm. The rapid reduction in air pressure caused the inferior pop-rivets, restraining the door of the cargo hold to release their grip.

In the hold, a weak weld in a container of corrosive material gave way. A stream of full strength industrial solvent sprayed its contents indiscriminately and settled on a plastic hydraulic pipe. The pipe performing under pressure provided control of the rudder at the rear of the aircraft. Circling the earth, a number of global positioning satellites are constantly receiving and returning information. Sensitive to the slightest disturbance, these million-dollar messengers are easily affected by space dust, detritus, meteorite showers or an overload of electronic information. Released from its captive core, the star burst released a concentrated stream of radiation. Rapidly travelling through space it reached and disabled Area One, the satellite responsible for relaying height and flight information above Greenland and the Arctic Circle.

Having regained control after the lighting strike, the Pilot readjusted the height of the plane according to the information displayed on the altimeter. The electrical storm, combined with the solar flare activity caused a communication breakdown between ground control at Godthab Airport and the aircraft.

Locked on to automatic, Hilda, already pregnant was in love, and looking forward to her wedding day. She had her head in the clouds as she drove the old blue Japanese Datsun car down the highway for the final fitting of her white satin wedding dress. Living south of the city, the journey had become second nature, a part of the regular routine. Driving to work, thinking of other things and then arriving at the day job, without consciously paying attention. The road to Amsterdam was not a problem, a journey she had completed a thousand times before.

Hilda, a dress designer could not decide on the final details. She needed to make a decision. An extra wide blue ribbon tied at the back into the shape of a butterfly, restraining her long blond hair, complimented her big blue eyes and emphasised her extrovert, outrageous nature. Or to present the opposite picture, a shy docile domestic creature willing to love, honour and obey? Wearing a demure pink floral print headband, identical to the smaller versions controlling her corn-coloured plaited pigtails, resting on the bright red roses embroidered on the shoulders of her dress. The rich red diminishing as the primary colour of the roses receded into the back ground and finally surrendered to give way to a subtle shade of pale pink, surrounded by a perfectly formed circle of hand printed, powder blue love birds. The width of the bodice, trimmed with taffeta and traditional Dutch lace, was emphasised by the short puffed up mutton sleeves and the pale pink shoulder pads. The floral design reflected years of study and hard work. Thinking of her husband to be, the northern lights unexpectedly lit up the night sky as Hilda rapidly approached the triangular single lane, road works ahead, slow down diversion sign. Pointing left, it directed traffic across the old rickety wooden bridge.

The green light showed and beckoned, as the Aurora Borealis bathed the heavens overhead in an irregular display of erratic colour. Red, pale pink purple, and an assorted collection of secondary tints. Colour, created by cosmic energy, transient and translucent, activated by the solar flare. For Hilda, it was a sign from the Gods. She believed in the power of prayer and divine inspiration. Hilda decided that pale pink was the colour she needed. The decision had been made for her. On her wedding day, she would wear that pink floral print headband.

On the road, a smooth and deceptive surface concealed the depth of the potholes filled by the recent rain. They reflected the confusing cosmic colours. After her momentary lapse of concentration, Hilda reacted automatically to the colour red, and rapidly applied the brakes of the blue Datsun. As the left front wheel sank into a hole continuing loose gravel, it momentary lost its grip. The steering failed to respond and the car began to turn, slowly sliding on the slippery surface. Facing in the wrong direction, it stopped and came to rest like a police roadblock, restricting and taking up the full width of the temporary alternative river crossing. Travelling behind, the driver of the forty-ton container truck had no chance of avoiding the unexpected obstacle, and nowhere to go. He locked up the rear wheels of the trailer and waited. As it began to sway from right to left, it removed the intricate lattice work that supported the handrails of the bridge, the wooden uprights also snapped like matchsticks, as the full weight of the container continued to demolish an significant part of the structure. He approached and watched in slow motion as the woman, brightly illuminated in his blaze of halogen headlights franticly fumbled and tried desperately to start the engine. Temporarily blinded, she stared hypnotised at the constantly moving display of warning lights mounted on the roof of the mechanical big MAC, increasing in size as they came closer. Frozen like a rabbit caught in the light, she was paralysed by fright.

The driver was so close to stopping, but the weight of his truck and its momentum continued to drastically reduce the distance. The bump could not be heard or felt, above the volume of the sound system in the cab as it played loudly, 'Nice day for a white wedding,' and slowly pushed the old dark blue Datsun off the bridge and into the black water.

Looking over the side of the broken balustrade the distraught driver watched helplessly as the woman reached for her rosary beads and began silently reciting and mouthing the words for 'Mother of God'. Her big, blue, bulging eyes stared in fixation at the face of the driver. Hilda held her last breath as the water reached the roof. The engagement ring on the finger of her right hand helped to locate the submerged seat belt buckle and release the restraining strap. Underwater, the locked door handle took too long. Tangled up in her long blond hair and encumbered with her rosary beads, she finally let loose a great sigh and expelled a multitude of bubbles. They were rapidly replaced by a copious amount of river water that filled her empty lungs and finishing her fight for life.

The pilot noticed the northern lights as they flashed erratically: a moving mixture of coloured lights displayed across the sky, blending and disappearing into the background, adding colour to the white top of the ice capped cone of the mountain. Revealed at the last minute, it loomed directly ahead as it appeared out of the snowstorm. The alarm bells rang in the cockpit. The plane was on a collision course. In Cabin class, Peter, white-faced and rigid with fear after the previous rapid unexpected descent of a thousand feet, was still recovering, sitting upright and securely held in place by a seat belt. Served by Susan, a member of the cabin staff, he violently stirred another extra strong cup of coffee in a plastic cup. After that previous experience, he decided there was no way that he would ever fly again.

The pilot tried to release all the power of the engines in a final attempt to gain height and turn right, but there was not enough time, the rudder failed to respond and a sudden unexpected blast of arctic wind created a cross wind. The wind shear moved the slow, low-flying aircraft, off its intended course. A wing tip hit a hidden outcrop on the side of the mountain, and the resistance caused the plane to spin. The plane, after a loud bang began to rotate. It revolved around an unseen axis and increasing its centrifugal force, the speed held him tight, up against the handle of the passenger door. Peter watched and waited for the outcome. Like a car driver in a slow motion movie, time slowed down as he prepared himself for the crash. The cockpit smashed into the rock-face and the 707 spiralled out of control like a sycamore seed on a warm summer day, it descending on a cushion of air, and eventually hit the ground.

Laying face down in the soft powder snow, Peter slowly began to examine his bruised and battered body. Nothing was broken. The snowstorm had finally released its multitude of frozen ice crystals and the wind had been reduced to a long, low, slow whisper. The cold night air carried the sound of crying and the smell of aviation fuel. At ground level Peter appreciated being alive. Illuminated by the light of the full moon, the pristine Christmas card, endless expanse of sparkling white snow in front of him, made him realise that there was nothing green about Greenland. Dressed in his green army camouflage suit, he felt like a fool and stood out like a sore thumb but it sent a comforting message to his brain. The uniform helped contain his body heat and inner strength.

After a brief moment or maybe an hour he began to regain his senses. The all-embracing silent snow had begun to fall again. Covered in the comfort of the white blanket, Peter woke up. This was not good, he had the ability to look and think in two directions at the same time. His lazy left eye was focused on the carnage caused by the crash. He began to remember. Like a T.V. cameraman recording its final resting-place, he slowly turned his head to take in the full picture. The majority of the fuselage had remained intact but dragging its belly across the frozen landscape it had disgorged and exposed from the cargo hold, a complicated collection of coloured entrails. The broken Boeing was losing its lifeblood from its severed arteries. As the plastic pipes released their contents a red liquid originally intended, under pressure, to control the brakes slowly dripped and added to the remaining drops of green hydraulic fluid that had long ago failed to perform its function in controlling the stabilisers and the rudder. Their contrasting colours were combining and sinking into the glistening, shiny, surface, of the frozen wasteland.

Laying on its side, the isolated tail fin and the rear third of the plane, including the toilet section remained intact. It had come to rest a short distance away from the bulk of the Boeing 707. Removed from the main broken body as if cleanly cut by an invisible force the plane from a distance, looked like a long French loaf with the end chopped off. The detached remains of the metal monster were scattered far and wide. Strewn across the crystal snow the left wing refused to resemble a recognisable part of a modern flying machine.

The cabin lights continued to flicker as Peter clambered on to a pile of discarded containers and carefully climbed over a tangled, collection of sparking wires. He scrambled up into the gaping, passenger compartment and made his way through the carnage to the cockpit. On his way with tunnel vision, he passed Ray in Business class. Peter wanted words with the pilot. He was a man on a mission, with one thing on his mind, and nothing would stop him as he wrenched open the remains of the door to the flight deck.

Peter looked in and saw the condensed shape of Dennis squashed into an impossible position. The head hung forward, it had no support from its broken neck but it was held in place by the bent knees that had been forced back into the upper body by a reinforcement rod, designed to protect the occupants of the cockpit. It still restrained his lower limbs and kept his lifeless body in place. With no supporting structure, roof, or restriction the left side of the flight deck had disappeared completely. The cockpit was exposed to the elements. His sightless eyes looked down through empty space to the ground below.

The dead pilot had been held, securely pinned to his seat in an upright position by the dividing centre pillar of the windscreen. On impact, the force ripped out the overhead bolts and bent the pillar back, as the momentum moved the pilot forward. They met in the middle. His left arm had been severed at the shoulder, releasing from his padded epaulette a quantity of polished white cut diamonds. They had fallen on to the open page of the New York Times at the feet of the pilot and stuck to the paper in a pool of sticky blood. The left foot of the pilot was firmly planted on the page, as if to prevent the wind blown, flapping paper, from falling off the jagged, ragged edge of the open cockpit floor. His blood slowly spread and seeped into and nearly covered the crossword puzzle, but still visible was the answer to the question. What is a four-letter word for a conveyer of contraband? The word 'mule' had been crossed out and replaced by the word 'fool'.

Peter returned to the main cabin, but passing through Club class he paused, a loud gurgling sound attracted his attention. The left side of the compartment presented an unobstructed panoramic view. Blowing through the gaping hole, the low intermediate whistling wind temporarily gave way, to be replaced by a long deep sigh, released from the lips of the dreadlock wearing rasta man, laying on the edge of and gazing face down into the black void. Peter rolled him back from the abyss, turned him over and took his pulse. The loose flesh on the remains of his face focused attention on to the untouched area of skin that still displayed a tattoo. On the right cheek a dragon, the mark of a member of a Chinese Triad. The last time Pete had seen that tattoo, the same man was standing on a street in the midnight mist, opposite the laundrette, pointing a gun in his direction. The weak pulse provided Peter with an answer to his moral dilemma.

Without a second thought, a quick push dispatched the body into the open air, revealing the still gurgling first class passenger previously pinned, prostrate underneath the massive bulk of his bodyguard. The man was desperately trying to suck great gasps of air into his broken body but to no avail. A rib-bone had pierced his lung and at the same time the sharp, detached end had opened up the stretched muscle of his upper chest, allowing the free flowing air to enter and exit the body without supplying the vital life giving oxygen. He began to turn blue as Peter found a piece of plastic cling film, originally used to cover the in-flight meal and pushed it into the open wound. Lifting the dead weight, Peter carried the body out of the broken fuselage and into the open air. He then pulled it across the snow to the safety of the tail section. Returning for Ray, he ran through a confused crowd of walking wounded that had recently slid down the emergency escape chute situated above the non-existent wing as instructed by their leader, a distraught member of staff. She followed, leaving the dead and dying behind as an increasing amount of toxic fumes and vapours of aviation fuel built up and forced her and her fellow passengers to flee. Reaching the ground and still issuing orders, she eventually surrendered to fatigue and sat crossed-legged at the bottom of the slippery slope. Looking back up into the remains of the plane, she continued automatically to perform the company's emergency drill procedure. Her out-stretched arms were pointing in different direction as she screamed incessantly, a memorised mantra, 'Exit the aircraft now, exit the aircraft now, exit the aircraft now.'

Ray had remained silent and secure in his seat. He was slumped over the laptop. It was still working and showing an old black and white movie, A Fortunate Life starring James Stewart. Peter, on his hands and knees, crawled up the thickening smoke filled isle. Coughing and spluttering he reached his destination and removed Ray's seat belt. As he ripped out the computer connections to make way for the removal of his friend the screen went blank. Ray woke up immediately. Wide awake, bright-eyed and alert he shouted loudly, 'I was watching that, and don't cough in my face!'

Peter watched in amazement as Ray, without saying another word stood up, picked up the laptop and walked calmly down the walkway, through the devastation without missing a step, he silently disappeared from view and slid down the escape chute. On landing, he bumped into the still weeping and wailing flight attendant, pointing her arms in different directions. Regaining his composure he apologised profusely and walked unaided to the isolated rear of the plane. Pete followed in his footsteps. He heard a muted sound and turned around, to see a long tongue of fire released from the belly of the Boeing, racing down the rescue chute. It reached the end of its range then paused, caught, embraced and completely covered the crossed-legged member of the cabin staff. Lacking in energy, it remained flickering at her feet, lightly licking at the reluctant figure. Quietly alight and still mouthing the unheard words for an emergency evacuation, she turned and faced her remaining passengers. This time her arms were pointing in the right direction.

The heat melted the supporting snow beneath her as she slowly began to sink into the permafrost. In the tail section an occupant had been trapped in the toilet, the timid tapping sound from the inside of the cubicle caught Ray's attention. The locked door refused to move as it indicated the engaged sign. He began to kick at it, swearing and shouting at full volume, 'Open this door immediately I need to wee!'

Still carrying his laptop computer his commanding tone caused the sign to change to vacant. A dishevelled female flight attendant emerged, apologised, and returned to the toilet to retrieve an emergency first-aid kit from the overhead compartment. Going about her business in a detected manner she calmly began to take care of the walking wounded.

Ray lost sight of her as the illuminated background provided by the flames, faded and died. The dark night descended rapidly leaving the survivors wondering aimlessly in the wilderness. In the still of the night an oppressive silence settled. It was occasionally broken by the cry of a lost soul calling out in vain for a missing loved one. As if to compensate for its previous instant violent behaviour, the arctic winds began to blow again with a low, slow, continuous restrained whisper.

Suddenly as if bored, it lost its respect for the dead and dying and rapidly increased in sound and speed. Replacing the audible muted mumbles of the wounded with a wildly shrieking wind. The destructive force of nature had returned with a vengeance. It was a convenient moment for Peter and Ray to communicate. The cautious conversation of the undercover cops was cut short and replaced by a strange uncomfortable silence as Ray listened to Pete explaining, how the unfortunate demise of the rasta man had occurred.

Precariously balanced on the exposed edge, in the remains of the first class cabin. Peter leaned out and grabbed the bodyguard. His head turned and as his dreadlocks fell away they revealed the sign of the dragon. In shock, Peter lost his grip and the body accidentally slipped over the edge. Ray did not believe a word of it but Peter had provided a simply answer to a potential complicated problem. Momentarily lost for words, Ray was speechless. His mouth was silently moving but he could not construct a suitable sentence. Thinking back down the tunnel of time when it came to administrating his particular brand of justice, Ray could not count the number of Peter's personal, illegal, positive results. Trying to formulate an acceptable verbal response, his train of thought was conveniently interrupted, by a rapidly increasing clamour coming closer, from the other side of the mountain.

Chapter Seven

At Godthab Airport, the emergency response team had just been stood down after a routine practice when the call came through as the Boeing 707 disappeared from the radar screen. Flight control responded immediately and put their emergency rescue procedure into operation. The intermittent wind relented long enough to open up a convenient window of opportunity, allowing the rescue squad time to climb aboard and buckle up in preparation for a bumpy ride. Reaching their maximum revolution, the twin rotating blades began to lift the helicopter into the hover position, followed closely behind by their identical back up. Twenty feet above the ground they turned and faced in to the right direction. With final clearance from the control tower, they took off and flew the fourteen miles that separated the safety of the brightly lit airport runway from the dark, misty, mountain.

In a temperature of minus twenty, plus a wind chill factor, a body begins to lose heat at an alarming rate. Stressed and confused, the isolated walking wounded survivors wondered off aimlessly into the unknown. Still calling for help as hypothermia set in they slowly lost their fight for life and froze to death minutes before the arrival of the rescue squad. Flying low over the crash site the choppers searched for signs of movement. The on-board infrared camera would register a remaining spark of life left in a motionless body. A residue of radiating heat displayed on the monitor was enough to locate a living individual. Nothing moved on the ground below, there was nobody left alive but on a second pass over, the lead helicopter hovered above the tail section as it recorded a heat source. The occupants looked down and stared in amazement as a uniformed figure, emerged, still wearing her company hat at exactly the right angle, she proceeded to indicate a safe landing zone for the rescuers.

On landing, the paramedics immediately dispersed to retrieve the dead and the dying. The life-support team reached and prepared the Club class passenger for hospital treatment. Strapped on to a stretcher they lifted his lifeless body. In a race against time, as the gale force winds returned, they took it to the wildly rocking helicopter. The female Australian flight attendant ran in advance to the open door and issued instructions. As she waited, the survivors approached in single file. She remembered (for no apparent reason), the name of the next in-flight movie (The Good the Bad and the Ugly). Ray walked unaided in front of the stretcher-bearers completely composed and apparently unaffected by his experience he was the first to climb aboard. Looking back, he saw the struggling stretcher-bearers. Lending a helping hand, he reached down to take over from the front man carrying the Club class passenger. A violent fit caused the casualty to regain conciseness but breathing erratically he was in a bad way. The medics began to perform emergency surgery. Peter, wearing his camouflage suit was the last to arrive slipping and sliding on his way to safety. Protesting loudly, he refused to never ever fly again. Dealing with an argumentative determined passenger in an ugly mood, was all part of the day job for an experienced member of the cabin staff. Listening quietly and politely replying occasionally to his irrational ranting, she left it to the last minute. Out of time and tolerance she grabbed the back of his belt and bundled him head first into the open interior of the rescue chopper. The big brave man was finally pushed aboard by the small thin flight attendant. The second helicopter had reached its maximum weight capacity. The pilot had a full load of safely contained corpses, securely sealing in their silvered body bags. Confirming with the rescue crew as they finally climbed aboard that that was the last one, he wrote down the numbers on his dispatch sheet and engaged vertical lift.

Transporting the intact bagged up bodies he could handle; the next stage of the operation, collecting and identifying the dismembered parts of the previous passengers he left to a different department the clean up crew and the crash site investigators. As long as he didn't see close up the carnage caused by a crash he was OK, but in the back of his mind it was still there. At home he never ate blood red steak it had to be well done. On landing, the bags were transferred to a refrigerated meat container truck, taken down town and parked in a corner of the hospital grounds for future investigation.

It was the first thing that Peter saw as he woke up in the observation ward. In the cold light of day, his bed facing the window gave an unrestricted view of the mortuary men unloading the truck. Kept in overnight, he and the rest of the rescued were surrounded in the early morning by a team of medical professionals. They were subjected to the routine tests, a series of probing and prodding before being allowed to sign their release forms. Lying next to each other like three peas in a pod, the man in the middle with the punctured lung had been operated on successfully. Securely sutured, the wound had been covered by a restrictive supportive bandage. Tightly wound around his torso, it looked like a Middle Eastern cummerbund worn by an ageing actor in a film from the late forties, or a big fat money belt. He leaned over grabbed Peter by the hand and said, 'I thank you, I owe you my life. I insist that you work for me as my bodyguard, you can call me the Boss Man.'

Ray dressed, and ready to go, he removed his laptop computer from the bedside cabinet. Adjusting his tie, he turned in time to see the arrival of the female flight attendant as she entered the ward with a controlled confidence. Banging back the double swing doors she advanced up the aisle between the beds, and reached Ray. Without a word she lifted his laptop, turned around and walked back to the exit with Ray close behind her. Passing Peter's bed, she threw him a jar of instant coffee. The plane crash had left a lasting impression in her memory, if it wasn't for the conversation of that boring, tiresome tin soldier (the caffeine freak), forcing her to escape to the tail end toilet, she would not be alive today. As he passed Peter, Ray said in a low whisper, 'Keep close to the Boss Man.'

Her name was Susan Jordan, and she lived in Sydney Australia. Drinking endless cups of coffee in the hospital cafeteria and talking incessantly to Ray, she opened up and released her repressed post-traumatic stress. Since the accident, she had silently carried her burden deep inside. Her emotions racing rapidly to the surface caused her voice to increase in speed and volume. It finally cracked as her composure crumbled and dissolved to give way to an uncontrollable flood of tears. Ray was a good listener. Susan had been talking continuously for two hours. This lady needed to take time out to recover from her ordeal.He led his crying companion out of the building and onto the pavement. Attracting the attention of the doorman, Ray explained the situation. The man recommended the local Turex hotel. He phoned in advance to reserve a room and requested a courtesy cab. Ray wrote down the name, address, telephone number and a financial figure, which he peeled from his fist full of paper folding. Ray gave the money and the written message to the doorman.

'If this is received in the next ten minutes, Peter in the observation ward will pay the same amount on delivery.'

The cab arrived to collect the travellers. Ray turned around in time to see the doorman already rapidly returning to the hospital interior. The promise of money motivated his aching leg muscles forcing him to climb the stairs. He would not wait to take the lift.

A young, bored and indifferent receptionist at the check in desk of the Turex Hotel continued her cell phone conversation. Pointing to the register, she completely ignored Susan's agitated appearance. Red-faced and flustered, Susan was still wiping her tear filled eyes and occasionally blowing her nose into the centre of Ray's white linen handkerchief. With one hand reaching below the desk, the employee retrieved a copy of the hotel's rules and regulations. Sitting in her swivel chair, she suddenly revolved and turned full-circle. On her way she reached out and removed a key hanging on the wall behind her but the movement kept her going. Still glued to her cell phone her head held at a ridiculous angle, she returned to face Ray and dropped the room key on to the desk. At the same time pointing to the lift, she silently mouthing the words, 'Have a nice day.' The chair and its occupant finally finished its rotation facing the wrong way. Not a word had passed between the lips of the persons involved. Looking at the back of her silently shaking shoulders she displayed an automatic reaction. Still whispering into the telephone, she flicked her long blonde hair subconsciously over the opposite shoulder. Ray recognised the body language. Lost in a world of love she was oblivious to any outside influence.

Love was the last thing on his mind as Ray opened the door to room

405. The first of the two-room apartment contained the standard fixtures and fittings. Susan, emotionally drained, staggered to the comfort and security of the bedroom. In the room the seven-foot, pine, octagonal waterbed beckoned. It dominated all the available space. Without a second thought, she stood in the open doorway, undressed, slipped under the black satin sheets and fell into a deep sleep. It was to late for Ray to try and organise, or explain to the giggling girlie on the front desk that he needed two separate beds. Closing the door a list of rules and regulations firmly fixed to the back of it caught his attention. 'In an emergency (fire or flood) please assemble at the front desk.' Ray focused on the small print; the last line read, 'Please contact for your own safety and satisfaction our local chemist. We provide a free 24-hour condom delivery service plus a free phone number obtainable in reception.' The hotel was not exactly what Ray had in mind. He lay down on the long settee and caught up on his lost sleep.

Hours later he was dragged back from his deep slumber by the sound of Susan calling his name. Caught in the diffused light of the bedside lamp she stood like a nude stature and slowly began to shiver as Ray approached.

'Please come to bed and hold me tight I need to feel wanted, I need to love and laugh again.' In a strained silence, Ray did not reply but quickly removed his suit. Sitting on the side of the bed and still wearing his boxer shorts, he bent down to remove his socks. Accidentally his elbow knocked over the small wicker basket on the bedside table. It contained a numbered supply of different coloured condoms. The majority fell between the legs of the bedside cabinet and into the half-exposed bucket of the plastic waste-paper bin, conveniently placed next to the bed by the hotel cleaning staff. Ray, red with embarrassment, crawled around on his hands and knees and fighting off a feeling of inferiority he found the last lost condom. Supplied with a complementary amount, the hotel charged for any extras. They were numbered and included in the final bill with telephone calls and cold drinks from the fridge. On all fours, he raised his head above the bed and looked at Susan. She was still trembling but not because of the cold or emotional expectation. Susan was desperately trying to control repressed laughter as Ray retrieved and held aloft the last, lost, condom. She reached out grabbed it and removed the cover. Ray had supplied the laughter now it was time for the love.

Finding love or making it had passed him by. Looking down at the body of a beautiful woman reminded him of the young receptionist and the way he thought that she might be feeling. Ray never had time for a love life, just the occasional prostitute. If only he could turn the clock back and start again. Maybe this time it would be different, a woman that wanted him for himself? Not for his money, or to use him as a reason for releasing her personal problems. She was young enough to be his daughter.

At 8:30 a.m., a loud knocking sound and a muffled voice made its way into the subconscious silence of Ray's relaxed brain. Ray presumed that room service had arrived with the pre-ordered champagne breakfast. Wearing his bright, blue, boxer shorts he answered the door. It was Peter dressed in a brown business suit, holding a breakfast tray and biting into a peanut butter sandwich. He put the half-eaten sandwich on to a plate next to an airline ticket and said, 'If you want it, it's yours. We leave in eight hours. And tell the Australian lady I said good day.'

Susan received a call from the company at 9:00 a.m. Their personal morning routine was performed in a shy subdued manner. Feeling a need to break the embarrassing unsociable silence, they both rapidly began to speak at the same time. Each apologised and continued to surround themselves in a cloud of controlled efficiency. The uncomfortable quiet gave way rapidly as a knock on the door announced the arrival of the hotel porter, pushing a trolley full of food. Relieved of the need to make unnecessary small talk they both consumed and communicated on common ground. Ray did not have the ability to understand a woman. Resisting the feeling of obligation for services received, he returned the folded bank notes to his wallet and placed them next to a copy of Peter's fingerprints. Returning it to his back pocket, Ray left Susan with a polite kiss on the cheek and a promise to return later. He took a cab downtown bought a collection of new clothes and a suitable suitcase. Walking past a charity shop, a well-worn shabby Mac displayed on the bargain rack at a cut down price caught his attention. Waiting in the window like a good luck charm, Ray had to buy it but first he bought from a local drug store a boy scout's emergency first aid kit that contained a knife for removing stones from horse's hooves. He returned to the shop, put the packet in the pocket of the raincoat. Had it wrapped in brown paper, tied it with string and wrote on the outside, 'From Red Rover, open later.' He knew that Peter would appreciate the present. Ray understood men but not women.

He returned to the hotel, left his luggage at the front desk and took a bunch of flowers to room 405 were he was greeted with a look of startled surprise by the cleaning staff. Susan had gone. He walked around the bed, found the waste paper bin and placed the bouquet in it, on top of the knotted, discarded condoms and gave it to an attractive, very vacant looking, forty something female, inefficiently flicking a feather duster at the bedside table.

'These are for you, they are second-hand and slightly soiled but they still contain a lot of life.' Her English was not the best and as Ray left the room, he was followed by a sincere thank-you for the flowers and a last minute reminder to please come again in the Turex Hotel.

At the entrance to the airport, Ray began to feel the silent pulsating vibrations in his left leg, emitted by Peter's personal bleeper. Both men had surgical implants and were electronically tagged. Peter had a microchip implanted in the eye of the tiger tattooed on his back. It responded to Ray's remote control transceiver and set of a regular return pulse, like submarine sonar, or a blue whale in the deep water of the open ocean the signal increased in speed as they approached each other.

Ray's picture cell phone picked up the signal, homed in and focused on his partner. In the men's ware department of Fly by Night Fashions, a retail outlet that relied on the last minute purchases of departing passengers. Peter selected a pair of denim jeans and took them to the changing room. Ray walked past the closed door of the cubicle and threw the parcel over the top of the partition. It was received with an explosion of verbal expletives.

To pass the time before take-off Ray sat in the cool, calm, quite, of the church, opposite the airport. He thought and found the words he needed to send a message to Susan. Having located the airline's company web site on his laptop, he sent an e-mail addressed to the Australian hostess on flight 101.

In the departure lounge, wearing his new brown, coffee-coloured suit and securely carrying the matching parcel like a fashion accessory. Peter passed through passport control and boarded K.L.M. flight 102 to Amsterdam. Ray, the last in line silently prayed that God would forgive him for his previous sins and deliver him safely to his destination. He then turned his negative thoughts around. The last digit of flight number 102 became a positive and the number two, signified a second chance to survive. He was not going to die on this flight, and he had the confidence that Peter and his parcel would make the difference between life and death.

On the flight to Amsterdam, Susan played the part of a consummate professional. Providing the passengers with a reassuring rhetoric, she ignored Ray completely and took his order for an in-flight meal with an aloof, detached impression of indifference. Not a word was said about their night of passion. Ray was confused. He thought that maybe he should have offered an amount of money for the physical fun. Because of his age, he felt embarrassed for taking advantage. He never mentioned it and returned to the business in hand. Connected to the Internet his laptop computer, he began to search and select more information on EMU Imports and Exports, Amsterdam, to prepare a case for the prosecution is a time consuming logical, legal progression. Arresting and successfully convicting a criminal requires research, determination and a dedicated, obsessive individually. Finding the facts, following a paper trail and locating offshore holding companies registered in different names. Using post office box numbers as an address in a tax haven, where the banks refuse to reveal the identity of the account holders depositing large amount of cash inconsistently and withdrawing an equal or lesser amount at a later date. Money laundering is big business. The Internet added to the information, Ray would spend a lot of time logged on.

Chapter Eight

Flight 102 touched down and landed safely two hours later. Ray followed the departing passengers off the plane at Schiphol International Airport. At the door, Susan gave him the standard 'Thank-you for flying with K.L.M. airlines and please come again' speech. Without another word, she placed a sealed envelope in Ray's right hand. On the Internet, he had previously booked a second floor, front facing room in Canal Street over looking the EMU building. Passing through the observation room on his way to the luggage recovery lounge, Ray saw Peter on the tarmac and could not resist the temptation.

After carefully closing the rear door of the white stretched Limousine with the blacked out windows behind the bulk of the Boss Man seated in the vast interior, Peter walked to the front and began to climb into the passenger seat. He stopped, straightened up, reached around his back with his left hand and gave it a satisfying rub between the shoulder blades. Ray had sent a rapid pulsating signal from his cell phone and activated the eye of the tiger. He immediately followed it with the cancellation code. Still slowly scratching and silently swearing, Peter looked around in all directions. He finally found and focused on the cause of his discomfort. Ray returned his gaze with a slight grin and a raised eyebrow. This could be the last time for a long time that they would be so close. Except for the impersonal remote controlled hi-tech surgical implants, they were on their own and completely detached.

Early the next day Ray went shopping for surveillance equipment.

Back in his hotel room, he assembled a collection of observation and recording items hired from a local Seen and Heard electrical shop. He made a note of the fact that they also supplied a varied collection of domestic electrical cleaning equipment. He positioned the tripod, attached the camera and focused it on to the front of the E.M.U building. The camera automatically activated by movement relayed the time day and date to the videocassette recorder. Ray slightly lowered the sash-cord window and attached a sensitive, directional microphone, to the side of the opening. Connected to the recorder, its selective hearing would only react to a hi-pitched sound.

A part of Peter's repertoire from an early age had been his ability to perform, without warning, a loud, high-pitched, ear-piercing whistle. It was nearly beyond the point of human hearing but for those unfortunately close enough, it caused considerable audio discomfort. They experienced a temporary moment of deafness. Dogs howled and ran away, causing chaos, as their elderly owners tried desperately to restrain them. Ray knew that Peter knew that he was not far away. Each member of a perfect partnership is adaptable and able in any situation to take the lead role. The chosen one in the frame follows the suspect, secure in the knowledge that his backup is close behind, hiding in the bushes or watching and waiting in a convenient location.

Ray telephoned all the hire companies operating a limousine service, situated close to the airport. It was a process of elimination, asking the same question repetitively, 'I am trying to trace the owner of an item of luggage left on board flight 102 last night from Godthab Greenland. Did you or a member of your staff pick up a passenger on the runway? A rotund man and his colleague wearing a coffee-coloured suit and if so please collect the left luggage and deliver it to the person concerned or supply the delivery address.' Carefully concealing his delight, he wrote down the name and address of the E.M.U. building opposite his hotel room and hung up.

Ray opened the envelope. It contained Susan's cell phone number her Australian address and the words write or phone me. He phoned. She was still in the city and gave him her temporary address. Ray set the video cassette player to record, closed the door of the room and smeared the door handle with a gossamer thin layer of hair cream, he left the rest of the internal doors wide open and locked the apartment. He walked down the road, passed a white camper van with blacked out windows and caught a cab on the corner of Canal Street. Ray arrived at a sleazy sex shop. On a stopover in Amsterdam, Susan shared the flat above with Sally, a permanent member of the airport office staff responsible for passenger departure lists obtained from the booking agents. Having reached maximum flight capacity, the computerised system automatically produced a printout of names, seat numbers, dates, departure time, destinations and a flight number. On completion, the information was passed to the dispatch department.

In the executive suite situated on the second floor of the E.M.U. building, Peter, in his new blue jeans and suit jacket met the other minder. Built like a mountain, the bodyguard was all muscle, complete with a tiny mind. They would take it in turns, twelve hours on and twelve hours off. Complete opposites: speed and mental agility, or moronic muscle. Feeling safe and secure with his personal choice of security staff, his employer gave Peter a cell phone and the day off.

Pete finished smoking a filter tipped cigarette and carefully holding it in the vertical position, with a delicate construction of cold grey ash still attached to the burnt butt, he returned to his own apartment passed through and closed the connecting door. At the same time he dropped behind it the dead remains of the American cigarette left on the carpet; the door could not be opened with out it being disturbed. Assuming that the room was wired for sound and vision, he closely inspected the bed sheets and threw them into the corner of the room. He phoned room service and requested a clean set of sheets. Two women arrived and replaced them. At the same time, taking advantage of the distraction, he opened the door of the walk in wardrobe and with his back to the room, unwrapped the brown paper parcel. Peter would not take the risk of revealing the contents of the parcel alone in a room under observation.

He then removed his jacket and hung it on a hanger, its front facing the front of his camouflage combat suit. He reached between the two and grabbed the far sleeves and at the same time he rapidly pushed the two hangers together, trapping the sleeves in between, making it impossible to search the jacket pockets of the suits. Wearing the raincoat with the brown wrapping paper stuffed in the left pocket, the right still contained an unopened item, which he would investigate later. Peter went to the bathroom and placed a small wet sample of soap on to his right wrist. He closed the door of the apartment, took a long strand of hair from the back of his head and passed it through the spot of soft soap. He placed it across the gap between the locked door and the frame. Peter would be reassured if that hair was still there when he returned.

He expected to be followed by employees of the Boss Man but a visit from an unknown, interested, intruder through the front door was another matter.

Walking out into the wind swept rainy day he felt like a celebrity caught in the spotlight. Leaning against the wall was a man reading a magazine in the rain, opposite a camper van with blacked out windows. Peter was about to paint a false picture for his followers and at the same time build a solid convincing character.

The man with the wet magazine moved and crossed the street in front of Peter and the man in the van followed close behind. After walking for miles to catch up on his caffeine intake, Peter stopped off at a coffee shop and picked up a copy of the daily news. Standing at the counter nursing a cold cup of cappuccino he turned around as the door opened. At last, his cold wet observer finally entered the shop and refused to return the look that Pete gave him. He sat at an empty table. As the waiter took his order, Peter walked over and sat down beside him.

'I noticed that you have followed me all day now its time to play. I am so pleased that you like to do it in a public place.' Under the table he rapidly rubbed his hand up the leg of the man. At the same time Peter whispered, 'In the rain, a man in a Mac that has a fetish and wears no underwear is uncontrollable, and there is no turning back.'

Reaching down, he unzipped his fly and Peter stood up and punched him in the eye, the table turned over as the man ran off and returned to the wind swept street.

Covered in coffee, Peter complained and sought the safety of the men's washroom.

In a closed cubical Peter removed the brown paper from his pocket, ripped out the words 'Red Rover', shredded them and flushed them down the toilet. He left the rest of the paper bundled up behind the U-bend. The small packet in his right pocket contained a collection of emergency medical supplies. Peter would never completely understand Ray. The way he thought made no sense at all but he kept the kit just in case. Having it made him feel better now it was time to put part two of his plan into operation.

Peter left the coffee shop and kept to the main streets still obviously followed by the white van man, he did not intend to lose his tail. In the city, he bought a street map and a multi-ride tram ticket to see the tourist sights and as night fell, he ventured into, explored and began to experience the sordid sex industry that attracted the lonely middle-aged man.

Leaving a massage parlour at midnight, he walked past a dark secluded doorway. It contained two argumentative individuals, one male and one female. As Peter passed by and approached the white van, her piercing scream shattered the silence of the night. He returned in time to see the man holding up the body of the woman and in his hand a blood stained serrated hunting knife. The man turned around as Peter hit him hard in the kidneys with a karate kick. He grabbed Peter's leg and lost his balance. They crashed through the glass door of the shop, taking the woman with them. On the ground, Peter rolled as the man with the knife lunged and missed, but it cut the neck of the lady lying next to them. The assailant dropped the knife and ran from the crime scene leaving Peter with a dying woman. At the same time the incessant, repetitive noise of the burglar alarm began to be replaced by the increasingly loud siren sound of a rapidly approaching police car, with blood on his hands he felt for her pulse but there was no sign of life.

Peter stood up with his hands in the air and looking down the barrel of a gun he slowly walked toward the police officer. Playing the part of a submissive criminal, he stopped as requested and turned around. The streetlight opposite illuminated the scene and cast the shadow of the approached uniformed officer on to the wet cobblestones below. Peter watched the shadow as it came closer from behind. It was close enough, with his arms still raised and with lightning speed he twisted his upper body. The left arm connected and deflected the carefully aimed gun. The first bullet missed but as he reached the other side of the street and disappeared into the darkness, a second bullet hit the lamppost and with its power spent at the end of its trajectory, it ricocheted and lodged itself into Peter's left arm just above the elbow.

Still running and momentarily lost in a labyrinth of dark alleyways he stopped, to refer to his street map and regain his orientation. Eventually he found his way back to the front door of the E.M.U. building and pressed the entrance button. At the same time, a quietly cruising police car turned the far corner of Canal Street. So close but so far from safety, Peter removed his raincoat, rolled it up and stuffed it down the front of his trousers. The security guard turned on the light and illuminated Peter. Close-up and looking him straight in the face, through the glass front door. Peter tightly crossed his arms reached around and began to sensuously caress the back of his body in full view of the passing police car. Seen from the back it gave the impression that he was romantically involved with a compliant woman. The security guard opened the door and kept his distance from Peter, having already heard about the confrontation in the coffee shop. Convinced that this was some sort of serious pervert, he swiftly returned to his side of the security section behind the reinforced observation screen. He had met many weird and wonderful people in his time but this one was something else.

Pete blew him a loud kiss as he passed by but the guard refused to respond, as he pretended to concentrate entirely on a news item on the TV about a murder committed by a man in a Mac.

Reaching his apartment, Peter opened the door and disturbed the hair still in place bridging the gap between the door and its frame. He walked into the room and immediately caught sight of the crushed remains of the discarded cigarette. It confirmed his previous assumption that the apartment would be searched in his absence, not through the main entrance but by an employee of the man on the other side of the connecting door. In the walk-in wardrobe separated by a searcher, the suit sleeves hung independently.

Peter removed the rolled up raincoat from his trousers and took the small packet containing the first aid kit from its pocket. The imbedded bullet was still protruding from his left arm, but a hospital visit was out of the question as the police were still searching for a man in a Mac with a lazy left eye. He carefully began to remove the bullet, cutting it out with the knife from the first aid kit. Good enough evidence to convince the Boss Man that he was one of the bad guys. Without a word of warning, the man from next door walked in, followed by his muscle-bound minder carrying a plate of raw meat. The minder sat down next to Peter and with his fingers he proceeded to swallow whole chunks of the cold congealing collection of liver and kidneys. At the same time, the Boss Man began to tell the story of an unfortunate former employee who brought unnecessary attention to his business organisation on this very day. He died of kidney failure.

Peter turned his head in time to see the minder mopping up the last remains from the oval platter. Held in both hands he raised it to his prominent lips and lost the last meaty lump as it fell into his lap. He rapidly retrieved it and with a satisfied smile he ripped it in two with both hands. He poked it in and closed his already full mouth, putting extra pressure on his already bulging cheeks. As he continued to bite on the uncooked offal, a mouth-full of blood escaped and ran down the outside of his double chin.

Peter looked away and into the eyes of the Boss Man, now holding a stainless steel Italian flick knife. He came closer and asked Peter, 'Do you like your kidneys red raw or cooked?'

Without waiting for an answer, he threw the knife at his minder, he caught it and began to extract morsels of dead meat from between his teeth. The Boss Man insisted that Peter joined him for dinner. He had previously ordered a sumptuous supper for two containing kidneys and lightly fried liver. Peter felt like a lamb being led to the slaughter.

In the executive suite the dining room table displayed a lavish presentation of culinary delights. The perfect host sat opposite Peter and began to instigate an intelligent, stimulating, general knowledge conversation; he showed no sign of dissatisfaction. At the end of the meal, Gouda cheese and copious amounts of Colombian coffee were consumed. Relaxed and replete, they adjourned to the lounge room.

Sitting in front of a wide screen TV, smoking a cigar and sipping a Courvoisier, Peter suddenly felt the hairs on his neck stand up, as he smelt the fetid breath of the minder who had moved up close behind him. It mixed, mingled and over-powered the pleasant aroma released from the bulbous bowl of the brandy glass. The Boss Man stood up and turned on the TV. He replayed a previous recording of recent events featured on the national news. A full-scale police investigation was underway as they searched the city to locate the man responsible for the murder. A suspect wearing a beige coloured rain Mac, had been seen leaving the scene of the crime. The Boss Man turned off the TV, his minder stood up and holding hands they both began to walk to the bedroom. On his way, the big Boss Man, breathing heavily, stopped, turned around and said, 'If you want a women pick her up outside on the street and bring her back here. Do not go out of this building without Bertie. We leave in three days. You won't need your raincoat for our destination.'

Bertie, the boyfriend, gave a benign grin as the Boss Man turned off the lights and closed the bedroom door behind them leaving Peter alone in the dark thinking about his future.

Back in the relative safety of his own apartment, Peter placed a chair from the breakfast bar up against the connecting door and wedged the top of it under the lever latch handle. He repeated the previous security manoeuvre, making an unexpected entry from the outside communal corridor almost impossible. Peter needed to attract attention and pass on the information. He turned the bath-taps full on, returned to the bedroom and fell into a deep sleep. Peter would not need an early morning wake-up call.

Ray returned early that night from Susan's apartment. He said good night to the man at the reception desk and waked up the stairs to his rooms. He stopped halfway and took a small nail file from his inside pocket and filed down a part of the door key. He returned to reception and complained that the door lock was jammed. A maintenance man appeared with a skeleton key and closely followed by Ray, he unlocked and entered the apartment. Behind his human shield, Ray quickly relaxed and turned on the lights, he announced loudly that he was tired and going straight to bed. The man mumbled a polite goodnight and returned to his quarters. The internal doors were still wide open, except for the one tightly closed containing the recording equipment. Ray removed a pressured can of cleaning fluid from beneath the kitchen sink and with his butane gas lighter he crawled quietly across the floor and took a closer look at the door handle. He looked at it from all angles with the illumination from his lighter. It appeared to be exactly as he had left it, not a trace of a fingerprint, or a slippery smear from a gloved hand, were visible.

Ray turned off the apartment lights, banged the bedroom door and walked quietly back across the lounge room. He approached the room containing the recording equipment with caution. Laying on the floor in the dark, he reached up and slowly turned the handle just enough to disengage the closing mechanism.

Ten minutes later he burst through the door brandishing a flaming, hissing, aerosol can. Any occupants would be temporally blinded and so would he, but thrown in the right direction towards an unfamiliar sound or movement he would regain the advantage. The observation equipment in the quiet, empty room still silently recorded the day's events. He stopped, rewound and played the VCR tape.

After Ray had left his apartment that morning, the equipment had recorded the movement of a man in a Mac leaving the E.M.U. building emitting a loud high pitched, ear-piercing whistle. With the lights still out, Ray adjusted the angle of the microphone and watched as Peter run into the shadow of the building opposite and emerged without his Mac. The passenger in the slowly cruising police car shone a hand-held spotlight; the moving light lit up the dark interior of the room. Ray looked on, as Peter appeared to perform an illusion. It looked like a couple of lovers closely entwined at the entrance of the E.M.U. building.

Ray removed the cover of his laptop commuter. He logged on and searched the Internet for any information that would help build a case for the prosecution. Hours later, the slowly growing dawn light lost its quiet approach and was replaced by an unexpected, early morning activity. The fire service arrived, parked opposite the apartment and began to pump out the flooded E.M.U. building. Ray wanted Susan's help; he phoned and gave her a limited amount of information, just enough to achieve a positive result. She arrived on time and took up her position outside the building. Wearing plain glass spectacles and a false beard Ray returned to the hire shop and selected an industrial waterproof suit, wellington

81

boots and a hot air, carpet dryer. Suitable dressed and looking the part he had himself and the dryer delivered to the E.M.U. building.

The Boss Man trembled with rage as he ineffectively tried to control his mounting anger. Peter felt like a naughty schoolboy singled out and standing in front of the headmaster. Standing up straight and holding his hands behind his back, he held his head in shame and looked down at the water logged carpet as the main man continued to rant and rave. Lost in a world of his own, Peter returned to reality when the sound subsided. Peter was becoming a liability and he knew it; he had brought too much attention to the Boss Man. He would have to back off. Peter left the apartment without saying a word in his defence. Emitting a high-pitched whistle, he walked out of the building followed by Bertie.

In a short red mini-skirt and hi-heeled black, leather boots, the working girl whispered to Peter as he passed her by, 'Hi, how do like your coffee, Ray sent me.'

He stopped and turned. Bertie, ten paces behind, began to catch up. As still as a statue and with a menacing stare, Peter looked him straight in the eyes and slowly shook his head from side to side. The bodyguard froze and became so confused he could not walk, talk and think at the same time. With his back to Bertie, Peter got straight to the point.

'I leave in three days with a new identity, destination unknown and I won't need a raincoat. Give me your phone number, slap my face and walk away now.'

Bertie was on the move again and coming closer. He heard the slap and slowly a childish grin grew and spread from ear to ear. Peter pointed to the red mark on his cheek, rubbed his jaw and started to laugh. He had to find a way to pacify this man-monster. Humour and fun rarely failed when dealing with a petulant child. If he could persuade Bertie that he was a friend and not a threat he would use it to his advantage. It was a dangerous game to play but he might need a plan B for later.

The immediate problem was to pick up a prostitute and take her back to his room to convince Bertie and the Boss Man. When you need one, you can't find one, then two turn up at the same time; Peter had a king size bed in his apartment.

The cleaning staff were still wiping up and drying out the remains of the flood as he led the ladies up the stairs to his rooms. He was not surprised to find the door of his apartment open. A worker, wearing wellington boots and a beard, was busy pushing a hot air carpet dryer across the floor, stopping occasionally to sprinkle a white powder on the carpet ahead. Peter left the ladies in the kitchen and returned to the bedroom.

On the floor the white powder had spelt out the words Red Rover. It was removed immediately as soon as Peter had seen it. The worker turned off the machine. Taking it with him, he gave a quick nod in Peter's direction and walked out into the corridor. On his way he stopped and picked up the do not disturb sign, closed the door after him and hung it on the handle.

In the next room, Bertie and the Boss Man monitored the movements of the man next door on the TV screen. Peter turned on the in house sound system and ignoring the hidden cameras he began to satisfy his sexual desires with the help of his compliant companions to the sound of Freddie Mercury and Queen. When the entertainment was over, Peter paid the prostitutes and took their phone numbers. The Boss Man opened the connecting door and walked into the room. One of the ladies had left a pair of red knickers on the bedroom floor the man picked them up and put them in his pocket.

'Your time for fun is over. Pick a name that you will remember for your passport and plane ticket and hand over your cell phone. You are still a wanted man and you will not leave this apartment again. Phone room service for your needs and give them my name.'

Peter had to think fast. He took time out to go to the toilet. His agile brain began to work overtime; he needed a name immediately that Ray would recognise if he came across it. Peter had not taken the risk of using the cell phone. To remember a number he connected it with a mental image and Peter had a photographic memory. There was no way that he would be able to communicate directly with Ray or Susan again. His mind was in turmoil as he recalled a whirling kaleidoscope of sights and sounds, 'Red Rover' in white powder, Freddie Mercury, red knickers, room service, fun over. It was obvious, it was all there, his new name, he just needed a reason to explain it.

Peter invented a fictional dead relative, an untraceable figment of his imagination. The Boss Man was satisfied and summoned a collection of people from his adjoining suite. They surveyed Peter in a professional manner and commenced to apply their individual expertises. He was measured from head to foot and side-to-side. The boot maker took an impression of Peter's feet and increased his height with the help of Cuban heels. Shoulder pads were added to his jacket, to extend the horizontal line of his upper body. His head was shaved and a silver stud inserted into his left ear lobe. The resulting close-up passport photograph showed no resemblance to the previous individual.

Ray needed information. He returned to Sally's apartment and saw Susan. Ray required the completed passenger departure lists for the next three days from Schiphol Airport. It was a question of elimination. Assuming that they would make a last minute booking in first or business class on a flight to the Southern Hemisphere was a long shot. Ray knew that if Peter had a new passport and if could look down the list something would stand out, he had nothing else to go on. The majority of flights were fully booked and had been for weeks. The next day Ray was running out of time when the list came through. Three first class male passengers to Bangkok, Thailand. He read the name Freddie Serover twice. It was two much of a coincidence he knew Peter too well and he was the only man that knew him as Red Rover.

Ray issued a continuous flow of rapid requests before he stopped to take a breath. 'I need a seat on that plane, security clearance to view the suspects before boarding, a photocopy of their passports and a single room in a Bangkok Hotel reserved in advance.'

Susan said, 'No, the first and last requests are not possible the rest I can arrange. You will need two seats and a double room because I am coming with you. Ray realised it was pointless to argue; he had to get a seat on that flight. Sally used her position to explain to a booking agent that the plane had been over booked. Susan successfully secured permission to allow Ray to undertake his request and booked a room for two in advance at the Shangri-La Hotel, Bangkok. Susan informed the airline that she was taking time-out to recover from post-traumatic stress, brought about by her previous experience in Greenland.'

Back in his hotel room, Ray packed his suitcase and dismantled the surveillance equipment. He arranged for it to be returned to the hire shop, paid his bill and took a taxi to the airport.

The Boss Man and his employees entered the building. Ray was ready and waiting behind a one-way mirror located in the first-class departure lounge. At the control desk Peter presented his new passport and the detailed information was immediately transferred to Ray in the observation room. The passport in the name of Freddie Serover bore no resemblance to the under-cover cop he knew as Columbo. When Peter entered the departure lounge, Ray did not recognise the man with the shaven head, wearing shades with a silver stud in his left ear. Ray needed positive proof that Freddie and Peter were one and the same. Due to a slight delay in departure time the airline provided an extra complimentary round of drinks for the first-class passengers. Shortly after, an announcement was made that the flight to Bangkok was now boarding so please proceed to your departure gate.

Ray entered the empty lounge and carefully removed three glasses. He applied a short length of transparent sticky tape to each one. On removal, the tape retained an identifiable impression of a fingerprint. A close up examination under a microscope provided a perfect match with the one in Ray's wallet.

He was the last to board the plane and intentionally headed to the first-class cabin with his cell phone in his hand. He had just enough time at the open door to transmit a pulse and with a sigh of satisfaction he saw the man with the shaven head reach around to scratch his back, before being directed to his seat in cabin class. Ray sat in the last row next to a lady with bleached blond hair wearing an enormous pair of false eyelashes.

Chapter Nine

Susan sat in the aisle seat at the rear of the plane close to the toilets. On the long flight, Peter eventually appeared from the first-class cabin and as he crossed her path she stood up and surreptitiously gave Peter a folded piece of paper containing the name, address and telephone number of Ray's hotel in Bangkok plus his e-mail address. She gave way and waited outside the closed cubical. When he emerged, he muttered, 'The next time you serve my coffee, make it twice as strong with two sugars, I like to fly high.'

Leaving the air-conditioned interior of the aircraft at Bangkok airport, the humid heat of the tropics assaulted and overwhelmed the senses. The close, cloying atmosphere reminded Peter of the oppressive conditions of an overcrowded housing tenement block on a hot summer night, situated on the south side of New York City.

Susan and Ray quickly removed their luggage from the oval rapidly moving carousel, as it relentlessly continued to disgorge a collection of deposited items from behind the plastic curtain. On his way to the exit, Ray caught site of a sign mostly written in an incomprehensible language. Except for the last line, 'Welcome to Thailand, Drugs are Death.' That he understood. It almost defied belief that anyone would risk death or a life sentence for a few thousand dollars.

They took the airport shuttle bus to the Shangri-La hotel. On their journey to the city centre, safely secure in the closed confines of the mini-bus, Ray looked through the window of the bus as they passed by and he saw for the first time the luxuriant opulence of the Oriental Pagodas, protected from evil spirits by the omnipresent Buddhist statues and in complete contrast the opposing, repressive, relentless, poverty. For the transient western traveller, it provided and confirmed their opinion of a slowly developing nation, a divided society the have and the have-nots money or misery. God Bless America, Ray thought.

At the hotel Susan an sent e-mail to Jodie Jordan, Bundaberg, Queensland, Australia. She had seen the sights of Bangkok before and using her accumulated free air miles, she reserved a flight for two to Thailand's northern city of Chiang Mai situated in the northeast state of Chiang Rai. Chiang Rai meets the Mekong River to the north and borders on both Myanmar (Burma) and Laos. It is internationally known as the golden triangle. Susan had four days left, two in Bangkok and two in Chiang Mai, a chance to experience a ride through the rain forest on the back of an elephant before flying home to Australia for the Christmas holiday. At the front desk, Ray arranged to keep his room empty and informed the employee of his destination and left the torn half of a hundred-dollar note. The missing half would be provided on his return on condition that all messages were recorded including the name, time, day, and date. In his absence they would be relayed to Peter, or Freddie Serover, if requested, together with the day and date of Ray's return.

Susan had a plan and a birthday in Chiang Mai. At the local indoor market, she resisted but finally gave way to Ray's request to buy her a present. Side-by-side, the local shops displayed an enormous amount of local products. Thai silk dresses embroidered with oriental designs. Intricate three-dimensional cravings of mountain scenes cut from a slab of solid black teak and imitation international designer goods, complete with their credible counterfeit labels and logos.

After what seemed like an eternity walking along, lost in a labyrinth of interconnecting lanes and walkways window-shopping, Ray had to make a decision. It was a choice between a gold ring and a SLR automatic camera with an extra attachment, a telescopic lens. Ray thought of wedding rings and persuaded Susan that she needed the camera for their jungle journey. She had no intention of requesting the ring. Susan had successfully achieved her objective and to Ray's amazement without hesitation or deviation she retraced their steps to Madame Cia's Camera Shop, an importer of Japanese electrical goods and computer equipment.

Early in the misty morning at 6 a.m., they arrived at the elephant camp. The flimsy enclosure contained a number of the five-ton gentle giants, being prepared by their Mahouts for another day of monotonous, regular, routine. Scrubbed clean and washed behind the ears, they were then given huge bundles of sugarcane and bananas and then left alone to enjoy twenty minutes of free time before being allowed to mix and mingle with the incoming members of the general public. Outside the fence, Susan stood in line and looked through, remembering Jodie, her daughter's first day at school, let loose in the playground waiting for her mother to collect and control her exuberant energy.

Going through the entrance gate, Susan bought a bunch of bananas. The sharp sense of smell of the elephant is its main information gathering ability, its vision is weak and near sighted. Tommy the elephant lifted his trunk to sample the air and then blow the sample into his mouth against the olfactory glands situated in his upper lip. The breeze was in front of him, a damp moist movement of air that carried the smell of ripe fruit towards his highly sensitive trunk. Enclosed in the compound, the typical ageing, retired female tourist will immediately wave a bunch of bananas at the powerful animals to attract their attention. An over-excited elephant running straight towards you at an alarming rate will change your mood immediately from benevolent benefactor to personnel panic as you realise that an uncontrollable force is rapidly approaching with no hint of hesitation or control. A busload of little old ladies on a day trip gave out a great scream in unison as they ran in all directions. In a desperate attempt to escape the rapidly advancing rogue animal, they gathered their skirts about them and uncovered a collection of white legs that had not been exposed to the elements for a considerable amount of time. Their lack of modesty also revealed a quick glimpse of knee length, grey flannel bloomers as they sprinted across the compound in their sensible shoes. Order was restored and they were finally convinced that the previous excitement had been deliberately arranged to give the visitors a day to remember.

Ray wanted no part in it but he was eventually persuaded to participate in the elephant ride. He carefully climbed aboard Tommy, the now docile, lead beast.

After leaving the sanctuary, the elephants, with ears flapping and trunks swinging, began a slow ponderous walk sedately through an enclosed claustrophobic part of the rain forest. Tommy stopped for no apparent reason and began to violently rip branches from an over-hanging tree. A heated exchange of loud sounds took place between the elephant and his Mahout. The man eventually regained control and explained that the animal was getting old and coming into musk for the last time. The elephant, full of male testosterone and frustration after a long working life would be given its freedom and released back into the wild to find a fertile female and live out the rest of its natural life. Ray could not resist the urge to look at Susan. Their eyes met at the same time in an embarrassed silence that signified their inner thoughts. She was still young enough to be his daughter.

They left the forest and entered a clearing of long, lush, verdant grass, which eventually gave way to a rocky mountain path leading to the distant summit. In single file, the procession of pachyderms climbed higher through the foothills. Ray was suitably impressed by the scenery and the sheer drop at the side of the track. It gave an unrestricted view of the valley floor far below. The only distinguishing feature was a collection of small bamboo huts safely contained in a compound, surrounding a larger central building of the same material. Tommy tentatively tapped the ground in front with his trunk to confirm a solid footing before deciding to take another step. Occasionally he stopped to remove a loose lump of rock. Slowly, they lumbered on lurching alarmingly from side to side. Ray, sweating profusely convinced himself that it was the tropical heat. Having reached the summit, the party dismounted and posed for the pre-paid photographs, a part of the original plan. Susan still sitting on top of Tommy took a photograph of Ray. Looking down from her high advantage point, she included in the background a village located far below in the valley. She insisted that Ray returned to Tommy and sit on the head of the Asian elephant, wearing a silly grin and Ray obliged. Sitting on the cranium the short sharp hairs turned the silly grin into a grimace. Up close, Susan took the perfect picture of a city dweller out of his depth desperately trying to contain his composure.

A sudden clap of thunder caused Tommy to trumpet loudly as he decided to run for the safety of the trees. Astride the large head, Ray, with legs wide apart in his floral Bermuda shorts suddenly realised that they provided inadequate protection from the rasping movement caused by the unexpected departure. Trying to control the uncontrollable, he applied maximum pressure from his inner thighs in a desperate attempt to stay upright and on top, as the pain and experience of sitting on a moving wire brush rapidly increased.

After a mouthful of incomprehensible language, the Mahout sitting behind, managed to regain his authority. Ray, recovering from his ordeal, completed the return journey lying face down in a comfortable howdah, situated on the back of the last elephant., thoughtfully provided by the company for the unexpected medical emergency, accidents or the occasional infirm tourist that needed a more secure comfortable ride.

Their last evening in Chiang Mai had been arranged to include a cultural entertainment a traditional dinner and dance. It is the custom and expected that the guests will sit cross-legged on the hard wooden floor. To stand above and look down on the assembled diners is to show disrespect. Ray could not sit or stand. Laying face down on the bed in the hotel room after his painful experience, he insisted that Susan leave him alone to recover. She attended the entertainment and returned at midnight to collect her luggage. Susan had a seat booked on the last flight to Bangkok to arrive in time to connect with a Qantas flight to Mascot Airport, Sydney, Australia.

Ray would return to the Shangri-La Hotel Bangkok the next day, to pay the bill and pick up any messages from Peter, then fly to Australia to join Susan in Bundaberg, Queensland, for Christmas. That was the plan.

She had no time left for a long goodbye or lingering kisses. Issuing a rapid, continuous, collection of do's and don'ts, she gave Ray his final instructions. At the same time, without a pause in the one-way conversation she gathered up and packed her possessions. Ray tried his best to respond at the appropriate moment. A quick 'yes' or 'no' at the right time seemed to please but it did not delay the continuous verbal flow. He heard something about Timmy the elephant trashing the compound and escaping into the tropical rain forest at the end of the day of their enforced acceptance. Ray tried to find the right answer to break the cold silent atmosphere that had descended. He could not decide if Susan was

91

blaming him and trying to make him feel guilty for the animal's unpredictable behaviour or if she was taking advantage of his inability to attend the entertainment. An unemotional friendly kiss on the cheek provided Ray with all the information he needed.

He was not the marrying kind. She turned out the light, banged the door on her way out and left him alone to enjoy the quite of the darkened room. As he turned around to say 'goodbye', he noticed a part of the birthday present. The untouched telephoto lens left behind on the bedside table, still safely secured in its white moulded, polystyrene container.

The police kicked the door in at 3 a.m. The loud crack of the breaking doorframe was rapidly replaced by the insistent strident sound of an authoritative figure in full verbal flow. A confusing collection of bright torchlights randomly moving in all directions in the small room, eventually settled on Ray's tired eyes as he was grabbed from his prone position on the bed and thrown to the floor. Roughly manhandled and restrained with his hands tied behind his back, he was forced to his feet. The room, now illuminated by the single over-head light bulb, contained a number of uniformed figures pointing a powerful collection of weapons in his direction. Safely secured and surrounded, Ray offered no resistance.

The man in charge immediately focused his attention onto the telephoto lens and conveniently produced a pocketful of precision instruments designed to unscrew the most complicated parts of the modern camera. To the amazement of Ray, the leader, in full view of his assembled assistants, extracted a number of carefully wrapped plastic, identical small items from the telephoto lens. It had revealed a significant amount of illegal substances. The leader, confident in his capacity removed a card from his top pocket and began to recite in broken English.

'You are under arrest for the transportation of prohibited drugs.'

Ray reacted automatically and began to resist. He took a step toward his accuser and at the same time, a sudden blow to the back of his head brought him to his knees. As he lost consciousness he realised that he had been set up. He would have to have words with Susan later.

Back in Bangkok, Peter had a day off to appreciate the finer things of life and sample the sex shops of Pat Pong Road. Playing the part of an interested tourist he hired for the day at a derisory price, a local type of transport a three-wheeled tuk-tuk taxi, complete with driver. Experiencing the crowded, polluted, city centre traffic, carefully crawling along the slow moving congested road, Peter stuck behind the continuous convoy of out of town trucks belching out diesel fumes, trying desperately to reach their destination in time to sell their produce at the local market. He soon realised that he was being taken for a slow ride. He had just seen for the second time the other side of the Golden Temple, situated in the grounds of the Grand Palace. Built for the King of Thailand in contains an impressive example of a collection of intricate artwork. Produced by local artisans and the expertise of distant village communities, that specialised in using their traditional knowledge and available materials to honour the Buddha and his earth bound representatives, the Royal Family.

Bored with the start, stop, slowly going nowhere, rolling roadblock. Peter left the tuk-tuk and boldly took his live in his hands. As the lights changed to green, he nimbly ran across the four-lane highway. Running recklessly, he ignored the honking traffic and the sudden squeal of resisting tires, trying desperately to get a grip on the slippery tarmac. He safely reached the other side and took time out to regain his composure.

Peter, with his arms folded on top of the dividing bridge structure. Looked down into the still waters of the canal that quietly flowed beneath the incessant, uninterrupted flow of the early morning traffic. Peter was lost with nothing to do. To pass the time he took a trip in a long-tailed water taxi to the floating markets. After completing the expected business of bartering, he had a collection of unwanted trinkets and tropical fruit, which he gave to the owner of the water taxi.

Back on dry land, he decided to take a walk through the back streets of Bangkok. The crowded bustling polluted streets were lined with stalls selling dried fish, cheap clothes and counterfeit cassette tapes. The smell of spices, fried food and contaminated waste was overpowering. Behind and above the stalls were several signs fixed to the nearest building advertising their goods, all of them in Thai, but he recognised a red and white Coca-Cola symbol and a sign advertising Kodak film. The narrow street was packed with sweating bodies. He saw old women holding on to trays of cigarettes and disposable lighters, and toothless men mumbling and muttering about the lack of business in charge of the change bag, while their wives stood guard over their stalls and way laid any passer-by in the hope of persuading them to part with their money; bare-chested and shoeless children running between the shoppers, giggling and pointing at the white-faced foreigner. It confirmed Peter's impression that he was in the wrong place at the wrong time.

Surrounded by an endless claustrophobic mass of humanity, he ignored the numerous serene statues of the silent Buddha displayed at the entrance of the local temples and rapidly found refuge and sanctuary in the nearest Western style watering hole. Sitting on a barstool in Dave's Discount Liquor Store, on the south side of Pat Pong Road, Peter still smelt the overpowering sweet, exotic, incense, wafting occasionally through the open door, combined with the polluted atmosphere caused by the black fumes emitted from the passing traffic. Consuming a number of Singha beers in the risqué bar, he was constantly approached by a steady stream of unsavoury characters of indefinable sexual orientation. The lady-boys of Bangkok appeared to be perfect in every way and the Thai girls were pretty enough with their soft brown skin and glossy black hair but Peter resisted the temptation and telephoned Ray's hotel.

The employee relayed the information that Ray had taken a trip to Chiang Mai. His return was already overdue. Peter put the phone down, he was not happy. He felt a restless uncertainty that the situation was rapidly spiralling out of control. He needed desperately to get in touch with Ray to exchange information. Walking back to his bar stool, a bird in a gilded cage hanging high above the smoke filled room caught his attention, as it suddenly screeched, 'Try again later, try again later!' The African Grey parrot carried out a restricted dance in its confined container. Moving its head up and down in a knowing way it also whistled as it shuffled from side to side on its bamboo perch.

Peter understood he needed to break out and take charge of the situation. He realised that he was getting old, the thin lithesome, perfectly presentable young Thai girls, did not interest him at all. He wanted to change his life and settle down with a mature big buxom woman. Not in a mood to enjoy himself, Peter paid the bar tab and returned early to his hotel room.

The big Boss Man walked unexpectedly into the room as usual and announced the fact that they were leaving and flying north to Chiang Mai. Peter felt a feeling of relief he was getting closer. He nearly smiled but that could have been a big mistake. Bertie, the ever-present bodyguard looked on and Peter got the message that he might be looking for a reason to react and protect his boyfriend. An irrational display of uncontrollable energy, released in a moment of madness by a jealous walking man-mountain, is a force to be reckoned with. Bertie would eventually need careful control and counselling in a maximum-security home, if he lived that long.

Peter felt completely isolated, securely contained and alone in a strange land without any chance of breaking out and exerting his pent-up potential. Coming to grips with the situation, he thought of the African Grey parrot and decided that he would not wait to make the next phone call or try again later. It was time to turn the tables to put in place and operate the back-up plan at the next available opportunity.

They left the hotel twenty minutes later in a blacked out limousine. Peter presumed that they were going to the Bangkok International Airport but he was not about to raise their suspicions by asking questions. He sat quietly in the back seat and tried to remember local landmarks and the time it took from A to B. The lengthening shadows from west to east gave him the position of the setting sun. They were travelling north in the right direction but taking back roads and side streets. Peter realised he was in the middle of a mobile protection unit and the vehicle in front and the one behind took it in turns to change positions. He stopped looking out of the window, fastened his seat belt and slid down in his seat below the level of the window hoping that the body of the limousine was bullet proof. They stopped outside a pre-cast concrete building. Bertie got out and stepped aside to allow four saffron-robed monks to walk by. The monk bringing up the rear whispered something to Bertie as he passed. Bertie returned to the car and the driver drove around to the back of the building and parked next to a loading ramp. More men dressed in saffron-robes surrounded the car and opened the doors. The occupants were escorted up the ramp to a steel shutter, which the leader banged on with the flat of his hand, five short raps followed by two more in quick succession. A door in the shutter opened a couple of inches and someone inside muttered a few words in Thai. The right words were spoken and the door opened wide. The Boss Man motioned for Peter to go in first.

It was dark inside and Peter blinked as his eyes became accustomed to the gloom. The warehouse was hot and airless. Directly ahead stood a small, plastic outdoor dining table and two chairs. The rest of the building was packed with wooden crates and cardboard boxes, which reached almost to the ceiling. A line of bare light-bulbs provided the illumination, but there were so many crates and boxes that much of the interior was in shadow.

Peter wiped his damp forehead with his sleeve. The Boss Man smiled sympathetically. 'We check, then we go,' he said.

The man who had opened the door was tall and thin with a handgun stuck into the belt of his jeans. He grinned at the Boss and nodded towards the far end of the warehouse. Four more Thais in T-shirts and jeans with guns in their belts materialised from the shadows. Peter looked at the Boss and together, with Bertie close behind, they walked down the aisle between the towering boxes. At the end, a large space had been cleared. A cardboard box with an international photographic logo and the message 'Made in Japan, Electronic goods and Equipment' had been opened. Half a dozen SLR automatic cameras with telescopic lenses had been taken out.

The Boss Man ignored them, after counting the boxes in the towering stack he pointed to Peter, 'You choose,' he said.

Peter picked out a box at the bottom of the pile. The doorman began to talk quickly but the Boss Man silenced him with a wave of his hand. Bertie said something in Thai but the man continued to protest.

'He says it's to much work,' Bertie translated. 'He says they're all the same.'

The Boss Man's eyes hardened, he was insistent. 'Tell him I want to see one from that box.'

Bertie turned to the man and spoke to him again. There was something pleading about Bertie's voice, as if he didn't want to cause offence. Eventually the man relaxed, shrugged his shoulders and smiled. He waved his two colleagues over and helped them take down the upper boxes until they had uncovered the one on the bottom. They carried it across the warehouse floor and placed it on the white plastic, outdoor dining table. The Boss Man made an incision with his Italian flick knife and removed from the cardboard box a camera, complete with a telescopic lens. He detached the lens and on command Bertie immediately provided the required tool that was needed to remove the restraining screws that concealed the hidden contraband. He pulled out three polythene-covered packages containing white powder.

There was a crashing sound from the far end of the warehouse followed by shouts. He looked across at Peter.

The tall, thin, doorman pulled a gun from his belt and ran towards the entrance. His two companions followed. The Boss Man yelled at Bertie to go with them. A gunshot sounded, and caught in the confided space it reverberated loudly around the enclosed space.

'What's happening?' shouted Peter.

'Maybe nothing,' said the Boss man as he handed Peter a powerful Smith and Western.

'Maybe nothing?' Peter shouted. 'This is a set-up!'

The sound of a second shot, much closer, was deafening in the confines of the building. There were more shots, louder than the first coming closer. Peter had reacted instantly at the sound of the second gunshot, and immediately he fell to the ground and rolled up into a tight ball. He rolled and reached the safety of the nearest stack of cardboard boxes. Hiding behind the boxes, he reached out and grabbed the leg of the Boss Man. Still standing, he was thrown off balance, and brought to his knees as a hot bullet whistled through the air and burrowed its way through a cardboard box at head-height. Blasting away at the approaching target, Peter rolled out from his concealed space and with both hands on the Smith and Western he rapidly discharged the contents of the handgun as he continued rolling full-length across the aisle, and into the relative safety, and security of an empty space behind another stack of boxes.

The obstacle, the dead body, was not enough to obstruct the progress of the pursuers. Peter pulled over a stack of boxes and blocked the path to impede their progress. He pulled the Boss Man to his feet.

'This way,' he said, pulling him down the aisle. They ran between the stacks of boxes.

'Is it the cops?' asked the Boss Man, gasping for breath.

'Maybe,' said Peter. 'I don't know.'

A bullet thwacked into a cardboard box above the Boss Man's head and he ducked down.

'The cops wouldn't just shoot, would they?' he asked Peter.

'This is Thailand,' Peter replied. 'The police can do anything they want.'

Still running, Peter kicked open the emergency exit fire door. They were both grabbed and bundled into the back of the limousine. It shot off immediately with the doors still open, turned a corner and collected a bruised and blood-splattered, Bertie. The Boss screamed out two words. 'Airport! Now!' Peter could think of nothing better. A night flight to Chiang Mai.

Chapter Ten

The whirling kaleidoscope of colourful confusion slowly gave way and subsided as Ray eventually regained consciousness and began to be aware of his surroundings; safely shackled and secured in the back of a moving van. He slowly opened one eye and lying on the floor in the dark, he had a close up view of a metal reinforced toecap resting against and indenting his right cheek. It was just one in an identical line of black, laced up military leather boots receding into the blurred distance.

Without a sign of movement, he closed his eye and tried to think. Suddenly the rear doors opened and forced to his feet Ray rapidly blinking in the early morning daylight was pushed in the back, by a member of the uniformed team. Sent sprawling, Ray landed face down in the dirt beside another booted foot. He received a swift kick to the kidneys before being forced to crawl on his hands and knees the short distance to the entrance of the notorious local prison.

Arriving on all fours at the door, he turned his head and looked up to see armed security guards stationed with their machine guns pointing in his direction, thirty-foot above the ground and surrounded with barbed wire in their unassailable towers. The last thing he remembered was seeing a low flying aircraft with flaps lowered in the bright blue sky preparing to descend and land at the local airport. It was Ray's last sight of daylight. A brutal blow to the back of the head sent his senses reeling and returned him to the whirling world of coloured confusion before the darkness of blissful oblivion took over.

He came to on a cold stone floor in a small empty cell and recovered his senses. The door opened and Ray recognised the arresting officer. Protesting his innocence, Ray was taken to an adjoining room this one was occupied by two brown-uniformed policemen sitting at a wooden trestle table. There was nowhere for Ray to sit and as he stood in front of them with his hands at his sides his palms begun to sweat.

This was a case for the prosecution. The only thing Ray understood was that the arresting officer relentlessly pacing the tiny room was producing a continuous verbal torrent of incriminating evidence. At the end of the strident diatribe caused by a lack of breath, a calming silence descended. The oldest of the seated superiors had a sheet of paper in front of him. He cleared his throat and looked up at Ray and slowly studied him with impassive, almost bored, eyes.

'You are charged with the possession of illegal drugs, how do you plead, guilty or not guilty?' Ray pleaded not guilty. The grey-haired man in charge nodded and began writing. The third man reached down below the table and produced the telescopic lens in the polystyrene container. He placed it on top of the table. The door opened behind Ray, and Madame Cia appeared. She identified Ray. The two seated policemen nodded in agreement and the grey-haired one continued to fill out the form. The arresting officer produced his pocketful of precision instruments and unscrewed the telescopic lens, to remove and display the previously hidden contents. The contents confirmed the fore-gone conclusion, Ray was found guilty.

The quiet grey-haired judge pushed the form across the table and tapped a space with his ballpoint pen at the bottom of the sheet of A4 paper.

'Sign,' he said, in perfect English, 'case closed.' Ray reached out and attempted to pick up the piece of paper but was rapidly restrained by his accuser.

'I just want to read it,' said Ray. The grey-haired judge tapped the form with his finger.

'Sign,' he repeated. Ray leaned forward and looked at the form. It was all in Thai and totally incomprehensible. He had no way of knowing if he was putting his name to a misdemeanour or signing his death warrant. He shook his head.

'I can't sign this, I can't read it. I can't sign something that I can't read. Get someone to read it to me in English, then I'll sign it.'

'Sign,' said the judge with a note of menace in his voice. He stood up slowly, as if he was playing a part in a pre-rehearsed theatrical drama. Eye-to-eye, he stared at Ray for several seconds. The slap, when it came, was totally unexpected. Ray took a step backwards and was immediately restrained by his accuser. Ray opened his mouth to speak but no words came out. He felt his left cheek redden.

'Sign,' said the judge, raising his hand again.

Ray looked around the room but found no compassion or comfort in the cold stares of the other occupants as they reached for their weapons. He knew without a shadow of a doubt that if he didn't sign, the piece of paper they would beat him to a pulp, or worse. He reached for the pen and signed it 'Freddie Serover.' The judge took the form away from Ray, scrutinised it, then spoke to the guards.

Ray was taken out of the office and led down a corridor to another door. Ray was pushed inside without a word and the door locked behind him. It was hot and airless and in total darkness; the only light in the room came through a narrow gap at the bottom of the door. Ray couldn't even tell how large the room was, or if there was anyone else there. He felt his heart begin to race and struggled to stay calm. He carefully approached the door, and feeling around the frame with his forehead he eventually found a light switch. It took several attempts before he could press the switch with his nose but he managed it and an overhead recessed fluorescent tube protected by a wire grid slowly flickered into life. He sighed with relief as the light illuminated his surroundings. Leaning with his back against the wall, Ray realised that he was in deep trouble. The small claustrophobic room was successfully designed to create a restrictive environment, devoid of windows, washings facilities and a bed. The toilet was a hole in the ground located in a far corner. The other inmates, a swarm of flies, were constantly returning to it and exchanging their body fluids. Accustomed to the unsavoury surroundings, they occasionally took off to explore their domain. The disorganised cloud of opportunists would surround and descend on Ray. Their mass attack and constant buzzing distracted Ray, as they settled on and absorbed the moisture from his sweating skin, before returning to the hole in the ground and its surroundings, to compete with the moving mass of crawling cockroaches. The bare earth was also a breeding ground for parasites. The handcuffs were hurting his wrists; they had been put on too tight. From the treatment that he had received so far, he suspected that the police had done it deliberately. He slid down the wall and sat on the floor. There had been no interrogation and no questions. It was if he was a part of a bureaucratic process that had no interest in his guilt or innocence.

Hours later, he woke up, his deep sleep interrupted by guards in brown uniforms bursting unexpectedly into his cell. Still in chains, he was dragged to his feet and propelled with a number of blows to his back, down a long corridor into a crowded room. A barrage of blinding lights met his arrival. The local press had been invited to attend in advance. As Ray was forced to sit in front of a TV camera, next to the grey-haired judge, they continuously fired their flashbulbs in his face. Ray was a prize catch; the cops had called the press conference to show off their latest arrest. A forty-something white westerner, an American drug dealer, obviously an international carrier as well.

Ray had no idea what was going on, so he repeated continuously, 'I am not guilty on all charges, I need a lawyer and to be allowed to make a phone call to the American Embassy.'

As soon as it began it was all over and the assembled media melted away. The pointless press conference had one consolation, when Ray was taken back to another claustrophobic room, the guards removed the handcuffs and leg irons with which they'd constrained him, before closing the metal door behind them. He stood up and stretched his arms, reached out and touched two bare brick walls at the same time. There was no window in the cell and the far wall consisted of floor-to-ceiling bars and overlooked a narrow corridor. Next to the bars on the bare floor, lay a stained, flea-infested mattress. Ray lay on his back on the hard concrete floor, his arms folded behind his head. He could hear far-off shouts and from time to time a metal door would slam shut. When he was arrested the police had removed his wallet and wristwatch, so there was no way of telling what time of day it was.

He heard the sound of shuffling and the rattle of leg chains in the corridor outside. Without warning the cell door opened. Another prisoner had arrived and was thrown to the floor to land at Ray's feet. The new arrival stood up and pleaded his innocence as the impassive guards hastily retreated and returned the cell door to the locked position. The prisoner sat down next to Ray with his back up against the cell wall, his knees drawn up against his chest. Something buzzed by his ear but he was too out of it to swat it away.

'You okay, Ray?' asked the inmate.

'I will be in a minute,' was the reply, 'when they deliver my next fix.' His smile seemed genuine, though Ray knew enough about prisoners to know that appearances could be deceptive and that an easy smile could just as easily be followed by a knife in the ribs. As if on cue, the cell door opened again and a guard carrying a transparent plastic bag entered the claustrophobic room. The bag contained all the necessary paraphernalia for an addicted drug-addict. Ray assumed that this man was a plant, an informer, sent in to gain his trust and secure any information available for the prosecution. In return he would receive a reduced sentence.

He kept quiet as the man said, 'I don't know why you don't buy your way out of here. They leave you in isolation for days with a bag of assorted drugs until the temptation becomes irresistible. The guards give it to you for free to prove you are a user when you are examined later by an independent doctor. Time is on their side, it might be five days or five months before you eventually weaken and give in to temptation. After the first taste, life inside seems a lot better, each day the bag is refilled with a more powerful drug of your choice. They increase the strength of your daily supply and then without warning they remove it. Days later, alone in your cell, you start to lose your mind and you will confess to anything just to get your fix and get out of there. When you start suffering withdrawal symptoms, shouting, screaming and trying to climb the walls the guards return to put you in handcuffs and foot restraints, then they take you to your trial.' Without pausing for breath, the continuous monologue finally finished.

Ray recognised a drug addict when he saw one. He did not understand addicts but he knew enough to realise that this man was capable of irrational behaviour. The prisoner took a syringe out of the bag, a metal spoon, an unrecognisable substance and a candle. Ray watched in fascination, as the prisoner placed the drug on the spoon and held it over the candle flame. He watched as it began to sizzle on the hot metal. He coughed a dry hacking sound that echoed around the cell. Ray watched as the addict carefully put the spoon containing the now colourless liquid down onto the concrete floor. He dipped the end of the needle into the liquid and drew it up into the barrel of the syringe, holding his breath as he filled it.

'Try some, time goes faster this way,' he said.

Ray refused and replied, 'It was drugs that got us in here. Why would I want to inject that stuff into my veins?'

The prisoner grinned and said, 'Because it feels good.'

Ray watched as the man prepared to inject. 'How long have you been using?' he asked as the man wrapped a shoelace tourniquet around his upper arm.

'Who knows, two months, two years, time is not important in here.'

Ray watched, fascinated, as the prisoner slowly, shoved the needle into the raised vein. He sighed and slowly depressed the plunger, pushing the drug into his system, then loosened the tourniquet. The man relaxed immediately, 'You should try it he said just once to experience the buzz.'

'Not me I can't stand needles,' said Ray.

'Suit yourself, like I said, it'll help to pass the time.'

'I don't want to pass the time I am not staying,' said Ray as the addict's eyes began to blink and glaze over.

'What are you talking about?' The empty syringe fell from his fingers and clattered on to the floor. As the man slipped into unconsciousness a large, shiny, black, cockroach scuttled past Ray's feet. It climbed up the right side, ran across the man's face and disappeared, into the darkness, behind and into the shadow of his left ear.

Adam Smith emptied the remains of his whisky glass and ordered another. Sitting, drinking alone at the long bar in the Coconut Club, he began to think about returning to Bangkok. He had to get back to work in the big city. An American by birth, he preferred and found it easier to use his English accent obtained from his five-year stay in London. It was his first foreign posting after graduating from Harvard University. Adam worked as a freelance independent. He had learnt that a journalist in Thailand with an English name and accent receives more respect than an American.

Watching without interest the news item on the wall-mounted TV, he began to pay attention as Ray appeared. It was the usual story; a drug carrier had been lawfully caught, or an innocent American abroad had been set-up by the local law enforcers. Adam knew from past experience that it could be either one. It might be worth a visit to find out from the man himself.

On his approach to the prison, he stopped at a small wooden shack and bought an assortment of tinned fruit, cigarettes, soft drinks and soap. It would be expected and accepted by the guards as an entrance fee. Every man has his price. At the end of the line, the prisoner would receive what was left, if anything. He drove slowly, down a long dirt road. At the far corner of the perimeter wall, ringed with barbed wire, was a large watchtower with a powerful searchlight. Higher and more obvious than the rest, it was open to the elements but with a circular metal roof held up by three legs. Isolated from the outside entrance by fifty-feet of bare ground, it contained a menacing machine gun. Under observation, Adam parked the car and walked with his collection of consumables to the main gate. He pulled the bell chain and a wooden panel slid open at head height. Adam showed his press credentials, spoke to the man in Thai and through the narrow opening, handed him a packet of cigarettes. Bolts were withdrawn from the inside and the door swung open. The guardian of the gate pointed his gun at Adam and invited him into the compound. A second guard grabbed him, turned him around and pushed him up against the wall. With professional indifference he went through the routine search. On completion he helped himself to a packet of cigarettes and a bar of soap. The grubby individual released nauseating waves of stale sweat every time he moved. Adam, close up, could smell the obnoxious odours of the uniformed officer. He hoped and assumed that the soap would be put to good use.

Passed on to another guard, Adam was escorted across the open space of the dry deserted exercise yard. At the far side they stopped underneath an ornate shady arch. Constructed out of soft sandstone it supported a serene, cross-legged seated statue: the all-powerful forgiving figure of a gold-coloured bloated, benevolent Buddha. The arch was inscribed with a collection of incomprehensible words, signs and symbols. Carefully cut into the stone by previous inmates. Adam recognised the English phrase: 'drugs are death.' The door was unexpectedly thrown open by another malnourished, skinny guard wearing a large key chain around his waist. The guard's uniform was several sizes too big for him. In his hand, he held and spoke into a mobile phone, at the same time he looked across the compound and waved to the guard in the watchtower. The man in charge of the machine-gun pointing in Adam's direction turned it around and returned it to its original position. He re-focused and aimed it at the bare stretch of dirt road that approached the prison. That was his killing zone.

Led down a long narrow corridor, Adam passed on both sides a number of identical cells. Each one contained a prisoner behind the floor-to-ceiling bars. Motivated and stirred into life by his passing, they began to shout and attract attention by banging their heads against the bars. The guard reacted by poking them in the head with his baton and screaming a torrent of verbal abuse in Thai. It reminded Adam of the time when he was a young boy taken to the circus. He remembered that the lion tamer controlled the animals with a long stick and a whip. Maybe whips were illegal now or just hidden away until later?

At the end of the row, the guard unlocked and opened a door and ushered Adam into a small room. Before he left him on his own, the guard carried out a search of Adam's bag of highly desirable items. He selected a tin of tropical fruit, a tin of fizzy Tizer and a plastic shrink-wrapped four-pack of Coca-Cola. Adam's presents for the prisoner were running low at an alarming rate. With a polite bow and a false smile the guard began to leave the room. On his way, he stopped at the open door with a hand on the outside handle, he turned around and said in perfect English, 'Have a nice day' and slammed the door shut. The sound of the key turning in the lock and the strident diminishing laughter from the guard returning down the corridor gave Adam cause for concern. He had no back-up and no one knew were he was, the room contained two empty chairs, a table and one troubled reporter.

The guard returned with two uniformed policemen. They had large handguns in black leather holsters on their hips and transceivers clipped to their belts. One was carrying an A4 folder, which he placed in front of Adam. They sat at the table and began to talk in Thai ignoring Adam completely.

He interrupted and said in English, 'I understand Thai.'

'Good,' replied the officer. 'In that case we will converse in English.'

Written in Thai, the folder contained two sets of identical papers, the originals and photocopies. The first document was an official charge sheet informing the accused that they were under arrest for the transportation of prohibited drugs. The bottom line had been signed Freddie Serover. The second sheet of paper provided a signed witness statement from Madame Cia's camera and computer shop in Chiang Mai. The third and final page had been prepared and signed by the arresting officer. It included an extra charge of resisting arrest. Adam suspected that Freddie had been framed, as the senior officer had suggested that Freddie should plead guilty as charged. His signed confession would guarantee a lighter sentence. Adam had heard it all before. He held on to the photocopies and requested permission to see the prisoner. The policeman talked into his transceiver, conferred with his colleague and returned the original paper work to the plastic folder. They stood up and made their way to the door.

Adam repeated his request, 'Can I see the prisoner?'

'Twenty minutes,' was the reply and 'make sure he has enough money for a good defence.' He winked and nodded as he emphasised the word 'money.' It was a thinly disguised message. If the prisoner had an acceptable amount of money it would mean that all charges would be dropped and Freddie would be a free man. It is the custom in Thailand to buy your way out of trouble.

The malnourished, skinny guard led Adam out of the room and down another long, dark, depressing corridor. They arrived at what could only be described as a wire cage. The guard seemed pleased and proud as he invited Adam to step inside. It was his living room. On the floor next to a pile of explicit pornographic magazines, a mattress took up most of the space. It left just enough room in the corner for a portable TV. The screen flickered and the picture occasionally rolled, as the set tried desperately to hold on to an inferior signal. A high wooden stool standing beside an old school desk gave the guard an uninterrupted view of the corridor.

The guard insisted that the prisoner be allowed only one of Adam's gifts. He would have to confiscate the rest. He lifted the lid of the desk and took out what Adam assumed was the visitors book. He made a mark in it and returned it, with the rest of Adam's purchases and locked the lid. The guard had a lot in common with the other inmates - they were all prisoners, confined and conditioned to lead a completely pointless existence. He took Adam back down the long corridor and stopped outside a cell with the floor-to-ceiling bars. He was carrying a clipboard and he ran his finger down it.

'Freddie Serover,' said the guard. When there was no response from the occupant of the cell, he repeated the words, louder the second time they carried more conviction and confidence. Ray lay on the floor in his cell and kept his eyes closed. He ignored the Thai guard as he banged on the bars with his baton and shouted the name, 'Serover!' Ray had decided to keep quiet, he had no intention of reacting. He needed to speak to somebody superior.

At the sound of Adam's English accent repeating the question, Ray stood up rapidly and reached through the bars to shake Adam's hand. Adam introduced himself and flashed his press credentials.

Ray visibly relaxed and said, 'Thank Christ you're here. I need someone sensible to talk to, I'm not guilty of any of these charges.'

Adam noticed the dark bags of loose skin under Ray's eyes, a sign of the strain that he was under. His mouth was set in a nervous half-smile, as if he was trying to reassure himself that everything was going to be all right. The strain was evident in his face and his hand was trembling. Adam saw a typical retired American male, fat and forty-something on a trip to the tropics and the Far East, in the wrong place at the wrong time and under arrest.

Adam passed the three photocopied sheets of A4 paper through the prison bars. 'Is that your signature?' he asked. 'Do you intend to plead guilty at your trial Mr Serover?'

'I won't be pleading guilty,' said Ray. 'I won't be pleading anything. There's been a mistake.'

'You have already signed a confession of sorts Mr Serover. It doesn't exactly help your position.'

'Confession? What confession?'

'This form you signed.'

'It's in Thai,' Ray replied angrily. 'How the hell was I supposed to know what it said?'

'You should have waited until you'd received a translation,' said Adam. Having lit the fuse, he stood back from the bars and watched as Ray exploded with rage and released all of his pent up frustration.

'You weren't there!' he shouted. 'You didn't have a uniformed sadist thug breathing down your neck as you were confronted by a couple of all-powerful control freaks deciding if you were to live or die!' The force of the verbal out-burst motivated the guard into removing his baton from its container. It also convinced Adam what he already suspected, that this man had been set-up.

'There's no need to shout,' Adam said to Ray. 'To survive this nightmare you must keep it together and control your temper. There is always someone ready to take advantage if you step out of line and make yourself a target. Do you have any money Mr Serover? Life can be unpleasant in a Thai jail, or it can be bearable. The only thing that makes a difference is money. If you are guilty or innocent you will need some sort of heavy financial or legal back up. It all depends on your bank balance.'

'They take drug smuggling very seriously here Mr Serover, more seriously than murder. A kilo of cocaine is worth much more than the life of a local and convicting a foreigner focuses the attention of the international press on to the progress being made by the enforcement officers, in eradicating the export of illegal drugs. It is a deception designed to placate the powerful Western rulers that pull the purse strings and provide financial assistance to those in control of this developing nation; on condition that they contain the drug problem inside their own borders and do not allow it to escape and influence the activities of the workers in Western Europe and North America.

In your case I believe it's a set up between the police and their informant, someone plants the drugs, informs the police that you are in possession and then they arrange to have you arrested. The police keep enough of the drug to convict you and then they return the rest to the informer; he or she takes their cut, sells the rest and returns fifty per-cent of the profit to the police. The informer places another illegal amount on another innocent victim and the financial result is guaranteed. The endless circle is secure and unbroken. It can be arranged for a foreigner to pay for his early release. If you trust me, I will return tomorrow with your release papers but I shall have to have access to your bank account to remove the money.'

Ray had to trust this man, he had no choice but he didn't need a curious reporter poking about in his business. If he uncovered the real reason why Ray was in Thailand it would jeopardise the whole operation and put Peter's life in danger.

'I agree,' he said. 'On the condition that you phone the Shangri-La hotel and leave the following message for Peter, Freddie, Serover.'

'I am in Chiang Mai prison. I need a lawyer that is conversant in Thai law, an advisor from the American Embassy and inform the captain immediately that I need a lot of luck. Leave your name, address and a contact number with Mr Serover, the lawyer will contact you with the required funds for my release.'

Adam agreed and decided to over-look the obvious. He removed a Parker pen from the inside of his top pocket and wrote down the instructions on the back of Ray's copy of the charge sheet. It didn't make any sense, if he was innocent? Why would this man use the same name as a man on the outside, unless he had powerful friends? Ray was relying on the fact that the confusion he was about to cause for the hotel would be noticed and remembered. Adam realised that this man was not what he appeared to be, he was not silly, and who was Mr Serover? There were too many unanswered questions. Adam decided to investigate further.

'Mr Serover, or whoever you are, I am not interested in your innocence or guilt. I suggest we discuss my fee for your freedom. I will accept the same amount as the authorities for your release. Sign here please.' He pushed the paper back through the bars, he had already written out the agreement.

Ray had no choice, he wrote the name Freddie Serover. Adam had no idea what he was about to become involved in. On his way out of the prison escorted by the guard, Adam was stopped and searched again by the guardian of the gate. Satisfied by his examination of Adam's anatomy, the guard unlocked and slid back the big metal bolts securing the exit and entry to this place of punishment and correction. The guard leaned against the wall, took out a packet of cigarettes and asked Adam for a light. He took his time and inhaled deeply. The strident sound of his cell phone shattered the oppressive silence as it stirred the guard into action. He retrieved it from a pocket in his prison uniform and talking as he went, returned down the long dark corridor.

Adam could see the sunlight shining through the small open aperture in the closed wooden door. It spread a warm square of comforting light, through the suspended dry dust particles as they moved listlessly through the powerful beam. Adam looked out on to a dry, empty, exercise yard. His idle gaze travelled up the legs of the watchtower and straight into the mirror-glass black reflecting shades worn by and concealing the eyes of a prison guard, pointing the machine-gun in Adam's direction. As the guard with the cell phone returned, Adam resisted the temptation to open the door and walk across the yard. Adam had not fallen for the oldest trick in the book. The guard opened the gate. He gave Adam a silly grin and waved to the man in the watchtower.

Adam had been released after a few hours; a few days would have driven him crazy. Waiting for him to return, Ray relaxed and slowed down his metabolic rate. He needed the time to pass as fast as possible. He cleared his mind of the immediate problem and forced himself into a state of transcendental mediation, by repeating continuously the mantra that drugs are death. Ray didn't need drugs to achieve a heightened awareness.

The guard shouting something in Thai broke the serenity of his inner silence. At the sight of a handful of something edible, resembling food, wrapped in a piece of newspaper being poked through the bars, Ray's stomach growled in anticipation. The paper contained cold cooked rice, and a small portion of an unidentifiable fish still attached to its tough, solid, inedible backbone, complete with its dorsal fin and long sharp lateral bones. The congealed mess was smothered in a thin insipid watery sauce. Ray gratefully devoured the glutinous, unsavoury meal and sucked the backbone clean; he saved it for later. It was the only thing he had been given to eat since the beginning of his ordeal. He washed it down with mouthful of lukewarm water from a plastic cup, supplied by a passing benevolent guard. After the meal, Ray rapidly returned to his state of meditation. If his cell was a room in the Bangkok Hilton he would have hung a 'do not disturb sign' on the bars.

Adam returned to his hire car and reversed the vehicle to a convenient turning space. He was watched all the way by the guard in the tower with the machine-gun. Adam tried to drive slowly but he could still see the watchtower in the rear view-mirror as his speed unintentionally increased.

At a small wooden shack, he stopped with a sigh of relief and lit a cigarette to calm his nerves. His mouth was dry and his hands were shaking; he needed a drink. Inside the shop, he bought a tin of Tizer and received change for the pay phone. He took the charge sheet from his pocket, lifted the hand-piece from the old black telephone and placed an index finger in to the round indented surface of the circle. He dialled the number of the Shangri-La Hotel. It was answered with the usual standard welcome speech and a promise to pass on the message. Adam insisted that it must be given the highest priority - it was an emergency. He repeated the message making sure that the listener was paying attention and that they understood every word. Adam was not convinced that the call would be passed on; he would have preferred to speak to the man himself.

He replaced the receiver and ripped off the ring pull top of the aluminium Tizer tin. He drunk the contents in one go but it was also not up to his expectations. The Tizer was warm, flat and tainted with a hint of aluminium. It failed to satisfy his taste buds and left a bad taste in his mouth. Adam felt uneasy. There was something wrong, he felt that he had missed an important part of the puzzle. He crushed the empty can in a fit of frustration. Slightly depressed, Adam returned to his hire car and carried on to Madame Cia's Camera Shop.

Adam eventually located the premises situated in a back lane of the indoor market. The young shop assistant denied all knowledge of the signature written on the witness statement and supplied a sample of her own handwriting; there was no comparison. She insisted that she could not recognise it and Adam instinctively knew that she was lying. The assistant gave Adam a convincing story that she was a part-time worker employed by a local employment agency on an hourly basis and that she had never met Madame Cia. Adam bent over and left his business card and a contact number at the Coconut Club on top of the glass display cabinet that also severed as the counter. The cabinet contained the latest collection of identical copies, of western electronic consumer goods, cameras, televisions and portable laptop computers.

Madame Cia, standing behind the bead curtain that separated the shop from the interior, carefully moved a part of the obstruction to take a better shot. As Adam stood up straight, she pressed the camera shutter, but he saw the movement reflected in the glass top of the counter. He turned around and began to leave the shop. He stopped at the door and said in a loud voice, 'Don't forget there is big money involved for the right answers.'

Adam, even more depressed, returned to his room above the Coconut Club to wait. After Adam had left, Madame Cia appeared from behind the curtain, and decided that she did not need reporters; they were bad for business. To put her plan in operation, she would have to check with her superiors. Madame Cia made a phone call to an unlisted number. They immediately arranged for an observer to be sent to the Coconut Club.

Chapter Eleven

As the private plane circled and prepared to land, Peter looked out of the cabin window and saw the prison. He heard the 'clung' as the landing gear descended and became locked in the required position. From his vantage point, he realised how big the city of Chiang Mai really was. The bumpy landing brought back bad memories of Greenland. The twin engines relaxed with a sigh of relief as the tires took over. It was their turn to control and stop the forward momentum. They tried desperately to get a grip on the bitumen, as the plane bounced its way along the short landing strip. The plane eventually stopped and Peter filled the cabin air with a profusion of four letter words. He was not happy flying. Peter, in a bad mood, was a force to be reckoned with.

Upon landing, Peter's unexpected irrational outburst gave Bertie and the big Boss Man cause for concern. Because of stress, Peter demanded time out to find a woman. He was given the address of the Boss Man's destination, with strict instructions to stay out of trouble and given four hours off. Peter had four hours to find Ray. He had no idea how to, or where to, start looking for Ray. Peter needed caffeine.

In the nearest coffee shop, he ordered a double strength black and sat back as the strong stimulant began to work. He was in an Internet Café; on the wall in front of him was a list of instructions on how to send an e-mail. Peter sent the following message: 'Chiang Mai (Colombo) addressed to Ray at the Shangri-La Hotel.' He needed to know that all messages were being held or passed on. He spent a restless twenty minutes before he reached for the phone; if this didn't work he would have to phone Susan, which he was reluctant to do. The fewer people that knew anything, the better the chance of success.

The receptionist at the front desk of the Shangri-La Hotel had just read the e-mail when Peter's phone call came through.

'Yes Mr Serover... No, Mr Ray has still not returned but we have received an e-mail for him from a Mr Colombo in Chiang Mai. We also have a message from Mr Adam Smith that you are in Chiang Mai prison, Mr Serover and that you need a lawyer who is conversant in Thai law, an advisor from the American Embassy and to inform the Captain immediately that you need a lot of luck.'

Peter wrote down Adam's contact number at the Coconut Club and explained to the confused receptionist that he had been released after a wrongful arrest, it was a case of a mistaken identity and that he would call back later for any messages for Mr Ray. Peter felt better now he knew were Ray was but who was Adam Smith?

He made an international, person-to-person, reverse charge call, to Captain Luck on his private number and explained the situation. The captain had connections in high places; he would persuade the police commissioner to call the embassy. He knew the right people his request would go straight to the top and be put into operation, without any awkward questions being asked. Peter had achieved his priority just in time. With one hour left he took out the crumpled piece of paper from his back pocket and hired a local black and yellow tuk-tuk taxi. He had to meet the Boss at Madame Cia's Camera Shop.

Adam slept the day away and woke up late as the phone finished ringing. He dialled the local re-call number for information. The caller had not left a message. On his way to the bathroom, the phone rang again. Adam ran back to the bedroom and lifted the receiver. The voice on the other end said, 'Adam Smith, we need to talk about money.'

Holding on to the phone, Adam heard a click and he knew that the call was being recorded.

'A friend will meet you immediately in the Coconut Club to discuss the transfer of the required funds for the release of our mutual friend. I suggest that you wear something outrageous to attract attention. Lady-boys in Thailand are not what they seem.'

Adam began to reply but swore as the line went dead.

Wearing a tropical Hawaiian surfer's shirt and a pink silk tie, he entered the Club and sat at the end of the bar in his usual seat. The colours he wore were so bright and beckoning, they attracted a constant supply of unwelcome attention. When the stunning blonde arrived, Adam was surrounded by what looked like a gorgeous group of giggling girls. As she approached Adam, the group realised that they could not compete and slowly they drifted away. Wearing a serene smile, she looked deeply with an unwavering stare into Adam's dark brown eyes. Up close and without saying a word, she rapidly reached out and grabbed him by the balls.

'We need to talk about money for our mutual friend. It has been arranged, you will receive a phone call and drive to this address.' She placed a piece of paper in Adam's top pocket and relaxed the pressure. She released her hold and walked away. Adam gasping for breath was lost for words. She left the bar and returned to the night.

Outside the club, she signalled to the observer that all was well as he surreptitiously continued to work on Adam's hired car. He placed the plastic explosive, a detonator, the tracking device, and a cell phone secured with sticky tape under the dashboard and locked the car door.

On completion, he returned to the Coconut Club for a well-deserved drink. He found an empty seat at the bar and sat next to Adam Smith. Adam, having read the address, returned the scrappy piece or paper to his top pocket. Adam stood up to go to his room and then the phone rang. The barman took the call. He wrote down the address of Madame Cia's Camera Shop and gave it to Adam, both addresses were identical. The phone call contained extra information: a command to leave now. As Adam walked through the open door, the observer made a call on his cell phone and arranged the inevitable outcome. Adam would not reach his destination.

Getting involved in the late night downtown traffic was a situation that Adam didn't need. The continuous start, stop, slowly moving people, isolated in their metal boxes becoming stationary, made no sense at all. Adam sat in a long line of traffic watching the red brake lights ahead. A three-wheeled tuk-tuk taxi overtook to take its place at the head of the cue. It stopped momentarily beside Adam's hired car. The driver applied the brakes, disengaged the gear and restrained the energy of the small tuk-tuk engine. As he pressed the go pedal down the engine built up its revolutions into a high-pitched scream for a quick getaway.

117

Madame Cia sat in the back seat, looking in Adam's direction and gave an inscrutable Asian smile. Adam smiled in return and reached out for a cigarette but he had no chance of lighting it. Madame Cia raised a hand and pressed a sequence of numbers on her cell phone. At the same time, the driver released the brakes, dropped the clutch and the engine delivered all its pent-up power in one hit, as the muted explosion lit up the night sky the force rocked the suspension and tipped the tuk-tuk on to two wheels. Madame Cia looked back and watched as the intense heat and internal pressure force open both front doors of the burning vehicle. As the frustrated inferno escaped its confinement it split into two identical orange-red fireballs. They rolled up from both sides of the burning mass of melting metal and met in the middle of the rapidly blistering blue paintwork on the roof of the Hertz hire car. They combined and rose slowly, relentlessly, onwards and upwards, taking with them the soul of Adam Smith.

The tuk-tuk taxi continued to travel in the right direction without losing speed and reaching the front of the line. It regained its stable position, on three wheels as the lights turned to green. Without hesitation or interruption it safely crossed the intersection. The driver of the taxi took the next left turn as Madame Cia pressed more numbers on her mobile phone. At the end of the block, he turned left again and travelled down a long dark street. After another left and at the end of the road, he reached a stop sign, in time to see the ambulance with its flashing blue lights pass by.

The fireball had left the car's burning doors wide open; the dead driver still sat in his seat as his facial flesh slowly began to melt. Suddenly, the cigarette tightly clamped in his dead jaws, spontaneously burst into flames, ignited by the intense radiating heat. A passing motorist slowed down and took his eyes of the road to look at the fire. Momentarily he was distracted and lost his concentration. He continued to drive forward and hit the rear of a stationary truck waiting in line at the red light. He applied the brakes too late, as his car began to slide uncontrollable towards the beneath the truck. He made a last minute desperate attempt to bend down and protect his head below the dashboard. The impact cut the roof off, like peeling back the top of a sardine ring-pull can it left the driver intact exposed and alive. Suddenly he sat upright in the driving seat preying to his god for his safety and salvation. The second unexpected impact from a car behind pushed him further forward and the resulting whiplash snapped his neck. The ambulance crew, as they picked up the remains of Adam Smith, made room for one more. Adam would not be alone on his final journey.

The police moved the traffic on and pointed them in the right direction. As the traffic began to flow again, they passed the temporary obstruction. Standing in the street, the truck driver answered all the necessary police questions before he was allowed to leave and continue his journey to Bangkok with his consignment of computes and camera parts made in Japan. It was a regular run, the police knew all about it and waved him on.

The observer dressed in a police uniform was sitting in his car, parked opposite the Coconut Club when he received Madame Cia's phone call.

'It is done,' she said. 'Mr Adam has been fatally injured in an unfortunate accident.' She repeated her previous instructions, 'Show the bar staff your ID and explain that you need access to his room for information, to inform his nearest and dearest of his demise. Go now, search the room and remove all trace of written and computer records. I shall follow the ambulance to the hospital or the mortuary and phone you from there.'

The room contained the minimum amount of necessary requirements for a transient traveller. The searcher removed a red address book and a pile of computer floppy disks. He deleted all information from the computer's hard-drive and set an incendiary bomb and a mechanical clockwork timer under the computer. He returned to his car to wait.

The expected blast blew out the first floor window. It was such a shame, he had enjoyed sitting at the long bar of the Coconut Club. As the crowd, in an organised state of confusion, evacuated the building, he received another phone call from Madame Cia.

'The body is burnt beyond recognition and has been delivered to the city morgue. Use your official seniority and your badge as a back up, but only if you have to. You have to get into the room with the body and make a thorough search of any remaining pockets. Remove all contents and

119

bring them to me, here at the shop. Use the expected excuse that you are looking for information to inform the relatives of the death of their recently lost loved one.'

He entered the premises without any awkward questions being asked. There were no questions, no security and nothing to steal from a mortuary. Entering the cold storage department, he removed a pair of surgical gloves from the self-service dispenser. The remains of the dearly departed had been placed in a bag, a hygienically sealed medical version of the black plastic, domestic bin liner. The searcher unzipped the body bag and emptied the contents onto a marble slab. He didn't need the surgical gloves; there was no way that he was going to examine the burnt body of Adam Smith. The skeletal bones still hung onto parts of barbecued muscle. The seared lungs and internal organs had been protected in the chest cavity by the restraining ribs resting on his drawn up knees. Sitting in the car seat, he had automatically reacted and instinctively crossed his arms and lifted his legs into the protective position. There was no need to search the remains of the man he had no pockets left or skin.

Madame Cia received the information with her usual oriental indifference. She immediately pressed button 'C' six times in rapid succession on her cell phone; it confirmed a for-gone conclusion. The signal sent an unspoken message to the department that the operation had been successfully completed. Adam Smith had been in the wrong place at the wrong time, an expendable irritant. The department could not take the risk of Ray or Peter being exposed at this stage of the investigation.

On the edge of the round hole that the prison authorities called a toilet, a black rat waited. Ray had to answer the call of nature. He approached carefully and removed the dead rodent by the tail. It was not the first or the last time that a life would expire in that restrictive, oppressive, claustrophobic cell, he had to get out now.

Ray was passing the time fashioning the fish bone into a lock-pick when his concentration was interrupted by the announcement of his name. With his back to the guard, he dropped the fish bone, turned around and became aware of a visitor wearing a grey suit, pushing a pen and a clipboard through the gap between the prison bars.

'Sign here Mr Serover, you are free to leave. I am from the embassy.'

The official looking release form, with the American eagle icon embossed and stamped on the top of the page had been written in plain English, without any legal language. It looked genuine. Ray read it twice. All charges had been dropped due to a lack of evidence.

He signed it as the guard inserted a key in the cell room door and slid back the heavy bolt and opened the metal access. The requisite bribe had been paid in high places and out in the corridor, standing beside the open cell door, Ray's shackles were removed. The man in the grey suit walked rapidly down the corridor with out looking back to the wire cage. Ray followed, and arrived in time to see the guard lift the lid of the wooden desk. He removed a sheet of plain white paper, an inkpad and a rubber stamp. Completing the formalities, Ray's rescuer counter signed the document and removed the carbon copy. They moved on up a long, dark passageway, passed the cells containing the remaining prisoners and emerged into a visiting room. It was separated from the general office and reception area by more floor-to-ceiling bars, over which was a double layer of chicken wire presumably to keep any contraband from being passed from the other side.

Through the wire, Ray could see the office area where half a dozen uniformed guards were deep in conversation, the rest were sitting silently at their desks with their feet up, watching TV. Caught in the small confined area, the accumulation of exhaled cigarette smoke silently rose to the nicotine stained ceiling. A young bored recruit, keen and eager to impress, continuously cleaned his rifle while smoking a cigarette at the same time, and blowing out the occasional smoke-ring. The released tar and poisonous particles slowly descended and irritated his right eye, causing the tear duct to release a constant stream that rolled down his right cheek. Refusing to remove the cigarette from his mouth, the youth made a manly effort to ignore the discomfort and carried on cleaning his rifle. The majority of the guards weren't doing anything constructive at all except for one. He was pecking away unenthusiastically at an old-fashioned, inadequate, mechanical black typewriter.

The door to the chicken pen was pulled open and Ray pushed into the reception room by the silent grey-suited man behind him. The man from the embassy had not said a word. He approached the typist and ripped out the final written release form from the typewriter with a dramatic flourish. With an air of superiority and inconvenience, he rapidly signed the document. Ray looked on in silence as he realised that the confirmation of this second signing cleared him completely.

The powerful man made his way to the already open door, Ray was not far behind as the guards lined up on both sides and bowed as a mark of respect. Ray could not contain his gratitude any longer as he walked free into the dazzling daylight. Halfway across the exercise yard he asked, 'What is your name and where is Mr Smith?'

The voice of authority, when the man spoke, was in clipped curt tones that conveyed a short sharp message. The man did not waste words.

'Mr Serover, you do not need to know my name, we will never meet again, and Mr Smith has unfortunately been delayed but he has been taken care of. Your personal financial situation remains the same and I am instructed to provide you with one thousand dollars in American bank notes.' He removed and opened his wallet, peeled of the correct currency from a bulging bundle and returned the rest to his inside jacket pocket. The man walked on, leaving Ray with a fist full of dollars in the dry, dusty, killing zone, under the eyes of the tower guard.

Ray ran and reached the main gate at the same time as the man. The exit gate was already open, on the other side a long, black limousine, menacing in its dormant, dominating position, prepared itself for a fast, secure getaway. The quiet hum of the restrained engine could not be heard above the heavy heartbeat pounding away in Ray's chest.

The four men in black, positioned at each corner of the vehicle with their guns drawn, made a defensive stand as the man in the grey suit reached the open doors. He entered and sat on the back seat, as the door was closed behind him by one of the hired hands. The big bulk of the bodyguard obstructed Ray's access and view of the grey-suited man as he realised that they were about to leave without him. The rear window was wound down at the last minute as the men in black climbed aboard.

'Mr Serover, I presume you have somewhere to go? Please accept a lift, I will leave you at Madame Cia's Camera Shop.'

Ray had to have words with Madame Cia. Reclining in the rear seat of the sedan next to Ray, the man in the suit ignored and refused to take part in Ray's one-sided conversation, the claustrophobic atmosphere forced Ray into a state of silent acceptance. In the quiet air-conditioned environment, Ray sweated profusely and picked absent-mindedly at the patterned fabric of the dividing armrest. The car turned a corner and stopped. A passing pedestrian pulled the car door open, grabbed Ray by the arm, dragging him out of the vehicle and onto the busy pavement, outside the indoor market the pedestrian raised a finger and pointed Ray in the right direction.

'That way, Madame Cia's Camera Shop, go now.'

Ray resisted the urge to say thank you, as he turned around the black back of the sedan was rapidly disappearing and merging into a congested, colourful, collection of commuter traffic. Ray turned around again but his temporary guide had also gone. Madame Cia's was not available but in the camera shop, Ray selected a new Japanese laptop computer. The salesman made an impressive effort to close the deal until Ray insisted that he removed the surrounding shell and expose the inner workings of the computer. Ray had no idea what he was looking at but he knew the interior did not contain a compromising amount of illegal substances wrapped in a protective layer of plastic cling film. The shop assistant was also relived that there were no technical, complicated questions to answer. It would test his non-existing knowledge to the limit.

As they both stared incomprehensibly into a complicated mass of microchips and modern technology, the embarrassing silence was suddenly shattered by an unexpected eruption. Peter had appeared from behind the bead curtain and thrown up on the floor, dressed in his designer suit and with his shaven head Ray would not have recognised him except for the lazy eye. The big Boss Man followed on behind and whinged like an old woman, 'What is the matter with you?'

Peter replayed, 'I need good American food, a Big Mac and a Budweiser. I am designed for a western diet. Oriental entrails and exotic eastern delights destroy my delicate constitution.' The Boss Man placed a comforting hand on Peter's shoulder. Ray tried not to look and laugh but he listened as Peter asked, 'Where do we go from here?'

'Back to the hotel and then we take a trip to the triangle before we fly out to Australia. There you will have all the beer-burgers that you can eat.' Ray could not believe his luck. Ray had never doubted Peter's sexuality but he knew that Peter was walking a fine line between the Big Boss Man and Bertie the jealous bodyguard following on behind.

As he over heard the conversation, Ray controlled his immediate reaction and suppressed his desire to deliver a shout of satisfaction; knowing Peter's intended destination completed another part of the puzzle and reconfirmed Ray's previous opinion. With the help of the useless sales assistant, Ray replaced the cover of the laptop computer.

As Peter walked out of the room, Ray relaxed and a wave of euphoria broke over him. He could not remember the last time he felt so elated. He took out a handful of Thai bank notes and gave the assistant the inflated asking price; he shook his hand warmly and added an extra, extravagant, copious, amount of currency. It was more than the local man would make in a month.

The monsoon season arrived at the same time that Ray was preparing to leave Chiang Mai. All flights to the capital were cancelled until further notice. Bangkok airport had been closed down due to severe weather conditions. The ceaseless, relentless rain ran down the outside of the protective walls that enclosed Ray's rented rooms. The self-contained single unit consisted of a bed, a breakfast bar and a bathroom. Located next to the airport and isolated from the main administration block it provided the bare essentials for an over-night stay. The tropical rain landing loudly on the corrugated tin roof tried to compete and disrupt Ray's concentration; he was oblivious and ignored the downpour. He continued to search for information on his latest acquisition. The laptop computer provided all the information he needed. Tax evasion is treated as a very serious crime; it attracts more intensive investigation than pre-meditated murder and will result in a longer sentence. In America, the gangster Mr Al Capone made that mistake.

Ray continued to research the history of EMU Exports; he had already put the pieces together from the beginning of their land grab in South America when the bullyboys took over and forced the local subsistent farmers into producing a constant supply of cocaine for the Western market. Concealed in a variety of innocent looking day-to-day objects, the illegal substances eventually arrived at a northern sea port and became part of a container full of family goods destined for the U.S.A. The rain stopped as the dawn broke. Ray had been awake all night; logged on to the Internet he had continuously searched the world wide web, looking for the Australian connection.

The endless search eventually revealed a positive result: the cartel owned and controlled a subsidiary of a Queensland distillery company beginning with the letter B and then the lightning struck. The computer immediately displayed a Red Cross termination sign and the following warning. The sign on the screen displayed: 'You have performed an illegal operation and this programme will now be shut down.' With no time to save, the information the screen went blank.

Chapter Twelve

The young girl knelt down and pulled a small, inferior poppy plant out of the ground. It was too weak to survive. Sprayed the day before by a passing government plane, it had already begun to whither and die. To account for the diminished harvest she had to put it in the big wicker-basket strapped to her back with the ones she'd already picked. It was backbreaking work, made all the harder because she had to take care not to damage any of the mature, robust plants, as May-Ling moved across the field.

The remaining crop would be harvested as soon as she had completed her menial task. The quicker the crop was cut, the more opium the poppies would produce, the more money her father would make. Surviving on a pittance, the poppy harvest provided their only income. Her younger sister, continuously complaining, struggled to keep up. Suddenly sixteen year-old May-Ling stopped working, turned and threw the heavy wicker basket to the ground. Relived of the increasing weight, May-Ling stood up straight and arched her aching back. Something clicked, like a small twig snapping. She wiped her hands on her soiled black trousers then rubbed the base of her spine with her red dirt-stained fingers. As she stretched her arms to their maximum height, the small cotton top she wore rose up to expose her firm tanned, mid-drift. May-Ling returned her arms to the horizontal position and expanded her chest muscles by reaching behind her back with both hands, to release her long, waist-length hair. Held in and restrained by the flimsy cotton, her pert young breasts protruded as the early morning sun shone through the fabric, it emphasised her curvaceous contours.

Using a pair of high-powered binoculars, the local warlord looked on in anticipation at his rapidly developing assets in the field below. Watching the silent scene from the top of a rocky out crop, he realised that this year's young untouched virgin sample would provide him with another financial asset. The poppy crop was looking good and the maturing merchandise would be easy to sell on the open market. From his elevated position, the warlord had to decide on his next move. To use it or sell it, he was a businessman, he could do both.

May-Ling picked up the basket and carried on with her work. She bent down and pulled up another plant. She jumped as she heard a loud snort from behind. As she turned quickly, she caught her foot in an exposed fibrous root, the weight of the wicker basket upset her balance and she crashed heavily to the ground at the feet of a large black horse.

Its rider was wearing an army uniform and a pair of dark reflecting glasses with a black beret on his head and strapped to his back was a rifle. She put a hand over her mouth. The horse snorted again and lowered its head. It began to sniff and she could feel its warm, moist, breath against her cold frightened skin.

The man smiled for the first time showing white, even teeth. 'Good morning, I think my horse likes you,' he said. The girl was suddenly embarrassed at the unexpected greeting and she averted her eyes. 'And your name is?' he asked.

The girl blushed furiously. Why did he want to know her name?

'Can't speak?' said the man amused by her silence.

'No, sir. I mean, yes, sir.'

'How old are you, child?'

'Sixteen, sir.'

'Stand up and answer my question. What is your name, child?'

She stood up, saw that he was still smiling at her, bowed her head and clasped her hands. 'May-Ling, sir,' she said.

'Do you know who I am?'

'No, sir.'

'Are you sure? Have you never heard of the Black Knight?'

She caught her breath. Of course, everyone knew of the Black Knight. The warlord, the opium king.

'Well?'

'Yes, sir.'

'Look at me, child.'

The girl looked up. The horse snorted as she did and she flinched.

'There's no need to be afraid,' the man said. He looked enormous, sitting on the back of the black beast. In his right hand was a black leather-riding crop, which matched his riding boots. They blended into the animal's shiny ebony coat. The horse stamped its feet impatiently. May-Ling looked up at the man's face. She could see her reflection in his sunglasses.

'Have you been up to the compound?' he asked. She shook her head but she knew it was where the soldiers were based, and where the opium was processed. 'I want you to come along to see me tonight. Your father will tell you the way.'

'But, sir, my father...'

'Your father won't mind,' he interrupted. 'Tell him you've spoken to me.'

'Sir, I...'

The Black Knight suddenly brought the whip end of his riding crop down and slapped it hard against the horse's neck drawing blood. The horse jerked away and reared up but the rider kept a tight grip of the reins and swiftly brought it under control.

'Do not argue, child.'

May-Ling lowered her eyes and said nothing. The rider ran the tip of his crop along her left arm, down to her elbow.

'That's better. Tell your mother you are to wear something special. If you do not arrive I shall return and take your younger sister.' He kicked the horse into action and they cantered off across the poppy field, leaving behind a trail of bruised and battered plants.

May-Ling sank to her knees and began to remove the remains of the damaged crop, she would still have to save the evidence and account for its condition.

Crawling on her hands and knees along the trail left by the black beast, she came face to face with her younger sister. The nine-year-old held a wilting pink poppy in her tiny hand, she thrust it forward and presented it as a token of reconciliation. She promised to be good if she could go home soon and prepare for her tenth birthday party. Full of excitement and expectation, the birthday girl explained that she needed time to try on her new dress and prepare herself for the party. All the local kids had been invited and as a special treat she was looking forward to her first disco dance. Arranged at a place the grown-ups called the compound.

May-Ling smiled and agreed, and as her younger sister skipped off happily and disappeared into the distance, she left behind a young, broken, pink poppy. Only then did May-Ling's tears begin to flow.

The warlord returned to his domain and read a list of peasant farmers under his control. They had no choice but to supply the required information and register their annual income. Last year May-Ling and her family had failed to meet the required quota. Their harvest had fallen short by a considerable amount. To make up for the short fall, it was an unwritten rule that the deficit, would be made up by depriving the family of their most valuable asset.

It was May-Ling or her younger sister that would be taken to Bangkok to pay off the debt and the warlord would receive extra money by informing the authorities that her family were growing opium poppies. The government troops would move in with their flame-throwers and burn down the house and the surrounding area. Opium poppies grew better on a burnt, barren land.

The cuts in the grey sides, at the top of the mature poppy pods had released a brown sticky substance that seeped from their open wounds. Collected by family and friends of the local farmer, it was then pressed into a convenient block and passed on to a central collection centre.

The two Thai technicians grunted as they manhandled the heavy metal drum off the fire, using pieces of wet sacking to protect their hands. They eased it on to the soil and stood back to allow it to cool. The boiling mixture contained raw opium, water and lime fertiliser. The blocks of concentrated opium, delivered from an unknown source, had been previously prepared. The fertiliser had been legally bought and brought across the border in trucks and then loaded on the backs of donkeys for the twenty-mile trek through the jungle to their secret location.

The Thais worked outside, downwind from the main part of the camp because the fumes were unpleasant. Not as dangerous as the later stages of the process, but the technicians weren't trusted to do that. The technicians were paid to turn the Black Knight's raw opium into morphine, nothing more. It was a loss of face for the technicians, but secretly they were glad not to be involved. They'd heard rumours of technicians being blown up when the process went wrong. Blown up or burned alive. Better to work with the drum and the open fire, better to be outdoors so if anything went wrong, they could try to out-run the hot sudden release of explosive energy.

One of the technicians looked at the two young boys who were sitting in the shade of a tree, fanning themselves with the leaves of a mature banana plant. He beckoned for them to come over. They eagerly stood up and ran over to help pick up the heavy drum. The four of them carried it to a nearby stream. The boys picked up the filter, a metre-wide piece of cloth, which had been stretched across a wooden frame. They held it a foot above the flowing stream while the technicians lifted the drum of opium suspension and carefully drained off the water. The technicians took the container over to another drum previously prepared by the boys and emptied the opium solution into it. The technicians left the dirty drum by the side of the stream for the boys to scrub clean later.

When the solution was boiling again, the technicians took six plastic bottles of concentrated ammonia and poured them into the bubbling mixture, one by one, after tying strips of protective material across their nose and mouth to protect them from the unacceptable fumes. The morphine began to settle out, sinking to the bottom and leaving behind a clear translucent liquid. They lifted the drum off the fire and shouted over at the boys to get the filter ready again. The technicians took the drum over to the stream and as the boys held out the flannel filter, they drained off the water. Left behind were globules of morphine, glistening wetly on the filter. They left the boys to press the morphine into blocks and wrap them with banana leaves.

The two technicians had more important things to do; they had to prepare more opium and fertiliser to complete another successful product.

131

The Black Knight was expected at any time to check up on their production out-put. They would face the wrath of their local warlord if they failed to meet the daily quota. The Black Knight's anger was a fearful thing to experience; the body of an informer was still decomposing on a stake protruding from a part of the wall surrounding the warlord's jungle compound.

The big Russian wiped his sweaty bald head with a grubby white handkerchief. He would never get used to the obsessive heat and stifling humidity, or the mosquitoes. He was more used to sub-zero temperatures and snowdrifts of the Siberian winter than he was to the unrelenting sauna that was the Golden Triangle. He tucked the wet handkerchief into the pocket of his lab coat and checked the timer on his workbench. Twenty minutes, long enough for the morphine and acetic acid to bond together. Simple chemistry, a child with a chemistry set could do the same thing - with an endless supply of the basic ingredients. The present crop would provide enough morphine to keep a thousand people in euphoria for a year.

He turned off the bottled gas burner and waited for the mixture to cool. The accumulated heat inside the hut made working almost unbearable. The walls and ceiling were of corrugated iron. A couple of cut-aways at head-height in each wall, designed to allow the noxious fumes to escape, also gave entry to the hot tropical heat. They combined to produce an even more intolerable environment.

The Russian wiped his head again and picked up the ineffective rapidly revolving electric fan from the far end of the wooded workbench. It did its best to keep the hot air moving, but it was fighting a losing battle. He moved it and placed it next to the glass flask containing the morphine mixture in a pointless attempt to speed up the cooling process. When the container was cool enough to touch, he called for his assistant, a young Chinese boy who was waiting outside. Born in the People's Republic of China, the child was a burden on the state and a drain on the resources of his already improvised, peasant family. Surplus to requirements, a Government dictate stated that all married women were only allowed to produce enough male children to work in the fields and gather the crops to support their own existence and supply the local commune. Living on the bare necessities scratched out from a small non-productive patch of exhausted land, the family could not afford to feed another hungry mouth. The boy was sold at an early age for the price of a new plough and a powerful workhorse.

Together they wrapped an insulating thick cloth around the heavy flask, lifted it and carefully poured its precious contents through a carbon filter to remove its impurities. The Russian watched as the clear liquid bubbled through the filter. Why take so much time and trouble to take the contaminants out? By the time the drug reached its end users, it would probably have been adulterated with baking powder, chalk, talcum powder, or any one of a dozen other substances. But that was no reason for him to take any less care. The Russian was a professional, and he took pride in his work.

As the cloudy liquid began to settle in the glass carafe, the young Chinese apprentice removed the contaminated filter and fell over as he caught his foot in the lead of the electric fan. Not concentrating, he was thinking of the night to come and the party at the compound. He immediately rolled up on the ground in a defensive position; he knew what to expect and received a severe kicking from the Russian. As he attempted to get to his feet, he found his escape route blocked by the appearance of his master the Black Knight, he who must be obeyed.

Standing in the open doorway half dressed, the man was obviously taking great pleasure in relentlessly beating the back of his big, bare, broad shoulders with his black leather riding crop. The Chinese boy had heard about fanatics practising flagellation as an act of religious purification but this son of Satan was something else. As the boy crawled quietly and carefully into a dark corner of the hot, claustrophobic hut to lick his wounds like a wounded dog, he made a life changing decision. To run away the morning after the party and stay with a member of his extended family, somewhere in Chiang Mai, a woman who he had never met with the name of Madame Cia. He would not be missed until the next day. They would all be to drunk to realise that he had disappeared. After having a heated conversation with the chemist, the warlord turned around and walked away, his back was covered in blood. With trepidation, the

Chinese kid slowly returned to the job in hand. The chemist had already weighed out the sodium carbonate and he nodded for the boy to begin. The boy sprinkled the crystals into the liquid and stirred it with a long bamboo pole. The Russian watched as the crude heroin particles solidified and dropped to the bottom.

He had bought his young Asian apprentice as a future investment to eventually do most of the work. His young assistant showed great potential. The boy was eager to learn and he had the ability to remember complicated, scientific, formula. Together, they waited in silence until the heroin had been deposited at the bottom of the big glass bottle. The chemist nodded; the boy smiled and grinned, pleased at the approval, then they poured the mixture through another filter and into an open container. The Russian used a stainless steel spatula to scrape off the crystals and deposit them in another flask, this one contained a mixture of alcohol and charcoal, another step in the purification process. He filtered out the charcoal then placed the flask on to a burner, positioned underneath the extractor fan. He turned the switch on and as the powerful fan slowly began to rotate it built up its momentum, eventually reaching its maximum revolutions it rocked the flimsy bamboo building to its foundations. Only then did he light the burner. The alcohol fumes could be explosive in a confined space - more than one of the Black Knight's jungle laboratories had gone up in flames before the Russian had arrived on the scene - to ensure that the conversion from opium to injectable heroin was completed successful. That was why he was receiving more money in a month paid into his Swiss bank account, than he could earn in a year back in Belorussia. The chemist worked for eighteen hours a day, seven days a week and he'd been in the jungle for six months without a break. He didn't resent the long hours, it was the unpredictable nature of the business that upset his desire to rely on a regular routine. Having established a well-run production line, he would be warned and informed at the last minute that he would be moving from one isolated location to another.

It took an hour for the alcohol to evaporate, during which time he prepared a new flask of morphine and acetic anhydride, ready to start the process again. The warlord kept up a relentless pressure for the finished product to be delivered on time. It was part of a consignment that had already been promised. The Black Knight was responsible for the end product, supplied by the many production units that he controlled, located deep in the interior of the Golden Triangle. The mule train had been pre-arranged to arrive on time and pick up the required quantity and transport the finished product to the uniformed deliverers. In Chiang Mai, the merchandise would be made ready for export. Concealed in containers, it would continue uninterrupted on its journey south to Bangkok.

At the far end of the laboratory were the drums of chemicals needed to complete the process, most of them with Chinese labels, the quality as good if not better, than the adulterated ingredients sold by the underground, black marketers, back home in mother Russia. They also bulked up their wares in the same way that street pushers diluted their drugs with whatever was available.

With the alcohol gone, the Russian was left with white granules of heroin. The final stage in the preparation was the most dangerous. It involved dissolving the granules in alcohol once more and then carefully adding hydrochloric acid and ether. Ether vapour is even more explosive than alcohol and has to be carefully handled. The Chinese apprentice looked on from a safe distance as the chemist poured in the acid. White flakes began to form in the mixture. He put out his hand and without being asked, the boy gave him the bamboo pole, like a nurse assisting a surgeon in a delicate operation. As he stirred, more flakes began to form, like a snowstorm. All that remained was for him to filter and dry the flakes and he would have another batch of pure heroin. He had produced more than the expected daily amount and turned off the extractor fan. His assistant could take care of the final, minor details. The Russian removed his lab coat and looked at his watch, it was time to get ready for the evening's entertainment. He had a special interest in one of the guests invited to attend the local disco dance.

As he prepared to light it, Peter poked both ends of his hand-rolled cigarette with a matchstick. The action restricted and compacted, the loose strands of tobacco into a confined space. Like a small, fully charged container of built-up addictive energy, Peter was about to ignite. The slightest spark would set him off. He had not consumed his daily amount of caffeine.

Sitting in the back of the open-top four-wheeled drive Ford truck, he swore again, as the vehicle hit a bump on the jungle dirt track. Forcing him to his feet, he grabbed on to the nearest roll bar, as an overhanging tendril from a tropical rain-forest plant missed his face by inches. As it passed by, it removed from his mouth and took with it his carefully constructed cigarette. Rounding the next bend, the sudden sight of an impassable roadblock activated Bertie's limited survival instinct. Sitting in the front seat, he stood up and presented himself as an obvious target. Peter grabbed him around the neck from behind in an arm lock, and forced him back into his seat as the first bullet bounced off the bonnet of the vehicle. Sliding to a halt with inches to spare from the barrier, the vehicle was quickly surrounded by a bunch of evil looking, gun carrying individuals intent on completing a pre-arranged plan. Aiming and pointing their guns in unison, their leader demanded that his prisoners follow him.

With their hands held high above their heads, Peter and his fellow passengers stood down onto the hard, rocky rubble of the jungle track, and followed the leader into the humid, claustrophobic, undergrowth of the tropical rain forest. Peter heard the loud sound of booming cannon fire from Tchaikovsky's '1812 Overture', echoing across the valley, before they reached the clearing.

As they emerged into the sunlight, the crescendo of cannon fire and church bells reverberated around the open space. Peter was presented with the sight of a well-fortified enclosure. In single file, they crossed the open space between the jungle and their destination. The sound died down, to be replaced by the incessant clicking of crickets, the buzzing of mosquitoes, and the barking of far-off dogs. Squelching his way through the sodden knee-high grass, Peter stopped to remove a blood-hungry leach, attached to his left leg. A mosquito landed on his leg at the same time, he slapped it. It splattered on his skin, leaving a mixture of black and red blood. He received an unexpected blow to the back of his head from the butt of an assault rifle. The guard responsible explained that it was nothing personal but his religion stated that all life was sacred. He aimed his loaded rifle at Peter and politely requested that he move on.

The circular walls of the compound had no obvious means of entry.

Protected by an outward-facing array of sharpened bamboo stakes and an under-growth of thorn-bush it looked impenetrable. Suddenly, a section of the wall opened up in front of them. The prisoners walking in a straight line with their hands held behind their heads were momentarily held up by Peter's interruption. In front of Peter, Bertie continued to walk on towards the entrance. The tempting invitation was cut short by a guard grabbing Bertie's legs from behind. The rugby tackle caused the man-mountain to crash to the ground. The guard slowly crawled forward over the prone body of Bertie and carefully parted the pristine grass ahead. Less than a foot away from Bertie's head, it revealed the location and pointed spikes of a hidden landmine. To prove a point, the guard stood up, picked up a stone and threw it aimlessly into the air. When it landed, the explosion completely wiped out the sound of the second playing of the '1812 Overture'.

The guard raised an arm and barred the way forward. Responsible for the captives, he pointed to his associate standing in the distance, the associate with a beckoning wave encouraged the prisoners to proceed down an uncharted path towards him. Keeping close to the compound wall, the visitors eventually arrived at the entrance. They were welcomed by a group of over-exited enthusiastic young children bearing gifts, each one trying to stifle and control an exuberant amount of giggling, repressed energy. Shyly and slowly they began to stand in line and approach the prisoners, they presented each one with a hand-made garland of poppies gathered from the surrounding area. Peter placed it around his head and thought of it as a drowning man wearing a life belt, desperately out of his depth and treading water. He had no idea where he was or how to escape from the compound. He turned around but the entrance had already been closed, it had become part of an impenetrable wall.

Looking on from the inside, Peter could not detect the slightest disturbance or inconsistency in the surrounding perimeter. A circular building in the centre of the enclosure was their intended destination. Led on by the guard, they took a circuitous route around three identical but smaller buildings, before reaching the roundhouse. As before, a hidden part of the wall swung open, not opposite the main entrance, but on the south side. Two guards emerged from the inside and escorted them into the gloom of the inner sanctum. Once again a door closed behind them without leaving a trace of its location.

The Black Knight stood in front of a half-finished canvas supported on a wooded easel. Wearing his black beret, a white smock splattered with bright red paint, and smoking a cigarette held in a long black holder, he completely ignored the prisoners. He continued to extract great globules of household, non-drip gloss paint, from a two-litre can. Attached to the end of a two-inch brush, the paint was rapidly transferred and smeared across the canvas. The impression and the child, like daubing of a field of red poppies bore no resemblance to a Monet or a Van Gogh. The artist's deteriorating talent could not compare with his previous paintings of poppies, displayed and hanging on all the available, surrounding wall space.

The concealed door opened unexpectedly behind Peter and admitted two uniformed Government soldiers, carrying a large heavy crate.

'AK-47s?' asked the Black Knight.

'All brand new,' replayed the soldier.

'I have M16s,' said the Knight, removing the cigarette holder from his tightly pursed lips. 'They are good weapons, M16s.'

The soldier shrugged his shoulders carelessly. 'Talk to me again in six months,' he said, 'after the jungle has got to them.'

As the soldier turned around to leave, the Black Knight called him back. Sitting cross-legged on a rush mat, he reached out and lit a cigarette with a gold lighter and exhaled before speaking. He held the cigarette between the thumb and first finger of his left hand, delicately, as if he feared that it might break.

'My men know how to take care of their weapons,' he said. The soldier sat down opposite the warlord.

'I didn't mean to imply otherwise, but M16s do not compare to the AK-47 in terms of reliability, not in the jungle. They will jam. Trust me, sooner or later they will jam. Why do you think so many of the American Special Forces used Kalashnikovs in Vietnam? They could not wait to get their hands on a superior weapon and lose their inferior M16s.'

The Black Knight flicked a long length of dead ash from his cigarette into a large cut-glass ashtray. 'You might be right,' he said coldly. 'How many did you bring?'

'One hundred and ten. With one hundred thousand rounds of ammunition.'

'I need more,' said the Black Knight.

'More guns? Or bullets?'

'Both.'

'I will see what I can do. I have brought fragmentation grenades. Six dozen, and anti-personnel mines, made of plastic in the Czech Republic so they can not be detected.'

The Black Knight nodded. 'Mines are good,' he said, 'and your price is as previously agreed?'

'As agreed,' said the soldier.

'And I will take it in heroin, but first, I have something else. A surprise.' He got to his feet and went over to the unopened crate he used a screwdriver to prise open the box. The soldier removed the lid, removed the bubble wrap and pulled away the rest of the packing material. 'Made in the Soviet Union when it was a union,' he said.

'How many?' asked the Black Knight.

'Five.'

'And you can show me and my men how to use them?'

'Of course, but you just point and pull the trigger. The missile does the rest. It goes straight for a heat source. Aimed at a helicopter or a plane, that's where it will go. It has a range of ten kilometres. Just over six miles.'

The Black Knight stood up and walked over to the portable ground-to-air missile launcher and stroked it as if it was his first and only son. He carefully took it out of its crib and held it high in his arms before hoisting it onto his shoulder.

'How much?' he whispered.

The soldier said, 'Expensive, but you can afford it.'

The warlord reacted like a protective farther, he turned around and pointed the projectile at the soldier and rapidly pressed the trigger continuously. For a moment the soldier feared that he had gone too far, but then the lips of the warlord set in a tight line, curled back into a cruel smile, he began to laugh loudly. He slapped the soldier on the back, turned on the '1812 Overture' again and at full volume, laughing hysterically, he began to dance dementedly around the room, only stopping occasionally to point the missile launcher randomly, at any one of his invited guests.

The man eventually slowed down and returned to a near normal state of social acceptance. He sat cross-legged on the floor and extended his hand in a friendly gesture to the soldier. On completion of a vigorous handshake he announced, 'The deal is now done you can go. I have to entertain. But you must return for the party.'

The soldier saluted, and escorted by the guards, he left the building. The schizophrenic Black Knight apologised for his momentary lapse of reason and became the perfect host. He explained that it was just a matter of business, and that he had to keep, and present a false sense of mental instability. Still tenderly touching and stroking his latest toy, he decided to share the experience with the assembled group. He insisted that they also appreciate his latest present. To express his friendship and willingness to bond with his visitors, he reluctantly let go and passed the rocket launcher around the group for their admiration.

When it reached Peter, he realised it was time to display an admiration of the product. He had the unnerving feeling that his life depended on it. In the police department, Peter had never come across such a thing, but he gave a convincing speech about its potential destructive firepower, and as he playfully pointed the weapon in all directions he finally aimed it at the warlord and adjusted the sights. Caught in the crosshairs, the Black Knight came into sharp focus - he was a perfect target. Peter pulled the trigger.

Chapter Thirteen

In his hotel room in Bangkok, Ray continued to search for the missing link. Logged on to the world wide web, he was deeply involved in his quest when his concentration was interrupted by a rapid, persistent, loud knocking noise on the hotel room door. Without waiting to be invited in, those responsible broke in.

A menacing group of men wearing black with their guns drawn rapidly moved in, and over powered Ray. They filled the small room and stood around him pointing their weapons at his head. Their leader removed the computer from its Internet connections throw it to the floor, and jumped on it. Ray looked on in amazement. He resented the fact that he would have to purchase another laptop and he began to complain loudly. His protests were silenced by the sound of the surrounding group activating and preparing their weapons. An aggressive silence descended and Ray relived his previous vulnerable situation in Chiang Mai. He could not believe it was happening again.

To his relief, the man from the embassy unexpectedly arrived. The man in the grey suit walked straight through the opening circle without any hindrance, and immediately dismissed the threatening force.

'Mr Serover,' he said, 'we meet again.' He held his hand out and as Ray shook it he heard the whispered words, 'Mr Ray, I have researched your history. To meet me a second time is most unusual but this is a matter of International importance. Please follow me and I will explain.'

Ushered out of the hotel and into the same long black limousine as before, he sat in the back seat again, and began to pick at the patterned armrest. Ray knew from his previous experience that it would be pointless to try and engage the man in a conversation. The journey lasted less than ten minutes. They stopped outside a nondescript, pre-cast, concrete building.

On the third floor, they entered a spacious room and stood in front of a large-scale map of the Golden Triangle, which had been pinned up on the wall. The map, predominantly light and dark greens, did not do justice to the area. Without any distinguishing features, the picture of the pristine jungle photographed from a great height, presented something primordial about the region, as if it belonged to a time long ago before governments, corruption and greed; a time when men were hunter-gatherers living off the land, in harmony and mutual respect, struggling to survive because survival was a fulltime job. Ray wondered how long he would last out there in the endless wilderness, armed with nothing more threatening than a sharp stick and a New York attitude.

'Mr Ray, unfortunately you been caught up in an International drug running operation, and I have been requested by my advisers to inform you of the situation, please pay attention. Most of the Mr Bigs are up in the Golden Triangle and they're pretty well untouchable.' The man in the grey suit reached out and pointed at the map. He circled an area with his finger, only a few square inches on the map but in the real world hundreds of square miles of jungle. 'Mr Ray, a local war lord known as the Black Knight has his poppy fields somewhere in this region, his heroin refineries, his army supply dumps, training grounds and bases. Fifty-percent of the Black Knight's heroin is refined on the other side of the border before being smuggled into Thailand. I say smuggled, but it actually comes across with the connivance of the Thai army. The Black Knight is not ungenerous with his associates. Several high-ranking members of the Thai military have grown very rich thanks to the Black Knight - very rich indeed. Moral standards in Thailand are not quite as, how shall I put it, in your face, as they are in America. In that, we are not interested. Our concern is the amount produced on this side of the border. A reliable colleague in Chang Mia has informed us that an acquaintance of yours a Mr Peter Serover is a guest of the Black Knight.'

Ray resisted the urge to smile. Both men knew that corruption was equally rife on both sides of the border. It is the way of life in Southeast Asia and permeates from the upper echelons of government all the way down to the man on the street.

'We have tried several times to apprehend him without success. Do you think he was tipped off? Almost certainly. The last time we came close to arresting him we closed down several of his refineries, burned some of his poppy fields, and sprayed the rest with a powerful toxin, but we've made no real progress. He moves too quickly. Have you been to the Golden Triangle?'

Ray nodded and remembered his painful experience with Tommy, the truculent elephant. Ray absent-mindedly rubbed his arse as the man in the grey suit continued.

'Then you know what the terrain is like. We can't travel in jeeps, or tanks, and helicopters aren't much use because his production bases are too well camouflaged. Unless we knew where to look, they can fly around for weeks and not see anything. Mr Ray, we now have information that your elephant ride included a photograph. Unexpectedly without cloud cover, it gave an unrestricted view of the valley floor far below. Mr Ray thanks to the photograph developed at Madame Cia's camera shop, we have at last located the warlord's permanent headquarters, and we are about to launch an attack to wipe out his operation.' As he spoke an unseen overhead projector suddenly lit up and illuminated the far blank back wall and began to display Ray's collection of holiday snaps. Captured on film, the picture of the peaceful-looking idyllic village surrounded by its encompassing, protective, wall. Included a small amount of transparent smoke expelling from the central, circular building. It was the perfect reminder of a happy holiday snap to show the folks back home.

'Mr Ray it all depends on your co-operation we cannot attack until we knew that Mr Peter Serover is safe and out of the firing line. The plan is to land a small force of American troops; you included, close to the compound, under cover of darkness.'

'How small?'

'We don't envisage requiring more than twelve.' Ray raised his eyebrows in surprise.

'You intend to take on one of the most powerful warlords in Asia with a dozen men?'

'Not take on, Mr Ray. Take out.'

'Your job is to inform Mr Serover in advance that the raid is about to take place, you will be in charge of the troops, and on your command they will attack the Compound.'

'I suggest, Mr Ray that you send a signal from your cell phone and activate Mr Serover's tattoo, the eye of the tiger. Mr Ray, the mission starts now. We have no time to lose. In the next room you will find an army uniform, a bullet-proof vest, a gun, ammunition and a map.' He turned to leave and stopped, 'One more thing before I forget,' he said. 'Please pay special attention to the map, it is marked with a number of crosses, the clearing around the compound is littered with landmines. Goodbye Mr Ray.'

The man in the grey suit walked away, switched out the light and left the room. The open door left enough light from the corridor to illuminate Ray's position. He was closely surrounded again by the guards who were still pointing their guns in his direction.

Dressed in a camouflage suit, Ray arrived at the location with the rest of the troops. At the end of the day the sun rapidly descended and disappeared, taking with it a multitude of natural sounds emitted by the insect and animal occupants of the surrounding area. It was instantly replaced by the still silence of the night. Ray waited until the creatures of the night began to stir, to replace the raucous noise of the day shift with their carefully controlled emergence into the threatening dark, jungle, night. The sound of their furtive, foraging began to increase as Ray lay in wait for the right moment.

A loud crack from a breaking twig close by and a snuffling sound sent shivers down his spine. He removed the gun from its holster, rolled over and looked up into the eyes of a wild pig. The pig poking about in the leave litter had presumed that Ray in his camouflage suit might provide a tasty meal. When the litter moved, rolled over and aimed a gun at a terrified pig, it ran off squealing into the night. Disturbed by the interruption, Ray stood up and heard another animal sound: the loud aggressive, trumpeting, of a distraught elephant. It was time for Ray to make his move.

He carefully crossed the exposed area, constantly checking the landmine map. As he approached the round wall of the compound, he intermittently stopped and sent a signal from his cell phone. Ray reached his objective without interruption. Keeping close to the wall, he moved quickly and quietly around its circumference, looking for any sign of a concealed entrance.

A sudden shaft of light illuminated Ray, caught in full view, he looked up and into the face of a decomposing copse impaled on a Bamboo stake. The full moon had suddenly broke through the dark, protective, cloud cover. Ray returned to the jungle to wait for daylight.

In the main house of the compound, Peter sat beside Bertie and the Boss Man, at a long, polished, dining table. It was covered with a white linen tablecloth. The table supported the weight of a variety of edible delights, small bowls and big dishes of eastern cuisine. The place settings were set out with a meticulous care for detail, each one the same, knives, forks and spoons, of shiny stainless steel. They sat opposite the Russian the soldier and two Oriental males wearing business suits, they eyed each other uncomfortably. Without warning, the threatening aggressive silence was suddenly broken by the sound of the '1812 Overture'. It announced the arrival of the warlord. The centre of the table featured a seven-pronged candelabra. It remained unlit until the arrival of the Black Knight.

He suddenly appeared from behind a hanging tapestry and with a theatrical flourish he entered the room, bringing with him two large, aggressive barking, black dogs. Each animal wore an identical spiked leather collar. Pulling powerfully at their restraining leads, the warlord suddenly let the dogs loose. They immediately jumped up on to the table, one at each end. Growling loudly, they began to eat the large lumps of raw, red meat, placed in the big porcelain Chinese containers. The Black Knight, wearing a dark blue full-length towelling robe, had a semi-automatic machine pistol stuck into his big leather belt and draped across his shoulders he wore the flag of the United Kingdom, the white ends securely tucked up inside a blood-red turban.

Without a word, he approached the candelabra and spat out a fine spray of volatile liquid, at the same time he used his gold lighter to ignite it. The flash of flame bent burnt and ignited the candles.

'Seven guests and seven candles,' he said. 'At the end of the evening I will extinguish them one by one,' he gave out a demented roar of uncontrollable laughter.

As they felt the heat of the flame the dogs began to whimper and yelping in fear they fled the scene, leaving behind them the smell of their singed coats. It lingered in the air as the Black Knight took his seat at the head of the table and said in a quiet, controlled voice, 'Please begin to consume.'

Ignoring the silverware, Bertie immediately stood up and with both hands he reached over and scooped out a large amount of raw meat left behind by one of the dogs. He began to eat before he regained his seat. As he sat down, the Boss Man slapped him on the wrist, to remind him of his manners. Peter picked unenthusiastically at a plate full of tropical fruits. With a piece of Paw-Paw halfway to his mouth, he felt the first irritating pulse in the eye of the tiger and rubbed his back. He looked around but no one had noticed. Bertie and the Boss Man were busy holding hands under the table. Having crept back into the room, the dogs were cowering in a corner behind their master. Occasionally, they came forward to retrieve a discarded chicken bone, tossed aimlessly over his shoulder before they retreated once again to safety. The warlord on his best behaviour was the perfect host. Engaging each one of his guests in turn in an intelligent, interesting topic of conversation. Full of food and imported wines, the guests feeling relaxed and comfortable inevitably slipped into a false sense of security.

A contented lull in the conversation caused the Russian to look up from his plate. He thought the dinner party was going well until suddenly, the Warlord leapt on to the table, took out his sub-machine pistol and started firing at the ceiling. The party tried desperately to take cover under the table. Laughing like a demented lunatic, the warlord, out of bullets, finally returned to his seat. He eventually settled down and apologised as the invited diners slowly emerged from their hiding place.

'I have a need for outrage and excitement,' he explained. 'A prolonged silence causes a painful pressure to build up inside my head and my only relief is to release the tension immediately. I am sure you understand?

Please accept my medical condition and as a token of my gratitude I will give you all a gift to enjoy, my latest acquisition.'

The Black Knight stood up, whistled loudly and excitedly clapped his hands, the hanging tapestry opened up to reveal a very tearful, and terrified May-Ling. 'You can go first,' the warlord said, pointing to the Russian. The big Russian would have preferred the Chinese boy. 'But before we leave the table, we must thank her majesty the Queen. Stand up and sing God bless our gracious Queen, long live our noble Queen and rule Britannia!'

Peter, with the rest of the group stood up and began to mouth the words of the Monarch's mantra. At the end of the embarrassing sing-a-long the warlord said it was time to go to the disco-dance. He led the way, closely followed by the Russian, May-Ling and Peter.

As they approached the dance floor and entered the room, the incessant booming sound increased in volume and assaulted Peter's ears from all directions. Temporally blinded by the flickering lights he headed straight for a dark secluded corner. At the far end of the room, the Chinese boy stood in the shadows with his back to the wall. The pulsating strobe light from the disco occasionally illuminated his presence as it bounced off the revolving mirrored glitter ball, hanging high up in the roof space. In a sudden flash of light, May-Ling appeared and walked into the room. She was the most beautiful thing he had ever seen. The Russian ignored her completely as he set his sights on a long-legged teen-aged transvestite wearing a short gold coloured dress laying provocatively on a leather upholstered antique chaise-lounge. With the Russian out of the way, the boy looked straight into the seductive deep, dark brown eyes of May-Ling. As he took her hand, he felt a hot rush of male testosterone, a brain-numbing wave of excitement flowed through his entire body he was speechless and lost for words as they began to dance. May-Ling returned him to reality as she whispered in his ear. 'Can we run away together?'

Locked in a close embrace, the boy began to explain his previous plan. 'I am going to leave in the morning,' he whispered. 'I have remembered the location of the concealed door. It is next to a pile of discarded sacks. I will meet you there at sunrise or before.'

A sudden blow to the ear took the Chinese boy by surprise and caught off balance, it sent him sprawling across the dance floor. He looked up to see a struggling May-Ling being led away by the warlord. As he looked on from the shadows, Peter resisted the urge to intervene but he made a mental note to seek revenge. The Chinese boy got to his feet and walked over to Peter. In a state of shock, he was uttering what Peter presumed was a continuous out-pouring of Chinese profanities. As he looked at Peter, he came to senses and shut his mouth in mid-sentence. He had no idea if Peter was a friend or foe, an informer for the warlord or one of the good guys.

Ray spent the rest of night on the damp jungle floor on the perimeter of the compound, listening to the sounds of the disco. It reminded him of a hot summer night in New York City but that was in a previous life. So much had happened in such a short time. He had no idea what day it was. Christmas could have been and gone without any obvious change in the seasons, this place was continuously hot and humid.

Peter threw up, apologised and made his excuses. He left the disco, returned to the dining room and lay down next to one of the sleeping dogs and waited for the expected signal.

Later that night, Peter's deep sleep was disturbed by a rapid, insistent, delivery of irritating pulses in his back. He had finally received a wake up call from Ray. It was four in the morning the party was over and the empty oppressive silence, occasionally interrupted by the snoring dog and the chirping crickets, were the only audible sounds. It was time for Peter to be alert and pay attention.

The Chinese boy had spent a long, cold, sleepless night, shivering under the sacks with a mixture of fear and anticipation. The thought of being discovered by one of the ever-present prowling guards made his blood run cold. But the promise of an intimate reunion with May-Ling had kept him wide-awake. He was so close to freedom but he had to make sure that he knew exactly where the concealed exit was. The full moon had disappeared as he carefully crawled out from his hiding place, stood up and felt his way with both hands, along the interior wall. It was only a matter of metres until he found the depression that separated the solid structure from the moveable section. With both hands still out-stretched and facing the wall, he heard a guard approach from behind. Shaking with cold and fear, his bladder suddenly felt like bursting, he reached down opened his zip and sent a stream of urine down the wall. The guard joined him to relieve himself and laughed.

'When I was a young man we used to have competitions and at your age I could reach higher than that.' The drunken guard re-adjusted his dress. The Chinese boy breathed a deep sigh of relief as the guard departed, he took two steps forward, stopped and turned around. The boy held his breath. He heard the sound of the guard loading his gun, at the same time he said, 'Drink more beer and before you know it you will be pissing over the wall.'

The Chinese boy replied, 'I will be pissing off over the wall before you know it.' The guard laughed again and returned to his rounds.

His pulse rate had increased rapidly but even more so when he saw May-Ling approaching. He grabbed her just in time as the light of the full moon broke through the disappearing cloud-cover and illuminated the compound. He held his hand across her mouth to stifle her startled scream and pulled her into the pile of sacks. The boy had arranged the sacks in such a way as to leave a small empty space in the middle. Just enough room for two people. Safely inside, they closed the entrance and waited for the right moment to make their move.

Peter knew it would not be long before something happened but he was not expecting the '1812 Overture' at full volume. The dog howled loudly and ran from the room as the warlord entered and announced that it was time to leave.

Assembled at the open rear exit of the roundhouse, the group climbed aboard the open-top truck.

Completely spent by their night of passion, the young lovers carefully emerged from their hiding place. The Chinese boy and May-Ling heard the truck coming, out in the open they rapidly returned to their place of concealment. A guard approached from the other side of the compound and came, closer and closer to the pile of sacks. The occupants held their breath and trembled with fear and trepidation as he stopped next to them, undid his trousers, had a wee and then whispered in a quiet voice.

'Be careful, I haven't seen you.' He then moved on and stood still beside the hidden exit. As the truck appeared from the back of the building, the guard reached out and plunged his hand into a part of the tropical foliage of the wall that concealed the operating mechanism of the entrance. At the same time, an annoyed cry uttered from the outside, disturbing the still-air with its aggressive verbal demands and as it insisted entry, the door slowly opened. The warlord, about to leave, ordered his driver to stop. He stood up in the back of the truck and removed his automatic weapon. Facing the exit, he took aim. The open door exposed a local peasant farmer ranting and raving as he approached the Black Knight the man said something about May-Ling. He was her father.

The man stared fixedly ahead, his lips together in a straight line.

'Do you have any idea what you have done?' he asked. 'You have dishonoured my eldest daughter. She is now unacceptable for a virgin marriage and in nine months time she will be unable to work in the fields and gather your illegal crop, and I will have another hungry mouth to feed.' The Black Knight took a deep breath. He was finding it difficult to stay calm. He had an overwhelming urge to step down from the truck and hit the man hard, very hard. He wanted to hurt him, to make his blood flow, to beat him to a pulp with his bare hands. But the warlord knew that to do so would be to lose face in front of the men who worked for him and that was not a price that he was prepared to pay.

'I have protected my daughter from the evils of life,' he continued, his eyes fixed firmly on the Black Knight. 'She has known nothing but peace and harmony, and you stolen that from her. She is not of your world, yet you have dragged her in, you have tainted her. Not a day will go by when she will not think of what she has done, what you made her do. For that alone you are going to die.' He reached down into his pocket for a concealed weapon and brought it into view. The warlord had had enough and immediately shot him dead. He apologised to his guests. 'Just a minor dispute with one of the workers I will have another one tomorrow but we must now continue without interruption.'

As the truck began to move forward May-Ling appeared. She had watched the unfolding scene from the safety of the sacks. In an irrational act of emotional despair she emerged from her hiding place, and much to the concern of the Chinese boy, she ran to the body of her dead father. She reached and knelt down beside the dying man as the warlord ordered the truck to stop. He reached out a large muscular hand, grabbed her by the upper arm and in one move lifted the struggling, distraught May-Ling, into the back of the vehicle.

'My dear we meet again. I am so saddened by your unexpected loss but we must put these things behind us and move on. I have already arranged an exciting new life for you. It might be uncomfortable, but I will make an exception and allow you to sit next to me on the journey we are about to take. Your unexpected arrival is very convenient, it will allow me to escort and present you in person to your final destination.'

As Ray watched the arrival of the peasant farmer, a concealed section of the wall next to the decomposing copse opened up. The silent warning at the door would send a memorable message to the local community.

As the truck came into view, Ray adjusted his telescopic sights and fixed them on to the frightened face of May-Ling. A slight realignment gave him a perfect picture of the rest of the occupants. He ignored Peter, Bertie and the Boss Man and set his sights firmly on the warlord. Ray calculated the time, speed, and distance of the approaching truck and informed the rest of the troops, he then sent a signal to Peter.

Peter felt a twinge in his back and he knew that Ray was somewhere close by, he settled down in his seat and tried to make himself a smaller target. Ray raised a hand; the troops raised their weapons and carefully took aim at the target.

Their organised efficiency was suddenly disrupted and shattered by the arrival of Tommy the frustrated, rogue elephant. Crashing through the jungle and trumpeting loudly, the animal appeared from nowhere and ignoring Ray and the rest of the troops, he continued to proceed at full speed across the open space. Straight toward the advancing truck, he attacked it head on. His powerful prehensile trunk and ivory tusks lifted the front of the truck and turned it on to its side. Bertie, the driver and the Boss Man were thrown from the vehicle and caught out in the open, they offered no resistance to the severely disturbed, rampaging, animal. The driver had no chance, as without hesitation, Tommy trod on him and continued on his way but Bertie held his ground. To protect his master, he stood in Tommy's path and made a futile attempt to stop the elephant by shouting and waving his arms about.

The enraged animal reached down and encircled the bodyguard's ample girth tightly in its extended proboscis and squeezed him in the middle. The elephant immediately changed Bertie's body into an hourglass figure. Releasing the rearranged shape, the animal dropped it on the ground and as a second thought coursed through its demented brain, and in a moment of continuing madness, picked up the dead body again and threw it across the clearing. Bertie ended up impaled on a sharp pointed bamboo stake, deliberately placed facing out of the enclosed compound to deter rogue elephants. It was the first and last time in Bertie's short life that he had reached his desired shape the perfect figure, broad shoulders, big buttocks, and a very small, thin, narrow, waist. With wide-open unblinking blue eyes he looked like a pinned specimen in a Victorian butterfly collection, now there were two silent sentries, one at each side of the concealed opening to the warlord's living hell.

Tommy let out a loud aggressive sound of satisfaction and stomped off through the long green grass and into the minefield. He stepped on one and it blew his foot off. Screaming with pain the large distraught animal fell on to its side and landed on another landmine.

Peter had managed to remain in the truck with May-Ling and the warlord. The Boss Man had taken shelter around the back of the vehicle. They were quickly surrounded by a rescue party from the compound and led back to safety.

With Peter in the line of fire it was impossible for Ray to get a clear shot at the warlord. He also realised that his men would be over run by the enemy if he exposed their position. They were clearly out numbered. Ray reluctantly lay down his weapon.

The second landmine detonation had confirmed the location on Ray's map, the place was clearly marked with a cross, he felt reassured but he was not about to presume that the rest of the crosses were marked in the right places. Ray was willing to wait for the right time, however long it took before he made his next move. He had an unrestricted view of the entrance to the compound he knew that it was only a matter of time before the warlord re-appeared. It would eventually be a head on, might-against-right battle on the narrow dirt strip road.

Ray assembled his troops and explained the situation. He was concerned and reminded them of the importance of the landmine map on either side of the approach road. It was an age thing. The fresh-faced young men had experienced more, close hand-to-hand fighting than Ray could ever possibly have imagined. They accepted Ray as an old advisor he was the man in charge.

For a second time that day the same section of wall opened up. It let out a convoy of three military vehicles. The first and last were armoured personnel carriers. In the middle of the escort, exposed to the elements, the warlord sat next to May-ling in the back seat of an old American Jeep. In the front, Peter was sandwiched between the driver and the Boss Man.

Ray resumed his position and readjusted the telescopic sights. He pressed a sequence of numbers on his cell phone and watched in satisfaction as Peter reached up and scratched his back, high up between his shoulder blades. A high-powered, shoulder-launched rocket grenade slammed into the lead vehicle. It exploded on contact and blew particles of the personal carrier high into the air. The missile had transformed and turned the transport into fragments of red-hot metal, which descended over a wide area and detonated more of the hidden landmines.

'Ambush!' shouted Peter as a bullet smashed through the driver's skull. Peter turned around and looked at the terrified warlord. Immobilised with fear, he had begun to lose control of his bladder. Peter reached out and punched him in the mouth.

'Out now or you die, hide behind the last vehicle.' May-Ling had already left the Jeep and was running in the right direction. Peter turned back and pushed the dead body of the driver out onto the track. He took over the driver's seat and at the same time grabbed the neck of the Boss Man and forced his head down below the steering wheel into Peter's crotch. It would be the first and last time he would be that close.

153

The remains of the burning truck had come to rest at the side of the track leaving a clear run to the rain forest. Peter did not hesitate; he put his foot down and drove like a madman towards the jungle. The last vehicle was rapidly reversing when the mortar attack began from somewhere close by. Peter reached the safety and seclusion of the overhanging trees and felt another irritating pulse between his shoulder blades. He was not in the mood for explanations or polite conversation. He drove straight on at full speed, swearing continuously and just missed a large camouflaged lump at the side of the road. Ray rolled over and out of the way, in time to see Peter disappearing into the distance down the long dirt road. He stood up and let out a loud four-letter word.

May-Ling kept on running and reached the entrance to the compound. She fell exhausted just inside the opening. At the same time the attack began to increase in its intensity, unknown to Ray, a number of Thai Government troops had arrived under the cover of darkness and concealed themselves in the long grass. As the troops emerged and approached the entrance firing indiscriminately, the Chinese boy left his cover and ran out into the open space. He reached May-Ling; their hands touched and locked together. In a desperate attempt to drag her to a place of safety, a stray bullet hit him. Shot by friendly fire, he fell dying, into the arms of May-Ling. He reached into his shirt pocket and took out a blood stained slip of paper. 'Go now,' he said, 'to Madam Cia's Camera shop.' They kissed as the Russian ran over and pushed May-Ling aside. She lay flat on the ground sobbing inconsolable. It saved her life. The Russian carefully gathered the limp body of the Chinese boy into his ample arms and began to cry. He sat on the ground with his legs crossed and rocked back and fore, he continued to weep and wail as he lovingly caressed the young boy's dead body.

Ray watched through his telescopic sight as a sudden burst of napalm flames erupted from a hand-held flame-thrower shouldered by an advancing member of the government troops. Its long trail of ignited dripping sticky liquid eventually settled on and set fire to both sides of the entrance and ignited the two dead sentries. It also engulfed a seated figure sitting in the middle of the opening. That was the first and last time Ray saw the Russian. It was then that he decided to pull his troops out and return silently to the pick-up point.

Peter had a responsibility, or was it a liability, to look after the Boss Man. Taking a corner too fast on the forest road, the truck lost traction as it tried to grip the uneven surface. Peter lost control as the Jeep continued in the wrong direction. It eventually came to rest at the side of the road. Having hit a sharp object, the front tire on the driver's side slowly, with a sigh of escaping air, began to deflate.

As the night approached, without water and lost in the rainforest, they began to walk at a fast pace. Peter took his bearings from his watch and the setting sun. He decided to head south. The Boss man, struggling from behind complained continuously about the heat and the humidity. Peter ignored him but eventually he gave in to the constant demands to stop and slow down. Huffing and puffing, the big man sat down and rested his weary body under a banana tree. He rearranged his position and made contact with his aching back and the trunk of the tree.

The slight vibration caused a venomous tree snake to slowly emerge from its slumbers. Leaving its concealed location in the upper leaves and tasting the air with its long forked-tongue on the way, it carefully descended the trunk. Its heat-seeking senses homed in on to the hot pulsating body of the Boss Man. The poisonous viper reared its head, rearranged its position and as it prepared to strike the Boss Man, who then unexpectedly lifted his left leg. The snake was already committed as it released its pent up power, it missed its intended target and sunk its fangs without hesitation deep into the inner thigh of the fat man's right leg. The white flabby flesh exposed below the baggy shorts immediately began to change colour.

Peter, keeping his distance a few steps ahead, heard a loud-pitched scream and turned around in time to see the snake disappearing. The Boss Man jumped up and hysterically began to run around in circles, unintentionally pushing the poison further into his body. Peter pounced on the victim and brought him to the ground. He stood astride the prostrate figure, took his shirt off and tore it into strips. From his prone position, the Boss Man looked up and smiled in admiration as Peter exposed his muscular torso. The last thing he remembered as he slipped into unconsciousness was the sight of Peter reaching down to suck at his inner thigh. Peter sucked hard and spat out the poison. He had heard of it before but he had no idea if it would work or not. He applied a tight tourniquet to the leg and lifted the unconscious man onto his shoulders. It was impossible to carry the dead weight any long distance without stopping. Peter's strength was failing as he fell forward on to the forest floor and hit his head. In a state of dehydration, concussion and total exhaustion he made one final attempt to get to his feet. As the darkness descended and overwhelmed him he passed out completely.

Chapter Fourteen

The Connection

The next day Ray booked the first available flight out of Bangkok to Sydney, Australia. He phoned Susan from the departure lounge and they arranged to meet in the south terminal of Mascot airport.

Flying across the red heart of central Australia, Ray began to have second thoughts. Sending a message to Susan might mean he had compromised the mission. If she had set up the situation in Chang Mai she would now be in a position to complete his permanent incarceration or elimination.

The wing flaps slowly began to extend as the plane held in a holding pattern above the airport began its long, circular, descent. Losing speed and altitude, it cruised quietly as it released the air pressure from underneath its aluminium arms. They flexed alarmingly as Ray looking out of the cabin window.

He watched as the vast isolated interior of the continent begrudgingly gave way to the rapidly increasing front line of sparkling bright blue, polished water, contained in the numerous back-yard swimming pools, located in the western suburbs of Sydney. The rapidly extending boundaries were marked out by a mixture of heavy, earth-moving machines backed up by the emerging structures of yet unfinished, residential properties. The relentless onward push into the hinterland, financed by the assets of individual property developers buying up the cleared land, had resulted in a building bonanza. Local contractors competed to build the perfect retirement village for a generation of senior citizens about to retire to the country. It also gave the green light and provided the incentive for a relentless progressing army, a countless numbers of real estate agents. The city had been expanding for years and had consumed all available fertile land in easy reach at an alarming rate. It was time to release more land for development and stretch the already over-burdened infrastructure to breaking point. The ancient Roman Empire had made the same mistake extending its supply line too far into hostile territory.

The interior of the Australian Continent contains an inadequate supply of fresh water for the extravagant demands of modern man. The top end of the Northern Territory and the swamplands of Kakado National park regularly receive a tropical downpour, as well as the rain forest of Daintree, Queensland, perched at the tip of the Cape York Peninsula. The rest of the continent can go without rain for years. Except for the occasionally wet weather generated by the surrounding oceans, forcing their saturated rain-filled clouds to their maximum distance two hundred miles in land. Finally, they release the rest of their depleted supply onto the parched earth and the withered remains of the wheat belt. Eventually they give up completely, disintegrate and their remnants float aimlessly onwards into the hot pristine blue sky, high above the immense Australian outback.

Susan, wearing her airline uniform was standing at the back of the assembled relatives waiting to receive their loved ones. She held aloft on a piece of cardboard a roughly drawn caricature of an elephant and a wire brush. Ray cleared by customs entered the arrival lounge and seeing the childish drawing he immediately pushed his way through the expectant crowd and prepared himself to ask a number of important questions.

Their brief encounter lasted long enough for a quick hello and goodbye and a promise to meet up later in Bundaberg. Susan was about to fly out but she had arranged for Ray to stay with her daughter Jodie in the Kings Cross district of Sydney. Susan gave Ray the address and the key of the door and then she was gone. He then became lost in a crowd of departing tearful passengers about to board their plane to foreign parts.

On his way to the exit, Ray stopped at the tourist souvenir shop. Browsing through a collection of acrylic transparent key rings containing miniature replicas of Australian animals, he came across a black emu. Hanging on the chromed display stand, it attracted his attention immediately and he knew it was exactly what he was looking for. It might come in handy and serve as a silent message to Peter if it was placed in the right place at the right time, if he ever saw Peter again...

Standing outside the airport terminal, Ray waited in a long line for the next available cab. As the fierce heat of the Australian noonday sun beat down relentlessly on to his unprotected baldhead, Ray began to feel the first uncomfortable signs of sunburn. He was approached by a tall, impressive looking native Australian Aboriginal carrying a didgeridoo. Wearing a brown loincloth and white war paint, the man began to blow down the hollow tube. Emitting a tuneless deep drone, he tried desperately to compete with the ever-increasing sound of a countless number of chirping cicadas, hiding behind the bright blue blossoms of an avenue of jacaranda trees. Then he disappeared into the distant the long line of trees pointed straight to the centre of the City.

'That will be ten bucks mate,' the man said breathlessly as he lay down his instrument.

Ray looked up and stared straight into the eyes of the towering figure and said, 'I will give you five if you want to get out of here alive.'

The man grinned and replayed, 'Good on ya cobber, no worries she'll be right mate. Hope your wombat wiggles well, welcome to Australia.' He took the money made his way to the end of the long line of parked taxis and climbed inside the last one. Ray watched and waited silently, sweating, as an excited group of new arrivals pushed past him and jostled for space at the front of the taxi rank. He was in no rush and eventually his turn came. Ray reached out and opened a rear door of the car. The cool air from the air conditioning unit was like a breath of fresh air. After loading his limited amount of luggage, he relaxed on the back seat and closed the door, but he could still here the irritating, incessant muted noise of the insects, infiltrating the sealed interior.

The driver, wearing a typical Australian bushman's hat, turned his head and said, 'I will turn on the radio if you like? It is better than that background noise.' It was the same Aboriginal man. Ray nodded in agreement. To meet twice in a matter of minutes could have been a coincidence but as the loud sound of the '1812 Overture' filled the confined space Ray's alarm bells began to ring, the driver engaged first gear and moved off without asking for the destination. Ray prepared himself to make an immediate exit. Looking out of the window and into the slow moving traffic he made a decision to leave the vehicle and run across the highway. He surreptitiously pushed a podgy finger onto the upright pillar of the rear door lock but with no result, it was central locking. He turned around in time to see a glass partition sliding silently up-wards, separating him from driver. Locked firmly in place, it prevented all communication. Ray's destiny was in the hands of a friend or foe, he did not know. Merging into the traffic, they joined the freeway and increased their speed. It rose with Ray's heart rate.

Jodie Jordan lay in a hammock sipping a tequila sunrise through a pink plastic straw. As she passed out, she slowly let the trashy magazine she was reading slip from her fingers. The empty glass followed and shattered on the concrete floor but she was oblivious to the sound. The black wrought iron ornate railings surrounding the balcony of the old Victorian building began to mask out a percentage of the sun's rays. After forty minutes, they had left a fine filigree pattern of red and white marks on Jodie's sensitive skin. The hot tingling sensation sent an alarm call to Jodie's comatose brain. It was reinforced by the repetitive strident sound of a car horn.

She woke up saw the damage to her previously unblemished white skin and swore. Working the late night shift at a local members-only drinking club as a pole-dancer put her under the spotlight, the management would not be amused. The after-hours activities meant she spent too much time awake partying, indulging in sex and drugs and rock and roll without enough sleep. The day job compounded the problem. Working nine-to-five at the fast food take away took all her remaining energy and now her dysfunctional mother had the audacity to phone her up out of the blue and request her help to look after and entertain another one of her countless lovers.

She retrieved her floral bikini top and enclosed her large bosom in the flimsy material. Looking over the balcony she saw Teri the taxi driver unload the contents of his cab: an old man with a rapidly peeling red baldhead, two plastic bags and a battered brown, leather suitcase. Jodie waved a perfectly manicured hand at Teri as he drove off with squealing tires and left behind him traces of burnt rubber on the Bitumen. She had a love-hate relationship with Teri but Jodie had to be nice to him; he was her local dealer.

Ray had arrived. He looked up and thought that Jodie was waving at him, he waved back. To successfully entertain this ancient geriatric would be hard work, but she might score some financial brownie points with her way-ward mother. Hopefully it would put her into Susan's good books and if she played her cards right, remove the financial burden of last month's rent. Jodie could not any longer afford the luxury of her expensive lifestyle and the rapidly increasing cost of the designer drugs that she so desperately needed to keep her act together. In the beginning it was almost cheaper getting high on coke than it was getting a buzz from beer and without the calories. But as her addiction increased so did the cost.

She quickly bent down, hid behind the balustrade and snorted up the remains of the Cocaine previously cut and placed on her vanity mirror. It was a part of an addictive pattern. Jodie always prepared a hit in advance. Day or night, the time was always right for another snort. Caffeine and coke and maybe a marijuana smoke started Jodie's every waking day. Once she had sniffed up the remaining substance from the surface she smiled into the clean reflection of the mirror and re-applied her make-up. The dappled light cast a dark shadow under her brown eyes and drew her attention to the first traces of a small amount of baggy skin hanging loosely below the lower lids. The elasticity of the ageing skin was no longer able to bounce back and the passing of time had begun to show. Jodie was getting older and losing her looks. In a moment of madness she threw the mirror over the balcony, it hit Ray on the head.

'What the - !' he shouted.

As she ran down the stairs the coke kicked in. Bright-eyed and buzzing she opened the door. Close-up, Ray looked all right except for a small trickle of blood.

'I am sorry, I am so sorry,' she said as she smothered him in kisses. 'It just flew out of my hand, please come in and let me look at it.'

'Susan said you were a bit of a wild child but I didn't realise how wild. I'm Ray. But if you smother me in kisses for a slight scratch, what do I get for concussion?' He winked with a mischievous look in his eyes and laughed out loud.

Jodie relaxed and immediately her embarrassment turned to suppressed relief. The happy infectious sound caused her to giggle like a little girl. She blushed and felt her face turn red. The more she tried to apologise and compose herself, the worse it got, laughing and crying at the same time with tears rolling down her cheeks, she picked up the suitcase and led the way into the sitting room. Jodie hadn't spontaneously laughed so much for a long time. So long in fact, she could not remember. This man was something special, maybe mother had made the right choice at last, she thought. Most of the men that Jodie met at the club were lecherous, lonely, losers, or married with a white mark on their finger, which had recently been covered by a rapidly removed wedding ring, contrasting clearly with the rest of a brown tanned hand.

Jodie left the room and went to the medicine cabinet in the bathroom and searched through its contents. She rummaged around and found an old bandage past its sell-by date, a packet of safety pins and a box of Band-Aid plasters. On her way back she stopped off at the kitchen and picked up a plate full of homemade cannabis cookies. Jodie opened the fridge door and took out a couple of cold tinnies, a bottle of vodka saved especially for medicinal purposes and a bottle of Greek Ouzo.

Ray, left alone in the lounge, sat down on the black and brown crushed velveteen pattern covering the G-Plan seating unit, designed and built in the seventies. The room contained an odd assortment of memorabilia. Fading posters of once famous film stars and celebrities adorned the walls. One of the corners contained an impressive looking hanging wicker basket chair, painted white. The chair looked down and across the room to an inferior comfort zone. A large blob of polystyrene filled beanbag, wrapped in a garish covering of cheap material lay passively in an opposite corner. On a side table, the obligatory transparent Lava-Lamp silently bubbled away as its colourful contents rose lethargically to the surface. Slowly reaching their limit, they changed their shape and serenely sank to the bottom of the vase in time to repeat the endless cycle. In an energetic contrast, the multicoloured optical fibre-light unit, positioned on top of a metre high, round rough-sawn section of a redwood tree-trunk, still displaying the stubby remains of two remaining branches, changed its electronically-programmed sequence of rainbow colours with a rapid boring repetition. On its wooden pedestal, the glass fibre light was situated next to and above the obsolete beanbag and provided a perfect example of opposites, the ancient and modern, trying in a futile, unsuccessful attempt to bring peace, balance, and harmony to the environment, a meeting of Ying and Yang and Feng Shui.

Jodie returned carrying a collection of items for Ray's well being. He immediately noticed the bottle of Ouzo.

'Don't touch that,' she said as she placed it between him and the Lava-Lamp. 'Try these, they are made to a traditional Australian recipe I made them myself.'

Munching on one of the sweet oatmeal biscuits, Ray slowly began to relax and sink into the upholstered seating unit. Exposed to the humid room temperature, cold beads of condensation were already beginning to form and roll down the sides of the beer cans. Reaching out for the nearest one, Jodie took hold of the ring-pull top and ripped opened the top of the flimsy tinny and poured its amber liquid into a midi-glass. At the same time, with her other hand she removed the cap of the Vodka bottle and suddenly with out warning began to pour the strong, potent liquid onto Ray's sensitive wound.

Ray, with a fine catholic upbringing, was not used to swearing, but the unexpected intensely painful stinging sensation, caused him to utter another unholy expletive.

'Why do men make such a fuss? It is only a scratch and if you are a good boy, you will get to drink the rest of the bottle. It's the only thing I could find to sterilise the cut.' Jodie placed a piece of cotton wool on the cut and began to wind the bandage around Ray's head she secured it with a safety pin which inadvertently pierced his skin. Ray let loose another loud four-letter word. In the company of Jodie, Ray realised that he had spent more time swearing than engaging in polite conversation. He reached up and pulled at the protective covering. Resisted by his left ear, the bandage slipped down and covered his right eye. Jodie began to giggle again. Ray was not amused. He felt uncomfortable and did not appreciate being made a figure of fun.

'Just take it off and stick a Band-Aid plaster on instead, like a postage stamp. You can then return the unwanted item to its previous location. I presume that even you can do that correctly.' Making eye contact, the two antagonists looked deeply into each other's eyes and playing the power game each one refused to look way. The potent unending silence that filled the room was occasionally disturbed by the entrance of a gust of warm wind through the open French windows. Its disruptive arrival slowly moved the hanging chair. Playing a placid part, the beanbag had no such problems, sitting quietly in the corner it contributed to the tangible silence of the humid room.

Jodie laughed and looked away. 'That's what I like, a man that can call my bluff.' She turned around and walked across the room to the other side. Ray removed the bandage.

The solid-looking wooden pedestal supporting the glass fibre light revealed a hidden secret when Jodie pushed a finger into one of its extended stubby arms. A small hidden door sprung open and Jodie removed an impressive looking oriental bubble pipe. The hollowed-out interior of the tree trunk also contained all the necessary drug paraphernalia for a habitual user. Placed on a silver tray, the pipe, a penknife and a large lump of something covered in silver foil was presented to Ray.

'This is what you need,' she said as she placed the tray at Ray's feet. 'It will change your mood completely. I hope you are not an under-cover cop?' Ray reached for the bottle of Vodka and took a mouthful. At the same time, Jodie slapped a postage stamp-sized plaster on to his head. Ray immediately ripped it off. He was going nowhere.

Jodie removed the ornate wooden upper-section of the bubble pipe, took off its brass top and cleaned it. She blew through a flexible tube attached high up into the side of the transparent glass bowl and then half-filled the container with Ouzo. Jodie then reassembled the pipe. She unwrapped and removed the silver foil from a solid block of black cannabis resin. Jodie picked up the knife from the tray and held its blade over the flame of her cigarette lighter. As she cut a thin slice from the black block, the hot knife transferred its heat to the resin, releasing a small amount of pungent smoke. Jodie rolled the warm slice between her right finger and thumb, and crumbled it into several small pieces above the brass top of the bubble pipe. A concentrated blast of heat from the lighter ignited the resin as Jodie sucked powerfully on the flexible tube. Glowing red and satisfied that the contents of the bowl were well alight, she inhaled deeply and held her breath for a considerable amount of time. Jodie eventually exhaled a copious amount of smoke with a contented sigh and passed the pipe to Ray.

Ray remembered the last time he had smoked dope, in the presence of his police instructor on the same day as the police academy passing out parade. It was a rite of passage. The final challenge: to present himself to the general public, as a perfect example of a law enforcement officer in complete control of his actions.

Before his acceptance as a police cadet, Ray had tried the occasionally joint on the college campus when he was a young man but that was a long, long, time ago, back in the dark ages, shrouded in the mists of time. His memory managed to delve deep and it came up with a long lost answer to the problem, do not inhale, hold it in your mouth. Filtered through the liquorice tasting liquid, the cool, smooth smoke disguised its harsh powerful potential and lingered on his tongue, tantalising and inviting. Ray resisted the temptation to breathe in and held his breath.

After an acceptable passage of time, he released a mouth-full of acrid-grey smoke. Held in his mouth, the powerful narcotic had begun to take effect before Ray realised. He felt a slight numbing sensation taking over his facial muscles as they locked into place to display a silly, benign grin. Ray focused his attention on Jodie as she began to involve him in a rapid, sensible conversation. Ray tried desperately to keep up and be alert, to nod and twitch at the right time and utter the expected reply, but he had no idea what she was talking about and he could not remove his silly grin. He took another swig from the vodka bottle as Jodie passed him the bubble-pipe.

'Talk to me about yourself,' he said as he reached out for another one of the home-baked oat biscuits.

So, she told Ray this story: 'My father, Jack Jordan is a habitual criminal, convicted again last month and locked up for committing armed robbery with an offensive weapon two weeks after his last release. Jack specialises in stealing from small town, suburban post offices. He has been arrested so many times I can't keep count. My mother had just arrived in Sydney from the United Kingdom as a ten-pound P.O.H.M. Young, naive and innocent she took the first available job offered, working as a waitress in a local hotel. That is were she met my father Mr Jack Jordan. Caught up in the heady atmosphere of a new life, a new job, and a new future, she was easily seduced into believing the promises of the dark-haired, smooth talking, handsome man. Each night he would return to impress Susan with another romantic tale of the wonders of the great Australian outback and his desire to rediscover a hidden vein of almost pure gold locally known as Lassister's Reef. Situated somewhere northeast of the Kalgoorlie Gold Fields, in the state of Western Australia, covered up by the continuously shifting sands but still occasionally accessible. My Father had a map and a plan. He was a dreamer and a compulsive gambler.

Before he met my mother, he made his money playing pool in isolated hotel and snooker halls. He would arrive on a Friday night, play the part of an inexperienced novice and lose a large amount of money. Insisting that he would win his money back he challenged the locals to another game on Saturday night, they eagerly agreed. He lost again but not as much. The word went around that the passing stranger had more money than sense. On Sunday, the venue was packed to capacity. The tension rose as the hours ticked by, Jack won a few games and lost a few, just enough to keep the punters interested. At four in the morning, a substantial amount of money was at stake as the local best boy bet his VW camper van in a last desperate effort to save face and win. He threw the car keys onto the table and watched silently with the rest of the onlookers as they slid across the green baize and disappeared into a far pocket. The game commenced without a sound. Jack took a deep breath as he prepared himself for the final shot. He judged the distance the angle of the shot and the required force correctly. The last ball left the tip of his cue and kissed the side cushion as it slowly and serenely made its way to the far pocket. It stopped and teetered on the edge for an excruciating amount of time, before it finally decided to drop into the pocket and onto the car keys.

It was the perfect sting. Jack had cleaned up completely; he was a professional. Still holding the pool cue for his security, he removed the keys from the pocket, picked up the pile of Australian dollars and made his way to the door. He broke the stunned silence with his final words 'I thank you and goodnight.' He ran to the camper van and started the engine at the second attempt and took off in a cloud of smoke. Looking in the rear view mirror, he watched as an angry mob of irate losers spilled out from the hotel.

He enticed and excited Susan so much that when he gave her a blue opal eternity ring, on the end of a Kalgoorlie gold necklace, she gave up her job at the hotel and they took to the road in an old, used, rusty, VW camper van. In the beginning, on their way across the continent, they stopped off at every hotel, roadhouse and homestead, looking for good honest work, they were in love and my mother was expecting. Jack and Susan were rapidly running out of money, as their futile search for work proved pointless. The empty wide-open spaces beckoned. The distance between east and west was vast and they had no financial back up. Jack stopped the van at an isolated outback town to buy a pack of cigarettes at a local store and to repeat the all-important question, 'good day mate, any work?' Fumbling through his nearly empty pockets all he could find was a small collection of loose change: just enough to buy a pack of ready rubbed, cheap, hand-rolling tobacco. The shop was deserted but the till was open and empty. From the back room a subdued murmur attracted his attention as he called out, 'Shop.' A large typical redneck Australian appeared, wearing a soiled sleeveless, sweat-stained t-shirt, cut off jeans and a bush mans hat. Jack paid for the baccy and a packet of papers. On is way out of the shop, he put his last cent into a poker machine and pulled the handle. The three wheels revolved and stopped at the same symbol, Jackpot. A cascade of coins overflowed the catching tray and clattered noisily onto the floor. The redneck rubbed his grubby hands together and said, 'City boy, if you want to make some real money, follow me.'

The hands of the man holding and dealing a deck of cards in the back room had been exposed to the unrelenting sun so many times that they had taken on the look of wrinkled leather. Jack pulled up a vacant chair and sat down opposite the stockman. Laying his recently acquired winnings on the table, Jack began to play poker. The redneck owner shut the front door of the shop, locked it, and displayed the closed sign. He returned to the room and sat down next to Jack, it was two against one. When it came to card games, Jack was the master; he knew all the tricks of the trade. Having learnt from an early age, he could play from dawn to dusk and not show a sign of emotion, or a lack of ice-cold control at the turn of a losing card. Halfway through his second losing hand, Jack requested that he change seats with the storeowner to improve his luck, the man begrudgingly agreed. As the tension grew, Jack locked into a fierce mental tussle, lost all track of time. Hours later, the shop owner folded and left the game. Then there were two, Jack faced the stockman head on, eye to eye across the table and called his bluff. At the late hour in the silence of the night, a sand fly settled on the sweaty, greasy nose of the stockman, which he completely ignored as he reached down and picked up a rifle from below the table.

He pointed it straight at Jack. 'This works well,' he said, 'show me your hand and I will let you have it.' Jack controlled his fear as he placed his card's face up. 'I don't have any bullets but it's worth a hundred bucks it's yours.' The man stood up reached across the table and shook Jack's hand. 'If you are looking for work there is good money to be made as a kangaroo shooter in South Australia.' Jack picked up the pile of money and the rifle, and returned to the camper van.

Susan was fast asleep, he woke her up and showered her with a large hand-full of Australian bank notes and pocket-full of change and excitingly explained another one of his many moneymaking ideas. Covered in money and caught up in the addictive adrenaline rush of Jack's enthusiasm, Susan drove all night without stopping, to the South Australian border.

The sun was coming up as they reached their destination. Susan was tired. A sudden gust of violent wind began to blow another bundle of dried up spinifex across the highway. It stopped in the middle of the road and Susan realised, too late, that the tumbleweed was sitting on top of the inner part of a discarded truck tire. She realigned the vehicle and passed over the obstruction with out losing speed. Underneath the camper van, the coil of steel tire wire had been briefly touched by the inside edge of the near side wheel. It stood up and wrapped itself tightly around the rapidly revolving drive shaft. The lose flailing end increased its grip as it wound itself around the back axle and poked its rusty point into a sealed section at the end of the prop shaft, bringing the van to a grinding halt. The pierced seal released a steady stream as Jack, lying on his back tried to remove the tire wire. As the warm oil slowed to a depressing dribble, Jack gave up. Stuck in the middle of nowhere, they needed help. He picked up the dollar bills and a couple of loose coins from the floor of the camper van, gave Susan the empty rifle and locked her inside the van.

The endless desert road disappeared into the misty horizon, only made visible by a long line of converging telephone poles diminishing in size as they approached the indistinguishable distance. Out in the open, the buzzards circled high up on the hot thermals and waited for the right time to descend. Any slow-moving object instinctively alerted the birds of prey to prepare themselves for easy pickings. The deserted road beckoned as Jack began his long journey.

Walking briskly along the hard, tarred highway, Jack eventually slowed down, and stopped at the side of the road unintentionally disturbing a kangaroo feeding her young joey under the shade of a tee tree. She immediately took fright, abandoning the juvenile to any prowling predators and bounced of into the undergrowth. The carrion crows and the circling vultures descended rapidly as the vulnerable creature broke cover and made an attempt to escape. It tried to cross the open road and for the first time in its short life it found itself exposed and alone. Trying to make a decision, it froze n the middle of the road. Jack ran over, picked it up and plucked it from the jaws of death as a black wedge-tailed eagle with a five-foot wingspan appeared from nowhere, swooped down, and tried to grab the tasty morsel with its powerful talons.

He put the joey in his jacket pocket, leaving its long gangly legs exposed as the eagle returned for another attack. The boomerang missed, but made the bird think twice about its intended victim. It gathered speed, gained height and gave chase, to a fleeing carrion crow left behind by the flock. The eagle caught it in mid-air.

'Crazy white boy,' the aboriginal muttered as he picked up the boomerang. 'You want death?' He was not alone, a small menacing group had emerged from behind the roadside bushes. 'You give me joey, him good eating, good tucker. I give you directions to phone, and number for rescue.'

Jack exchanged the infant for a dirty, grubby, business card. Printed over a picture of a tow-truck the name Garry's Garage, and a telephone number.

The man pointed south. 'Two hours walk,' he said, 'and we will take good care of your woman.' He laughed out loud. Jack had no choice. The bush telegraph had already passed the news of his predicament far and wide. In that desolate land, the unseen locals knew every move made by a passing traveller.

Jack found the phone-box and phoned Garry. After an unbelievable amount of time, the break down truck eventually turned up. Sitting in the limited shade of the phone-box, Jack was hot, exhausted, and dehydrated. He was slowly sinking into a sun-stroked pit of despair but rapidly brought back to full consciousness as a cooling stream of water descended from Garry's canteen, with the words, 'Wake up mate its time to go.'

Gazing out of the closed window of the camper van, Susan appreciated the vast panoramic view of the empty wilderness, locked inside the close confined space enhanced her feeling of security. The small mobile love nest carried all their personal possessions and a promise for the future. If only they could complete the journey. Jack feared the worst as he approached the van and saw Susan slumped over the driving wheel showing no sign of life. An agitated Jack knocked repetitively on the windscreen and rudely interrupted Susan's romantic dreams of a wonderful life.

'I thought you were dead, how did you deal with the aborigines?' he said as she opened the door.

'What aborigines? I haven't seen another human being since you left.'

Garry took a quick look underneath the van and immediately attached a steel cable to the axle. 'This is going nowhere mate it's a lump of dead metal, it looks like major damage. I can take it back to my place and repair it for a price or do a straight swap at the garage with another second-hand van, plus the towing charge. How much money do you have?'

In a no-win situation, Jack was stuck between a rock and a hard place for the second time that day. He had no choice and handed over a bundle of dollar bills. Up on the back of the breakdown truck and safely secured, the van obscured his view as he climbed inside the cab of the recovery vehicle and sat next to Susan. Garry in the driver's seat had a quick look back out of the open window, as an aboriginal emerged from the bush. With a surreptitious wink and a grin he made eye contact with the main man as the rest of the gang reappeared. Garry engaged first gear and drove off.

Jack drove out of Garry's garage with a pocketful of loose change, a replacement camper van, a tank-full of petrol and a pregnant woman. They were broke again without enough money to buy food or bullets.

They finally arrived in the battered van at an isolated town south of the border. The annual kangaroo cull had already taken place. That was when Jack, a law-abiding citizen unintentionally changed the rules and became a wanted man.

Jack parked the van outside a local pawnshop, situated on the corner of Main Street and Western. He took his rifle and approached the entrance. The door suddenly flew open as a couple of bearded characters emerged and ran down the side road. Inside, on the floor behind the counter, the distraught occupant with his hands bound behind his back visible shook and shivered with fear as he saw Jack's rifle.

'Look leave me alone haven't you had enough already? There is a bit more money hidden under that coffee pot in the corner take it all and go.' Jack could resist anything except temptation.

He took the notes, returned to the van, lent through the open window and lied to Susan. 'There is money to be made in the next town, that's why I kept the rifle. Their pawnshop displays a list of information for men looking for work.' Jack was thinking of easy money as he passed the rifle to Susan. The risk was minimal and without bullets, the rifle was harmless but it would be a powerful persuader.

Jack's thoughts were interrupted by a loud shout of 'Stop! Thief!'

A man had suddenly appeared running from the entrance of the shop waving a six-inch knife. Jack turned in time to face his attacker and raised his right arm. He received a long flesh wound down its length as the point of the knife sliced open the protective surface. The separated skin began to release a steady flow of blood. With his left fist, Jack hit the man in the face. As he fell to the ground Susan pushed open the driver's door and pulled Jack inside. In a state of shock, he closed and locked the door, at the same time he desperately tried to start the van.

Susan screamed as the man reached through the window to grab the ignition keys. The man turned his head and froze as his wide frightened eyes fixed on the rifle pointing straight at him. With a squeal of tires they took off in a cloud of dust, Susan yelled at Jack, 'What have you done?"

Chapter Fifteen

Returning to the shop, Bruce Bennett spat out a broken, bleeding, tooth. Working quietly alone in the back room, the teenage assistant took great care filling in the information of the day's business transactions into Mr Pike's personal ledger. Examining the last item to be listed, a bone-handle bowie knife, the silence out in the shop was suddenly shattered by an aggressive shout.

'Open the till now and give us the money!'

Bruce still held the knife as he hid under the table and held his breath. The hair on the back of his neck stood up in fear as he forced himself to remain calm and collected. Time stood still as silence descended, he waited and waited for what, he had no idea. The fear gradually subsided and anger took over. He carefully crawled to the door and peered through the keyhole into the empty shop. Full of bravado, testosterone and adrenaline, he reached up to turn the handle as Jack entered the building. Bruce had second thoughts as Mr Pike pleaded, 'Leave me alone haven't you had enough already? There is a bit more money hidden under that coffee-pot in the corner take it all and go.' Bruce began to boil with rage and saw the red mist descend, as he looked again through the keyhole to see the back of a man carrying a rifle leave the premises. He pushed open the door and holding the knife ran out into the street.

Back inside the shop, Bruce removed the rope from the hands of the frightened owner. Mr Pike shaking with fear, too weak to stand and hyperventilating, indicated his right hand pocket. Bruce heard the words 'Heart pills,' found the bottle and gave him one. He placed Mr Pike in a sitting position and phoned the police. Having completed the call, Bruce turned around in time to see Mr Pike slowly slide onto his side and release a satisfied sigh of relief as all the fear and heart-stopping tension left his exhausted, lifeless body.

Susan ripped off a part of the white linen bed sheet and tightly wrapped it around Jack's arm. Parked up in a deserted lay-by they decided to take to the back roads. Jack wasn't going to do that again, from now on he would be on the straight and narrow and squeaky clean. He had learnt a lesson and had too much to lose.

They spent four days in the back of beyond before they ventured into the nearest town for supplies. Susan shopped at a local supermarket and bought a copy of the daily paper. The front page headlines announced the fact that another pawnshop robbery had taken place the day before and the police were still looking for those responsible for a previous raid, which had resulted in the death of the owner. They had an eyewitness description of a man with a rifle and a wounded right arm caused by a knife. It was now a murder hunt.

Moving rapidly west, they arrived at the isolated Ross River homestead situated in the outback, which still close enough to the central town of Alice Springs. The Homestead employed my mother as chief cook and bottle washer and made her responsible for providing the packed lunches for the over-night paying guests desperately waiting for the thrill of a lifetime.

Riding on the back of an aggressive complaint camel at the crack of dawn, for another pointless wander into the surrounding desert, Jack was employed as a maintenance man, and outback assistant. He made enough money to play poker and pool in the clubhouse all night and every night. At last, life was looking good and they were saving enough money to move on, and find their pot of gold at the end of Lassister's Reef.

The pawnshop robbery gang had driven Police Inspector Jeff Metcalf to despair as the endless reports of sightings of suspicious characters and false information had led his limited team of dedicated officers on too many pointless pursuits across the state. Looking forward to a part of his annual leave, Jeff had already booked a week of rest and relaxation at the Ross River Homestead. He left the investigation in the capable hands of his second in command Craig Compton. With two small boys to take care of on his own after a disastrous first marriage to a mail order-bride from Thailand, Jeff needed money and lots of it. Picking up the occasional pocketful of money with no questions asked from an illegally parked motorist, or letting off a local lad caught committing a slight misdemeanour helped to swell his unearned income, but he wanted more. He had applied for a transfer to the traffic transport highways police department in a town called Collector N.S.W., situated on the Federal Highway, southwest of Sydney between Goulburn and Canberra. The traffic cops in charge of motorways controlled and were responsible for all-interstate heavy-goods commercial traffic and foreign trucks. Jeff knew a man in the federal police force based in Canberra who needed a friend in New South Wales that could do a thing with accidents, especially international container trucks from Thailand.

Playing the part of a North African Arab for the benefit of the tourists, Jack, in charge of the camel train, wore a long-sleeved white Bedouin robe. He adjusted the saddle strap on the last camel and helped a man up onto the disgruntled animal, inadvertently exposing his scared arm. Jeff Metcalf made a mental note, he was on vacation but he was still a cop working on an unsolved case. Jeff was looking for a man with a scared arm.

'Smile and give me a salute,' Jeff said to Jack as he grinned and raised his right arm again and touched his temple with his right hand. 'Hold that pose,' Jeff said as he took out his photo phone and pressed a button. 'Take one of me,' he said as he carefully wiped the cell phone clean and handed it to Jack.

Jack wanted to move on. He had the promise of a permanent job as an out-rider on a five thousand acre, sheep station repairing the surrounding dingo fence and now he had enough money to buy bullets to shoot the wild dogs. Today would be his last day.

Back at the Homestead, Jeff followed Jack's every move from a discreet distance. It was payday for the employees and as he entered the office, Jeff waited for his opportunity. Inside, Jack handed in his notice, picked up his pay and left the building. Jeff watched him leave and as Jack approached the on-site shop, Jeff made his move. He arrived in front of Jack and held the door open. They stood next to each other at the counter. Jack bought a substantial amount of ammunition from the store. Jeff purchased an entire roll of unnecessary freezer bags but one would be essential for forensics. He listened intently as Jack bought the bullets and announced his decision, destination and time of departure.

Jeff, still standing at the counter had to buy time, he mentioned the price of his purchase and complained loudly.

'I only wanted one, for the price of that roll I could have played a hand of poker!' At the word 'poker,' Jack pricked up his ears.

'If you reckon you're good at the game mate, I will catch you later in the casino room, ten o'clock on.'

Jeff followed Jack's flowing robe as he walked out of the room. He paused at the door, beside the transparent canopy containing the landline telephone. He ripped a bag from the freezer roll, placed it on the small shelf next to the coin slot and wrote the day, time and date on to its plastic surface. He then carefully slipped his photo phone into the pristine bag, sealed it and made a call on the landline.

In the casino room, Jeff played poker opposite Jack. With a copy of the fingerprints from the coffee pot, Constable Craig arrived wearing a pair of jeans, a white t-shirt and a denim jacket. He stood next to Jeff without a sign of recognition. Jeff lost as soon as possible and left the table. Outside the building, he passed the securely sealed freezer bag to Craig. Craig had five hours to compare the fingerprints and organise a roadblock.

The travellers took off at first light. Jack and Susan managed to make it a mile down the dirt road before their world fell apart. Around the next bend, the road was entirely blocked by a heavy earth-moving machine. Hiding behind the shovel of the bulldozer, the armed police stood up and raised their rifles as one. With their guns supported on the top edge of the two-inch thick steel, they took careful aim. Stating the obvious, Craig standing at the rear bellowed down the megaphone. 'Come out with your hands up. This is the police. You are surrounded.'

Behind the top of the steep high piles of red earth on both sides of the road, two concealed groups of officers readied their weapons, and made their presence known as they showed their faces and looked down at the camper van through telescopic sights. In the rear view mirror, Jack caught sight of a stationary line of armed officers wearing bulletproof vests, also pointing guns in his direction. There was nowhere to run to. Jack slowly opened the door and stood down with his hands held high.

That was when, in a state of shock, Susan's water's broke prematurely, and I was about to be born in the front seat of a VW camper van. How's your head?' she said.

Without waiting for an answer, Jodie returned to the hollow tree-trunk, took out a plastic bag full of grass, a packet of cigarette papers and a box of matches.

'It's good for headaches. I grow my own on the back balcony. The best fertile seeds come from Thailand. It's natural, clean and environmentally friendly and I need a joint before I go to work.' Jodie removed three papers from the pack of green Rizlas, licked the gum on one and stuck it on to the adjoining paper. She then licked and applied the third paper horizontally to the other two. Jodie placed the papers on the side table, and added a small crushed handful of the dried green leaves from the plastic bag and laid them along its length. She carefully rolled the thin, white papers around it, stuck them together and poked both ends of the cylindrical tube with a matchstick. Satisfied that the contents were safely contained, Jodie ripped off a piece of the Rizla pack, rolled up the thin strip of cardboard and inserted it into one of the open ends. She returned her attention to the other end, and twisted the white papers into a tight ignitable point and lit it.

'It's good,' she said letting out a lung-full of smoke. Jodie passed the joint to Ray. One quick puff and he passed it back. He was losing the plot completely, already feeling nicely numb and unable to speak coherently. Ray wore a silly grin and suddenly acquired an intense craving for sugar. He reached out and helped himself to another one of Jodie's homemade cookies.

'Please continue what happened next,' he said as he stuffed his mouth with the sweet-tasting biscuit. Ray listened without paying attention as he contentedly munched on the tasty mouthful. After all his years, he still did not understand how a woman could take so long to tell a story that could be told in five minutes. Jodie needed no encouragement and began again.

'Where was I? Oh, yes, my father Jack. Sensing a successful

conclusion, Jeff Metcalf had cancelled his remaining holiday and returned to work to prepare a case for the prosecution. He pulled rank and took over from Craig Compton. Susan was interrogated by Jeff Metcalf, stripped of her personal possessions and locked up in the hospital wing of Alice Springs remand centre, under constant surveillance. I lay next to her in my own small private prison, a confined premature, baby unit. In the warm transparent plastic tent I was attached and wired up to a number of life support systems. Looking back, it was like nurturing a small delicate plant under a protective gardener's cloche, sealed but easily accessible from both ends by ripping open one of the plastic zips. It was my earliest recollection, the first time that I became aware of my surroundings.' Jodie picked up and aggressively shook the small plastic bag. She emptied the required amount of dried, green, grass into her hand and rolled another joint. Well alight and glowing red, she passed it to Ray. He shook his confused head and took another bite of his biscuit. Jodie continued.

'My mother, weeping and wailing, appeared in the dock holding me in her arms. She had already done a deal with Jeff Metcalf. He would look after mother and me on condition that she married him and took care of his two kids. In court, he defended her position and dropped all charges for the prosecution as she renounced all responsibility and involvement, and blamed Jack. For Susan, it was the perfect answer to her predicament. When it was Jack's turn to appear before the Judge, Susan did not arrive to substantiate his defence. Jeff appeared for the prosecution wearing Susan's opal eternity ring, hanging on a gold chain around his neck, in full view of the assembled crowd. Jack saw it from the dock and was physically restrained by the guards as his sentence was read out: six years for manslaughter and robbery with a deadly weapon. That verdict destroyed my father. Jeff arranged for Susan to visit Jack in jail the next day under his supervision.

I still remember my father reaching out a large white hand between the solid black bars of the prison cell and sucking on his first finger. My mother cried and began to shake with uncontrollable emotion as a female office appeared and took us away. Jeff remained behind, and then the sadistic bastard rubbed it in. 'I have your future wife but your future is finished, don't forget this eternity ring is mine as well, and your unwanted kid, but it's a small annoying price to pay for your woman and a map of Lassister's Reef.

When Jack was released four years later for good behaviour, he had nothing left and nothing to loose. So he took up armed robbery for a living. By that time the transfer to the highways police department had come through and we were living in N.S.W. He is now a corrupt cop on the take with friends in high places with the Federal cops in Canberra, and the underworld Chinese triads in Sydney. But that's another story. I must get ready for work.'

On her way to the bathroom, Jodie picked up the pipe and the rest of the paraphernalia and returned it to the hollow tree-trunk. Above the sound of the shower she called out, 'I haven't seen Jeff since I was six years old. He is a violent man and used to beat my mother black and blue for no apparent reason. One day on the school run, Susan stopped at the local bank and withdrew all the money from their joint account. She then used his credit cards and cash cards to complete the job. We never went back. Don't forget my mother will do anything if it's to her advantage. She will use you, and sell her own soul if there is money to be made. Susan will do anything for money. Beware of that woman.'

Ray remembered Madame Cia's Camera Shop and his time in the Thailand jail. Jodie shouted, 'You can wash my back if you like?'

It cleared Ray's mind completely of the narcotic effect. He stood up and walked to the bathroom as Jodie emerged wearing a short white towel, they met in the hall. She pressed him up against the wall and looked deep into his eyes. As the towel began to slip she breathlessly began to undo Ray's shirt buttons. 'You look after me and I will look after you, forget mother.' She placed a kiss on Ray's forehead and left a bright red lipstick mark. Suddenly a key turned in the lock and the front door flew open. A tall aboriginal man entered and walked straight towards them.

'Are you ready?' he said.

'Ray, meet Teri, my boyfriend,' Jodie said. Teri had left the front door wide open and the door of his car. The taxi was still playing the '1812 Overture'.

Jodi left to get dressed, leaving the two antagonistic men together, eyeing up each other from close quarters like two rutting male stags in the mating season. Teri and Ray made light, polite, inoffensive, small talk. They both had a lot of information and aggression to conceal and control.

Jodi returned. 'It's nice to see two admirers competing for my favours.'

With his back still against the wall, Jodie took Ray's head in her hands and placed her bright red lips on to his unresisting mouth.

'Keep it warm for later, I will return and give you the best night of your life, it will be an unforgettable experience, and that's a promise.'

Teri visibly bristled with the unwanted information.

'And as for you young sir, I want you to take me now, as fast as possible until I tell you to stop, but I don't think that will last long, your engine over-heating already.' Jodie pointed to a faint white emission of steam, escaping from under the bonnet of Teri's taxi.

They departed at last, leaving Ray alone. With his laptop and a large measure of Bundaberg Rum, he settled down to the task at hand: locating the Australian business interests of EMU Imports and Exports. Oblivious to the passing of time, he finally found what he was looking for: E.M.U. Imports and Exports, located in Newcastle, New South Wales. Licensed and approved by the New South Wales Government for the Importation of Corrosive substances, volatile materials and computer technology. The company's finical interests also included land in the Sydney suburbs and a substantial amount of real estate in and around the Queensland town of Bundaberg. They also held a license to import Colombian coffee beans from South America. Two independent sources of supply competing with each other would keep the cost down and cut the profits of the producers, making them produce more, leaving more money available for the organisation. The head office was situated in the Chinese section of Sydney known locally as Happy Valley. Another piece of the puzzle had fallen into place. Ray made a phone call.

Four hours later, Jodie returned with Teri. 'There's a change of plans. We are leaving now, for a week-long party at Sheila's place. It's just north of Bondi beach at a place called Dover heights. It's on the map, I will catch up with you at mother's place on Christmas day, but if you stop off at this address on your way and I am not completely out of it, or I have already had enough you can give me a lift.' Jodie scribbled down the address and a phone number on the back of a green Rizla pack. 'Lock up when you leave and bring the keys with you.'

As she left the room, Jodie stopped, bent down and began to nibble Ray's ear, at the same time whispering, 'I haven't forgotten my promise its in the pending tray.'

'That's enough of that, I think it's time to go,' Teri said as he appeared in the lounge doorway, filling its inadequate space with his long, lean, wide, muscular body.

Sitting on the seating unit, Ray stood up straight and aggressively as Teri entered the room, he held out his hand and enclosed Ray's in a vice like grip. 'So long mate, it was good knowing you, I don't think that we will meet again.' Looking hard into Teri's eyes, Ray realised that the slight twitch and softening of the intense stare did not convey the same message as the macho man's body language. Ray was receiving conflicting signals from Teri. As he turned and left the room behind Jodie, Teri displayed an open hand, thumbs up sign, and a wide grin. Ray was totally confused by the mixed messages. Teri slammed the street door on the way out and left Ray in an uncomfortable silence. Ray wasn't happy about Teri.

He went to the bathroom and found some cotton wool balls and in the kitchen, a pair of rubber-glovers. Ray returned to the lounge room and picked up the remaining ouzo in the near-empty bottle. He applied an adequate amount to the soft absorbent material, and returned to the hallway to remove all trace of his presence in the property. Ray carefully applied the impregnated cotton wool to the wallpaper where his head had made contact. Back in the lounge room, he removed the discarded bandage from the waste bin and removed the bubble pipe from its secret location wiped its surface clean and replaced it. He used the last remaining drops of the powerful spirit to clean the outside of both the ouzo and the Bundaberg rum bottles. He paid particular attention to his empty glass and removed all traces of fingerprints. The top of the table received the same treatment and with a quick wipe, he cleaned the edge of the cookie plate. In the toilet, he wiped the handle clean.

Still wearing rubber gloves, Ray found the vacuum cleaner in an alcove under the stairs. He cleaned the hall carpet, lounge room, his seating unit and then changed its position, replacing it with an identical seat from the other side of the room. He removed the dust bag from the cleaner, filled up its remaining space with the empty beer cans and the bandage, and then placed the bag in his suitcase. Ray returned the machine to its original position, left the apartment and locked the door.

Out on the street, he hailed a passing cab.

'Where you going mate?' the cabby called out.

Ray replied, 'Somewhere downtown near Happy Valley.'

'Wearing those pink rubber marigolds mate, you can't go wrong. Climb aboard.'

Chapter Sixteen

Peter woke up in a bamboo hut and looked straight into the eyes of the big Boss Man, sitting astride him slapping his face.

'Wake up. We go now, I have already arranged transport. We are lucky to be alive, the government troops are on their way and time is running out. Hurry, hurry.' He moved his vast bulk and Peter got to his feet.

Peter had a slight buzzing sound in his ears. It rapidly increased in volume as an old DC-3 propeller driven, twin-engine Dakota landed on the jungle airstrip. A wing tip missed the bamboo hut by less than five metres as the plane slowly rolled along the dusty runway and turned to face its previous path. The pilot judged the distance perfectly and with its propellers still turning, parked the plane outside the hut.

For a man of his size, the Boss Man moved extremely quickly at the sound of gunfire. As the first shots rang out, he grabbed Peter and pushed him through the open doorway in front of him. The pilot increased the engine's power, released the brakes and the plane began to move. They reached the plane in a matter of minutes. The cabin door was already open. Peter scrambled aboard as the fat man lagging behind lost his footing.

The swirling dust stirred up by the rapidly revolving propellers almost obscured the prone body except for one fat podgy hand, extending above the descending dust particles. The pilot applied the brakes. As Peter bent down, a row of bullet penetrated the skin of the plane from its tail to the top of its cockpit; they had missed him by inches. He reached out and grabbed the man's hand. Peter pulled the fat man aboard as the pilot released the brakes and continued the take off.

The DC-3 banked alarmingly as it took a tight right turn to avoid incoming fire from the ground troops. A ground to air missile passed harmlessly overhead, as the plane adjusted and regained its equilibrium.

The pilot confirmed the time, destination and original flight plan, Bangkok Commercial Airport.

Sitting behind the pilot, next to the Boss Man, Peter asked the important question.

'What happened? How did I get here? I thought I was dead.'

'We were found just in time, dehydrated and unconscious by the village people. They are friends of May-Ling's late father. The good guys looked after us in our time of need and we are still alive to tell the tale. You sucking out the poison from that snake bite saved my life.'

Peter looked out of the cabin window and down onto the Thai army diminishing in size but increasing in numbers as they emerged from the surrounding jungle and encircled the small village. The man in charge apparently issued an order. All the young men of fighting age appeared from their huts with their hands above their hands and assembled on the airstrip. The first in line was shot on the spot. As he fell to his knees, Peter looked away. The Boss Man said, 'Nothing can go wrong now, I have already arranged a safe sea passage from Thailand to Australia.'

The Pilot turned his head and gave a loud congested cough. He looked at Peter as a small dribble of red blood escaped from his mouth. 'I think I need help,' he said, 'I have been hit. You will have to fly the plane.' The pilot passed over a note-pad and pen to Peter. 'Write this down now, the flying instructions and landing procedure in case I don't make it.'

The rapidly delivered stream of technical information was cut short by Peter insisting that the pilot slow down, so that he could write and remember it in plain English. At the end of the monologue, Peter reached over the pilot's shoulder and took hold of the joystick. They carefully changed places. Coughing up copious amounts of blood, the pilot climbed over the back of his seat and collapsed next to the Boss Man. The big man immediately prodded the pilot and asked, 'Where do you keep the parachutes?' The pilot smiled in response, rolled his eyes, lowered his lids and passed out.

Talking to air traffic control on the intermittent, crackling, radio, Peter confirmed the flight plan, and requested assistance. On course and flying low, the plane approached the sparkling waters of a vast inland lake. Peter could not see the far side. The site triggered a latent subconscious memory that caused Peter's right hand to move involuntarily and pull back the joystick to gain more height. At the same time, he instinctively applied more power to the engine. Peter felt that an outside force had become involved and intervened. Making sure that they successfully reached the other side, Peter then recalled that day at the lake in New York's Central Park on his son's sixth birthday. Peter checked the day, time and date on his watch. Today would have been his dead son's birthday.

The near-vertical climb had forced the Boss Man to let go of his tenuous grip. As he rolled to the rear of the plane, he upset the balance. The plane, at the end of its climb veered violently to the left and began to descend at an alarming rate. The Boss Man rolled back down the cabin like a bowling ball and crashed into the back of Peter's seat.

'For Christ's sake, if you don't sit still you can leave now.' Peter levelled out the plane, which by this time was flying in an entirely different direction. The sudden erratic departure from the prearranged flight plan had been detected by a ground-based radar unit placed in a secret, sensitive military establishment. They immediately alerted the Thailand Air Force.

Cruising comfortably at ten thousand feet, Peter was suddenly aware of the presence of two accompanying, menacing MiG fighter planes flying within touching distance of the wing tips of the DC-3. The pilots of the Thai defence force flew closer and positioned the wings of their planes into the flip position, one above and one below the wings of the DC-3.

The calming voice of air traffic control was cut short as the intermittent distorted sound, gave way to a loud clear command.

'You are flying in a restricted air space. Follow us immediately to a designated runway or we will be forced to shoot you down.'

As he followed them in their descent, Peter read aloud the landing instructions from the notepad, to reinforce his lack of confidence.

'Line up the landing approach, make sure it's level with the horizon, decrease speed, throttle back the engines to the red line; don't stall. Extend the undercarriage and lock the wheels into the landing position. Prepare for a bumpy landing. If you have too much speed and you think that you might overshoot, increase power, reverse the previous procedure, leave the wheels locked in the landing position fly around and try again.'

At the same time, Peter muttered continuously to himself, 'I can do this, I can do this.'

The Chinese MiG fighters made a low pass over what seemed at first to be a highway construction site cut into the dense jungle, complete with a collection of mechanical diggers and earth moving equipment. A ribbon of black bitumen had been laid down from an opening in the side of a nondescript hill. At the far end, it terminated in a large mound of boulders and broken rain forest trees. The radio crackled into life

'We land now, immediately.'

A slight movement caught Peter's eye as he made the approach. A hidden camouflaged anti-aircraft gun, situated at the side of the road under the branches of a Banyan tree, adjusted its gun barrel and locked the DC-3 firmly in its sights. The plane had too much power and the road came up to fast. As the plane landed heavily and bounced twice, Peter heard an alarming loud crack and a big bang. With too much speed, the end of the road was approaching rapidly. He immediately increased the engine's power, pulled back on the joystick and made another vertical climb. The anti-aircraft gun opened fire and missed.

Peter shouted at the radio, 'I have overshot the landing strip stop firing. I think I have broken something. I am going around again for another go.' Peter added more power to the engines and the resulting high-pitched sound caused the pilot to regain conciseness. He said, 'Extend the wing flaps, I forgot to tell you about the wing flaps.' Peter tried again and approached for his second and final attempt. He landed the DC-3 as the pilot died.

The plane, with a damaged undercarriage and a blown tire, rolled down the road on two wheels. Leaning to the left and dragging one wingtip on the ground in a shower of sparks, the plane headed for an uprooted, hard wood tree at the end of the road with a big broken branch pointing in its direction.

Eventually the plane came to a halt. It stopped just short of the tree, but as the plane's last remaining unassisted momentum carried it forward, they came closer and closer and made contact. The wilting, dying leaves on the end of the branch touched and wiped the cabin window clean. The warm summer wind blew at them for the last time. Releasing their dying grip, they took their remaining nutrients and joined the dead pilot's spirit on a quiet journey to another place.

The plane made one more involuntary lurch forward, causing the branch to break the cockpit window. The stunned silence in the plane and the slowly receding adrenaline rush were in perfect harmony with the diminishing hot ticking sounds of the over-heated, cooling engines.

A rescue squad arrived and surrounded the stationary aircraft. Their leader climbed up on to the branch and pointed a pistol through the broken windscreen at Peter's head.

'You are under arrest for violating Thailand's national air space in a military zone. Leave the plane now with your hands above your head and follow me.' The Boss Man, in the back, babbled incoherently as he was physically removed from the plane's interior. On the ground and still protesting their innocence, they were both forced at gunpoint to enter a military ambulance. The medics on board with drawn guns took over. It was a formality.

The main man took over and with a bright light he looked into Peter's eyes and asked silly questions.

'Do you remember your mothers name and the day of your birth?' Peter replayed in the affirmative.

'Please stand up and turn around twice.' After the pointless exercise, Peter sat down again.

'In my professional opinion, Mr Serover, you are of sound body and mind, and well enough to stand trail in front of a military court. I am only doing my job Mr Serover please sign here.' The man handed over a white sheet of A 4 paper attached to a cardboard clipboard. Peter refused.

'A wise decision in your situation Mr Serover, I agree entirely, but you will be taken to a military establishment to await your trial.'

'And if I sign?'

'The same rules apply Mr Serover, the same rules.'

Locked together by a pair of hardened steal handcuffs, Peter and the Boss Man made a comical picture, tall and thin, and fat and short. They were taken to the prison block and read their limited writes.

Still handcuffed together in a back room, a member of the military police took great delight in subjecting them to a full body search. The Boss Man obeyed without comment. Peter protested and received a stunning blow to the back of his head.

'Your life is in my hands, Mr Serover, and I can inflict terrible damage with my truncheon, bend over.'

The door opened and a loud voice intervened. 'There is no need for that. Mr Serover you and your friend are free to leave. I am from the embassy. You both have clearance to leave the country immediately. I have arranged for your departure as persona non-gratis. You will be taken directly to Bangkok on condition that you never enter this country again. There, you will board a ship as previously intended to Australia.'

Wobbling about on one fat white leg, the Boss Man put his other foot into the right side of his discarded trousers, and said, 'Trust me Mr Serover, I have friends in high places.'

Finally fully dressed, they both walked to the open door. Peter followed the man in the grey suit. On his way out, the Boss stopped momentarily and smacked the military policeman hard on both cheeks, the resulting red blows caused an appreciative grin to appear that extended to the ends of his bristling brown, military cut, moustache.

Pleased with his display of limited control, the big man left the room and took a wrong turn. Peter, walking along the passage in the opposite direction turned around and shouted out 'Follow me you fool, this is the way to freedom.'

Arriving at Bangkok's international cargo container dock, the government helicopter slowed down, reduced its power and lost momentum. It landed carefully, facing into the erratic wind. Another blast of air took over and increased in speed, the occupants descended into a hot tumble dryer of turbulent unstable air. They were welcomed at gunpoint by an army sergeant and an armed guard. He invited them to follow him with a one-word instruction, 'Move.'

The calm, lifeless polluted water of the harbour had already begun to move. In a sluggish attempt to remove their thin covering film of waste oil, the small lethargic wavelets reached up and deposited their unwanted slippery substance onto the plimsoll line of a fully laded rusting container ship. The top deck supported two layers of closely packed cargo containers. Below deck, the ship accepted an assortment of vehicles in its capacity as an international roll-on roll-off ferry.

'I am not going on that, I can't swim. This is not my idea of a sea cruise. I prefer a crashing plane any day.'

The Boss Man replied, 'You worry too much.'

The guard said, 'Move' and took out his pistol. As they walked up the gangway, the guard remained behind with his sergeant, who shouted into the increasing wind.

'Hurry up! Hurricane's coming, have a nice day.'

On board, they were suddenly confronted by a figure emerging from the shadow of a decrepit lifeboat. A demented man with bulging eyes, babbling incoherently, waving a machete made straight for them. Another pair of eyes also took advantage of their arrival. As the individual quickly followed by members of the ship's crew approached, Peter and the Boss Man stood aside.

He ran past them and said, 'You crazy fools, this ship is about to sink! It will never make it! I'm leaving now, may your gods go with you.' He reached the gangway hotly pursued by the gang of irate muscular men. A black rat, with its sharp eyes, timed its departure perfectly and jumped from his secluded position onto the shoulder of the fleeing machete man. As they arrived on dry land, the man stopped, looked back and made a sign of the cross. The rat ran down his back and disappeared into the dark violent night.

The followers froze in their tracks as the first strident warning call of an immediate departure sounded from the klaxon of the rusting metal monster. The stern doors were slowly closed and locked into position as the ship prepared to leave the safety of the harbour wall.

On board, a hive of activity had broken out. The pursuing men returned and took their part in preparing the vessel, releasing the grip from

189

its dockside restraints. They removed the gangway, and the thick woven ropes attached to both ends of the container ship. As the final 'all clear' signal sounded, the captain appeared and held out his hand.

'Welcome aboard I will do my best to make you comfortable and give you an experience that you will never forget.'

The restrained vibrations of the diesel engines far below decks gathered pace, built up and released through the smoke stake, like a volcanic eruption, a contaminated belch of noxious gases, fumes, soot, black smoke and hot sparks, giving off enough light to illuminate the big Emu logo on the side of the ship's funnel. The air became saturated with the heavy, pungent, cloying smell of hot diesel fumes. The visitors were invited below and shown to their quarters, in contrast their adjoining cabins were the last word in luxury, complete with air-conditioning, satellite TVs and Jacuzzis. On Peter's bed lay a dinner suit, white shirt, bow tie, and an invitation to dine at nine, at the captain's table.

Heading out into the full force of the storm after leaving the shelter of the secluded harbour, the ship entered the unprotected waters of the South China Sea. The open ocean showed no mercy as the threatening storm increased its power, and gathered together a collection of black ominous clouds. Suddenly the lightning struck. It flashed past the porthole and briefly illuminated the interior of Peter's cabin. The double strike also caused a momentary loss of power. The cabin lights flickered and dimmed, but eventually they received enough constant energy to regain their controlled intensity. Peter suitably booted and suited, closed the door and left them to it.

The captain's dining room lurched at an alarming rate as Peter arrived and took a seat next to the Boss Man. A full-length crimson curtain on a hanging rail, moved incessantly and nosily from one side to the other, as it ineffectively tried to conceal the workings of the catering staff situated in the adjoining galley, desperately trying to prepare and present an acceptable dinner.

Peter removed the linen napkin from its restraining monogrammed, tortoise-shell ring, and placed the cloth in the required position. The ship gave an unexpected roll and moved the crystal-cut Waterford glass goblet, which was placed in front of him, slowly to the end of the dining table. It teetered on the edge and then the ship reversed the movement and returned it to its original position. Its momentum continued on the polished surface. Peter reached out and grabbed it as it moved past. The ship's movement caused the rest of the glassware to leave the table at the other end and crash to the floor. An accompanying sound from the catering department was followed by an outburst of profanities uttered by the oriental staff. The head chef appeared and whispered in the captain's ear. The captain nodded in agreement. A cold dish of assorted seafood arrived: slices of Japanese sushi, squid tentacles, and tiger prawns. Attempting to consume the unusual food increased Peter's feeling of nausea. But he was soon saved by an exceptionally large wave, which moved the plate and its contents into the lap of the Boss Man, the captain stood up and apologised.

'Gentlemen, we appear to have a slight wind problem. I suggest you return to your cabins and have an early night.'

Back in his cabin, Peter was violently sick and threw up, but this time, not on cue. He preferred flying instead of the endless pitching and rolling of the creaking, flexing, overloaded metal monster.

A watery sun pierced the scudding clouds as a new dawn broke and revealed the heard but not seen remains of the violent cyclone, adding to Peter's feeling of misery and impending doom. As he made his way to the wheelhouse, the storm was still raging intermittently, but the mountainous, relentless waves, kept up their assault and pounded the ship consistently.

'Good morning Mr Serover, I trust you slept well.' The captain seemed oblivious to the vibrations of the deck plates and their resisting rivets taking the strain as another fifty-foot wave hit the vessel head on. Untold tons of water broke across the ship's bow as it descended into a trough and ploughed deep into the raging torrent. It reared up again to repeat the performance and face another oncoming wave. The wave slammed into the wheelhouse and obscured all forward vision as the wiper-blades, working at full speed, tried inadequately to clear the window. The deck was awash, and as the water boiled and seethed in its angry fury, it finally found an escape route and cascaded over both sides of the ship in a continuous flow.

'Mr Serover, you will be pleased to hear that if we continue to be pushed along at this rate with a following wind we will reach our destination ahead of time. Please appreciate this experience is a most unusually occurrence.' The captain's face showed the first signs of an obsessive mad man. Peter returned to his cabin as another heavy wave crashed over the wheelhouse and sent a shudder throughout the entire ship.

Down below, he knocked on the door of the Boss Man's quarters and heard through the closed door what his distressed employer thought of the sea cruise.

The wind eventually relented and left the ship to continue on its intended course, leaving the powerful waves to roll the vessel from side to side in the heavy swell.

On the king sized bed, Peter's troubled sleep was interrupted by a timid tapping sound on the other side of the cabin door, and the pathetic voice of the Boss Man. 'Please help me, I need help to go upstairs. I need fresh air, these diesel fumes are making me ill.'

On deck, a clear blue sky dispersed the remnants of the storm clouds, the intermittent restless wind dropped to a whisper, allowing the comforting regular muted sound of the ship's engines to take over.

The engines stopped, without power the ship began to wallow alarmingly in the rolling sea. The sudden silence drew Peter's attention to a cargo container ten feet above his head. Out of position and precarious balanced, it emitted a strange knocking sound. It began to move again, and as it reached the point of no return it's restraining straps finally gave way. Peter jumped on the Boss Man and threw him to the deck just in time. The container broke free and slipped slowly with a loud metallic grinding noise over the side and disappeared below the surface, it missed Peter and the Boss Man by a whisker.

As it fell, it broke through the deck rail and left a gaping hole, the remains of the bent railings, twisted into an outward facing direction. One end of the container briefly reappeared, it rose up from the deep, shedding its covering of disturbed water from all sides and blowing out a number of bubbles on its way. As it settled down and prepared to sink finally into its watery grave, a lone albatross arrived and circled the sinking container letting out a blood-curdling scream, identical to the sound of a dying, desperate, human being. With its long outstretched wings, it flew low and level. Gliding silently, it approached Peter at head height. The magnificent bird with its piercing black eyes locked them on to Peters. It came closer and closer and finally changed direction at the last minute. Gaining height, it reached the funnel and left behind a deposit, the gooey mess dribbled down the last letter of the word E.M.U. Peter did not believe in an all-powerful God, but seeing the letter U split in two by the bird's droppings he turned around in time to see the blood red container disappear below the waves. The Boss Man was also having a religious moment, and surreptitiously made the sign of the cross. The wind dropped completely and left an uncomfortable calm.

'Come on, follow me.' Peter led the way to the nearest lifeboat. 'Stay here and don't move, I am going to find the captain.'

'Mr Serover, I have no intention of going anywhere without you.' Satisfied that he could remember the location, Peter left him alone and made his way to the bridge. The Captain, deep in conversation with his second in command, looked up as Peter entered the room.

'Mr Serover, what can I do for you?'

Peter replied, 'I have a question. You have just lost a container overboard. What was in it?' The phone rang, and as the Captain answered Peter looked at the radar screen. The revolving sweep on the green screen illuminated another approaching storm.

The Captain replaced the phone. 'Mr Serover, that was damage control. I have been informed that we have a badly buckled stern door that has developed a serious leak and is allowing water to enter the ship at an alarming rate. If this second storm hits before we have regained engine power we will not only have lost a container but we will also lose the ship. Mr Serover may I suggest that you keep your pointless questions for a more appropriate time and prepare yourself mentally to abandon ship if necessary.' He turned his back, and as Peter left the wheelhouse he heard the communications officer send out an S.O.S.

Peter began to explore the unseen secrets of the floating colossus. Below deck, he ventured into the bowels of the ship. He needed to know the extent and condition of his surroundings. The heavy metal waterproof door on C deck, inscribed with the words 'Drivers Only', was wide open. A quick look inside showed the depth of the water. Slopping slowly from side to side it reached halfway up the wheels and hubcaps of the intercontinental trucks. A long cylindrical tanker attached to its tractor-unit displayed the company's logo, a big black EMU and the words 'International Imports and Exports.' Beneath the symbol, a red warning triangle emphasised the following message: 'Customs Sealed Government Cargo, toxic and inflammable. Contains Liquid Petroleum Gas under pressure, refrigerated and highly explosive.'

The men down at the deep end were still desperately trying to seal the damaged stern door. To keep the incoming flood under control, the powerful water-pumps working at their maximum capacity, were fighting a losing battle. Peter heard a shout.

'You, don't just stand there and stare, come here and gave us a hand, if you don't want to die!'

The ship struggled to survive but slowly it began to sink even deeper into the turbulent water. To lose weight and gain more buoyancy, the captain gave an order to jettison the cargo containers occupying the main deck at the rear of the vessel.

The nearest deep-water fishing boat had received the International distress call. Its crew immediately pulled in their net and began a desperate race against time to reach the stricken ship.

They arrived a nautical mile off the rear starboard side of the stricken vessel and stopped their engine. With a raised sail, a following lethargic wind and the aid of the ocean current the fishing boat finally drew along side the ship's bow. The occupants assembled on the fore deck of the Chinese junk as their leader raised a megaphone to his mouth. In the hot sultry silence, his voice carried across the water, reached up to the lofty heights of the wheelhouse and entered through the open window.

'Captain, we request your help, we have travelled many miles to answer your distress call and now we are also in distress. We are holed below the water line and are taking on water. Please do we have your permission to come aboard?' The captain agreed and issued instructions for a deck hand to lower the pilot's ladder.

The rotting wooden boat was forced up five feet as an unexpected swell arrived, announcing the beginning of another threatening storm. The protective obsolete car tires facing outwards, suspended from the boat's inadequate deck-rail, became squeezed between the old traditional form of transport and the modern metal monster. An unkempt collection of sweaty ruffians ascended the ladder, reached the deck in minutes and entered the wheelhouse. Their leader, wearing a white stained headband with black Chinese symbols, drew his gun first, followed swiftly by the other members of his motley gang.

'Captain I am now taking charge of your ship, you will not be harmed if you and your crew do exactly as I say.'

The captain had met pirates in the South China Sea before, and adjusted his balance. He carefully placed his right foot over and pressing a slightly raised identical rivet, located on the corner of a deck plate under the protruding console, out of sight of the intruders.

'We need your money, rings, watches and passports to sell, to make enough money to buy another fishing boat, to feed our parents and our poor starving children. We are desperate men, but we will not kill you, it is against our religion.'

A shot was fired from the direction of the open window; the captain fell to the floor with the dead body of the man wearing the headband. Bullets found their targets, as close up, the fully armed members of the ship's crew opened fire, from both sides of the wheelhouse, putting into action a pre-rehearsed plan. One of the fishermen jumped onto the captain and put a gun to his head.

'Stop firing if you want him to stay alive, open the door and back off! I do not want to see anyone between here and our fishing boat.'

The door opened and swung silently in the breeze as the rest of the intruders regained their feet. One took up a position for rear guard action as the captain was forced to his feet and sandwiched between the two men. The man in charge made it safely to the deck with his hostage.

Taking advantage of the calm conditions, the Boss Man, unaware of the unfolding drama, was sunning himself in a make shift hammock tied between a stairway and the lifeboat support.

In a lull before the storm, Peter arrived and said, 'I think we are sinking but very slowly. No need to panic. The stern of the ship has risen up and the pumps are adequately coping.' The Boss Man seemed unconcerned as he readjusted his position in the hammock and returned his attention to the financial section of the Singapore Straits Times. Peter's reassuring statement sounded acceptable but he did not believe a word of it. He had seen the desperate men down below fighting for their lives and his. He needed time to think and study the abandon ship procedure. The last thing he needed at this time was a hysterical man on his back. A long lifeboat is an impossible thing for one man to handle. Plan B became the only alternative.

Peter found two circular, red and white inadequate, deteriorating life belts. With a man the size of Boss, a life belt would be like a necklace. He would immediately plummet to his death and feed the fishes. Peter rolled a cigarette and took in deeply the comforting smoke. Leaning over the side of the ship to judge the drop, he saw the ladder and the fishing boat. To the untrained eye, it looked inviting.

He poked the Boss Man. 'Pay attention, I suggest we leave now and get on that.'

'What's that?' the man asked.

'A rescue boat. Take this life belt just in case.'

'But you said there was no need for concern.'

'That's because I lie so convincingly and that is why you are still alive, follow me.' Peter led the way as the big man attempted to remove himself from the hammock. Every unsuccessful move increased its oscillations.

Their eyes met for a split second as the pirate appeared with his gun forced up underneath the captain's jawbone. He turned it towards Peter. 'Down!' he shouted instinctively as he hit the deck and began to roll under the lifeboat. Swinging wildly from side to side the increased activity caused the Boss Man to land face down on the metal deck as the bullets whistled over his head. Below the boat, Peter saw a pair of legs and heard a shot as the gunman opened fire. The hostage-taker fell to his knees.

At close range, the high-powered bullet had destroyed a large part of his cranium and released a substantial amount of grey matter. Lying on the deck close to Peter, his eyes remained wide open, and what remained of his head resembled a broken eggshell. The first shot was immediately followed by a second from a different direction. Another body fell and lay across the leader. The carnage continued as Peter, risking his life, emerged from his place of safety to drag the unwieldy weight of the traumatised Boss back into limited security.

'Keep your head down, shut up, and don't say a word.' In those few seconds, exposed to the blood bath, he glanced over the side of the ship in time to see the rescue boat slowly sink below the waves. The fishermen had no escape route and nowhere to go as the crew of professional killers continued to hunt them down and shoot them on the spot.

'Mr Serover, you and your friend can come out now, all is quiet and I think what we are doing now is what you Americans call a clean up operation.'

The captain smirked and displayed a wide grin. On his knees, his face was close to Peter's closed fist, he resisted the temptation and took his open hand.

Standing upright on the blood-splattered deck, Peter watched as the dead and dying bodies of the desperate fishermen were thrown over board; they were joined by lifeless members of the ship's crew, without a prayer or a respectable farewell. The Boss Man emerged as Peter, leaning on the ship's rail rolled another cigarette. He watched as another ominous collection of threatening storm clouds gathered their strength on the far horizon.

Peter looked down at the dead bodies floating in the open ocean; they occasionally touched each other as they bumped together in the increasing swell. The patch of rapidly spreading crimson sea attracted the first black dorsal fin. It surfaced slowly, cutting a small path in the resisting waters; it left a very small wake. It encircled the rich red mixture, returned to its original position and disappeared back into the deep. The big man stood next to Peter and placed a comforting arm across his shoulders.

'Will you roll me one of those? I have never smoked in my life but I think its time for a change and I have a lot to tell you, the hard part is I don't know where to start.' It was music to Peter's ears, after all this time the Boss Man was about to open up.

In the deep, the shark analysed the information received from its hyper sensitive senses and prepared to attack. Its nose had detected one part in a million, the important part that triggered an attack response, confirmed by the erratic movement of a dying body, twitching convulsively in its final death throes. The escaping electrical energy emitting from the dying man was received on both sides of the shark's body, it added to its positive decision. From below, it calculated the distance with great care and gathered its latent strength for the perfect strike.

With a quick flick of the powerful tail it released its awesome power and rapidly reaching the surface. It broke through and closed its eyes as it hit the target. The powerful blow pushed the fisherman four feet into the air. Like a limp rag-doll, he returned to the open mouth of the shark. Peter heard the crunch of bone as the denizen of the deep closed its powerful jaws around the black-man's middle and took the victim back to its underwater world. The attack had alerted a number of bloodthirsty predators, their black dorsal fin's criss-crossed the crimson patch. Involved in a frantic feeding frenzy, the sea boiled red as they relentless fought over each remaining tasty morsel.

The captain returned. 'You must be hungry. It is time for tea and tiffin, an old Indian custom. Black tea and crunchy biscuits.'

They followed the captain to his quarters. On the way they passed surviving members of the crew carefully cleaning the deck, with high-pressure water hoses, removing all traces of the violent encounter.

Presented on a silver platter, the delicate porcelain cups were surrounded by a number of dry biscuits, and an adequate amount of cucumber sandwiches. The waiter returned with a boiling hot pot of freshly brewed tea. He filled the china cups to their capacity. Suddenly a comforting rumble passed through the ship, the start of the engine had caused the tea to vibrate, spill over the golden edge of the oriental design, and run down their transparent sides.

Immaculate, in a clean uniform, the captain arrived. 'God willing you will both receive your place in heaven when the day comes. Until then, I wish you good luck and a long life. We shall now continue on our journey, and I will personally deliver you safely to your desired destination.'

Down below, the engineers had worked franticly to repair the engine. Regaining its mighty power supply the ship began to move, slowly at first but rapidly increasing its strength to full speed ahead. The shaking and shuddering finally settled down as the ship made unrestricted headway toward the calm waters of the Coral Sea.

Chapter Seventeen

Arriving off the Australian coast, the container ship slowed down and anchored off shore, waiting for the arrival of a river pilot and permission from the harbour master to cross the congested shipping lanes. Newcastle, north of Sydney, New South Wales exports a large amount of the country's produce. Manufactured goods, wheat, wool, steel and machinery.

Waiting in line for a docking slot in the crowded port, the ship's crew took advantage of the down time and consumed the contents of their illegal imports. The drunken sailors staggered alarmingly around the ship as the river pilot climbed aboard. His dark brown eyes had sunk back into the flabby folds of bloated skin that surrounded them, a definitive sign of overindulgence. Heaving his heavy body on to the deck, he was welcomed by the captain.

He took a furtive look in both directions and said, 'Your men are not in a fit state, or responsible enough to carry out their duties efficiently. May I suggest that we retire to your quarters and discuss this matter further.'

The rehearsed speech had been provided for the benefit of Peter's ears. River pilots the world over have a reputation for their ability to lead a ship's captain in the right direction, and deal with any potential problems. They emerged later with bright sparkling piercing eyes. The pilot sprightly climbed a ladder to the wheelhouse, closely followed by the captain. The Boss Man had also noticed an amazing rapid change in the man's condition.

In charge of thousands of tons of unyielding metal, the two men managed successfully to steer a designated course between the constantly arriving and departing container traffic, avoiding the hidden underwater reefs.

Close to the port, the ship's engine reduced speed as the powerful tugboats arrived to attach their steel hawsers to the compliant vessel. The ship passed a lighthouse on the headland and entered the harbour, on its starboard side it kept a safe distance from a danger buoy. Agitated by the wash created by the lead tug, it increased its lonely occasional despondent sound, and began sending out a constant alarm signal from its salt encrusted warning bell. Like a concerned mother, the small boats carefully pulled and pushed the large container ship into a place of safety. In the required position, the tugboats released their towropes and left the ship to perform its docking procedure. Safely berthed and tied up at the dockside, the busy terminal provided a kaleidoscope of colour as a multitude of international ships loaded and unloaded their valuable cargoes. Looking at the hive of activity, Peter, deep in thought had no idea what his next move might be.

'Mr Serover, I think it's time we continued our interrupted conversation.' The Boss Man had appeared suddenly from nowhere, carrying a collection of clothing. 'I cannot explain in great detail, but I need you to dress up in this uniform just for me. If you refuse it is unlikely that we will leave this ship alive. We have twenty minutes before disembarking from C deck. It is safe to assume that your papers are in order and that your new identity will go unchallenged. One more thing Mr Serover, have you ever driven a heavy goods vehicle before?'

The ship's bow door slowly raised its beak-like head. Allowing, at first, a restricted shaft of light to illuminate the embroidered words: 'Employees of E.M.U. Exports' on the uniforms of Peter and the Boss Man as they walked across the wet surface of C deck. The big man had decided to make a fashion statement and wore his black and white cap back to front. Peter grabbed it and threw it to the ground.

'Are you a complete idiot, or just practising? One of these days you are going to get us both killed. That is not the impression a man of your age needs to give to the guardians of a foreign country's borders.'

The bow door reached its maximum height and as the setting sun's golden glow flooded the ship's interior, it struck the side of the stainless steel tanker still safely secured on the lower deck. Peter stopped and looked at the man.

'That?' he said.

'Yes, Mr Serover, that.'

Peter shook his head in disbelief. The black EMU symbol became even more prominent as the red warning triangle placed below it absorbed the fading light and reflection its powerful message. Bathed in the sun's diminishing shine, Peter reached up and opened the driver's door of the tractor-unit. Inside, he leaned over and released a lock on the passenger's side. The big man entered the cab and took his place next to the driver.

With the landing ramp locked firmly in position, Peter turned the ignition key and the big rig roared into life. A Toyota pick-up truck parked next to the tanker started its engine and stalled. Peter began to engage first gear.

'No Mr Serover, stop. I insist we let that truck go first.' At its third attempt, the truck finally managed to harness its energy into a constant state of delivery and slowly it climbed the ramp and reached dry land, closely followed by the tanker.

The one-way exit road from the dock led straight to the Customs Post. It consisted of the usual identical tollbooths situated on both sides of the dual carriageway, with another one in the middle isolated on its concrete island. The red and white double-stripped barriers and round stop signs raised themselves alternatively as if saluting the passing traffic entering Australia.

It was formality, as each vehicle drove over the increasing white distance markers on the black bitumen, they reduced their speed and waited in line before entering a black and white hatched box area beside the checkpoint. In Peter's lane, the barrier remained in an upright position as private motorists presented their papers through the window of the Customs Post. Returned with the necessary stamp, they continued their journey. Peter came to a halt on a double white line behind the Toyota. As it moved off and entered the box the stop barrier descended. The driver handed over the requested documents and waited for there return. An armed customs officer appeared and approached the vehicle. Peter overheard the conversation.

'Please step down from the vehicle sir and follow me, just a formality you understand.' The driver entered the building, leaving his truck door wide open. The minutes ticked by and as Peter began to sweat he became increasingly uneasy for no apparent reason. Something was not right; he needed a strong cup of black coffee. His thoughts returned to the streets of New York City. An abandoned car with an open door would not contain enough explosive material powerful enough to blow the vehicle apart, only in exceptional circumstance but it would cause concern amongst the onlookers and act as a warning.

'Down!' he said as he grabbed the Boss Man again in a headlock and forced him to the floor. The muted explosion rocked the tractor-unit and as an orange glow lit up the cab Peter sat up in his seat. The flaming vehicle quickly attracted the attention of the Customs officers. Emerging from their singed building the first on the scene rapidly dispensing the contents of an inadequate fire extinguisher. His junior partner performed the task of traffic manager and read the words highly inflammable on the side of the tanker. Without hesitation he stopped the oncoming traffic, and franticly waved Peter and the volatile liquid toward an unrestricted exit on the other side of the road. Peter raised a hand in salute as he passed under the raised barrier.

'Mr Serover always remember the rules of the road. Let the small stuff go first, that could have been us. Keep in this lane and turn left at the next intersection, I know the way,' he said as he reversed his cap.

After the left turn, he gave the tanker driver another direction. 'Turn right at the next set of lights and follow the signs to the E.M.U. Industrial Estate. Stay on the main road and take the last turn on the left.'

Peter reached the end of the road slowed the tanker down, and entered a cavernous corrugated iron shed belonging to E.M.U. Imports and Exports. Inside, Peter applied the brakes, released the compressed air with a satisfied sigh and parked the Tanker on a weighbridge. Another uniformed officer approached the vehicle. Without giving his name, Peter complied with the officer's request.

'Please, Mr Serover, step down and follow me, we need to check your entry papers.' The Boss Man nodded in agreement as Peter gave him a quick look with his lazy left eye.

In the office, his time was taken up by a pointless conversation. The

Immigration Officer asked Peter if he understood the local language and
if he had any intentions of offending or conspiring against the lawfully
elected Government of Australia? It was obviously a delaying tactic. A
sequence of frozen pictures on a bank of monitor screen clearly showed
Peter's face as he stepped down from the tanker, followed the officer, and
passed by the number plate. Peter's papers proved to be in order and were
stamped without further question. He returned to the tanker checked the
condition of the tires, walked around the back of the vehicle and trod on
a red silk handkerchief.

Back on the bitumen Peter received more instructions from the Boss
Man. 'Take Highway One, the Pacific Highway to Sydney, then head for
the City of Goulburn on the South Western Freeway. Our destination is a
place called Collector, a small town on the Federal Highway south of the
city.'

Malcolm Metcalf picked his nose absent-mindedly as he waited for
the phone call. Leaning up against a wooden support in the shade of the
local delicatessen, he reflected on his pointless life. Watching the endless
stream of trucks passing by on the interstate highway made him feel
isolated and frustrated. He needed to join them, hitch a lift to anywhere,
to get out of Collector and live the real life. Dear Daddy was up to his
neck in illegal dealings and young Malcolm was slowly getting caught
up in the unsavoury business.

He responded immediately to the ring-tone emitting from his cell
phone, hoping it was the reply to a text message that he had recently sent
to his latest girlfriend. Malcolm walked the short distance to the corner
of Main Street and the intersection. On the way he stopped and retrieved
a concealed sign lying in the long grass.

Standing at the end of a line of transients hitchhiking was the nearest
Malcolm ever came to getting a lift. He held the recovered cardboard sign
high above his head. 'Diversion, E.M.U. Transport this way.' Feeling like
a bogus traffic cop, he waited for the arrival of a highly toxic tanker.

It had begun as a one-man operation. Storing damaged goods in a
small lock-up for later scrutiny by the insurance assessors. In charge of
traffic control, Jeff Metcalf was the first to know of a major accident on

the fast following freeway. Since his arrival, his section of the highway had provided him with a more than adequate income. With a selected band of trusty transport cops, he managed to reach the accident scene before the paramedics; Jeff specialised in damaged goods. He built another bigger warehouse down the road and kept the first one for legal reasons.

At a crash site, overturned trucks occasionally lost a part of their cargo and strew the contents across the highway. Playing the part of a clean-up squad, the cops trashed a further percentage of the freight and threw its remains on to the road and into the undergrowth. They took another ten percent of the damaged goods to Jeff's legal lock-up for later inspection by the insurance assessors, and the rest of the intact merchandise to the main warehouse. Jeff later filled in an accident report and informed the transport company that the majority of the goods were damaged beyond repair. The insurance assessor arrived in due time and inspected the damaged goods, confirming Jeff's opinion that the remaining merchandise were a complete financial write-off. Mr Jeff Metcalf had made his decision. It was time to pull the plug on the whole illegal business and shut up shop.

On forklift trucks pallets of various merchandise were transported to their selected locations and loaded into the waiting fleet of interstate furniture vans, identified by their individual independent company names. The Aladdin's cave of recovered goods contained a complete selection of untraceable items destined for the open market. Computers, fridge-freezers, trail bikes or televisions, they would all eventually reappear in a local paper in the for sale section at a boot or garage sale, or sold on for an acceptable price by a casual acquaintance in a public house. Slightly damaged goods were also up for grabs, two for the price of one. All the items from the highway crashes were rapidly dispatched to order. That, he could handle but when the stolen cars began to arrive, he wanted out.

The elevated office overlooked the constant arrival and departures. Jeff Metcalf had just finished flushing torn up incriminating evidence down the toilet, situated next to the back door. It opened unexpectedly. The accountant had arrived. Jeff returned to his desk and continued to fill in the latest false accident report sheet when he received the phone call.

The tanker arrived ten minutes later. This was a part of the job that was out of his control and to which he turned a blind eye. Too many powerful people were involved and he was just a prawn in the game, he was small fry. He could be and would be used to their advantage.

'Mr Serover, your numerous abilities continue to amaze me,' the Boss Man wiped his sweaty brow as Peter carefully drove the tanker into a restricted space between two fuel pumps, and parked it with inches to spare, facing a huge diesel storage tank. He turned of the power-unit and allowed his racing heart rate to return to normal before he spoke.

'That was the first time that I have driven anything so big and dangerous, next time I will be the map-reader and you can do the driving.' Peter aggressively jumped down from the cab, slammed the driver's door shut behind him, and set out to search for a strong hot pot-full of caffeine-laden coffee.

Jeff Metcalf had already prepared their departure vehicle with false plates and papers. As the big man began to ascend the wooden stairs, Jeff placed the ignition keys on a logbook lying on the centre of his desk and left the room by the back door.

While he was southwest of Sydney, Peter decided to take the scenic route back to the capital city and made his way across country to the coast road. With the wet stuff of the Pacific Ocean on his right-hand side, he continued to drive north on Highway One. Peter had no need for a map-reader. The Boss Man suddenly demanded another comfort stop. The man was rapidly becoming an annoying problem.

Sitting silently on his own in the four-wheeled drive vehicle, Peter thought seriously about his future. Sooner or later he knew that the Boss Man would get him killed by accident, or design. He felt isolated and alone and took the opportunity to send a signal from his cell phone to Ray. There was no reply. Peter had looked forward to receiving an irritating itch in his eye of the tiger.

Sydney's Happy Valley Chinese quarter is a closed section for the inquisitive tourist. A thriving independent law-abiding community, it prospers and remains isolated from the commercial mainstream centre of downtown Sydney. Behind a false façade of happiness and harmony, it contains a ruthless business principle of conformity and control at all costs.

Peter drove though the electronically operated Oriental gates. They closed quietly and securely behind him. He had entered a very quiet, secretive, society. On each side of the deserted courtyard, two giant stone ornamental Chinese dragons, painted in an impressive contrast of red and gold guarded the inner sanctum. A rapid slamming and closing in unison of window shutters shattered the serene silence. The sound brought Peter's attention to the concealed occupants of the surrounding buildings. He looked up and around and felt a thousand hidden eyes peering down at him through an identical number of narrow wooden louver slots.

From out of the shadows, two large muscular, heavily tattooed men emerged and they approached the vehicle from each side. An extra bulge to their bulk had been added by wearing partly concealed shoulder holsters, containing what Peter assumed were fully loaded handguns. In perfect synchronisation, they reached out their hands, they were both missing a part of their small right hand finger, and opened the front doors of the four-wheel drive. Peter instantly recognised the sign as a bond of brotherhood. Peter and the Boss Man stepped down from the vehicle. Like identical twins, the ushers bowed from the waist and escorted their visitors to the main entrance hall. The Westerners had been welcomed by members of an all-powerful ruthless Japanese crimes syndicate the Yakuza. In Peter, it triggered a latent memory. He recalled an unsavoury street gang of Puerto Rican misfits proudly wearing their colours and sleeveless shirts, controlled by Jimmy White, a black South African with a tattooed cheek. They patrolled and prayed on the unfortunate inhabitants of the South Bronx district of New York City and displayed the same signs of mutilation, solidarity and fraternity but they were playing a big man's game in a small boy's park. In the junior amateur league only in their wildest dreams could they be compared with these immaculately dressed, designer suited, fully qualified and programmed unemotional killing machines.

Peter had met cold-blooded murderers before. Coupled with a warm welcoming social handshake, the meeting also required an exchange of primitive body language: an eye-to-eye friendly exchange of non-aggressive facial expressions. Peter looked deep into the eyes of the man.

The blank stare that returned, sent a cold silent shiver down Peter's spine he adverted his gaze. Like a hungry pup in a wild wolf pack, he gave way to the dominant male. Peter could wait; his turn would come later, but what was the connection between members of a Japanese crime syndicate, the Chinese Community of Sydney, and the Boss Man?

Peter had his suspicions but he needed proof. Another tattooed member of the Yakuza met them at the open door of the inner sanctum and barred their way, backed up by a slowly advancing group of menacing Chinese gunmen. The word 'triads' sprung to mind. Peter immediately and instinctually, looked for an escape route and rapidly evaluated all possibilities. He prepared to reach for his hidden weapon as the Boss Man laid a hand on his arm and restrained him.

'I am quite safe, you can leave me now. I have a private business meeting arranged with an old Chinese friend of mine, but you are not allowed. Mr Serover, you have twelve hours to satisfy your carnal desires, I suggest you enjoy the delights of Sydney's Kings Cross red light district, but be back by midnight. Then we depart and fly to Bundaberg in Queensland, where I have to attend another meeting to discuss my interest in the distillery business. I always try to sample and promote my favourite liquor.'

Peter could not protest but he was frustrated and convinced that the answer to his problem would be revealed behind the closed doors of the secure reunion. He came to the conclusion that the three powerful organisations were having a world summit meeting.

Surrounded by Chinese bodyguards, the Boss Man was at their mercy and extremely vulnerable. They entered the elevator and as the lift doors began to close, the Boss Man, standing forlorn and looking pathetic, waved a limp wrist in Peter's direction. Peter felt inadequate and isolated; he was beginning to feel responsible for the international criminal.

Standing in front of the girlie bars of Darlinghurst Road, close to the corner of Roslyn Street, a doorman beckoned as Peter walked past. Peter stopped and surveyed the seedy scene and gave way to temptation. With the word 'visitor' stamped in black ink on the back of his right wrist, he left the bright lights of the boardwalk and seduced by the thought of exotic dancers, he descended into the murky depths of the underworld.

At the end of the stairs, Peter banged on a brown door. At eye-level a small closed shutter slid back, it reminded Peter of a different life as a small boy confessing his sins at the local Catholic Church. Protected by a wire grill, the oriental face demanded money. At the same time, a rollover money chute opened up at waist-height. Peter placed the required entrance fee into it, and entered a hot, humid room full of semi-naked female Filipino dancers. The oriental barman stamped his dance card, at the same time in a well-repeated speech of broken English he laid down the law.

'Four minutes for five dollars, no touching and no refund.' In small print the card informed the carrier that the management were not responsible for lost items or contagious diseases. In the middle of a small dance floor a stunning twenty-something curvaceous woman wearing a small, white, lacy thong, lit by an ultra-violet spotlight, gyrating to a constant supply of incessant African rhythms provided by an inadequate, distorted, sound-system. Peter was drawn to her like a moth to a flame.

Close up, he inspected the goods on offer. Convinced that it was not a transvestite toy-boy Peter passed her his card and began to perform his pathetic out-dated dance routine and his sadly lacking seduction technique. Four minutes were not enough time to secure a romantic attachment. At the end of the dance, breathing heavily, Peter bent over and whispered in her shell-like ear the powerful words, 'Cash or credit card?'

She immediately responded and changed her bored blank look of indifference to one of an animated money-grabbing animal. 'Do you have protection?'

Peter replied in the affirmative, 'Yes, a pocketful.'

His latest love grabbed him by the hand and led a way through the pulsating crowd. She stopped at the bar with Peter in tow and took out a number of dance cards concealed in her knickers. Cash changed hands with Peter's credit card. The barman took the American Express card and poured Peter a drink.

'On the house mate, no worries.'

He tried to reach below the bar with the card, but Peter stretched out a steely hand and grabbed him around the neck. 'Put it on the counter mate, I have heard about card cloning before. Let me see the procedure and the way you do it, and your name is?'

George reluctantly complied with the command.

The sounds of sexual satisfaction surrounded and assaulted Peter's ears as he climbed the old rickety stairs following the rear of the Filipino lady. They eventually reached a room at the top, guarded by another Chinese gangster.

'Money in and money out. You don't pay her, you pay me in advance.' Peter paid the required amount and the man pressed a button on his mobile phone. The door swung open. Peter entered a divided lounge room decorated sparsely in the Japanese fashion. Met by a Madame wearing a traditional Kimono dress and bowing continuously, Peter was taken to one side of the paper-thin wall, and given the number 'sixty-nine'. He sat on a soiled white leather sofa, and waited for the Madame to call his number, like a customer in a downtown New York deli waiting to buy a pound of meat, or a patient in a doctor's waiting room. In silhouette, his lady could be seen on the other side of the wall, her defined outline obstructed by the thin opaque membrane. The flimsy material stretched between supporting bamboo poles temptingly obscured Peter's view.

The Madame returned and exchanged his number for a key and a white woollen bathrobe. She led Peter to a changing room. It contained the usual information above a row of lockers: 'The management is not responsible for lost or missing items.' Peter undressed and wearing the robe, he opened a door at the far of the narrow room. It opened on to a Japanese-style bathhouse. The hot steamy scene suggested an ancient Roman orgy. Members of both sexes were committing indecent acts on each other and copulating with gay abandon.

Peter could not wait to disrobe, he dropped his garment to the ground were he stood, and joined in the sexual excitement. The compliant link in a depraved daisy chain, Peter felt a repetitive tapping on his bare back. He turned his head around and his eyes settled close up on to a pair of high-heeled silver stilettos. His gaze began to look up the long brown legs of a naked woman.

'You could have waited,' she said. 'I want you to come with me, I have something special in mind for you.' Peter had not recognised her without her knickers.

The walls of her small room bulged with a hanging collection of black full-length leather bondage gear, for every shape and size. Held in line by an identical row of cheap D.I.Y. coat hooks, each costume had it's own perverted attraction. Suspended at head height by small restraining throat straps, the evil looking empty facemasks looked down from all directions. Each available item displayed a half-hour price tag; the rest had been booked and paid for in advance. A mirrored ceiling made an identical image of the eight-foot octagonal waterbed suitable covered in black satin sheets. Situated on a small shelf at the top of the bed within easy reach, a tight fitting Lycra helmet lay next too a pair of pink, furry, handcuffs, and a long leather whip. Above each item the same price tag. Four minutes for five dollars. The lady pulled the matching satin curtains closed and shut out the light of the full moon as it shone between the iron bars of the bedroom window.

'Or would you prefer that I leave them open?' she said. 'Some men enjoy being watched.'

Peter left the soundly sleeping lady spread-eagled on the bed, took the pink furry handcuffs and quietly closed the bedroom door behind him. At the sound of the closing door, she immediately opened her mascara-lined eyes and reached for her mobile phone.

Without his clothes, Peter retraced his footsteps; on the second floor he opened the wrong door, and momentarily looked into a shooting gallery. The room contained a coloured multiracial mix of dedicated drug addicts, sharing needles and shooting up. A pair of professionals sitting below the iron-barred window had tied a length of cloth to each other's arms after passing it behind one of the metal uprights. They took it in turns to inject each other. Strung out, one would suddenly wake up, fill a syringe with another fix and lower his tied arm, causing the tethered arm of his close friend to rise and reach the required height. The man with the needle would then peer through half closed eyes at the raised limb and ineffectively puncture the skin continuously until he found the main vein. A couple in the corner were busily cooking and preparing a quantity of crack cocaine.

'Would you like to join in?' suggested the Madame, suddenly appearing from an adjacent room.

Fully dressed and back on the street, Peter, insatiable, continued to prowl the red light district. He could resist anything except temptation. Needing a strong shot of caffeine, he crossed the road and entered Shane's all night bar and disco. Dancing on an elevated platform high above the heads of an admiring crowd, the long dark haired, coffee coloured lovely attracted Peter's attention immediately. It was May-Ling.

The recognition had been mutual, she smiled and after the dance routine she descended down a slippery brass pole and joined Peter at ground level.

'How did you get here?' Peter asked.

'When I am not working at the brothel, I do this in my spare time for cash in hand, no questions asked. To save and send money back home for my family.'

'But how did you escape, I thought you had been burnt alive?'

'No, the Russian took the full-force of the flame-thrower as I rolled up into a tight ball behind his burning body. I survived with minor burns. Before the second burst of fire, the Black Knight appeared and ran across the compound. Without stopping, he scooped me up in his arms and saved my life. He carried me to a place of safety at the rear of the main building and we left by the back entrance in a military vehicle. To make up the lost money from the opium harvest, I was sold into the sex trade of Bangkok and introduced to a man called Jeff Metcalf. He was looking for a mail order bride, and I wanted a way out. Jeff had signed up on the Internet to an introduction agency. My photograph had previously been taken and placed in a glossy magazine, the marriage was a minor detail. After the wedding of convenience in a room next door, Jeff paid a man in a grey suit for the license, and my temporary visa to enter Australia. As we left the building, Jeff and I were approached on the steps of the civic hall by a man of the Chinese people. He made an offer that we could not refuse. They told us 'You have been sold to the Chinese triads and if you attempt to leave Thailand you and your family will be shot, but you Mr

Metcalf, have the good fortune of being able to return intact to your own country of Australia. I have instructions to pay for all your expenses and a substantial amount on top in return for May-Ling's Australian entry visa and passport.' Jeff realised that it was a good painless and profitable business deal, he could return to the glossy magazines later, and try again to buy another mail-order bride.

Without an exit permit, I left Bangkok in the back of an E.M.U tanker on a container ship, and spent the journey locked up in a cabin with the other illegal females. We left the ship the same way, secularly sealed inside the stainless-steel tanker. I gasped for air as we were finally released from the stifling confounds of our mobile coffin. Inside a cavernous warehouse, as I climbed down from the back of the vehicle I remember a blinding flash of light, and then we were brought to Sydney to work in a Japanese brothel. They took and kept my passport and identity papers. My fellow travellers are still there and I must return, but you can buy me if you like...' She flicked her hair seductively and pouted her bright red lips. Peter needed May-Ling as a material witness. He was prepared to offer her a place in a witness protection programme, change her name, identity, and arrange for her to start a new life back in the U.S.A. That would come later, he still had a few hidden cards up his sleeve. He would not show his winning hand until the final game.

May-Ling was expensive. Back at the brothel, Peter parted with his remaining cash and his depleted credit card for a twelve-hour sale and return arrangement. To complete the financial transaction, he left his false passport as collateral. As they swiftly began to leave the building with May-Ling tightly held by Peter's arm around her back, she stopped and whispered in his ear.

'I can't leave now I need my over-night bag.' The freedom of the street was so close. A big, heavy, Japanese doorman appeared, stood in the way and blocked their exit.

'Mr Serover, I have been looking for you follow me.' He led Peter to the half-enclosed canopy picked up the quietly buzzing black hand-piece and gave it to Peter.

'You have an incoming call, to receive it, press seven.' An audible pause suggested to Peter that the message was about to be recorded. 'Mr Serover, I recommend that you bring your latest purchase to the Regency Hotel on the corner of Russell and Sydney Street and introduce her to our mutual friend.' The line went dead to be quickly followed by a loud click as the listeners pulled the plug.

Chapter Eighteen

In his room at the Regency Hotel, Ray continued to use his laptop computer to search the Internet for information. Interrupted by the strident ringing of the telephone bell he received an anonymous phone call.

'Follow my instructions exactly. Attach your room key to the black Emu key ring with your name and room number; add the words E.M.U building Amsterdam, and deliver the key discreetly to your friend Mr Serover, who, as we speak, is sitting in the hotel bar below you with an attractive lady friend from Thailand. Be careful Mr Ray, you are being watched, you always have been.' Before he could reply the connection had been cut.

Ray returned to his computer and deleted all the latest relevant information. He had a good memory. Ray dressed for the part in a pair of black pants, white shirt and a bow tie. He left the room unlocked, walked down the corridor and descended the back stairs following the signs to the emergency exit. On the ground floor, he found the push-bar on the fire door exit but continued down the passage. He passed a locked street door on the way and ended up opposite a changing room for catering staff. Looking through the circular window into the empty room, he saw what he was looking for. He went in and took a white waiter's jacket put it on, and left the building by the emergency exit. Ray re-entered the hotel by the main entrance. As he walked through the lounge room, Ray saw Peter and May-Ling and completely ignored them. Adjusting his bow tie, he made straight for the bar, and walked behind it.

'Sorry I am late mate, I have been sent from Contract Caterers. A last minute panic by the company, the agency gave me twenty minutes notice to get here. You obviously know that we are expecting the arrival of a crowd of international celebrities to celebrate the completion of their latest blockbuster movie.'

The bored, bemused, bar man replied, 'No mate they tell me nothing.'

'Look over there, the star and his leading lady have already arrived as you can see. I insist on buying them a round of drinks and getting their autographs. Watch this.' Ray took a pen and order pad from behind the bar and walked across the floor. Reaching Peter's table and without a sign of recognition, he laid his keys on the table and whispered to Peter, 'Don't go, it's a set up. Get out of here now and phone Bundaberg later, but sign this first. You and your leading lady are in the movies.'

Peter picked up the order pad, took out the pen from Ray's top pocket, and wrote a fictitious name underlined by the word actor. On a separate page he wrote down a phone number, and a request: 'Safe house for May-Ling. Arrange immediately, I am flying to Bundaberg.'

Ray ripped of the second sheet and surreptitiously slid it down the inside of his shirt, and at the same time he removed an amount of a malleable, pink, pliable material. 'Before you go, take this, it is imbedded with a twenty-minute timer.'

On the order pad, Ray wrote down a sequence of numbers. 'When you arrive at the distribution centre, place this lump in a volatile situation, stand well back and press these numbers on your mobile phone.' It was a small packet of plastic explosive. Ray returned to the bar, opened a bottle of champagne, and turned around in time to see Peter and May-Ling leaving the building.

'It must have been something I said, but I have the autograph. They have promised to return in disguise and by the rear entrance after the rest of the crew have arrived. You must remember that these celebrities are so unstable and sensitive without their entourage they will do anything to keep there private lives secret. Some of them have been known to kill inadvertently if their security has been threatened. Keep that signature safe, it's worth money and drink the champagne. Before the rush begins, I am going to inform the press and arrange for a photographer to be present. In the morning, your story of serving a super-star will be in the paper.'

Ray rapidly walked back to the changing room, taking his tie off on the way and at the same time retrieving the request from the inside of his shirt. With time on his mind, he made a mistake. Without stopping and looking through the circular window in advance, he automatically pushed open the swing door, and entered a room full of men changing into their work uniforms. The night shift had arrived. Ray had to steal a coat, but he had no idea which one belonged to whom and time was running out. Refusing to look into the eyes of the inquisitive men, he averted his gaze and escaped to the safety of the nearest toilet cubical. The waiting was intolerable. Eventually the sound of movement diminished, and Ray returned to an empty room. After many attempts, he took the first jacket that fit and left the hotel by a fire exit.

Ray walked across town and on the way he stopped off at a corner shop bought a Christmas card for Susan and one for Rodney in Western Australia. The electrical store next door attracted Ray's attention. He had a weakness for the latest mini surveillance equipment and bought a substantial amount. Ray entered a late night diner next to a hire car company and made a phone call to Bundaberg.

'Happy Christmas holiday,' Susan said. 'Of course you can bring May-Ling, I have enough festive food for a fortnight and a special treat for you, and don't forget to bring my darling daughter.'

He then phoned Peter's number. Peter and May-Ling arrived thirty minutes later. 'She's all yours,' he said. 'I have to return to the Boss Man.'

Out on the street, Peter was grabbed from behind and roughly bundled into the back of a black cab. Hooded and held by two powerful unknown assailants who refused to speak, he was taken to an out-of-town location and dumped with his hands tied behind his back, beside what he assumed from the sounds was a busy motorway.

Up on his feet, he felt the cool wind of the night air and carefully began to analyse his surroundings. Suddenly a voice said, 'Mr Serover, may I be allowed to assist you?' A man in a grey suit removed Peter's hood. 'Mr Serover, I suggest that you come with me, and all will be revealed. I apologise for our unconventional meeting, but one can not be to careful in our line of work.'

Peter controlled his desire to lash out and ask questions. He allowed himself to be led past the towering skeleton of a building under construction and a ready supply of girders, scaffolding and concrete beams. Peter, closely followed by two threatening men dressed in black, headed to the illuminated open door of a worker's Port-a-cabin, parked on what was obviously an isolated building site. After the man in the grey suit, Peter entered the portable unit.

'Mr Serover, welcome to my small temporary office.'

Inside, the walls had been covered in a bulky soundproof material. 'Don't be alarmed Mr Serover, you will be not here long enough to become claustrophobic. Your visit will be a very, very short one. What I am about to say or do will never be heard outside of this room, and I will not be held responsible for my actions.' Peter looked around for an escape route in time to see one of the heavy minders securely lock the cabin door behind them.

The man in charge removed his spectacles and carefully cleaned them with the end of his red silk tie. It matched the identical material in his top, right side breast pocket. After the treatment, he laid them down on the top of a gunmetal coloured filing cabinet, opened its bottom draw and took out a bottle of malt whiskey, two glasses, and a manila folder he placed them on the desk in front of Peter.

'Mr Serover, please join me in a toast to our mutual success.' He filled the glasses to over-flowing, opened the folder and removed a copy of The Amsterdam Times. 'Mr Serover, I only wear my bifocals when I am trying to look intelligent, sensible and less threatening. I find it much easier to read a newspaper's small print without them. You will of course correct me if you disagree with the written word? I quote: 'A full-scale police investigation was underway as they searched the city to locate the man responsible for the murder. The suspect wearing a beige coloured Macintosh had been seen leaving the scene of the crime.' An operative of mine, Mr Serover was also severely embarrassed by your unsavoury approach in a local coffee shop. To add to the list of anti-social and criminal behaviour, I have proof of another illegal activity that you were recently involved in.' He let out a loud sneeze and took out the red silk handkerchief. The man wiped his nose and passed the soiled item to Peter.

'Mr Serover, I believe you will recognise this. It still contains minute imbedded particles from the bottom of your right boot. A scientific investigation by the forensic department has reached the conclusion that you and only you could be responsible for leaving those remains behind you from your contaminated foot-ware. That silk handkerchief Mr Serover is the same one that you trod on at the back of the tanker when you released your illegal immigrants and I have a photograph to prove it.' He took it from the folder and slapped it down hard on the table. The fabricated photo clearly showed the date, time of day, and other incriminating evidence: Peter's foot on a red silk handkerchief, the superimposed picture of a Thai lady leaving the rear of the tanker, and at the bottom of the photograph the vehicle's number plate was clearly visible.

'I also have proof of your involvement with a Thai national, involved in an international drug smuggling operation with American CIA connections, but Mr Serover, you are now outside of America's protection and subject to the laws of the Australian Immigration and Federal Police Department. I have the power to cancel your entry visa, confiscate your passport and arrest you immediately. Mr Serover, you are in serious trouble for trying to commit a lewd act in a public place and are wanted by the Dutch police for an unsolved murder, assisting the entry of illegal immigrants, and I forgot to mention Mr Serover, that your tanker also carried a number of computers made in Japan, each containing a prohibited amount of the class A drug, cocaine. A reciprocal arrangement with the Dutch police will assure your imprisonment for a minimum of fifteen years in an Australian prison. The Australian courts Mr Serover, are not known for their leniency in such matters. Or, after you have completed your sentence here, deportation to Amsterdam to stand trail on a separate charge of murder. That could mean twenty years in jail Mr Serover. While you ponder your predicament, may I offer you a refill?' The man returned to the cabinet took out another bottle of whiskey and a 45 Smith and Western. 'Old, obsolete, and untraceable Mr Serover, but still in perfect working order.' He raised the gun pointed it at Peter and pulled the trigger.

Peter instinctively dove to the floor, and unintentionally took the table with him. At the same time, he heard the click as the hammer landed on the empty chamber.

'Mr Serover you can get up now, I am pleased to say that your reactions are as fast as I have been led to believe.' The man took a tissue from his coat pocket and carefully cleaned the gun before passing it to Peter. 'This, Mr Serover is the only way out from your present predicament. All charges will be dropped on condition, with no questions asked if you eliminate an undesirable international criminal, who at this moment in time is arranging a meeting of powerful members of his underworld associates in the Queensland town of Bundaberg. It is a do or die situation Mr Serover. You will do and he will die. On your way out, my efficient guardians will supply you with enough bullets to complete your mission. For your convenience, I have previously arranged transportation to deliver you safely on time to your destination. There is no need to thank me Mr Serover, it is my privilege. It is the least that I can do for such an important guest. I have many friends in Happy Valley, and one more thing before you go Mr Serover, may I wish you good-luck, and may your God go with you.'

Ray's hire car was a load of rolling rust, but time was tight they had to leave the city immediately. On the road to Dover Heights to pick up Jodie at Sheila's place, they stopped for the night at the Halfway Motel. Ray arranged for the local paper to be delivered first thing in the morning, and tried to get a good night's sleep. At six in the morning, a copy of The Daily Record was silently pushed under the door. Ray read it at seven, with his hot buttered toast, a pot of coffee, and a bowl full of chopped banana.

On the front page, the headlines in bold print announced the fact that an unidentified body had been found in a room at the Regency Hotel. The page also had a photograph of the barman holding up a signed autograph of the suspected killer. Ray allowed himself a satisfied smile as he realised his plan had come to fruition. The second page contained an article of a great white shark attack that had occurred the previous night, off the headland of Dover Heights. It was reported that a distraught male had witnessed the violent assault and death of his long-time girlfriend. The newspaper quoted the male saying, 'I was in charge of the beach barbecue when she decided to go swimming. Jodie had swum out about forty metres. I finished filleting the fish and throw their inedible innards into the sea. When she cried out my name, I turned around and saw a dorsal fin break the surface just meters away from her. It disappeared, and the next thing I knew it had reappeared with Jodie's left leg tightly clamped in its massive jaws, its unrelenting momentum forced her upwards in a vertical position leaving behind them, a descending stream of fluorescent, frothing bubbles. Almost completely clear of the water, the savage killing machine began to shake and separate the yielding flesh. The frenzied, frantic, thrashing, attack continued as Jodie raised her right arm to the night sky. She presented the perfect picture of a sea goddess reaching up to heaven. The monster released its grip, rolled on its back and at the same time it opened an evil black eye and looked straight at me before returning to deliver the next fatal bite. Jodie's dying screams intensified and reverberated around the enclosed sheltered bay. I recall that the sound was so loud and close, it set up a vibration in the portable barbecue, and dislodged the precariously balanced serving tongs. They fell to the ground at the same time that Jodie finally fell victim to the denizen of the deep, and finished her fight for life. She was finally dragged under. The last thing I remember was a severed, handless arm, pointing straight up at the silent shining stars of the Southern Cross.'

On the back page, the paper had printed a late item. The remains of an unidentified female had been washed up and recovered from a beach south of Dover Heights. After a preliminary examination, the coroner's office had issued the following statement. 'A shark attack had obviously taken place but on one side of the torso the remaining internal organs were still intact. They contained contaminated traces of an overdose of a class A drug. Needle marks on the victim's remaining arm, confirmed the fact that the person had used and injected an illegal stimulant. The arm also showed signs of a fine, filigree pattern of recent sunburn.'

Ray folded the paper as May-Ling entered the room.

'Take this and your bag to the car. I have to pay the bill and make a phone call.' Ray phoned the police, gave them a false name and number, and left a message.

May-Ling, sitting in the passenger seat, reached over and sounded the car's horn as they arrived at Susan's Bundaberg home. Susan opened the front door, wearing a bright red paper party hat, and at the same time blowing loudly on a recoiling carnival whistle. Susan ran down the front steps of the house and reached through the open driver's window of the car. She gave Ray a big, long, lingering kiss and he reciprocated. After the affectionate welcome, he introduced May-Ling and tried not to answer the next inevitable question.

Susan asked, 'Where is my darling daughter?'

Without saying a word Ray passed her his copy of The Daily Record and said goodbye to May-Ling. He closed the passenger door behind her, put his foot down on the fast pedal and in a cloud of loose gravel he spun the wheels, turned the car around and headed back to the city. Ray had to find Teri the taxi driver.

The Sydney Airport concourse contained the usual collection of registered cabs for hire and independent free-lance operators, lined up for business in front of the main terminal. Despite his enquiries and a detailed description, Ray drew a blank from the assembled drivers.

He drove downtown to the transport licensing department of the city council, paid a search fee and found the name Mr Brown, registered for a parking permit for one day only at Sydney Airport. The address written down as his place of residence, on the same day that Ray had arrived in Australia, was Jodie's. The license plate had been issued north of Brisbane, Queensland, in the town of Bundaberg. The alarm bells rang in Ray's head as he ran down the steps of the municipal building and drove north again to Bundaberg.

Susan, still wearing her paper party hat, was alone when the front door burst open. She pointlessly tried to resist her over-powering assailants as they quickly applied a tranquillising-impregnated cloth to her nose and mouth.

May-Ling had left the house minutes before and walked to the corner store at the end of the street. She returned to the empty house and read a hastily scribbled note.

'We have the woman if you want to see her alive again, come to the grain silo now.' The outside of town, the silo was a local landmark and depending on the time of year and a good harvest, it was a hive of activity, combined with the continuous delivery of recently cut sugar cane carried on the narrow-gauge trains that criss-crossed the small town. The silo provided a vital ingredient to the continuing success of the town's major employer, the distillery. Out of season, the isolated construction would be completely deserted.

May-Ling returned to the mini-mart and entered the gun shop next door. She bought a small pistol and a supply of bullets. May-Ling had decided to stand up and fight for the people she liked and loved. Back in the house, she rang the number of Teri's Taxis. The business card was stuck on the wall above Susan's telephone. Ten minutes later, a tall mean looking lean, impressive native Aboriginal Australian, knocked on the screen door.

'I am Teri Brown, I can take you to places you have only dreamed of. So where do you want to go to in our beautiful country?'

Ray returned to Bundaberg and entered Susan's deserted home. The lights entwined on an imitation Christmas tree situated in a far corner of the lounge room continued to blink in sequence. It was the only movement in the house. The incessant strident sound of the ringing telephone broke through Ray's melancholic thoughts. He picked up the red receiver.

'Mr Ray, if you need enough information to complete your undercover investigation, I suggest you meet me immediately at this location.'

Before he left the house, Ray replaced a bulb at the top of the tree with an identical looking spy-hole camera. Activated every thirty seconds by a regular electrical pulse, it was designed to transmit the information to a transceiver at the slightest sign of movement, disguised as an adapter inserted into the nearest power supply socket. Ray attached the plug of the Christmas tree lights and programmed his cell phone accordingly. The mini-screen lit up immediately and presented a picture of a lifeless room. He left the blinking lights behind him, made a phone call to America and went to meet the mystery man.

In the cane field there was no sign of human activity. The eight-feet-high plants prevented any observation of the surrounding area. As instructed, Ray followed a well-trodden path and ventured deep into the unknown growth. Pushing his way through them, he dislodging their brittle, sunburnt crispy leaves, crushing them under foot and eventually reached the centre of a cleared circle. With identical paths leading off in all directions, he stood and waited in the middle of the meeting place and had the uncomfortable feeling of being watched. From the four primary points of the compass, identically dressed individuals appeared from out of the cane field and raised their rifles. Not a word was said to break the stressful silence until a man in a grey suit arrived.

'Mr Ray we meet again. Do you realise that with your constant meddling, you have yet again jeopardised an ongoing undercover international government drug investigation operation?' The man, ranting like a mad man, continued to issue a stream of verbal threats. Finally he stopped for breath and whipped out his bifocal glasses. Ray took advantage of the quiet pause and had his say.

'You assured me that the situation in Thailand was under your control. So explain the sudden appearance of government troops and as a result, the bloody massacre of the local village people.'

The man replaced the end of his red tie into the top of his grey trousers. The two opponents stood their ground and remained silent as the setting sun providing an appropriate background at the far end of the field. The sun slowly slid below the horizon, turning as it went in to a radiating ball of aggressive crimson. In the distance, local workers assembled in the gathering gloom and prepared to clear the undergrowth of the dead and dying vegetation. At dusk, they set fire to the fallen leaves of the sugar cane plants.

The rapidly darkening colour of the indigo sky was suddenly brilliantly light by the distant energetic flames that enhanced the outline of the man's head. The man removed his glasses carefully and placed them in his top pocket. He than continued to rant and rave again waving his arms about and exposing the damp patches under the armpits of his designer suit. Lit from behind, he resembled a raving lunatic character let lose from hell.

'Mr Ray, can you imagine the amount of paperwork that I have had to complete to get this far? That was a perfect example of two government departments failing to communicate. It was a slight over-sight that compromised the operation, resulting in a most unfortunate, and regrettable incident.'

Ray controlled his mounting blood pressure; he could fell his face turning angry.

'But Mr Ray, you must realise that in a war situations, casualties as a result of friendly fire and collateral damage will occur. You will pleased to hear that I have filed a full report and notified the appropriate authorities. The Thailand government are very understanding when it comes to matters of accidental death concerning their citizens.'

Ray was boiling red with rage, but held it all together and asked a non-threatening question.

'You must learn to trust me Mr Ray, I guarantee your friends are in safe hands and that they will join us later, but first I must attend to a minor detail. Please come closer Mr Ray, with your knowledge of modern technology, I know you will appreciate what I am about to do.' The man removed a cell phone from his suit pocket, illuminated the small screen, and pressed a sequence of numbers. The display of digital information remained frozen as he diverted his attention and stared intently at the watch he was wearing on his right wrist. As the second hand reached its zenith, he pressed the send button on the mobile phone. 'Technology, Mr Ray is such a wonderful thing. At the press of a button, I have just eliminated another member of the opposition. Mr Ray, we will now go to meet your remaining friends.'

The tall stainless steel edifice shone brightly, and reflected the harsh, hot, dying light of day. It appeared to shake and shimmer as the heat dissipated, to be replaced by the intruding cold night air of the South Pacific Ocean.

Peter and the Boss Man shivered as they entered the deserted structure and felt the falling temperature. The big man, wheezing loudly stopped, turned around and sneezed. He began to complain. 'I hope you realise that these dust particles are not good for my health; I need my inhaler. In this environment I might not live long enough to get old.'

'You're right,' a female voice replied. 'You will never get old, where is Susan?'

Peter spun around and dropped to the floor. Down on one knee he looked up into the eyes of May-Ling. She had appeared from out of the shadows and was pointing a small pistol in the direction of the Big Boss Man's head.

'No, this is wrong,' Peter said as he rolled forward and grabbed May-Ling's legs, forcing her off balance.

'The man is right my dear, she is up here, there is no point in you trying to play big boy's games outside of your girlie world. I suggest you come up and take the place of this undercover harlot. I do believe her name is Susan.' At the end of the overhead gantry, the flamboyant warlord, wearing a full-length leather coat of many colours, held a knife close to Susan's throat. The cold steel blade glinted and reflected a sliver of light through the dust-filled air. 'It's a fair trade, youth and virility for age and experience. I am a businessman, I can have both, but I shall allow you to make the choice. I promise you one will live in constant pain and poverty and die in despair.   The other one will experience a life filled with luxuries and endless adventures. I suggested we meet halfway and exchange our assets.'

Peter reached down, grabbed May-Ling by the arm and forced her to her feet. She protested loudly as he pushed her forward up the circular stairway. He had to get close enough to disarm the madman.

Using Susan as a human shield, the warlord approached the centre of the walkway. As the exchange was about to take place, the deathly silence of the standoff was shattered. A sharp single shot rang out and echoed around the cylindrical building. It was enforced by the words, 'Don't move!' and left the stunned opponents motionless in the middle of the narrow gantry.

Peter turned around and saw the Boss holding a smoking gun. At the same time, the dying bodyguard concealed behind the warlord fell forward. The unexpected push caused the warlord to loose his footing and lean to one side. Up against the inadequate handrail, their combined body weight caused it to give way.

Susan screamed as they both slowly began to teeter alarmingly on the edge. Letting go of the knife, the warlord wobbling precariously on the walkway franticly looked around for a handhold, but finally he lost his balance. Susan threw herself across the passageway and lay with her arms and legs dangling from its sides. Looking down into the wheat grain, she felt an excruciating pain in her right ankle as her body began to be pulled back across the gantry. In a last minute desperate attempt to survive, she wrapped both her arms tightly around an upright support. It began to bend as the Warlord lost his grip on Susan's leg. He fell thirty feet into a thousand tonnes of loosely packed barley. Each ineffective frantic movement caused the struggling man to sink even deeper into the all engulfing shifting embrace of the life-giving grains.

Ultimately buried by the overwhelming mass the warlord eventually disappeared below its surface, leaving behind him an ascending cloud of suffocating corn dust. May-Ling reached out for Susan as Peter returned to the traumatised Boss Man. The man was crying, shaking uncontrollable and emotionally unstable.

'I have never killed a man before. I feel sick, are you sure he's dead?'

'I will be if you don't give me that gun now, you are in no fit state to be in charge of a firearm.' The Boss Man passed the pistol to Peter and pulled the trigger. The bullet missed Peter by inches and hit the bent metal upright of the gantry it continued upwards and entered the rising cloud of barley dust. In a brilliant flash, the multitude of concentrated particulars ignited.

Out in the open, the force of the resulting explosion blew Peter off his feet. He landed on the Boss Man as May-Ling and Susan at the far end of the gantry safely shielded from the full force of the blast, ran screaming hysterically down an identical circular stairway. Lying on the big man's body, Peter waited for the reverberating shock waves to subside. His ears popped, as at the top of the silo the frustrated fireball confined in a small, restricted space looked for an easy exit. It reversed its assent and as it descended it absorbed the underlying oxygen. The flames of the energised fireball engulfed the walkway as Peter dragged the Boss Man down the spiral staircase.

'In answer to your last question, if that man wasn't dead after you shot him he is now.'

On the second landing the Boss Man regained his feet and stood up.

'But I thought the gun was empty,' he said.

Peter replied as they ran down the steel steps. 'I have told you before you are a public liability, and a health hazard you should be forced to ware a warning sign tattooed on your head. Do not approach, this is a danger zone.'

On the ground floor, Peter, Susan and May-Ling quickly followed by the Boss Man left the burning building and ran to the safety of a parked flat bed truck. An unexpected burst of automatic machine gun fire at close range penetrated the driver's cab, as Peter was about to climb aboard. Still holding the pistol, he let off a shot in the general direction of the gunman. With more luck than judgement, the bullet hit the Chinese bodyguard, the same man that had earlier driven Peter and the Boss Man to the grain silo received a fatal wound to the heart and dropped silently to the floor.

'I thought that man was on our side,' the Boss said.

Peter replied, 'There are no sides in this game. Get in the back of the truck, sit down and shut-up.'

The Boss Man protested to Peter, 'But were are we going?'

'On a cross-country ride in a bullet riddled vehicle. If we were seen on a major highway by the authorities or the underworld, our futures would be at risk. We are going back to the distribution warehouse to get a clean untraceable vehicle.' From his pocket, Peter pulled out a collection of small instruments attached to a wire ring. Designed for watchmakers and dental technicians, Peter selected the appropriate tool from the array and picked the lock of the driver's door. Inside the cab, he reached over and opened the passenger door for May-Ling and Susan. Peter hot-wired the engine, turned its road lights on and placed the pistol back in his pocket.

At four in the morning, Malcolm Metcalf had lost all interest in the passing traffic. Sitting beside the window in the all-night diner, surrounded by the warmth of the over cooked burgers and french fries, he sat over a cold cup of coffee and flirted outrageously on his mobile phone with Sahra, the love of his life. Malcolm failed to notice a white van with it's blacked-out windows turning slowly and quietly off the main highway. His concentration was finally interrupted moments later by the arrival of a big man on the back of a flat bed truck.

Temporally parked beside the petrol pumps, the rotund figure, illuminated by the bright lights of the overhead canopy, climbed down from the pick-up and ran through the restaurant to the toilets. Malcolm recognised the man immediately, and made a phone call to Jeff Metcalf.

As the big man returned and left the restaurant, Curly, the counter-hand turned off the coffee machine and wiped a greasy cloth over the work-top. Curly, the local source of information, kept a low profile. He would not reveal any indication of his extensive knowledge, unless it was a private one to one conversation to his financial advantage.

Malcolm left his seat and said 'goodnight' as Curly counted the meagre amount of dollars and cents in the open till. With the door locked behind him, outside on the deserted back road, Malcolm Metcalf turned around as the long neon strip lights illuminating the interior of the empty room began to lose their light one by one. Standing out of sight behind a supporting roof post, Malcolm watched as Curly made an animated priority phone call. He knew that Curly worked for both sides and was a conduit passing information to the best buyer. Out in the dark, still night, he texted a message to Sahra: 'Meet me at the back of the warehouse now, we are leaving immediately.'

Malcolm had to see dear daddy one last time to settle the debt once and for all before he took to the open road. Wearing his biker black leather uniform complete with patches, he blended into the background, took out his gun and began to walk quietly to the end of the dirt track road. He approached silently and surprised his unsuspected prey.

A bright-eyed rabbit nibbling contentedly at the remains of the dying vegetation at the edge of the freeway was shot immediately by Malcolm. He understood the preservation of the natural indigenous animal population, but imported wildlife, coloureds and aborigines were the exception. Malcolm was a white extremist who believed in the superior race, and had a personal problem with coloureds. They were at the top of his hate hit list.

Deserted at an early age by one of them, he had never known his natural birth mother, just her name May-Ling, a common name for a woman from an improvised rural background. The child bride from Bangkok had taken his naïve Daddy to the point of bankruptcy. She had left the happy white weather-board home silently in the early hours of the morning, taking the contents of the food cupboard with her, including the tins of powdered milk for her hungry twins and the keys to the pick-up truck.

Jeff Metcalf woke as the dawn broke to the cries of his newborn babes. Without food or transport, Jeff was on his own in the middle of nowhere with two small boys and a pile of unpaid bills. Distraught and crying uncontrollably in a disturbed state of mind, he reached out for his cutthroat razor and inefficiently tried to slit his wrists.

Lying in a pool of congealing blood, he eventually came to as the insistent crackling noise issuing from the citizens band radio slowly infiltrated his subconscious. He crawled to the receiver, pressed the send button for the flying doctor service and said, 'I need help now.' As daddy picked him up, Malcolm stopped crying, he felt touched and tasted the still flowing warm congealing red blood. It was his first bonding memory.

Without any obvious dark skin pigmentation, Malcolm looked like any normal Australian suntanned male but on the inside he knew he was not pure; his blood had been contaminated by an inferior, foreign gene. Malcolm had borne a grudge for as long as he could remember. He kicked the lifeless body of the dead rabbit with unnecessary force and replaced the diversion sign with a no entry road closed board, before returning to his motorbike. Astride the machine, he took another snort of cocaine and made a fast short cut journey to the warehouse.

Jeff had just finished cooking the books when he received the call. News that the big man was on his way was bad enough, but seeing the unexpected arrival of the white van as it entered the warehouse caused his blood to run cold. A visit from the man in grey always gave him cause for concern. As the visitors entered the office, Jeff felt his heart race as he reached out and shook the cold slimy hand of the accountant.

'Mr Metcalf please meet my new financial assistant, Mr Ray. It's time for another instant audit; I assume all your accounts are in order as usual?'

Chapter Nineteen

The accountant took over and removed the computer disk from Jeff's PC and replaced it with an identical disk. He downloaded information from the deep, hidden, inner-core memory of the computer's hard drive and with an amazing ability to instantly absorb facts and figures on sight. The man in grey rapidly scrolled down to the end of the relevant section and pressed the save, paste and print buttons. The information transferred to the new bright shiny disk contained all the proof he needed. He inserted the previous CD into his portable laptop and compared the on-screen display with the paper printout and analysed the result.

'Mr Ray I believe I have discovered an indiscretion. Please prepare yourself to restrict the reactions of that man.'

The room was filled with a heavy overpowering silence. Ray met the eyes of Jeff Metcalf in an unblinking stare from the other side of the room. Suddenly, Jeff relaxed and let out an exhausted sigh like a deflating balloon. He sat down and offered no resistance. Ray recognised a defeated man when he saw one.

Malcolm parked his bike at the back door of the warehouse, pushed his identity card through the letterbox and pressed a number of buttons on the intercom. On the inside, he rushed past the security guard and took the wooded steps two at a time to the elevated office. Ray and the man in the suit were still bent over, scrutinising the latest E.M.U accounts in great detail when Malcolm came in an agitated state and walked straight over to his daddy.

'Where's my money? No more excuses, you owe me. I need it now, I'm leaving tonight.'

The accountant slowly removed his glasses and stood up straight.

'Mr Metcalf, it sounds like we have another unsettled account that is missing from your records. We need to discuss your cash transactions or the lack of them immediately.'

Peter, Susan, May-Ling, and the Boss Man arrived ten minutes later. Driving along the long approach road, their presence had been detected by hidden security cameras. The digital image of the big Boss Man, fed to the central computer, made a perfect match. When they arrived at the closed entrance, the reinforced roller doors opened automatically. Peter drove the bullet-ridden pickup truck into the huge cavernous warehouse and left it under the harsh interior glaring lights. The ladies and the Boss Man descended and congregated around a tea and coffee machine.

They bought a selection of liquids as Peter chose a new, clean, untraceable form of transport from the vast collection. Completely ignored by the energetic workers carrying out their allotted tasks, he walked in front of and inspected the steel teeth of a monster mechanical digger. The teeth and the machine were strong enough to do job he had in mind.

Peter climbed aboard the metal monster and started the engine. The bulky beast carried a backhoe, which Peter locked into the upright position. Slowly, the big machine lumbered forward to the fuel pumps. As it reached its destination, it accidentally touched and slightly bent the last in line. Peter jumped down from the driver's cab inspected the damage, and as he filled up the getaway vehicle, he surreptitiously placed the plastic explosive next to the weakened base of the slowly leaking fuel pump. He returned to the driver's seat and drove the heavy ponderous earth-moving machine close up to the roller doors. Peter parked it and walked back to join the rest of the party at the drink dispenser. On the way, he entered a sequence of numbers into his cell phone. Peter had twenty minutes.

In the elevated office, young Malcolm stood in front of, and towered over the old man. Issuing a constant stream of pent-up emotional baggage, he banged his fist on the table and continued to rant and rave. He stopped his verbal outburst of intimidation in mid-flow as Peter, Susan, May-Ling, and the Boss Man entered the highly charged aggressive atmosphere.

Confined in the small room, a tangible silence descended as the occupants prepared themselves for the inevitable outcome. Ray moved slowly away from the man in grey as Peter approached.

'Stop there, Mr Serover,' the man said as he took out his pistol. 'Don't be afraid to communicate, I know we are all good friends, that is why I have arranged for you all to be here at the same time to discuss our differences.'

May-Ling, small and petite, had been hidden behind the vast bulk of the Boss Man. When she emerged into the light Jeff recognised her immediately, he ran to her, and in a tight loving embrace swept her off her feet. In a romantic state of euphoria he lifted her high above his head waltzed across the floor and sat her down on his empty seat.

'Malcolm, my son may I introduce you to your future mother, my new Thai bride May-Ling.'

Malcolm grabbed the gun from the man in grey and shot May-Ling where she sat. Jeff exploded in a fit of manic fury and launched himself at the biker. Caught by a rugby tackle, Malcolm dropped the gun as he made an unsuccessful attempt to escape. On the floor, the two family members, in close combat, fought like two demented advisories. Jeff reached the discarded gun first. Without a second thought, he picked up the lethal weapon and pulled the trigger as Malcolm stood up and began to leave the murder scene. Shot in the back, the bullet had no effect as Malcolm turned around and kicked his father unconscious. Malcolm made it to the glass-panelled door of the office before he finally lurched forward and fell headfirst through the fragile transparent entranceway.

Malcolm Metcalf rolled down the wooden staircase and finally came to rest as he hit his head on the hard concrete floor. The last thing he remembered was his mobile phone emitting an incessant answer tone, lying next to his loaded handgun. With blurred confused vision, he reached out and on the bright illuminated screen read the words: 'Don't go without me, I might be late, see you soon Sahra.' It was the last thing that Malcolm ever saw.

Ray held May-Ling's hand as she murmured her last dying breath. In a slow, concentrated effort, she issued her final words. 'That man in the grey suit, after my wedding, at the civic hall in Bangkok, stamped my visa to enter Australia.'

Peter overheard and took the gun out of his pocket. He aimed it at the accountant. 'You! Stand still and don't move.' With the other hand, Peter removed the untraceable gun from his waistband and gave it to the Boss Man. 'Take this and go now, leave by the back door of the warehouse and wait for me outside. If anyone gets in your way or approaches you shoot them, you can do it, you've done it before, and remember on the outside you are still vulnerable so save your bullets.'

Jeffery Metcalf regained consciousness, reached for the concealed weapon under his prone body and fired a shot in Ray's direction. The bullet whistled past Ray's ear and imbedded itself into the woodwork. Jeffery, dazed and confused got to his feet and pointed the gun at Peter. 'Don't try to stop me, I will use this again.' Moving the weapon from side to side he slowly backed out of the office and ran down the stairs, at the bottom Jeffery Metcalf jumped over his son's dead body and headed for the back door.

'That bullet nearly killed me,' Ray said.

'All in a day's work,' Peter replied. He reached into his pocket, pulled out a pair of pink, furry, handcuffs and threw them to Ray. 'Catch, cuff him, and arrest that man now.'

The man in the grey suit protested loudly. 'Mr Serover, you don't understand, I work for the federal government.'

'And you don't understand that I can prove that you have used your position of power to import class-A drugs, concealed in electrical goods, and that you have turned a blind eye to an illegal immigration operation. Under your command your operatives in charge of a protection racket operating in Chinatown for a substantial fee ignored their cocaine distribution, on condition that they allow you and your people to control the New South Wales cannabis market. A majority of their fees I believe are generated in this warehouse. And one more thing that my colleague has discovered is that you have an off shore bank account in Columbia for reasons of tax evasion. You are the executive officer in charge of a holding company exporting sacks of coffee beans from South America to Amsterdam.

A regular refuelling stop in Cape Town, South Africa, allowed a superior employee of the local customs service to select and remove, for further inspection, a sealed sack that carried the black E.M.U Import and Export tag. In a laboratory, the sack was weighed, and its contents emptied into a separation tank. The genuine articles floated to the surface, leaving behind the identical, rapidly sinking, moisture-resistant coffee coloured rocks of crack cocaine, previously prepared in a southern suburb of the Colombian city of Medellin. They were destined for a flight on a private EMU executive jet, in a broken coffee grinder in the catering section of the aircraft, ready for their removal at Brussels International Airport by a member of the cleaning company.

After the plane crash in Greenland and the death of his well respected but discredited smuggler father, Jamie Johnson junior began to slide on the slippery slope and occasionally he would pocket a heavy imitation coffee bean. He scooped up and removed the floating layer of coffee beans and placed them inside a hot-air tumble dryer. He drained the tank, picked up and counted the remaining sunken heavy beans, weighed them, subtracted the required amount from the dried beans and made up the deficit with an equal amount of illegal exports. Before collection, the rough, uncut diamonds of a standard size had been prepared in advance by a fully qualified tablet technician, employed by a local back-street pharmaceutical company. The enthusiastic, well-respected man worked overtime on his own, and made a substantial undeclared income. The special exports were placed inside a small sample, revolving coating drum, rolled around and covering in the same coffee coloured sealing solution.

The process would be reversed at their final destination. The warm, dried beans, plus Jamie Johnson's furtively included valuable additions were mixed together and returned to the sack; deep inside, they became unidentifiable. The same separation technique would be used later in Amsterdam.

Mr Johnson called for his young assistant. The innocent lad reached into the beans and enthusiastically rummaged around with both hands looking for any foreign object. The sharp eyes of the assistant never missed a thing. Jamie closed the sack and applied a customs seal for the forward flight to Amsterdam. The diligent adolescent, a black African, weighed and wrote down in a departure book all the relevant details, and confirmed with his signature, that he was the man responsible for the final dispatch.

On the day of Jamie's arrest, his young assistant, working undercover for the internal security authorities had carefully placed an uncut diamond in Jamie Johnson's pocket and informed his superiors. Mr Johnson is now serving five years in a South African prison.

EMU Imports and Exports, Canal Street, Amsterdam ship to America a regular supply of superior Dutch/Belgium liqueur chocolates for the connoisseur. Each hand-wrapped coffee-flavoured item supported on top a hard rock of crack cocaine, disguised as a dark brown coffee bean, presented on layers of indented, black plastic trays. The stack of shrink-wrapped covered exports carries the message: 'Perishable goods, do not expose to light, air, or moisture.' They are placed inside a smoked Perspex carrier, which is sealed and stamped with the same EMU Export message and logo. Destination: EMU Foreign Imports Emporium, Fifth Avenue, New York.'

Peter, performing his adversary role with his fingers tucked firmly under his armpits and locked his lazy left eye on the man. 'I know all about coffee, and I suggest that you hand over those computer disks immediately.'

The man in grey was visibly shaking, sweating profusely and wiping his ashen face continuously, with a red silk handkerchief. The exploding fuel pump suddenly shattered the prolonged silence.

On the warehouse floor, a number of the energetic workers - undercover agents of the federal government - revealed their hidden weapons, and began to open fire on the criminal opposition. The rear doors of a recently arrived interstate removal van opened up and disgorged another group of heavily armed protectors of the peace. In the noise and confusion, Jeff was shot by a pump action shot gun as the guard at the rear door of the warehouse failed to recognise the rapidly approaching individual waving a handgun in his direction. Jeffery Metcalf returned fire, and stepped over another fallen body.

Rapidly losing blood from a multitude of small wounds he managed to reach and open the exit door. The loud internal sounds were replaced by a strange deathly silence as Jeffery made it out into the open air. He could not see his way the descending blood from the shotgun blast blurred his sight. As Jeff stumbled out into the scrubby vegetation, he did not recognise the short fat body that stood in front of him, until the bullet passed through his chest. Only then did he remember the name of his killer.

Peter, ignoring the fire fight below the office, passed his pistol to Ray. 'Take that and point it in the right direction; don't pull the trigger that gun's empty, but I might be lying, I do that sort of thing on special occasions when it involves someone I don't like.'

The handcuffed logical accountant could not comprehend the conflicting information; he was not a man to take unaccountable risks. A loud powerful detonation rocked the wooden supports of the office and blew in its elevated windows.

Peter grabbed Susan's hand and ran down the burning stairs, closely followed by Ray and the restrained man. On the ground, Peter picked up Malcolm's discarded gun, checked its contents and gave the loaded weapon to Susan. 'If anyone attempts to stop us, shoot them on sight without a second thought.'

The organised efficiency of the warehouse had rapidly descended into a scene of complete chaos and had become a battleground of intense struggle between the opposing forces. The frustrated flame issuing from the fractured fuel pump was well alight and roaring fiercely. As it increased in its volatility, the contained rising pressure built up, and eventually an aggressive, explosive roar discarded and ejected the melting protective covering high into the air. Unrestricted, the powerful jet of concentrated flame reached up and touched the underneath of the warehouse roof. Brightly shining, the red-hot remains of the fuel pump descended and set fire to a stack of cardboard boxes, behind which, Peter and his party were hiding from the incessant gunfire. Ducking, diving and dodging the flying bullets, they finally made their way safely to the metal monster. Ray and the man in grey climbed into the backhoe.

Peter said, 'Keep your heads down, don't make a move and prepare yourselves for a bumpy ride.'

In the cab with Susan by his side, he started up the powerful engine, raised the backhoe to its maximum height and lowered the front bucket of the big digger to near ground level. Peter selected and engaged the forward drive gear. The machine slowly moved toward the roller door. An enthusiastic member of the opposition suddenly appeared from nowhere, firing his automatic weapon. He then stood still in front of the advancing vehicle. With his back to the roller door, in the rapidly decreasing space, he let off his final round. The windscreen shattered and left a gaping hole as Peter hid under the dashboard and applied more pressure with his right foot to the accelerator pedal. At the same time, he raised the bucket for protection and heard the man's dying scream as the heavy metal bucket bit into the upper body, and squashed him tight between the two unyielding metals. Under pressure the man's exposed, ruptured, adrenaline-filled heart, still pumping fast released the last of its supply of oxygenated red blood. In a final squirt, it covered the remains of the shattered windscreen and entered the driver's cab.

Peter reversed and stopped the vehicle. He looked at Susan; she was deathly quiet and had slumped to one side in the passenger seat. The ruby highlights in her long blond hair had been intensified; their split ends were now covered in and dripping with, bright red blood. Peter swore loudly, engaged forward gear, applied full power, and drove straight at the splattered roller door. The metal monster peeled open the aluminium entrance like a sardine can with a ring-pull top. Through the large jagged opening, a well-prepared back-up force of imported American government agents rapidly entered the building.

Led by a personal friend of Peter's, they identified their individual targets and became engaged in the fierce fire fight. On the outside and out of range of the internal mayhem, Peter stopped the metal monster. In the quiet night, he reached over and ripped open Susan's shirt. He began to apply heart massage and mouth-to-mouth resuscitation. She woke up suddenly, shook her damaged head and gave Peter a hard slap.

'Pervert,' she said as Ray opened the driver's door.

'No he's not,' Ray replied. 'He's not wearing his dirty Mac.'

Shackled to the man in grey, Ray reached up and pulled Peter to the ground.

'You set that up, that situation in the office. You knew that the Boss Man had a loaded gun and that Jeff Metcalf would try to escape from the nearest exit.'

'It never entered my mind,' Peter replied. 'I suggest we go and find out.'

The government agents had rounded up the walking wounded and the rest of the bad guys. Under arrest and contained in a corner of the warehouse, their number did not include the big Boss Man. Peter and his party walked to the rear door of the building. The body of a dying man, sitting on the ground and leaning his back up against the wall blocked the open exit. Susan held his cold hand and felt a weak pulse.

'I tried to stop him,' he said, 'but he took the motorbike and made off across the flat lands toward the interior, heading west. Maybe he is trying to make it to Perth?' He laughed at his own joke and suffered a coughing spasm.

Susan said, 'No worries mate he will never make it.'

'Nor will I,' he replied, 'I was only in it for the money.' He gave a final congested cough and fell forward.

The word 'Perth' stirred a dormant memory in Ray's mind. It was time to cross the vast continent and visit Rodney, his long lost cousin as previously promised. He left the man in grey in the capable hands of New York's Chief of Police, Captain Luck. The international arrest warrant signed by the Commissioner and a member of the CIA gave instructions for the immediate extradition of the offender to the United States of America, to stand trial for conspiracy in illegal immigration, drug trafficking, tax evasion, dealing in stolen goods and money laundering.

On the day of their separation and departure from Sydney, Susan had no desire to return to her bungalow in Bundaberg. Peter had nowhere to go and nothing to do but he refused to fly or drive anywhere. After a heated conversation, Ray booked three seats on the Indian-Pacific passenger train to Perth, Western Australia. The long journey from east to west across the desolate Nullarbor Plain gave him time to relax and remember.

Ray recalled the last words of his dying mother, 'Don't forget to send the Christmas cards and keep in touch with your Australian cousin.' The recollection gave Ray a small crumb of comfort, he was about to fulfil and complete her last positive wish. His recent negative experience with death, and the destruction of innocent lives would be his last. There was no way that he would ever again get involved in another criminal investigation.

At the end of the line, the interstate train, huffing and puffing, finally arrived exhausted and in the covered terminal, it carefully bumped into the resilient, reinforced buffers.

On his arrival, Ray was met by a local solicitor, a senior member of the West Australian police service, and the solicitor of the last will and testament of Rodney Patrick Conner. Ray's cousin and next of kin had died two days before and left him the Happy Homestead, on condition that he accepted, provided for, and looked after until her dying day, a local lady of mixed race named Fay. Without a second thought, Ray signed the legal papers and became a landowner.

Fay had escaped the commune as it fell apart after the death of Dez the biker, and had been taken in by Lightning Bob's extended family up in the stone country. Bob continued to deny all knowledge of her location and suffered the constant verbal abuse of his white employer. Working for a weekly pittance on the improvised land, he decided that he had enough and went to wake up the sleeping drunk. The bush flies had already gathered around the open, dried, encrusted, breathless mouth of the late Rodney Patrick Conner. Lightning Bob complied with Aboriginal folk law, and lowered the lids of the lifeless staring eyes to contain the dead man's spirit. The death of a white man would cause a multitude of impossible questions. He needed someone who was familiar with the white man's world. Lightning Bob left the Happy Homestead in the flat bed pickup truck, and went to fetch Fay.

When Susan, Ray and Peter arrived at the property, Bob and Fay were there to meet them. Fay handed Ray the official death certificate signed by a registered member of the flying doctor service. The cause of death stated that Rodney Patrick Conner had died the night before his discovery from an excess of alcohol and suffocation from inhaling his own vomit.

Peter was not interested in the formalities; he had his eyes set on Fay. It was love at first sight and he instinctively let out an ear-piecing loud wolf whistle. Bluey, a part of the welcoming committee, replied with a painful howl and immediately retreated to his dark quite place of confined safety under the leaking, rusty, water tank.

At the beginning Ray planned for the future and poured money into the rundown property and renamed it 'Dun Roaming'. He restored the homestead to its original condition with hands on determination and a dedicated bunch of local workers organised by Lightning Bob. Ray Conner enjoyed the life of a landowner for a while, until the novelty wore off.

The first serious winter rain brought a sudden flash flood to the parched land, and drowned the surviving drought stricken members of the property's thirsty herd of dehydrated cattle. It also destroyed the year's entire crop of recently planted corn. Only a small number of waterlogged sheep had managed to survive, they faced a bleak future. Ray realised that it was time to change the rules, without a potential income for the coming year, he called his solicitor and signed over a piece of the property to Peter.

Peter had nothing, so he had nothing to lose. Living with Fay at the end of the approach road in bush country, Peter had built a temporary shelter, painted his body with tribal colours, wore a loincloth and had gone completely native, but he kept in touch by mobile phone and the occasion text message to the amazement of his mate Lightning Bob. The Aboriginal admired Peter for his uncanny ability as a white man to issue an ear-piercing whistle that could be heard for miles. Susan had enjoyed the experience of living in the outback but becoming bored, she wanted to return to her place in Bundaberg. Ray admitted he also missed the city life and put his part of the property on the market.

The call came late at night. Ray, asleep in bed, became aware of an insistent ringing sound. He rolled over, picked up and answered his cell phone. It was Captain Luck.

'Jimmy White has just shot and killed your dead mother's carer Mrs Mason. He has a Chinese Dragoon tattooed on his right cheek. Maybe he's the same man who killed your mother, used the drop-in centre and ran from Peter outside BB King's blues club on the night of the explosion? We need Peter to make a positive identification so that we can lock him up for life.'

Ray phoned Peter and relayed the information. 'I thought you might be interested,' he said.

'When do we leave?'

Ray left Peter ranting on the end of the phone, set his alarm clock and went back to sleep.

Before the clock rang, he was up, showered, shaved, and dressed. He rapidly packed his battered brown leather suitcase and waited for the inevitable argument that would begin after the expected energetic knocking on the front door.

Ray ignored the first violent, loud assault on the solid closed wooden entrance and opened it five minutes later as Peter, in full flow, fuelled with strong black coffee, rapidly ran out of expletives and paused for breath. Standing in the doorway, Peter began to berate Ray again.

'We agreed back in America with the captain that this would be are last job but he's still your puppet master, pulling your strings. I can do it on my own and I don't need you.'

Ray replied, 'This is personal, I'm going with you if you like it or not. You know you are completely useless without me the only thing you are good at is making coffee, and wash your face it's still covered in tribal war-paint, put a shirt on and a pair or pants we are about to rejoin the humane race, we leave in one hour.' Ray slammed the door in Peter's face.

'Susan, that man is a liability or a responsibility and I am not sure which, but he needs looking after. I might have to arrange a maximum-security home if he keeps playing up. Restrained in secure accommodation, he might come to his senses.'

Susan had come to the same conclusion they were both in need of help that she could not supply. She was not prepared to waste any more time with the two inseparable and insufferable men. Ray and Peter were the perfect pair and always would be. There was no place for her in their future plans. Ray's final instructions confirmed her decision.

'If in my absence, we have a buyer for the farm, contact my solicitor and sell it for the right price. I will see you later, some time in Bundaberg.'

Deep in thought, I drank the last warm drops of my Bundaberg Rum. My reading was interrupted as a hard hand gripped my shoulder. I looked up at a male figure standing in front of me. My blood ran cold.

Ray Conner immediately sprung to mind, with his back to the setting sun, blocking out the light, the tall black aboriginal spoke.

'I have been looking for you, I'm Teri. I am an agent of the real estate office, a licensed taxi driver and your local tourist guide. We fly to the town of Broom in the Kimberley region named after a comparable state in South Africa. It is the nearest airport to Dun Roaming. Do you know about South Africa and diamonds? Follow me, we will go now to see the property and meet the owner Mr Johnathon Bee. You are Aussie John I presume?'